GREED AND LUST
BROUGHT THEM TOGETHER

SAMANTHA: The Heiress. She had money and power but hungered for what no man could give her.

PAUL: The Writer. Desperation plunged him headlong into a second chance at life.

SHELLEY: The Movie Star. A self-destructive sex queen who wore her tragedy like a second skin.

THEO and **CHARLES:** Millionaire and Son. Money divided them. Disaster would set them free.

HARRY: The Producer. Crude and ruthless. His gamble would be their salvation—or their destruction.

ACAPULCO

....

BURT HIRSCHFELD

A DELL BOOK

Published by
DELL PUBLISHING CO., INC.
1 Dag Hammarskjold Plaza
New York, New York 10017

ISBN: 0-440-10402-5

Reprinted by arrangement with
Arbor House Publishing Co., Inc.
New York, New York 10017
Printed in the United States of America
Previous Dell Edition #0402
New Dell Edition
First printing—August 1977

Some say the world will end in fire,
Some say in ice.
—ROBERT FROST

If you are alone, you are
your own man.
—LEONARDO DA VINCI

ACAPULCO

1

Bristol opened the road map and traced the route with a fleshy, well-manicured forefinger. Reassured, he dropped the map into the lap of the woman alongside him in the rented Cadillac.

"I was right," he muttered, releasing the brake. The car eased ahead, picking up speed. "These Mexicans don't know their own country. No sense asking them for help."

The woman folded the map neatly and placed it in the glove compartment. "I wish I had your sense of direction, Harry."

"It's a gift, a blessing. Somebody up there likes me. That was *some* picture. Did you see it?"

"Paul Newman was a prizefighter from the Lower East Side? An Italian?"

"That's the one."

"I don't like fighting, Harry."

"The trouble is, you don't accept life. Fighting is part of living."

She gazed at him with no change of expression. There was a suggestion of concern on her face, even when in repose, the look of a woman who expected the worst. Her skin was almost translucent, faint blue veins scoring her temples, a gentle angle from cheek to chin. Her features fit smoothly together, as if assembled by the sure hands of a master sculptor. Her lips were parted and her dark eyes were languidly wary, expectant. She called herself Shelly Hanes.

"I accept life," she said in a mild voice. "But I don't have to like fighting."

Bristol glanced at her and she looked away, unwilling to meet his eyes. "Violence is part of life, all kinds of violence. Everybody talks about love, but where is it? Tell me where it is. People are out for what they can get."

"I mean that we shouldn't hurt each other. I don't want to hurt anybody."

He laughed, a harsh, heavy exhalation, carefully restrained. As a young man, Harry Bristol had a full raucous laugh that came out of him uncramped and loud. It was a laugh that embarrassed him, made him uncomfortable, convinced him that he was attracting unwelcome attention. Early on, Bristol had discovered that to remain unnoticed was smarter, safer. So he taught himself to moderate all his reactions, including the laugh, to make them smaller, more "polite." There were other things to learn; how to use the proper utensils, how to chew with his mouth closed, how to talk without swearing every other word. And so much to unlearn; and still the process went on. Bristol thirsted for swift and general acceptance; he longed to be rich and respected. Both goals continued to elude him. But not for long, he was sure. This time around he would get everything he wanted.

"Yeah," Bristol said. "You don't want to hurt anybody. Only you might hurt me. It could happen."

The soft corners of Shelly Hanes' mouth lifted in silent apology; she *really* didn't want to hurt anybody, didn't want to argue.

The Cadillac sped past eroded hills patched with muted vermilion, pink, soiled white. The road twisted and turned, climbed and dipped as they threaded their way through the Sierra Madre del Sur. The name pleased Shelly, the gentle musical sound of the words.

Spanish was a beautiful language, she remarked to herself, and vowed to learn to speak it. What better place to learn than in Mexico? Twenty-five words a day. She would buy a book, one with pictures and explanatory captions. Every night before going to sleep, she would study a certain number of pages. By the end of the month, she would have seven hundred and fifty words!

No. Too much, too fast. This was not a vacation. In the days ahead there would be so much for her to think about. Lines to memorize, a characterization to develop. Learning a new language would simply get in the way. After all, the picture came first.

Ten words a day, then. At the end of the month, she would own a vocabulary of three hundred words. Very good for a person working without a teacher.

"Look at that, Harry!"

"I'm driving."

"Have you ever seen anything like it?" She leafed hurriedly through the guidebook to the section titled: "Mexican Flora & Fauna." "Organ cactus, Harry! They're called organ cactus."

"Thanks for telling me."

"You can see why. They look just like an organ in a church."

"Well, let me know when they start playing hymns," he said. "Taking this road was a good move, saves me nearly an hour's driving."

"The *tamarindo* said . . ."

"*Tamarindo*. That's something else, naming traffic cops after a fruit. What a country! Look up there! Now that's something to see!"

A solitary vulture soared with ominous grace out over the valley ahead, the bright Mexican sun shining off its ebony feathers.

"Ugly character, isn't he?" Bristol said.

Shelly had always thought so, but this bird possessed a kind of proud grace as it searched the valley floor; and it fed only off creatures already dead, unlike the human vultures she had come in contact with. But she said nothing; Harry didn't like to be argued with. He became angry, wouldn't speak to her for hours. Afterward, she always felt guilty, as if she'd committed some terrible crime.

"Sonofabitch!" The Cadillac came to a sudden halt and Bristol pressed down on the horn. Within the air-conditioned car, it sounded faint and foreign. "What kind of a country is this!"

Ahead of them, a dozen goats milled aimlessly about on the road, nibbling at moss sprouting out of cracks in the asphalt.

"Oh, Harry, they're adorable!"

"They're a pain in the ass!" Bristol hit the horn in an angry staccato.

A slender boy in white *calzónes* materialized on the high ground along the road, inspecting the long, black car with wide-eyed curiosity.

Bristol opened the window and leaned out. "*Vamos, señor!* Get those damned goats off the road! *Vamos,* will you please!"

The goatherd grinned and lobbed some pebbles at the goats. They ambled off the road in prancing little steps.

Shelly waved at the boy as they drove on and he waved back. "He was so *sweet*, Harry. And did you see the baby goats? They were *beautiful*."

"The trouble is you're too soft, Shelly. You gotta learn. Kids like that, they'd steal your eyeballs if you gave 'em the chance."

Shelly slumped back. Sometimes Harry seemed like every other man she'd ever known, selfish and ambitious, without concern for anyone else, careless and ordinary. But other times he was charged with energy and excitement, outlining plans and projects that included Shelly, that promised her the full, rewarding life she wanted. He was a complicated man, difficult to understand, and trying to made her weary. She allowed her eyes to close and reached back to recapture the penetrating scent of the goats, the pungent corn-and-chile smell of the boy. But all that remained was the cool rubber odor of the conditioned air.

Jiquilisco was set down in a natural bowl formed by four hills of varying heights. Pink and white and yellow houses stepped up the slopes overlooking the village in neat *barrios,* each one arranged around its own church. There were fourteen churches in Jiquilisco, five restaurants, three bars and twice each week movies were shown on the west wall of the Federal office building.

In the middle of Jiquilisco, the *zócalo;* a large sandstone church loomed up on its north rim. It was always referred to as the cathedral, a local boast that no one ever questioned. Opposite the cathedral, the municipal building with ironwork balconies and a shaded promenade under high archways. To the west, another promenade. Here Indians squatted, protected from the elements, their goods spread out, waiting for buyers: milk cheese, oranges, sisal bags and rope, live chickens, tortillas, and dried fruit.

The remaining side of the *zócalo* contained the local branch of Banco de Comercio, the police station, Jiquilisco's one pharmacy, and the post office.

In the *zócalo* itself, under trees artfully trimmed in the

shape of tall pine cones, old men slumped on benches of
iron lacework. Lovers strolled, children wrestled on the
grass, and shoeshine boys searched for customers. Two
long-haired Americans sat on a bench facing the bandstand, warming themselves in the sunlight, legs stretched
out, their feet dirty in open huaraches, eyes dull and still.

The ringing of the bells in the cathedral steeple announced vespers and as if responding to a signal flights of
black birds zoomed down on the *zócalo*, fluttering into
the trees, the air vibrating with their aggressive chirping.
The old men, the lovers, the shoeshine boys, left the protection of the trees; the two Americans remained in place
and were shit on.

The bells woke Foreman. He lay without moving, struggling to locate himself in time and space. Vespers.
Jiquilisco. Jenny. And the bed he was in was his own. The
waking panic receded and he lit a cigarette, heaved himself into a sitting position. Blue-gray light trickled between
the shutters and cool air brushed against his skin. He tested
his stubbled cheeks and promised himself a shave before
day's end.

On the floor, next to the bed, a glass containing mescal.
He drank it in one swallow, sucking air to lessen the sting,
and balanced the glass carefully on his belly, used it for an
ashtray.

The cigarette smoked down, he swung up out of bed, a
rangy man, thicker around the middle than he used to be,
but otherwise in good proportion. Hips narrowed, legs
well-formed, he moved with a graceful indolence, his
shoulders stooped, head angled forward. His face was long
and bony and his green eyes were guarded, as if hunting
for something half-forgotten and afraid of finding it.

The mescal burning in his throat returned. "Salt," he
grumbled. "Where is the salt?"

"In the medicine cabinet," offered a sleepy voice from
the bed.

"Ridiculous. Why would a man keep salt in the medicine cabinet?"

"Why, Foreman?"

He went into the bathroom and located the salt in the

medicine cabinet. He shook some into his palm, licked it up. The fire in his throat eased and he went back into the other room.

"This house is due to be reorganized," he declared.

The girl in the bed sat up. She was a slender Oriental with hair that came to her waist and small brown breasts. "You talk about organizing your life, Foreman, but you never do it. Has it occurred to you that you're not an organized man?"

"Mescal is a threat to a man's physical well-being. An outspoken woman can result in complete ruination."

She pulled up her knees, began combing her hair. "Why do you drink that vile stuff?"

"Absolutely right, Jenny. Starting tonight, back to pulque. It's cheaper and goes down easier."

She made a face and stood up. With one hand, he pulled her close, pressing his mouth against her stomach. He nibbled at the firm, warm flesh.

"More, please. More."

He bent lower and kissed her, inhaled audibly. "There's something about the way you smell after sex . . . rouses the beast in me."

"Degenerate," she said.

"Chinese food. An hour later and you're hungry again."

"Racist," she said, going into the bathroom.

"Yellow menace," he called after her.

"Mao Tse-tung *über alles . . .*"

He lit another cigarette and listened. "That's great, Jenny. The sound of you taking a leak."

"Foreman, you're the most anal man I've ever known."

"And you're the most ignorant woman I've known. You flunk biology? Still, think on it. A chick dropping her stream in the water without subterfuge or conceit. Here you are, a female creature and you've got to pee so pee you do. None of that coy shit about letting the water run to cover up. I make it out to be a very human attitude. Wholesome. Natural. Politically progressive. You don't even think to close the door. You're all right."

"One thing I would like to know, Foreman."

"Ask away."

"What were the last words your shrink had for you before you split?"

" 'Adjust,' she told me. 'Fit in.' What crap! I don't want to fit in. I want to connect."

"What with?"

"What a lousy thing to ask! I don't know what with. Sometimes I feel like some kind of a wacky pilgrim looking for a single conviction that is going to unravel the mystery for me."

"What mystery?"

"If I knew, I'd unravel it myself. There. There it is. The shrink told me I'm not serious enough about getting better. I told her I thought better might be worse and she said I was wasting my money but that she'd be glad to keep listening. That shrink was getting rich off me."

"She's right, you're not serious enough. Especially about your work."

"What work is that?"

"Your *writing*."

"Oh, yes, I remember. To be serious about writing requires an artistic commitment. Maybe I'm not an artist at all. Or maybe my entire life is an artistic expression. Think of it, Jenny. You may be an important element in a great work of art. A streak of exquisite color. A perfectly written and played musical composition. A sweet line of poetry. You're all of that to me, Jenny."

She appeared in the bathroom. "Have you seen my panties?"

"Didn't you hear what I said?"

"I heard." She kneeled down, peered under the bed.

"Well?"

"I'm a pretty good piece of ass to you, that's all." She stood up, panties in hand.

"Don't knock it," he muttered. "My creation, I'm living it out. Do you know what Jacob said when he wrestled the angel?—'I will not let thee go before thou bless me.' "

"When did you become a religious, Foreman?" She put on the panties, slipped quickly into her dress.

"Life is my angel," he replied, "and it's one hell of a tough match. Sorry, that's pretty fancy talk . . ."

"Go back to the States. This expatriate bit is not for you. Go home, Foreman."

"Fuck you, Jenny," he said affably. "Home is where the heart is."

"Where is your heart, Foreman?"

Almost before she had finished speaking, he was remembering. A grand swoop back in time to when he was married to Laura and what it had been like. That constant pervading desire that never lessened, was never sated. Her flesh was a bottomless reservoir to revel in, to explore and enjoy, never twice the same, giving off sexual energy enough to wear out a dozen ordinary men. A hundred dozen! A thousand. There she was, spread out, tanned skin on a white sheet, humping away in happy abandon, calling for greater efforts from her lovers, diminishing a man, raising him up in all those soft brown secret places, enveloping him in that rich smell of mingled sex and piss and sweat. Oh, Jesus, that hateful bitch.

Jenny kissed Foreman on the cheek. "Come and see me later."

"I'm going to do some work."

"Yes, do some work. Come around after, when you want some Chinese food again."

"*Adios.*"

"*Ciao.*"

Foreman wrote a paragraph, read it, and ripped it out of the typewriter; tried again. With glum concentration, he went over the words. Whatever he had meant to say wasn't said. He balled up the page and heaved it aside. Another clean sheet of paper went into the machine and he typed rapidly.

BY WHOSE INVITATION DO YOU WRITE?

"My own," he answered.

WHERE DID YOU GET THE IDEA YOU COULD WRITE A NOVEL?

"In the dark bottom of a deep depression, it came as a way out."

THERE IS NO WAY OUT.

"Cheap philosophy is no substitute for booze."

PAUL FOREMAN IS A HACK, A COMPOSER OF MERELY CLEVER TELEVISION COMMERCIALS AND A GLIB DIRECTOR OF SAME.

"Man cannot live on forty thousand U.S. dollars alone."

He left his desk and put on a pair of faded blue jeans

and an old army shirt and went out. He walked up Calle Insurgentes to B. Juarez with his head down, cut over to the *zócalo*. On an empty bench out of range of the trees, he smoked and contemplated St. George slaying the dragon carved into the pink stone facade of the municipal building.

A shoeshine boy spotted him and pointed to his scuffed loafers. "Shine?"

"No."

"Good shine," the boy insisted.

"Okay," Foreman relented. *"Sí."*

The boy worked fast, head swiveling about, obviously less than dedicated to his work.

"Do you think of yourself as a craftsman?" Foreman said in English.

The boy looked up and blinked.

"You take pride in your work, don't you? You're not ashamed to shine shoes for a living, are you?"

"Señor?"

"But your English isn't so hot, kid, which makes you definitely inferior to me whose Spanish after a year is not so very hot either. Tell me this, if you're so smart, why does the box have a mirror on the side?"

"Señor?"

Foreman repeated the question in halting Spanish.

The boy grinned. "That is the way they are."

"But why?"

"Fíjese, imagine it, I do not know."

"Fíjese, neither do I, good buddy."

The boy completed his labors and rose, hand out. *"Un peso, señor."*

Foreman paid and the boy went away, leaving the American to admire his polished shoes. Tiring of this, Foreman raked the *zócalo* for something of interest. At the far corner two Mexican girls stood close together, whispering and giggling, glancing surreptitiously at some young men who were watching them. Closer in, a handsome Mexican youth and a middle-aged Scandinavian type were earnestly engaged, obviously striking a bargain. Nothing new there. Foreman transferred his attention to the near corner. A man and a woman looked uncertainly around the plaza. *Gringos.* What attracted tourists to Jiquilisco continued to puzzle Foreman. Except for the cathedral, and a ranch or two outside of town, there was nothing to see. Nothing to do. They came nevertheless, as if on the trail of some great undiscovered secret.

These two—the man was powerfully built, his dark hair tinged with gray, his skin permanently tanned, his nose blunt and broad, his eyes puffed and pouched; the face of a man who might have been a prize-fighter. He wore an expensive sports coat and a blue-and-red ascot was looped around his neck.

The woman was a prize, Foreman decided. There was an anticipatory expression on her fine features and a fluid pliancy to her body, which moved as if her bones were all marrow. She was the kind of a woman, Foreman decided, that a man would want to please.

They were advancing across the plaza toward Foreman, a salesman's grin on the man's rugged face. Foreman braced himself for the encounter.

"You're an American," the man began in a voice that couldn't be ignored. "Spotted you as one of us right away. Let's introduce ourselves. Bristol's the name, Harry Bristol. This is Shelly Hanes, my star."

Bristol reminded Foreman of Chicago, a cold and violent city that existed only for making money. Shelly Hanes was a different piece of work. At close range she was even more attractive, with a kind of flawed beauty, a sad softness that wore tragedy like an outer skin.

"Is Shelly Hanes the kind of star you get when you're good in school?" Foreman said to Bristol.

"What? Whatayamean?"

"Or is she a heavenly body? She has a heavenly body."

"Listen, fella—"

"Or maybe Shelly is a Belle Starr?"

Shelly Hanes giggled. "That's funny. I saw a movie about Belle Starr once with Yvonne deCarlo."

"Not her real name," Foreman confided.

"Yvonne deCarlo?"

"Belle Starr. Myra Belle Shirley. If you were a legend in your own time, a frontierswoman and outlaw, would you want people to go around calling you Myra Belle? Wouldn't do at all."

"Say, what is this?" Bristol said. "I'm here on business. No time to waste horsing around. Maybe you can help.

Maybe you know a guy named Foreman? Paul Foreman."
He pronounced his words in a self-conscious way, without
the elided speech of ordinary conversation.

"Now what would people like you want with a no-good
character like Paul Foreman?"

"Whatayamean no good?"

"Harry is making a movie," Shelly Hanes said. "He
wants Mr. Foreman to work for him."

"Yeah," Bristol said. "If we can get together, I'll make
him a good offer. So if you're a friend of his—"

"Can't figure it out," Foreman said. "Foreman just
hangs around. Drinking, rapping, wasting time. What do
you want him for?"

"It's not your business, but okay," Bristol said. "Foreman's a director and I'm making a picture. I want to hire
him. Tell you what, fella, put us in touch and I'll slip you
something for your troubles. A finder's fee for you and a
favor for Paul Foreman."

"Harry Bristol," Foreman said. "Should I know the
name?"

Bristol's mouth flattened out. "Doesn't matter that you
know me. Only that Foreman comes to work for me.
What the hell is this! I'm trying to give a guy a job and I
get a cheap drifter who makes jokes. Let's go, Shelly.
We'll try the police station."

"Harry . . ." Shelly said tentatively.

"Let's go, I told you."

"Harry, I think this is Paul Foreman."

Bristol glared at Foreman. "No, I don't think so. He
don't look right. Well, are you?"

"What's your best guess?" Foreman replied.

"Look, fella, in my life there's no time for games. If
you're Foreman, say so. What the hell are you ashamed
to admit it for?"

"That's an interesting question," Foreman said. "Some
day maybe I'll consider it. Meanwhile, I'm Foreman. I admit everything . . ."

Bristol shook his head. "Well, come on then, Paul, let's
go somewhere and I'll buy you a drink. You're a pretty
funny guy. Sense of humor. I got a feeling you're my kind
of guy."

"You really think so?" Foreman said.

"Believe me, Paul. I really got a feeling."

El Grillo was a dimly lit bar patronized almost entirely by the small foreign population of Jiquilisco. The drinks were always inexpensive, the food occasionally edible; and it was the only place in town that offered a choice of three salad dressings.

Foreman led Bristol and Shelly to a round table in front of the fireplace in the rear room. A waiter appeared.

"What'll you have?" Bristol said expansively.

"Scotch," Foreman said. "It's expensive in Mexico."

"Listen, I'm not pinching pennies. I intend to do right by you." He ordered a screwdriver for Shelly and *cerveza obscura* for himself.

Waiting for the drinks, Bristol drummed impatiently on the table top. "Whataya say, Paul, this is your chance to go big time." He made a gesture that seemed to encompass not only El Grillo but all of Jiquilisco. "You're not exactly riding high in this hick town."

Foreman gazed at Shelly from under ridged brows. "Your face is something special, ideal for the movie camera."

"That's part of it," Bristol said. "You get to work with Shelly. The way I see it, you two would fit together."

"What do you think?" Foreman said to Shelly.

"I think I like you, Mr. Foreman."

"I think I like you too."

The waiter brought the drinks and Foreman instructed him in Spanish to bring a refill as soon as his glass was empty.

"Give me an answer," Bristol said.

"Tell me more," Foreman answered. "Who are you? Why are you *here* hunting a director with only one film under his belt? Make your pitch and I'll give you my undivided attention."

"I put my new picture into production a week ago in Acapulco," Bristol began. "Everything seemed okay until shooting started. This idiot I hired to direct, Harrison's his name, he worked for two days and drew a blank, a complete blank. Every frame was overexposed, out of focus, terrible stuff. I canned the bastard and the cameraman he had me hire.

"Then I got on the phone and back to the States looking for replacements. I found a cameraman named McClintock. He's no James Wong Howe but he's solid. A director was something else. I had to be sure, right? I needed a guy with *some* kind of a record. A guy in L.A. gave me your name and I tracked you down through Sam Wittstein in New York . . ."

"My agent still loves me," Foreman said. He finished the Scotch and held the glass aloft. The waiter brought the bottle.

"Yeah," Bristol said. "He said you were first rate and told me where you were living. What do you want to bury yourself in a crummy town like this for?"

"Okay. Sam told you I was good. What else would an agent say? Maybe he's a better agent than I am a director . . ." Foreman delivered one of his mildly awful grins in Bristol's direction, lips pulled back, teeth exposed to the gum line.

"I know what I'm doing. I flew up to L.A., saw some of the footage from the picture you did—"

"*Last Man Down,*" Foreman said. "An apt title."

"I loved it," Shelly said.

"You may be the only one. It is one of the unseen cinematic masterpieces of the age."

"It's okay," Bristol said. "A little fancy for my taste, but okay. I screened some of your commercials. Now they're really good. That's what convinced me, the series you did for Beauty Bar soap . . ."

"You've got an eye for art, Bristol."

"Art my fanny! I asked around. Those commercials of yours sold a ton of soap. Beauty Bar wanted you to do another series. That means you did what they wanted done. You can do the same for me."

"You're selling soap, Bristol?"

"Very funny. I mean you can make the picture I want you to make. You're gonna direct *Love, Love* for me."

"That's what you call it?"

"My own idea. Nobody's gonna miss the point. Foreman, I'm prepared to make you a firm offer. Three weeks shooting and a week to edit a first cut. Five hundred bucks a week. That's gotta sound good to you."

"I'm still listening," Foreman said. He stared into his glass; it was empty. "If you're still buying."

"Well, sure . . ."

The waiter returned with the bottle.

"Tell me all about Harry Bristol," Foreman said.

"What's to tell! All my life I've been buying and selling things. A couple of years ago I got overextended when people stopped spending."

"You went broke."

"Broke is nothing. I been broke a dozen times since I started opening cab doors for tips at Penn Station. I was fifteen then and I been hustling ever since. The point is, whenever I needed a new line I figured out where the action was and jumped in."

"Harry went into the movie business," Shelly offered.

"I made skin flicks," Bristol threw out challengingly. "Why not? The Supreme Court said okay to just about anything. I looked at a couple of dozen of those lousy pictures and right away I knew I could make stuff that bad myself. I found some jerks with a camera and some lights, and a dame or two. Any dame comes for fifty bucks a day. Just tell her she's going to be in movies."

"Dirty movies," Foreman said grinning.

"My pictures were good! I did it right. With writers and a real script, everything. Each picture was better than the one before. I even made a couple in full color."

"You didn't come all this way to ask me to direct a stag reel."

"Of course not. Skin flicks are okay for a starter. That's over now. The way things are in the business today anybody can make movies if he's got the brains and the guts."

"And you've got both?" Foreman said.

"In large amounts, fella."

"Harry wants to make a truly outstanding picture," Shelly said.

"The commercial market is big," Bristol went on. "All you got to do is read the signs right, give the people what they want. That way they can't wait to stand in line with dollars in their hot little fists talking about 'Cinema' and 'Art.' All I know is that if I can bring a project in at budget or under, I've got it made. No way to lose.

"Take *Love, Love.* I've already got about twenty min-

utes of color film, processed and ready to go. Good, clear
footage. Maybe it needs some editing. Some fancy lab
work. The kind of thing to impress the kids who go to
movies.

"I'll spell it out for you, Foreman. You did a couple of
plays off-Broadway that got you nowhere fast. One or
two good reviews, and no dough. But you direct film fast
and I guess you're smart. That's what I'm after—smart
and fast."

Even without hearing any more, Foreman knew he
wanted to accept the offer. This was his chance to make
another film, to prove what he could do. What the con-
sequences might be if he was successful, well, he chose not
to consider that. Not now.

No doubt, though. He knew he could make a *good* film,
a film that entertained, yes, and also hopefully said something. No blatant social message, just a comment on the
world he lived in, a world in something less than perfect
shape.

What about Harry Bristol? No evil genius he; an ordinary man, his breed scattered throughout the business
world. Lacking any special talent, any intellectual gift, he
compensated with drive and hard work and vast determination—and what was so wrong with that?

Foreman recognized in Bristol an ingredient that he
lacked himself, the ability to begin a project with nothing
but his own ambition, his own guts, and gall. Foreman
had always needed someone else to provide that first spark,
that continuing energy. Welcome Harry Bristol—

"Go fast, Foreman, go cheap. Like you did those commercials. You've got it in you. Do it for me."

"You want me to blueprint a movie, plan every step,
minimize the set-ups . . ."

"Right! You can do it. Hitchcock does."

Hitchcock, Foreman started to say and didn't, is a genius, able to conceive an entire movie in his head and then
produce it, step by step. But Paul Foreman was another
breed of director—

"Improvisation, freedom to move my camera, my actors,
that's where I'm at. I won't make a static picture."

"Do whatever you want as long as you do it fast
and—"

"—cheap." Foreman pressed the heels of his hands

against his eyes, trying to order his thinking. "I told myself I'd never work with anybody again."

"Paul," Bristol said in his most winning manner. "You can work for me, I promise you."

Foreman's eyes shifted from Bristol to Shelly. "Alone and afraid/in a world I never made . . ." He waited for her to react.

"Did you write that?" she asked, her voice low and warm.

"No. Somebody else, somebody looking for a piece of ultimate truth. Will that serve as a theme for *Love, Love,*" he said to Bristol, "the search for the ultimate truth?"

"What I care about is have we got a deal?" Bristol answered. There was a smile on his mouth but his heavy eyes were bright and chilly. "Talk business now. Talk books and authors later. *Have we got a deal?*"

"About those twenty minutes of color film you've got? That good, clear footage."

Bristol's expression changed; the blunted features were animated. "I put Shelly here in a beach house out at Malibu with a good-looking stud named Jim Sawyer. He tries to make her, she holds out. The action moves. In the house, in the bedroom, on the pool table, in the john. Outside on the sundeck, on the beach, day and night. Bit by bit she gives in . . ."

"I'll have to look at the film."

Bristol hunched forward, lumpy fist held aloft. In threat? In victory? Foreman couldn't tell. "I was going to shoot the whole thing around L.A. but California is nothing new. People like different scenery. So I picked Acapulco. Sinatra, John Wayne, Cary Grant, guys like that make the scene. International jet set. Playground for the world. Bodies and bikinis. All flash. All sun and sea and sand. Also, Acapulco should be a good match for the footage I've already got."

"There's no written script, is there?"

"I roughed out the story line, scene by scene. And a shot plot. To hell with a script. The less talk the better, like that French picture—" He turned to Shelly inquiringly.

"*A Man and a Woman,*" she supplied. "It was lovely."

"Yeah. Later, I'll loop in any extra dialogue it needs. Maybe I'll hire some bushy-headed kid to do a rock score for the sound track. Have we got a deal?"

"I'll want a thousand a week . . ."

"Jesus, you think I'm MGM! Okay, a thousand it is. Then it's settled."

"Sliding up to two thousand if it goes over four weeks . . ."

"Four weeks is all. We're not going over."

"And one more thing," Foreman said, studying the remaining Scotch in his glass. A nerve pulsed irregularly at the base of his throat and there was a foul taste in his mouth. "In the contract, in clear language, I want the final cut."

The lumpy face settled into place. He recalled to Foreman's mind a Roman statue seen in some museum in some American city—"Head of a Gladiator," the same obdurate fearlessness.

"The money you can have," Bristol said in that precise, learned way of his. "The overtime clause. But no final cut. Control your own business, is my motto. Take it or leave it."

Foreman wanted to argue, to make a fight, and knew that he wouldn't. He'd been shot down and bagged. His guts were cramped with hunger to make this film, any film. Apprehension and anticipation made him feel more alive than he had in months. In years. He drank the last of the Scotch.

"I'll direct your picture."

"I'm so glad," Shelly said.

There was no change on Bristol's face. He leaned back in his chair. "Good. The minute I saw you, I told myself I could depend on you. First thing in the morning, we leave for Acapulco. You'll share the driving with me, and along the way I'll fill you in on all the details."

Foreman stood up. "I said I'd direct your picture. You want a chauffeur, find another boy. I drive my own car. Be in front of the cathedral at nine o'clock and you can follow me all the way. We'll go the long way, it's quicker—"

2

By late afternoon, they were in Mexico City, checked into the Maria Isabel. At Foreman's suggestion, they had dinner at La Fonda del Recuerdo, where they listened to the white-clad musicians play Veracruz music on guitars and a harp and drank *Torito de Mamey* and ate tacos filled with pork and beef and cheese. Bristol refused to eat any salad.

"I'm taking no chances," he declared loudly. During the meal, he handed the contract to Foreman. "The usual clauses, all standard stuff. The money, first cut, I wrote it in. Initial all the changes and sign it."

Foreman put the contract into his pocket. "I'll read it tonight. If it's okay, you'll have it back tomorrow."

"You don't trust me," Bristol said.

"Think of it this way—my paranoia surfaces whenever I have to put my name on a piece of paper. Stay loose, Harry. For the next four weeks, I'm yours alone. Let's talk some more about the picture."

"It's not very complicated. A married guy latches onto this single dame. At first, he just wants to get a little. She likes him and she fools around, only she's not as easy as he thinks. That's the plot, you see."

"Some plot," Foreman said.

"He stays after her until she gives in. They make it all over Acapulco. In hotels, in the country, on the beach. Remember Burt Lancaster and Deborah Kerr rolling around on the sand with the tide coming in. What was the name of that picture? Give me that kind of artistic touch, Foreman, and you'll make me happy."

"I want you to be happy," Foreman said. "But not if it makes me unhappy."

"What's that supposed to mean?"

Foreman dropped the contract on the table, and spoke

carefully. "Either I'm the director or you are, Harry."

"Listen, you—"

"Harry . . ." Shelly said, mildly warning.

Bristol shrugged after a moment. "Okay, you direct, I'll produce. But it is my project. I am the boss."

"*Love, Love,*" Foreman said softly, retrieving the contract.

"Just keep the budget," Bristol said. "Keep the shooting schedule. Give me a neat picture with plenty of flesh. Make it so the critics think it says something important, a statement for the times. Does that make you happy?"

"Positively. And to prove it I'm going to order something special in celebration of this momentous occasion—*café de olla,* coffee from the pot. Black with sugar and cinnamon. A real Mexican treat, Harry."

"Skip the treat. I take my coffee straight, lots of cream and sugar—that is, if nobody objects."

Foreman lifted his hands in agreement. "It's a small thing, Harry . . ."

At ten minutes to four in the morning, Bristol woke to the sound of his own moans, his guts clenched and hurting. He fled to the bathroom.

During the next four hours it was firmly established; Montezuma was taking his revenge on Harry Bristol. Shelly called Paul Foreman and described the situation before turning the phone over to Bristol.

"The trip's out for me today," the producer muttered, the powerful voice a feeble imitation of itself. "You go on. Get started. Check the location list I gave you. Talk to McClintock, my new cameraman. Gary McClintock. He's at the Señorial Hotel. There's a room booked for you there. If I'm okay by tonight, I'll be in Acapulco tomorrow. When I get there, I want to see signs of action. Check in with me at the Hilton in the afternoon. Listen, Foreman," he said, gathering a reserve of energy, "I'm going places with this picture. Stanley Kramer did it. Joe Levine did it. I'm gonna do it too. You can have a free ride. I'll carry you along on my back. . . ."

"Harry, working with you is going to be a real education."

"What's that mean?"

"Only that I'm going to give a great deal of thought to what you just said."

"You do that. And don't forget to leave the contract at the desk before you take off."

"Harry," Foreman said. "Lettuce is very good for the digestion. Eat salads more often." He hung up before Bristol could answer.

Out of Cuernavaca, *la carretera cuota* aims directly at Acapulco. Foreman drove the noisy red Volkswagen reflexively, reaching back to his conversations with Harry Bristol. Traditionally producer and director were supposed to be in conflict, Foreman reminded himself, one concerned with profit, the other with esthetics. Or so the theory went.

Honesty made Foreman admit he wasn't entirely disinterested in material success. And he'd had his share. His achievements in the theater, for example. Harry Bristol's opinion notwithstanding, Foreman's accomplishments off-Broadway had attracted a great deal of favorable comment; and a number of producers from uptown had asked about his next work. But he had no new play to show them, no work in progress. Time expired and so did all theatrical interest in Paul Foreman.

He went back to making television commercials, in order to support his expensive theatrical habit, he told himself.

Then, *Last Man Down*. An actor Foreman knew had decided to produce films. He'd taken an option on a little-known novel, gotten the author to do a treatment on speculation, collected a group of actors willing to work for scale, and asked Foreman to direct. They shot the film on weekends in and around New York, took six months to edit and score it and another six months to make a distribution deal. The critics praised it mildly and those people who came to see it seemed to enjoy it, but without either star names or an advertising budget or *something* to convince a sizeable public it was worth viewing, *Last Man Down* went down and out.

Nevertheless, Foreman, the director, was in vogue. He

had two offers from Hollywood, another from an independent producer in New York, and another from a French critic who had written a screenplay and wanted Foreman to direct. He turned them all down in order to return to the theater, to his first love. He was going to write a full-length play. Only three short scenes ever found their way onto paper before he ran out of money.

He went back to making commercials. Madison Avenue displayed a rich appreciation for Foreman's skills and his speedy, intelligent application of them. They paid him well, offered him big jobs, but he preferred to stay loose and free-lance.

Looking back, Foreman could see that it had all gone bad at once. First, the work dried up. The stock market turned sour and many companies cut back on their advertising budgets. Abruptly forty-year-old directors who too often were unavailable when needed now became expendable. Account executives who had earlier been pleased to buy him long, expensive, three-martini lunches, were never in when he called.

And the marriage. Reality blurred, a liquid memory casting selective flotsam to the surface. Twenty-odd years of writing advertising copy, of directing commercials, down the drain—with little honor and less profit. Except that Laura had profited.

Being a wife and housekeeper hardly strained her restless, active mind. She yearned to do something *creative*. So Foreman agreed to teach her to write ad copy. Night after night, he reviewed the philosophies behind advertising, the techniques of applying them. He helped fashion her thinking along professional lines, directed and criticized every word she put on paper. He was an excellent teacher, demanding but patient, urging her constantly to bring her own background, her own very hip tastes into play. And finally his efforts were rewarded; her work became *professional*.

Convinced that she could handle a copywriter's job, Foreman arranged for her to see Milton Wallenstein; he put her to work on some small accounts. Within two years she was a section chief and two years later she was promoted to account executive. Shortly after that, she went to work for the Thomas Childress Company. Three months passed before Foreman learned that Laura was sleeping with Thomas Childress, had been for almost a year. In a reversal of the usual roles, he tried to save the marriage, offered such blandishments as having a family, buying an old house in Connecticut.

Laura found it more funny than convincing. What followed was a good deal of bad behavior in which neither party exactly distinguished themselves, including bad language, threats, Paul striking her, she heaving a marble ashtray at him that glanced off his head and literally put him down. When he was able to stand up again, she was gone.

He charged out to the nearest bar, and then the next and the next. Twice he was thrown out of bars for creating disturbances, and once he was punched unconscious; he fell asleep in doorways and alleys. Once he was arrested and put in the drunk tank; released, he got drunk again. After three days and three nights, he went home bloodied and reeking. Laura was not there; a note informed him that she intended to institute divorce proceedings.

Days later, or was it weeks, he awakened in restraint at Bellevue. A pleasant black man in a white jacket told him that he'd been drunk in some bar, had gotten into a fight, a knife had been flashed and there was a struggle. Foreman had ended up with the knife, had stumbled into the street and apparently had tried to cut his wrists. Foreman shook his head at the news of *that* failure. . . .

During the next two weeks, he had four sessions with a staff psychiatrist, a plump, cheerful woman who seemed to enjoy his bitter humor (at least she wasn't offended) and assured him that he wasn't crazy. She conceded, however, that he was trying very hard to become so. She invited him to visit her privately five times a week at thirty-five dollars a visit. Foreman knew he wasn't *that* crazy, but for strategic reasons agreed to her suggestion, and the following morning he was released from the hospital.

With a thousand dollars borrowed from an advertising friend, he purchased the red Volkswagen from a dealer in Queens and left for Mexico at once, determined to put his life in working order. His intentions had been good; his execution, as before, not exactly matching up. Maybe *Love, Love* was a turning point, a constructive change. He hoped so. . . . He'd try like hell to make it so. . . .

Once past the toll gate at Iquala, he pulled into a Pemex, had the tank filled with Gasolmex. While a boy cleaned his windshield, he used the john and drank a Coca-Cola, tried to ease the stiffness across his shoulders.

"On your way to Acapulco?"

Foreman looked up. A tall American stood a few feet away, looking like George Custer reincarnated in sombrero, boots, and a fringed leather jacket. Lean, with long, yellow hair and a sparse mustache to match, he peered at Foreman out of watery eyes. His voice was demanding, almost accusing.

"I'll bet that's where you're going," Foreman replied.

"You know it."

"And you want a ride?"

"That's it, man."

"Somehow I get the feeling you've been waiting in ambush for me to come along."

"Existentially you may be right. But I've been trying everybody all morning."

"And?"

"There's very little love in the world."

Foreman grunted and pointed at the red VW. The bearded man climbed in and sighed. "These small cars. A cat my size needs space for his legs."

"Sorry," Foreman said, getting back on the highway. "Catch me on the return trip. Maybe I can do better for you."

Soon after crossing the Río Balsas, the road began to climb and the VW lost speed. Foreman shifted into second.

"That's the trouble with these bugs," the bearded man said. "No *cojones*. At this rate, we won't make it to Acapulco till dark."

"You should've held out for a Cadillac."

"Oh, man, no. The fat cats are too spooked to pick up a freak. My style bugs 'em."

"Well, the way you look doesn't build up a man's confidence."

"Here is Leo, take him or leave him."

"Leo what?"

"Just Leo."

"Okay, Leo. I'm Paul Foreman."

"I suppose you're booked in at Las Brisas or like that?"

"The Señorial."

"Uhuh. How straight can you get!"

"What's your recommendation?"

"Try the beach. All that sand and silence, the whole universe. You know what Galileo said?"

"You're going to tell me, I think."

"Get this—'He who gazes highest is of the highest quality.' Outasight!"

"Been in Mexico long, Leo?" Foreman said.

"Time's so artificial, man, 'Just live,' you dig it? I paint when the mood's on me. Pluck a guitar. Burn some grass. Grooving, baby, that's where it's at. You won't find many like me in Acapulco. That sandbox is for the rich. Tinsel orgies and like that. Even when they make it it isn't real. For the true action, the swingingest chicks, come to Leo. He knows the path to ecstasy."

"I might want to take you up on that. Where do I find you?"

"Here and there."

"Like *where?*"

"There's a dude at the bus station, name of Franco. He'll know where I'm at. That Franco, he knows *everything,*" Leo inspected Foreman as if he were a microscopic specimen. "What are you, man, some kind of a business type? My old man was in paper boxes, how does that grab you?"

"I'm a director—I'm doing a picture in Acapulco."

"For real!"

"For real."

Leo stroked his goatee solemnly. "A word to the wise, man. Watch the cats at the gas stations. The natives are notorious. When they start to pump, make sure the numbers say zero. Never trust a Mex, I tell you—"

Foreman said he'd be sure to remember the advice, and noted Leo's sudden lapse from oneness with the universe— if it included untrustworthy natives, and a father in paper boxes.

The Royalton was the newest hotel in Acapulco, standing for less than a year. Twenty-two hot pink stories in three wings, forming a huge letter *Y*. Each suite had its own

balcony overlooking Caleta Beach and the small sheltered
bay that was always dotted with boats. The Royalton
boasted three Olympic-sized swimming pools, both an indoor and an outdoor gymnasium, five tennis courts, handball, shuffleboard, and a game room. There were three
restaurants in the hotel, one in each wing; and six cocktail lounges, three at ground level, three more on the
roof. The Royalton was among the most expensive hotels
in Acapulco.

"That's why I picked it," Theo Gavin explained to his
son, Charles. "The point about people with money, Chuck,
is that they just naturally understand its value. When a
man has money he can relax, appreciate another man with
money for what he is, his true character. In an atmosphere like this, I don't have to be always on guard, worried about being taken."

"I see. So just make the poor rich and everybody can
trust everybody."

"This is a vacation, Chuck," Theo said. "Let's try to be
pleasant."

Without answering, Charles went out onto the balcony.
The ripe afternoon sun made everything below seem almost antiseptic. But Charles suspected no place in Mexico
could be described that way. Acapulco seemed remote,
sleek. Picture-postcard pretty. All a pleasure-courting vacuum, staged for maximum effect.

Charles almost laughed at his own before-the-fact cyn-
icism. He might have said the same thing before leaving
New York. He wanted Acapulco to be empty and super-
ficial, a pile of expensive glitter. He wanted to confirm his
prejudgment. Prejudices, he corrected silently.

Still, he'd been eager to come to Mexico, to know an
alien land and culture, to meet people unlike himself; at
the same time he felt peculiarly reluctant. At first he put
it down to his hostility toward his father, and finally conceded it was more his own unease with the unfamiliar,
the risk of being forced to discover himself. But eventually
his curiosity about famous infamous Acapulco won out
and he accepted Theo's invitation.

Behind Charles, in the sitting room of the suite, Theo
was busy. He ordered some food from room service, asked
for a bellhop to take his dinner jacket to the valet, made a

reservation for dinner, and inquired about car rentals. Theo Gavin was organized.

"Hey, Chuck, bring it in here, boy! Let's talk a little, kick it around."

Charles arranged a pleasant expression on his face and went back inside. He walked with a syrupy looseness, bouncing up and down as he went, up and down, arms flapping at his sides. It was not, Theo Gavin had often remarked to himself, the walk of a real man. Nor was there much else about Charles that pleased his father. For one thing, the boy was not as tall as Theo, and his shoulders looked narrow, underdeveloped. There was an almost indecent softness about Charles's body, too slender, too fragile; and his triangular face was unformed, his mouth slack, his luminous brown eyes glistening as if he were always about to cry. And his hair; so damned *long*. There was too much of Julia in the boy, her indulgence and weakness. Theo had wanted a son like himself: a masculine boy who would *do* things. Theo doubted that Charles had even been laid yet.

What was it Julia had said? . . .

"Charles is our son. He needs the attention of a man, of his father. He's drifting, Theo. He exists in a world of dropouts and addicts. He's not even nineteen and he disappears for days at a time. He won't tell me what he's doing, where he's been. Something has got to be done. . . ."

"This is a bad time. I'm going off to Acapulco on holiday—"

"Take Charles along. Spend some time together, get to know your own son, Theo. . . ."

It seemed like a reasonable idea, a chance for Chuck to learn the kind of a father he had. There were more than twenty years between them, but Theo was certain Chuck would have a difficult time keeping up. In every activity . . .

"How about this suite!" Theo said, when Charles appeared. "Travel first class all the time, the only way to go. And there's no need for us to get in each other's way here. Plenty of room."

"I won't be any trouble, Theo."

"I know that. All I meant was—well, we're both men and men are entitled to privacy once in a while. Wouldn't you agree?"

"Yes, sir. I suppose I would."

"Well, there you are. You've got your room and I've got mine. Whatever you want to do in there is all right with me and I expect I'm entitled to the same privileges." His accompanying laugh startled Charles. His father was not a man who often laughed. "The main point is, Chuck, that I want us to understand each other. That's not unreasonable, is it?"

"No, sir, it's not unreasonable."

"That's the why of this trip, isn't it?"

"I guess it is."

"Well, sure it is." He stripped off his shirt and filled his lungs with air. His stomach was ridged with muscle and his shoulders and upper arms bulged and strained under the skin. He stood with his legs carefully positioned, chest thrown out, eyes grim and purposeful. He reminded Charles of a boxer waiting for the opening bell, or a man who'd forgotten his childhood. "We're in Acapulco, Chuck. All that fresh air and sunshine out there. Plenty of time for father and son talk. Why don't we hit the pool? I'll race you for beers. . . ."

Charles nodded. "A swim sounds good," he said. *But I don't drink beer,* he added between clenched teeth, and went into his own room to change.

Theo posed on the high board, assessing the people sprawled around the pool. What a pathetic lot the men were, bloated and flabby, gone literally to pot before their time. Well, all right. It just made the play easier for Theo Gavin.

He went off the board in a perfect jackknife, slicing into the water with scarcely a splash. He wasted no time coming out of the pool, getting back up on the board. Wasted motion was wasted energy. Theo knew how to make it look easy, scorning theatrical flourishes that might draw the applause of the unknowing.

This time he did a back flip. But his knees failed to straighten soon enough and he entered the water at a clumsy angle. He hoped no one had noticed, drew himself out of the pool, and stood up. In a deck chair two strides away, a stunning redhaired girl. No more than twenty, she had a small, inquisitive face with bee-stung lips and a lush figure encased in a crocheted black bikini. It was obvious to Theo that she had witnessed and recognized his failure.

"My bad day," he offered.

"The jackknife was good."

"You dive?"

"Not really. A little bit in high school."

"You can't be long out of high school."

"Three years."

"That makes me feel like an old man." He flexed his arm, kneading the swollen bicep.

"You don't look old to me. My name is Betty Simons."

Theo told her his name. "Just arrived an hour or so ago. Traveling with my son. That's Chuck across the pool, the one with the long hair."

"He looks sweet," she said.

"I'd like it better if he didn't," Theo said. "I don't mean to sound like a professional father, but I wish he was a *little* more rugged, athletic."

"Like you," the girl said. "You look like you were a professional athlete."

"I'm afraid not. Went to work right from college. Of course, I was pretty sports-minded in those days—football, boxing. Now plenty of tennis, some handball, working with the weights once in a while, just enough to stay toned up. Professional athletics are a short-term deal. I opted for the long view, for more—you know—solid accomplishments."

"And have your accomplishments been solid?" She looked up at him with interest.

"No regrets, Betty. Not a single one. But I'd like to hear about you. You're here with your parents?"

"I'm not that young," she protested cheerfully. "I entertain a little."

"Sing for your supper? That's what I'd've guessed, good-looking as you are. You'd have to be in show business."

She made room for him on the deck chair. "Why don't you sit with me for a while, Theo?"

He hesitated, glancing over at Charles. "Why not? For a few minutes." He sat down at the lower end of the chair, his bare thigh against the bottom of her foot. He was pleased she made no effort to move away.

Samantha Moore felt about Villa Gloria as she did about her own body—showpieces intended to present her at her best.

When viewed from a passing yacht, Villa Gloria was hardly visible against the stark cliffs opposite Roqueta Island. Closer inspection revealed a sophisticated man-made work, intricate stone bracings, supports, levels, layers, turrets, facades. Some forgotten Yankee lumberman had built Villa Gloria in honor of his wife when these cliffs were sparsely settled. Subsequently sold and sold again, the house eventually passed into the hands of Ahmed el-Akb Sikhoury, then husband to Samantha Moore. He presented the deed to her when the marriage was in its early, or affectionate, stage. Ahmed, prince of Saudi Arabia, with a substantial income from oil royalties, was anxious to indulge his very beautiful, very desirable American wife. His attitude would radically change, but not until after his detectives had discovered Samantha bedded down in Big Sur with a Spanish painter. The shoot-out that followed caused no permanent damage either to the painter or to Ahmed; but it did produce an international scandal which enhanced Samantha's desirability to everyone but the painter and Ahmed.

Shortly after the divorce, but before she married the movie actor, Samantha enlarged the swimming pool at Villa Gloria. A full year of blasting and the pouring of considerable cement followed before her aesthetic requirements were satisfied. When completed, the pool was a bathing palace appropriate for a Roman emperor, with hand-painted gold-and-blue tiles gleaming through heated water, concealed illumination for night bathing, covered promenade with fluted columns, an Italian marble terrace that reached out over the bay, and a glass-walled room below water level so that those inclined might drink in dry comfort, studying at the same time the body movements of the swimmers from below.

Through the years, Villa Gloria burgeoned organically. Six months after the pool was finished, and one level above it, the Japanese garden was added, tranquil, exquisite, miniature, complete with two authentic Japanese gardeners. Angling off to the southeast was a maze, meticulously trimmed, the hedges ten feet tall; a popular playpen during Samantha's many parties. Higher still, the land was terraced and planted with bougainvillea, tulips, poinsettias, oleander, and a dozen maguey cactus. Also the red-brown shrimp plant. The firecracker plant. The heavy triangular-stemmed night-blooming cereus, its scent so rich and fragrant. And looking down on them all, a double rank of coconut palms.

Wings and stories had been built, patios added, lawns created, until Villa Gloria sprawled up and down the cliff in a succession of textures and colors. Walkways led to elegantly fashioned cul-de-sacs decorated with fountains and statuary; one wall had been erected in exact duplicate of the geometric designs of the ancient priests of Mitla; and balconies reached out to the sun. A narrow staircase had been chiseled out of the rock wall, descending to a cove below where some of Samantha's hardier guests occasionally swam.

Samantha looked upon Villa Gloria with all its parts and extensions as an expression of herself, of her own expansion and growth. "The beauty within is reflected without," she liked to say. "True beauty grows more impressive with time . . ."

"But sadly neither the house nor I are what we once were," she confessed ruefully to Bernard Louis Font, on an afternoon shortly after her return from Switzerland. Font, a Frenchman, had resided in Acapulco for nearly twenty years; he was Samantha's business adviser and long-time friend. "The house and I," Samantha went on without bitterness, "display signs of wear, of tear, dear Bernard. The cost of repair increases yearly with a diminishing return on the investment."

Font was a small man with a fine, round stomach and yellow-gray hair, small eyes that bulged with nervous inquisitiveness, always peering into corners. Pale flesh hung in folds along Bernard's jawline and his ample lower lip was a damp, tremulous appendage.

He spoke Spanish with a French accent. "You become more lovely each year, my dear."

"How nice to hear it. But I wonder, Bernard. The trips

to the clinic in Geneva grow more costly each year and what, I ask myself, is the purpose of it all? The regimen is rigorous, so very dull. Beauty and health reborn is Dr. Koenig's promise and I have no cause to accuse him of any substantial default on his promise. Still, is it worth the effort?"

"But of course! You are the delight and envy of your friends. And no one would ever think for a moment that you are past twenty-five."

"Thirty," she corrected wistfully.

"As you wish. I see no purpose in allowing age to take its dreadful toll when one can prevent it. You are a beautiful woman, dear Samantha, and you owe it to us all to remain so for as long as possible. When I die I shall insist that the box remain sealed so that no one can say 'What an ugly corpse the Frenchman is!' You on the other hand shall retain your loveliness through death and on judgment day shall be judged on that beauty."

She blew him a kiss.

"And I love you, Samantha."

She frowned, quickly smoothed her brow, remembering how much damage frowning could do to a face so delicately stretched and stitched and gentled into its present wrinkless cast. "Life teaches us many things, Bernard I have learned that a woman without sufficient funds will find only despair and ugliness." A vision of Kiko faded into view before her eyes—*that beautiful whore!* "As much as I detest discussing it, Bernard, I am forced to confess, my funds are running low. We both know that."

"The market is uncertain . . ."

"I am beginning to be afraid, Bernard."

"Some caution is indicated," he replied, trying to restore her confidence. "Some minor economies might be in order, at least until conditions right themselves."

"Economies!" Samantha straightened up in her chair. They were seated on a small patio lined with vermilion and bright yellow flowers, overlooking the Roman pool. Samantha pointed toward the pool, toward the elaborate dressing rooms at the far end of the promenade. "What shall I do, Bernard? Advertise for boarders? Open the pool to the public, ten pesos for the day, including a *comida?*"

Bernard's jowls shimmered in amusement. "Nothing so

drastic is necessary. Still, economy can be a good thing for us all."

"For example?" she challenged.

"Your staff. *Four* gardeners, Samantha, and four maids. Plus—"

She brought him to silence with an imperious lift of her well-wrought chin. "To live at Villa Gloria without help is quite impossible. The house is entitled to proper care."

His Gallic countenance continued empty.

"You mustn't sulk, dear Bernard," she went on. "I solicit and consider your advice in all matters but certain things are *fundamental*. More tea?" She fingered the call button and a small Mexican girl in a black skirt and a white apron appeared.

"*Sí, señorita?*"

"*Mas té para el señor.*"

"*Sí señorita.*"

The girl returned shortly with a tall glass of iced tea. When she withdrew, Samantha went over to the low stone wall at the edge of the terrace. Below, Vicente, the handyman was cleaning the pool. It was always kept filled, clean, heated. Yet she doubted that, even during her absence, any of the servants would breach the boundaries of class and have the bad taste to swim in it. And rightly so, each to his own place. She turned, sleek and cool in a white silk jumpsuit, yellow hair flaring in a loose mist around her lean face.

"If you'd care to elaborate, Bernard . . . ?"

He dropped his chin almost to his chest. "Economies?"

"I will *entertain* each of your suggestions. But no promises—"

"Ah, good. The key to economizing is self-descipline, an ever-watchful eye on the purse, so to speak. Be strict in the smallest expenditures. To begin, the stocks you hold are not performing up to expectation and certain of your investments have not been as fruitful as we had a right to anticipate. It would not be unfair of you to believe that Bernard has failed you."

"Oh nonsense, dear friend. Remember I was the one who insisted on putting such a large sum into the chain of health clubs. I was *sure* they would be terribly successful. That mistake was my own."

"I blame myself for not being able to see the pitfalls.

Perhaps it is time you chose another adviser, someone younger, with a surer grasp of matters as they are today."

"Please, Bernard. Such talk upsets me." She sat back down, taking his hand. "Optimism in all things. It was you who taught me that. And it is the only way. Worry brings lines to one's face and does nothing for the spirit or the pocketbook. That last, dear Bernard, are the words of Dr. Koenig, the wizard of the Alps."

Both of them laughed.

Bernard extended his lower lip before speaking. "When money is in short supply there are only two alternatives for the individual."

"And they are?"

"Economize, as I have already said—"

Samantha raised her brows in dismay.

"The other way is to make more money."

"What a lovely idea. But how?"

"I intend to apply myself diligently to the question. I am not yet bankrupt—forgive me—of ideas."

"I have never doubted you, Bernard."

Yet that night as she soaked in her green marble tub, she did have doubts. Perhaps Bernard *was* too old, out of touch with current trends and techniques. Someone younger, with more vitality and drive, might be better equipped to operate in today's money markets, to solve her financial problems with greater dispatch. She decided to give the matter serious consideration. There was no denying her dependence on money. The advantages of wealth were many, emotional and physical. Villa Gloria, for example, Dr. Koenig for another; her Paris and New York wardrobe, designed especially for Samantha; all the lovely amenities of her existence; everything cost money.

Samantha had appreciated the advantages of being wealthy early on and so had arranged to marry not only men who were rich, but also men not afraid to spend money. All her husbands had known how to live well and Samantha was an excellent student; she learned quickly, and her appetites increased along the way.

But during the last few years the circumstances of her life had changed. Subtly at first, then more blatantly, the balance of power had shifted. Now it was Samantha who made it possible for men to live well, men who would otherwise be unable to put well-tailored clothes on their handsome backs. In the beginning it had been a game, a break in the pattern—*she* called them, *she* paid for taxis, *she* purchased tickets to entertainments. The novelty factor lasted a short time; once the pattern was established, she felt helpless to alter it.

Young men still came to her. They remained for a while—a shorter time these days—collected their gifts and weekly allowance, were fed well, and handsomely dressed. And when they grew bored or a more promising situation presented itself they moved on.

Kiko, that beautiful bastard!

Samantha was tired. Tired of looking after *other* people, tired of being *responsible*. She craved attention, affection, longed to be cherished and cared *for*. Loneliness had been a frequent visitor in the last months, loneliness and fear. Her years weighed and she began to project a bleak future crowded with infirmity and ugliness. Was it too late? Had time played its ultimate dirty trick on Samantha Moore?

She climbed out of the green marble tub and stood in front of the gold-framed wall mirror. Her face was still handsome in that cool blond style that came naturally to so many Americans. The faded-blue eyes were set wide apart, remote but all-seeing; her nostrils flared only enough to lend her short, thin nose a graceful line; her lips were full without being gross, wide, and always under control.

And her body. Lean without being skinny, the skin still taut and smooth, her breasts small but perfectly formed, the nipples responsive and dark. And her buttocks, the backs of her long legs; no signs of disintegration there.

Damn Kiko!

Damn all the takers who had used her!

I am still a beautiful woman. A *woman,* yes. That was the operative word. A woman attractive to *men.* Surely someone will want me, someone solid and respectable— even thinking the word startled her. Respectability was something Samantha had always associated with ordinary people, stuffy, absurd people whose names one never saw on the proper pages of the newspapers.

Perhaps that was what she needed now. A reliable man, a man willing to assume responsibility for a real woman. Someone who knew how to love.

It was not too late for Samantha Moore. Not too late

to make one last good marriage. Not too late to have a family. What a marvelous idea! A child would give substance to the marriage. Meaning. Substance.

She tried to imagine herself pregnant, that flat, tan belly distended and ugly. Out of the question. Nine months of discomfort and ugliness. They would have to adopt. That was the best way. A child would alter her life radically. Very well, she was prepared. Samantha Moore: mother and wife. She would cook and clean herself. Well, not really. That would be going a bit too far. But she would supervise the servants closely. To expect her to be an ordinary woman, a simple housewife, was absurd. But she certainly knew how to please a man, make him happy. All she had to do was find the right man. It was merely a question of putting her mind to it. That was all . . .

Gary McClintock was a serious man with a round, brown face and gray hair cut close to his skull, the perpetual squint of a professional cinematographer. He drove the rented pickup truck carefully, keeping a safe distance between himself and other cars on the Costera Alemán. At the Diana Circle, he swung back toward the center of town.

"No point in going further this trip," he said to Foreman in a crisp voice. "There's a golf course, another hotel, the airport. Also a Mexican naval base and Puerto Marqués Bay. A pretty place but not built up much. That's where folks like Jackie Kennedy do their swimming, and some of Mexico's ex-presidents. Well, what do you think? You've been here almost twenty-four hours."

Foreman shrugged. "The hotels are all Miami Beach. And Denny's, Shakey's Pizza, Kentucky Fried Chicken. Reminds me of a suburban shopping center in the States."

"My sentiments exactly."

"Still, even with the junk, there's a great natural beauty. It's lush, tropical . . ."

"Yeah. Like stunning. But so damned commercial."

Foreman looked out at the bay. The water was alive with points of brightness under an almost transparent sky. Green, rugged headlands framed the harbor, and looked to Foreman like a movie mockup.

"The sunsets here are special," McClintock was saying, "*Pie de la Cuesta,* Sunset Beach it's called. About eight miles or so out of town. Terrific natural back lighting and a great afterglow. But the tide is strong. Some fool's always getting drowned out there. Hornitos, another beach, gets big breakers. Very dangerous, I'm told. That's where the native fishermen hang their nets out to dry. Might make a good shot, using the nets like a scrim. Move in, move out, blurring the focus."

Foreman scribbled something in his notebook.

"They've got bullfights here," McClintock said. "Also jai alai and rigs called *calandrias,* which are just horse and buggies, like in Central Park. Then there're the high divers. Those kids climb up to this cliff a hundred and thirty feet or so above the ocean. It's pretty well staged. Dramatic lighting, deliberate timing. The diver says a prayer at a small shrine before he goes off, sometimes carrying a torch or two. What makes it spooky is they dive into a cove and unless they time it so that the incoming waves fill the cove, make it deep enough, they're in for a busted neck at least.

"The days are all sunbathing and water sports, checking out the female population. The dames are beautiful, plentiful, available. Trouble is I'm a happily married man.

"Other sports—game fishing and hunting up in the mountains. But I hear the hill people are a hard-nosed bunch who don't appreciate strangers. The way it's told, everybody up there packs a gun and thinks he's Pancho Villa."

"Bandits?"

"Also guerrillas. The fuzz think they're into bank-robbing and kidnapping to finance their dreams of revolution."

"Sounds like a fun place to visit."

McClintock nodded solemnly. "The local mountain boys have some very cute tricks. One gig I heard about goes like this—a couple of dudes get hold of an orphan kid, there's lots of them roaming around. Then they hang around the Mexico City highway, at night mostly. When they spot a tourist coming down the pike, they shove the kid out in front. Maybe he gets run down, maybe not. Either way the tourist is scared shitless, and figures to stop. The dudes wave a pistol around and help themselves to his roll."

"Nice people."

"Difficult. Still, if you want to go up into those badlands, count on me."

"We'll see. I've got a few ideas I'm trying to fit into Bristol's scenario, such as it is. When I work it out, I'll let you know."

The cameraman's round, brown face showed nothing. "Funny about Bristol getting the runs. A careful guy like him. Drinks bottled water only. Won't even take ice in his booze unless he knows the cubes are made with purified water. Reckon I should feel sorry for the poor bastard."

Foreman glanced sidelong at McClintock. He judged him to be quietly efficient in his work, a professional with a sufficient knowledge of angles and lighting and lenses. But McClintock would bring no special flare to the job, no singular vision that would enhance a scene, intensify its impact. He was a journeyman and would do what was expected, what he was told to do. The magic in *Love, Love* would have to be found elsewhere. Maybe in himself . . .

"Okay, Mac," he announced. "The tour is over. You can let me out here. I'm going to hit the pavement, pick 'em up, lay 'em down."

The pickup truck pulled over to the curb. "Infantry?"

"Something like that," Foreman said, climbing out.

"We can swap combat lies over beers some night."

"I'll go for the beer but not the American Legion stuff."

"I'll buy."

"If Bristol shows, Mac, tell him I'll get back to him later on."

"Will do."

The pickup pulled away and Foreman crossed the Costera, stood at the back of Caleta Beach. Out on the bay, a sailfish skimmed swiftly along, piloted by two young boys. Foreman watched as they fought against a crosswind that almost put them into the water. They handled the tiny craft with skill and speed, righting it and sailing on. Pleased by their victory, Foreman moved along.

When he came to the Royalton Acapulco, he went inside. The lobby was cool, the furnishings very new, all
polished chrome and glass and leather, with potted cactus
plants in every corner. Foreman located the bar and ordered a Cuba libre. Out of concealed speakers, Sinatra was
singing "Little Green Apples" and a bleached blond at the
other end of the bar kept time with her head, a rapt expression on her flaccid face. Two middle-aged men in
swim shorts and flowered shirts sat at a table with their
wives, all of them laughing, strong, loud—the women eye-
ing Foreman speculatively. He took his drink and went
out to the pool.

He sat at a metal table under a striped umbrella. In the
pool, a lone swimmer, a slender youth who seemed to be
enjoying his own company.

A girl in a pink bikini moved by. She measured Foreman out of her eyes striped with dark make-up and
smiled. He turned away, thinking how much she reminded
him of Laura, though they were anything but look-alikes.

Laura had kept him honest, obsessed. Anyway, his pants
zippered up. Funky Laura, that mocking smile fading onto
her thin face, the sudden birdlike gestures. Laura was
darkness. Her black eyes, the olive skin, the shadowed
voice, the graceful hands.

Great hands!

No one had hands like Laura's. One touch and everything came loose, including that craziness that terrorized
him and entrapped him, made him *her* man, not his.

She pulled all of it out of him. With her hands. With
her mouth—"Would you like a special consideration?" *A
special consideration* . . . a codified reference, one of many.
A word from her and he became hard and ready, anxious
—hell, desperate. She took him to the heights, and then
she buried him . . .

There was the familiar crotch-shift and he sat
straighter, angry at himself that across all the time and
distance, beyond so many other bodies, she was able still
to reach him.

The boy in the water drew Foreman's attention. His
thin arms thrashing until he reached the side of the pool,
hanging on, gasping. Foreman watched, grateful for the
diversion.

"If you're drowning," he said—"but only if you're

drowning—I'll lend you a hand."

"Life is killing me," the boy said with difficulty. "But I suppose I can still make it out of a pool." He struggled out of the water, collapsed on the concrete, chest heaving.

Foreman lit a cigarette. "That's all there is to it," he said gravely. "You have to quit smoking."

"I don't smoke," the boy said after a moment.

"Figures. You have to be one of the world's greatest swimmers."

"You a connoisseur?"

"Man, I was weaned on Johnny Weissmuller and Buster Crabbe."

The boy sat up, fingered his hair back off his forehead. "Who're they?"

"Looms large the generation gap," Foreman sighed. "Johnny Weissmuller was Tarzan. *The* Tarzan. Crabbe was his backup man."

"In the flicks?"

"Every Saturday along with the Shadow, Mr. Moto, and a few others. None of that campy crap like Batman on TV. This was *it*." Foreman finished his drink and ordered another. "Join me," he said to the boy.

"A Coke, maybe."

The boy climbed to his feet, made it into an empty chair. Under the heavy wet hair, his face was smooth, with a guileless smile. It was, Foreman thought, the kind of face girls described as "cute."

"You remind me of Peter Fonda," Foreman said.

"Thanks."

Foreman raised his hands in mock surrender. "I give up. Besides, it isn't Peter Fonda at all . . ."

"*Jane* Fonda?"

The waiter arrived with their drinks.

Foreman lifted his glass. "To tell the truth, you don't look like anybody I've ever seen, or hope to see in the distant future."

The boy sucked Coke through a plastic straw. "I'm Charles Gavin, a person of absolutely no consequence."

Foreman said his own name.

Doris Day had replaced Sinatra on the Muzak.

"How do you find Janis Joplin?" Charles said.

"I lean toward Aretha."

"Really?"

"But Bessie Smith, she is *the* all-time greatest."

"I heard of her," Charles said, "but I never heard her."

"Long ago I had some of her old discs—'Work House Blues' and 'Weeping Willow Blues.' My ex-wife heaved them at me one night."

"What did you do to her?"

"Nothing worth mentioning. I was an exemplary husband."

"Your wife didn't approve of you?"

"That's a safe assumption."

"My father doesn't approve of me."

"Why?"

Charles shrugged. "Because I collect Janis Joplin records and the Stones."

"Yeah, but why does your father disapprove?"

"Janis, Mick, long hair, grass. Would you like it if your son was a head?"

"I don't have a son. I thought Janis was real but Jagger strikes me as pretty showbiz. I don't believe him."

"Like Altamont?"

"Like Altamont."

"Mick, down—Janis, hair and grass to go. You know what I think? Theo, that's my father, I think Theo thinks I'm a fag."

"Are you?"

"I won't relieve his uneasiness on the subject, so why yours?"

"Suit yourself."

"Some very first-rate dudes were gay. Michelangelo, Alexander the Great . . ."

"Also Plato, Tchaikovsky, Oscar Wilde. So what?"

"Theo's very strung out on *accomplishment*. Everything has to have a purpose, show a profit. Not my style."

"But here you are living off Theo's bread."

"Bread's got no conscience. Besides, it was a chance to get down to Mexico. When this scene wears, I'll split."

"Be careful. Mexican fuzz can be rough on kids with long hair. And possession of pot can get you seven years. Local jails are no fun."

"How do you know?"

"I was there."

Charles finished his Coke and stood up. "See you around."

"Right."

"Thanks for the Coke and the advice."

Foreman smiled carefully. "You haven't heard a word I said."

Charles pursed his lips, then left, up-and-down, up-and-down. From where Foreman sat, he appeared very much alone, not so tough. A very easy mark.

Foreman continued to explore Acapulco. He wandered through the *zócalo,* into the public market. From a cheerful woman nursing an infant, he bought a slice of freshly cut pineapple. It was sweet and the juice cooled his throat.

He allowed himself to think about *Love, Love.* The title was beginning to please him. He might even get some spin off from the straight *Love Story* market. And depending on what he could put into the edited film, it had an ironic undertone that would safely evade Bristol. The producer had his points, but subtlety wasn't one of them.

At first, Foreman had grandly hoped to capture the essence of Mexico on film; he acknowledged now that it was a presumptuous idea. Mexico was too complex, too contradictory. This marketplace, it was Mexico. The plush glitter of Acapulco's hotels, that was Mexico. So was Jiquilisco, and the Paseo de la Reforma in Mexico City, with its chic shops and expensive women, its flinty-eyed businessmen. And Monterrey with its stripped granite hills and dust-laden air; and the port of Veracruz; and all those ragtag villages named after saints. The contradicting strains of blood and culture and history. The proud and shameful past, bloody and tender; the miserable present, still alive with optimism. Mexico was a nation that could call out its army to slaughter student demonstrators, yet allocate two-thirds of its national budget for education. Mexico, Foreman decided, was beyond all reason. Which was also its most attractive quality.

Foreman climbed away from the market, found himself in a *callejón,* a little street. No sidewalks, no pavement, only a stirring rise of dust that coated the small adobe buildings. A family of pigs rooted in the ditch, some chickens squawked and scratched. The rich scent of fresh tortillas floated on the air. He turned the corner.

"Hey, man, how'd you discover me?" Leo filled the narrow doorway of a faded yellow house, the hairy face blank, the watery eyes remote. "You are off your beat, man. This part of town is not for the tourist."

"I'm no tourist."

"Gonna make your flick up here?"

"Could be. This where you're staying?"

Leo gave a lipless grin, brushed his mustache out of his mouth. "Would you believe it, this is where I crashed last night. Maybe tonight. I'd show some hospitality, man, but the lady of the house is not receiving callers."

"Your discretion is admirable."

"A Mex," Leo said. "They got no real style, otherwise I'd invite you to share the wealth."

"Thanks all the same."

"How's the flick coming?"

"Slow, steady. I'm trying to get the feel of this town."

Leo straightened up. "You oughta have a guide on your payroll. Somebody reliable."

"Like who?"

"Like me, baby. In the interests of art, I'm available."

"For how much, *baby*."

"I trust you, man, to do right by ol' Leo."

Foreman made up his mind. "Tonight," he said. "Let's start early."

"Food?" Leo said with mounting interest. "Drinks, the works?"

"The works. Be at my hotel at eight o'clock."

"Count on it."

"Guides come and go, Leo. Remember, promptness counts."

Theo woke flushed with his own physical well-being. He stretched and rubbed his chest, flexed his arms. From the bathroom, the sound of the shower; a girl clean about the outside of her body would be clean in every other way also. He clasped his hands behind his head and lay back, waiting.

Betty Simons came out of the bathroom bright-eyed

and gleaming, looking younger than her years. She had wrapped a towel around herself.

"Oh, you're up! Did I wake you? I tried to be quiet, you were sleeping so peacefully."

"You provide a powerful sleeping pill," he said.

"Then you approve?"

"Without qualification. You're a very good thing." Looking at her now, so young and fresh, so naturally beautiful, the seep of excitement trickled back into his loins. Nothing started the juices flowing like a good screwing, absolutely nothing. He pulled back the sheet. "Come here," he muttered.

When she didn't respond at once, he became afraid that she might refuse, that he had failed to please her; but the moment passed and she advanced in that slow, tantalizing way, tongue appearing in the corner of her mouth.

"Is there something you want, Mr. Gavin?"

He reached out and yanked at the towel. It came away in his hand. Fantastic, that body, her breasts full and heavy, her skin unblemished, young, perfect.

"I'm not one of those single-shot guys. I came for more."

"Be my guest. I love to go first class."

"Luxury class," he corrected. "Nothing's too good, nothing's too expensive." He patted the bed beside him. "Put it there."

Instead she stood on the bed, legs planted firmly on either side of Theo, hands on her hips. "Do you approve of the view?"

"Sit down," he said, voice back in his throat.

She obeyed, buttocks warm against his thighs. Her hands rested lightly on his stomach.

"I try to give full value, Theo."

"One hundred cents worth on the dollar."

Her fingers fluttered along the length of his penis and back again. He felt himself stiffening, felt proud.

"Can I depend on you, Theo? While you're here in Acapulco? It would be nice to know that you'll visit me again, and again . . ." Her hands went faster, fingers dancing skillfully over the receptive flesh.

"Depend on it," he said, on his elbows, watching closely. His hand reached out to her.

"Don't," she said. "Just relax and enjoy." She shifted

around on all fours, small belly hanging, breasts brushing against his almost totally erect manhood. "This is extra, sweetie, because I know how nice you're going to be to me. Because you're such a terrific guy, something I never, ever do."

"Never?"

"Never the first time."

Mouth open, her head went forward, tongue flicking out, her lips reached out for him.

He buried his fingers into the soft flesh of her bottom, rising up to meet her. She contained his lunges, not listening to the words he said, the names he called her. Not that it mattered; she'd heard them all before.

Theo put on his swim shorts and terry-cloth shirt. He counted off some bills, figuring dollars into pesos, dropped them on the tall chest. He went to the door, turned back.

"I left some money on the bureau."

She lay still under the sheet, eyes closed. "That's sweet of you, sweetie. And I'll arrange that little something for you."

"Make sure she's special."

"I will."

"Let me know when it's settled."

"Maybe tomorrow."

"See you."

"See you."

Charles slumped in a chair on the balcony of his bedroom, burning grass and struggling with the concept of an expanding universe. The idea was a mind-blower and eventually he put it aside, concentrated on the joint until it scorched his fingers. He stripped it down and scattered the remains on the good people below.

"Chuck!"

Theo was back, calling from the sitting room. "You out there, boy? Ah, here you are! You shouldn't be by yourself. This is *Acapulco*."

"Look at the sky, Theo. No skies like that in New York."

Theo glanced upward. "I suppose so. What're you doing out here in the dark?"

Charles touched the book that lay in his lap. "Thinking about this. Tripping out to Andromeda and back. Fantastic!"

Theo frowned. "I wish you wouldn't read in the dark. You'll ruin your eyes."

Charles, eyes round, stared up at his father.

"What are you reading?" Theo said, annoyed by his inability to have a conversation with Charles. Talking to his son made Theo feel as if he'd done something wrong. "Let's go inside. Talk to me while I shower."

Charles followed his father into the bathroom, settled himself on the john. A cloud of steam rose from the shower and Theo said with pleasure, "Nothing like a hot shower to bring a man back."

"Back from where?"

"Oh. That girl at the pool. Betty Simons. We had a few drinks. Time goes fast when you're having a pleasant conversation. Sorry I had to leave you alone."

"No sweat."

A long, silent interval followed. Theo came out of the shower, rubbed himself briskly. "You were going to tell me about the book you're reading?"

"I was?"

"If you'd rather not talk about it—"

"Oh, I don't mind talking about it. In fact, I like to talk about it."

"What's it called?"

"*Siddhartha.*"

Theo repeated the name. "Never heard of it. Is it very new?"

"Not very."

"Who wrote it?"

"Herman Hesse."

Theo repeated the name. "I should know it, I suppose. What's it about?"

"It's about a man who's looking for something."

"Does he find it?"

"The search is the important thing, not the finding. I

think Siddhartha's trying to find the one thing that's true for him. The meaning of being."

"Sounds interesting." Theo went into his room, put on a bathrobe, sat down on the edge of his bed. Charles faced him, a faint smile lifting the corners of his mouth. "Yes?" Theo said.

"What?"

"I thought you were about to say something, Chuck."

"No."

Theo steadied his voice. "This is as good a time as any Chuck, for a serious talk, unless you'd rather not."

"What would you like to talk serious about?"

"We've drifted apart. A father and son should be close, don't you agree?"

"I do agree."

"No blame on anybody. I want to make that very clear. Not on you, or your mother. We have a problem and every problem has a solution somewhere. It's up to us to find it. I know you think this is corny, but I believe that a man can do just about anything he sets his mind to, if he tries hard enough. You agree?"

"I'll think about it."

"Yes," Theo said forcefully. "Think about it. And in the meantime let's get to know each other better. Do things with each other. You know, Chuck, the fishing here really is superb. Why don't we rent a boat . . ."

"Sure, but I don't want to fish."

"Oh. What do you say to hunting, then?"

"I just don't want to catch anything. Sorry if *that* sounds square to you."

"All right, what about this? I was talking to Betty Simons. She's got a friend, a real beauty, Betty tells me. Why don't the four of us have a night on the town?"

"Maybe we'd better not, Theo."

A shadow settled over Theo. He felt under attack. He wanted to strike back, but where was even a sporting target? Maybe the boy *was* a fag—well, if so, a night with a swinger would at least help straighten him out.

"Chuck," he said, presenting his most sincere expression. "I told your mother I'd look after you. I wouldn't want you telling her your old man ignored you."

"Don't worry. I won't."

Theo laughed nervously. "Tomorrow, Chuck, we'll spend the day together. You and me, around the pool. We'll talk—about *why* you don't want to hunt or fish or—"

"I thought I already told you—"

"Yes," Theo said coldly. "But maybe you could help your benighted father understand . . . look, forget it. Let's discuss that another time. Tomorrow, Betty may bring her friend around. If she's not your type, say so. A man's entitled to shop. I'm sure Betty has more than one friend. Take your time, slow and easy. Remember, Chuck, it's really your world!" He looped an arm across Charles's shoulders, moving him into the sitting room. "This little talk means a lot to me. Maybe we're coming closer. After all, we're two of a kind, flesh of my flesh and all that. Sleep well. Tomorrow's going to be a big day. For both of us."

Foreman arrived to find Harry Bristol in bed, the normally tan face drained of color, bloated puffs of skin supporting his eyes. His lips began to work.

"I called you fifteen minutes ago," he sputtered. "What took so long?"

Foreman kissed Shelly on the cheek, told her she had never looked lovelier, located a straight-backed chair, and drew it over to the bed. He straddled it, arms folded across the slatted back, chin resting on his hands. "Harry," he said with concern, "you look terrible."

"How do you like that! The joker's here! Well, if I look lousy it's because I feel lousy. My asshole's on fire and my guts haven't been still since Mexico City. On the way here we had to stop six times . . ."

"Five, Harry," Shelly corrected.

He glared at her. "What difference does it make? Five, six. All I know is I got no strength left and my fanny hurts from where I stabbed myself on a cactus."

The vision of Harry under simultaneous attack from a cactus and his bowels made Foreman feel pretty good. Good enough to laugh, which was a rarity with him these days. "You've gotta admit, Harry," he said, "it is funny."

"Yeah, well, maybe. Only not when it happened. The

least a sick man ought to get is some pity."

"Harry, you're just not a man one would associate with pity."

Bristol mulled it over. "That's for damn sure. Ever since I was a kid, I took pretty good care of me. Right. Screw that pity shit."

"Send to the drugstore for Entero-Vioforme, Shelly," Foreman said. "That'll plug the man up."

"You do that," Harry said to Shelly. "Now let's talk business, Foreman. Fill me in."

"Not much to tell. I've been soaking up the ambience, checking possible location sites. I'll be doing it again tonight."

"As long as shooting starts day after tomorrow. Got that?"

" 'For some must follow and some command,' " Foreman recited. "Chaucer said that, Harry. You know Chaucer, Harry?"

Bristol's swollen eyes seemed to turn inward. "Maybe hiring you was a mistake."

"We can tear up the contract. Merely say the word. After all, Harry, the only good producer's a happy producer. If I make you unhappy—"

"Nobody said anything about tearing up any contracts. The way to make me happy is to get going on *Love, Love,* to make it great. I depend on you, Paul. Who else have I got, right? Do right by me and when the time comes you'll find me right there. . . ."

Foreman let it pass. "You'll get my best shot."

"You're okay. I know that."

"As long as you don't expect me to be what I'm not," Foreman said.

A brief, hard smile touched Bristol's mouth, and there was a faint note of recognition in his eyes. "Sure. An artist can only do his own thing, right? I know that. And you've got complete freedom on this picture. Just deliver—" He broke off, grinning. "Look at us, knocking it back and forth over nothing. Everything's going to be terrific with us, I can feel it. Tell me about tonight. Where are you going?"

Foreman told him about Leo, that he intended to get a personal version of a hippie's eye-view of Acapulco night life.

"That's great!" Bristol enthused. "Night life is part of the scene I want in the picture. I got an idea. Take Shelly with you. The star of this epic might as well know about the action."

"Oh, Harry," she protested. "Maybe Paul's got a date—"

"So what! Did I tell him to try and score with you? Whataya say, Foreman?"

"An evening with Shelly would be my pleasure."

"There," Bristol said. "It's settled. Now let's go over the shooting schedule. I think we can cut out a day at least . . ."

Bernard Louis Font picked his way cautiously down the wide steps that led to the Roman pool, trundling past a fragrant line of red and orange bougainvillea in pursuit of the little Mexican maid. A pretty girl with excellent skin and a coquette's smile; her legs were remarkably well-shaped for a Mexican, Bernard remarked to himself. The Frenchman fancied himself a connoisseur of women's legs and bottoms, having spent the better part of a lifetime researching the subject, by sight, touch, and otherwise.

Bernard was willing to make allowances for faulty bottoms; too big or too flat, slung too close to Mother Earth. Bottoms could be concealed, disguised, sat on and otherwise removed from public view. But not legs. They were always on display. Pillars of support, the beginnings of grace and beauty. This pretty little *muchacha,* what kind of thighs did she have?

"Bernard!" Samantha greeted him at the pool.

"Samantha!" He took both her hands in his, kissed each in turn. "My dear, you're lovelier than ever."

Samantha wore only a white bikini, her lean body brown and shining with oil. She deposited herself back on the deck chair. "How good of you to come, Bernard."

"How good of you to invite me."

"Are you famished, Bernard?"

"Absolutely."

Samantha addressed the maid. "María, *traiga la comida, por favor.*"

Sí, señorita."

Bernard watched the maid depart. Her thighs he concluded would be excellent, strong and round, precisely joined.

Samantha took the opportunity to wipe the wet spots on her knuckles where Bernard had kissed her; if only he didn't drool so! She placed a wide-brimmed, green straw hat on her head and donned large, round, dark glasses. Samantha had been wearing them for years, had actually presented a pair as a gift to Princess Grace one season.

"Would you like a swim, Bernard? The sun is stifling and—"

"Never. My figure without clothes is less than beautiful. I prefer to conceal it from the elements and the eyes of the curious, except at night. And I, of course, sleep in the dark."

"I do believe you're being naughty."

"As a Frenchman, I should admit it. As a French gentleman, I shall ignore the suggestion."

Samantha's face lengthened. "Bernard, I asked you here today for purely selfish reasons. Since our last conversation, I have been troubled. My economic plight is a heavy one."

"Come now. Everything is comparative. Samantha Moore is a woman of property, not close to the edge of starvation."

"That isn't good enough, however." She straightened up, swinging round to face him, voice neatly formed and edged. "To get by doesn't suit me. It is vital that I continue to live as I've been living, at the same level. I *intend* to do so."

"And it is my intention to assist you."

"You suggested last time that in order to accomplish this my income must increase."

"Or else dip into capital, which I must severely advise against. With inflation—"

"So we come to the second stage—eliminating certain expenses." Her manner softened and she leaned back in the deck chair. "Very well. But my essential life style must not be affected."

The maid appeared with lunch. She arranged two glass-topped tables and served the food, then withdrew. Bernard admired her efficiency; Samantha had trained her well.

"What am I to do?" Samantha said.

"Begin at the beginning," he replied, chewing delicately on small bits of chicken. No rice, however, in consideration of his expanding middle. And definitely no *bolillos*. As one grew older, he reminded himself, temptation was everywhere but the sensual pleasures exacted a heavy toll.

"Where is the beginning?" Samantha asked.

"The staff at Villa Gloria. You employ too, too many servants. The girl who served—she's new?"

"Relatively."

"There! It is you who have been naughty, adding help when economies are in order. Let us face realities. How many automobiles stand at this very moment in your garage?"

"Bernard!" she cried, obviously alarmed.

"*Three*, three automobiles. This chicken is superb. How is it done, my dear?"

"A splash of rosé and Lupe, my chief cook works magic in the kitchen. May I serve you another breast, Bernard?"

"I mustn't."

"A leg, then."

"The small one."

She settled back, watching him eat. "A woman without transportation is a peasant."

"*Three* cars . . ."

"When you say it like that it does sound extravagant. What do you suggest?"

"The Daimler would bring a substantial price."

"Bernard, I *love* the Daimler. I *revere* it. Let me keep the Daimler."

"Very well, but only if the Rolls and the Thunderbird go in its place."

Very slowly, she lifted the dark glasses away from her face. "That I reserve tears is testimony only to my self-control, Bernard."

"I've always considered Samantha Moore to be a woman of sterling character."

She returned the glasses to their perch, began to eat again. "The chicken is good, isn't it?"

"The *Starfish*," Bernard spoke in a penetrating voice.

Samantha arranged knife and fork on her plate, patted her lips. "Not the *Starfish*."

"A yacht is the supreme luxury."

"The *Starfish*—weekends along the coast. Fishing expeditions. What memories!"

"For three hundred days of the year it lies idle and the crew draws full salary. Add to that upkeep, repair, painting."

"My morale is rapidly plummeting."

"I'm not suggesting you sell the *Starfish*. There is another way. Put it up for charter. Let the boat earn its way, show a profit."

"Am I to go into trade, as our English friends say?"

"The income would be considerable."

"I shouldn't know how to arrange such a situation."

"But I do. Just give me the word—"

She sighed and gave him a wistful smile. "The word is yes, I'm afraid."

"Good."

"Bernard, a dessert. A tart, strawberry, and wonderfully good."

"Ah, you mustn't tempt me."

"Coffee?"

"Black. Without sugar."

Samantha rang and María materialized. "*Dos cafés, María.* Are you sure about the tart, Bernard?"

He threw up his hands helplessly. "Men my age are notoriously weak, self-indulgent."

"*Y traigale un pastel al señor, María.*"

María went away.

"There is more fat to be sliced away," Bernard said.

"Tell me the worst."

"The household staff—fifty percent of the servants must be released."

"How cruel, Bernard! Those poor people, simple *rancheros*. Little more than children. Without me they'd be lost. I am father and mother to them all. What would they do, where would they go, how would they live?"

"Sentiment must not be allowed to interfere with business. Be firm."

"You're right, of course."

"To be fair, the last shall be the first to go."

"Poor Carlos," she breathed. "Poor Hermano and Juanita and Marucha . . ."

"María," he prompted.

"Poor María."

He patted her brown thigh reassuringly. Firm for a woman of her years but too slender for Bernard's tastes. "Perhaps I can ease the blow somewhat. It happens that at this moment I am understaffed. My gardener ran off to Mexico City . . ."

"Hermano! What a lovely man he is. And a very good worker."

"There. It is settled then." He raised his brows. "Perhaps I can find a place for another maid. The girl who served us, what was her name?"

"María! Oh, Bernard, if only you could."

"I can, I shall. Hermano and María. Send them to me at your convenience." He massaged his palms together in satisfaction. "Now to the matter of your entertainment budget. A blight, I'm afraid."

"Bernard," she said severely, "would you cloister me in Villa Gloria, alone and forgotten? My reputation as a hostess, my social life. You must at least leave me those!"

"You are too modest. Samantha Moore is a decoration at every villa in Acapulco, at every party, a prize for every hostess. You have always been in demand, always will be. Women admire and envy you, their husbands adore and desire you."

"How sweet you are, Bernard."

"Truth is self-evident."

"I accept your advice, dear friend. Otherwise why call upon such a good and faithful adviser. Oh, but I am sad, and concerned. No more parties. Oh, Bernard! It is too much to ask, I cannot go through with it. What purpose remains in life if one cannot entertain one's friends? I shall grow depressed, sink into melancholy, become *old* before my time. Still—Bernard! I have a splendid idea! I will no longer entertain as before. My goodness, ten, twenty parties a season, plus two or three dinners each week. You're absolutely right. I have been extravagant."

"Your idea?"

"Ah—starting this season I shall limit myself to one party each year."

"One party," he insisted, with an accountant's lack of humor.

"One," she agreed, smiling mysteriously.

Later, when she was alone, Samantha unclasped the bra of her bikini and exposed her breasts to the sun. She wanted no unsightly lines to mar her tan. Under the warm sun, she considered that one party she would give. What a beautiful affair it would be! Very special. The most dramatic, most talked of party in all the history of Acapulco parties. Samantha's Annual Gala! The start of a new tradition. It would, she warned herself, need truly to be distinctive. Yet not too expensive. The thought sobered her. How to solve that problem? She would put her mind to it, think hard, seriously. She lifted her face to the sun and waited for a solution to present itself . . .

The evening began in a small restaurant in a narrow street behind the *zócalo*. Leo, Foreman, and Shelly Hanes were the only non-Mexicans present. The food was ordinary and the service erratic; Leo bragged about both.

"This isn't one of your dumb tourist traps. This is authentic Mexican, no phony sauces, no fawning waiters. This is the real Acapulco, pure Acapulco gold." He stared at Shelly as if trying to beam some silent message to her brain.

Uneasy, she busied herself with the food. "Has Acapulco always been a resort?"

"Run it down, Leo," Foreman said. "You're the guide."

Leo stuffed the greater portion of a beef taco into his mouth, began to talk. "The word is this place got going around 1927. Up till then there was nothing except a burro trail through the mountains. Then the government put through a single lane road."

"And that turned Acapulco into a popular resort?" Shelly said brightly. In black silk slacks and a black-and-turquoise overblouse, her black hair pulled straight back off her almost translucent brow, Shelly seemed less vulnerable to Foreman, more the chic, sophisticated woman one saw in expensive restaurants and nightclubs. Still, tension corded her pale throat and her eyes were never still. She seemed, he told himself, to walk in a haze of

fear, with a sort of stricken air about her that heightened
—or diminished, according to one's taste—the soft, warm
femaleness of her, afraid, a woman blessed, a woman
cursed. How to capture all *that* on film? If it could be
done, *Love, Love* just might be a living portrait of a
woman, a woman apparently running away, or toward,
something . . . what? He wondered if Shelly had any
idea.

"With the road," Leo was saying, "some of the sharper
locals began taking in guests. But the first real hotel didn't
get built until about seven years later. Good-bye unspoiled
innocence, hello Yankee dollar."

"But didn't it help the people too? Didn't they begin to
make more money, to live better?" Shelly asked.

"Wow," Leo said. "Are you for real!"

"Be nice, Leo," Foreman said mildly.

"Dig this place," Leo said. "Crawling with tourists.
Spending a fortune. But money goes to money. Profit-
mongers abound. People taking, only taking. Nobody just
grooves. There ain't no love. The toll road finished the
job," he ended.

"When was that?"

"Around 1950, and bingo—a Mexican Coney Island!"

"If I felt the way you do," Shelly said, "I wouldn't come
here."

"Score one for the good guys," Foreman said.

"Maybe not," Leo answered, rolling his watery eyes
back toward Shelly. "Out in that world is not where I
exist. No lust for profit, no ache to take, just groovin' on
the beauty of the day is all. I am with the people, the real
people, all one big tribe. We love . . ."

"I'm sorry," Shelly offered, and meant it.

Leo caressed his chin hairs and displayed his profile in
resolute disdain.

"Could we meet some of your friends? Shelly said.

"Oil and water," Leo chanted. "Oil and water."

"That means," Foreman said, "that Leo is a snob. We're
not good enough to mix with those loving friends of his."

Leo opened his mouth to speak, clamped it shut, and
stared into space.

"Cheer up," Foreman said. "You can't expect to deprive the world of your true, loving nature forever." His
pale skin drew tight, seemed to gleam in the soft light.

"Okay, I've had it with this joint. Let's split. Lead on, noble Leo . . ."

Next was a nightclub tucked into the wine cellar of a private home. Thick, stone walls, high archways, low couches and mariachis singing romantic Latin songs marked the place. They sipped brandy and Foreman grew impatient.

"Turn a corner and you trip across mariachis in Mexico. Do better next time, Leo . . ."

A twenty-minute taxi ride took them to the far end of the Costera and a discotheque. Foreman switched to Scotch and watched the dancers and imagined he was in New York, or Chicago, or San Francisco. The amplified rock beat throbbed inside his skull and he tried without success to close it out. He ordered another drink.

A man with the shoulders of a football player danced close to their table, attention focused on his partner's jerking pelvis. He backed into Shelly, danced on without missing a beat.

Foreman came to his feet, spinning the dancer around. His speech was by now slurred and heavy. "Watch it, fella!"

The football player grinned. "What's your problem?"

"If you're too drunk to watch where—"

The football player blinked. "Looks like you're the drunk of the crowd, mister."

Shelly reached out. "Please, Paul, it's all right."

"That's right, Paul," the football player said. "Be good, boy."

Foreman punched out. A hand flashed up to deflect the blow and suddenly Foreman was helpless in the big man's grasp, almost lifted off the floor.

"Oh, my God!" Shelly cried.

"Peace," Leo said, prudently moving aside.

The football player heaved Foreman backward. "Peace," he echoed cheerfully. "Or a busted face, if you want it." He went back to his partner, who had never ceased gyrating.

Foreman slumped into his seat, chin hanging.

"Are you all right, Paul?" Shelly said anxiously.

"Wow," Leo said. "You were lucky, man. That cat would've laid it on you."

"Let's go," Foreman said thickly.

"Where to?"

"Let's go," Foreman repeated. "Let's go!"

Leo said, "I know a place . . ."

The cab circled the cathedral, charged up a steep incline, narrowly missing a pair of coupling dogs. The hill crested and they rattled down the back side, crossed a highway, and went bouncing along a dirt road. The taxi swung left, then right, and right again.

"Where the hell are we?" Foreman asked sullenly. His rage had subsided and only shame remained, shame and the urge to punish someone for his humiliation.

The cab stopped alongside an ancient stone wall. They got out.

"What is this, Leo?"

"Faith, baby. Follow the yellow-brick road. This way." The wall ended and they found themselves on a cobble-stoned walk. Fifty feet farther along they confronted another, newer wall, the top spiked with glass shards imbedded in cement. A carved wooden door swung open in response to Leo's knock and a husky Mexican in a red-and-blue uniform with brass buttons inspected them sourly, before standing aside.

"*Pase, por favor.*"

"*El Tiburón,*" Leo said, leading the way.

They crossed a broad patio lined with cactus, yellow lanterns swaying from high wires overhead. A fountain dribbled without conviction and a painted shrine to an obscure saint stood in one corner next to a wild orange tree.

"How beautiful," Shelly said. "Peaceful, sort of gentle. I'd like to live here, eat under the open sky, always surrounded by beauty."

"I figured you'd like this place," Leo said.

A short, stone passageway took them into a garden redolent with flowering bushes and trees. Up six shallow steps and they were on a wide terrace fronting a massive house built in the colonial style. French doors opened into a spacious chamber with couches scattered about. Flickering candles made the room seem smaller and more intimate than it was. Voices echoed softly and shadowed figures seemed to glide through the dim light.

A woman in a flowing gown seated them, took their drink order. Minutes later a Mexican in a white lace shirt and tight pants served them.

"How about this!" Leo said.

Shelly spoke in a whisper. "I never saw . . . it's so strange . . . mysterious."

"Exotic," Leo added. "Put this in your flick," he said to Foreman.

Foreman made an effort to penetrate the haze that blurred his vision. "Leo," he said, the words coming slow and ponderous. "Remember Little Big Horn . . ."

"Man, you are bombed out of your skull!"

Foreman pressed the heels of his hands against his eyes; he shook his head, peered into the darkness. The world had been transformed into a supercolossal Cecil B. De Mille production.

Magnificent! Massive! Monumental!

A cast of thousands!

Starring—

A woman floated into view and Foreman imagined she was naked from the waist up. He blinked, trying to bring her into focus; she was gone too soon.

Foreman desired to be drunk. Blind, crazy drunk. Safely drunk, with a clear excuse for making a fool of himself, some good external reason for the numbed state of his senses, for his angry frustration, his inability to be the man he wanted to be—needed to be. Which was . . . ? A waiter went by and Foreman clutched at him, ordering another round. Tension built in him, took hold along the inside of his skull. A sharp ache lodged above one eye. Invisible cords fastened him in place and the Lilliputians gathered around, giving off soundless cries of joy and jabbing him with pointed sticks.

A guitar sounded back in the dark. Foreman strained to identify the melody.

" '*Estrellita!* '" he shouted, voice breaking.

"What?"

"The song, the song, dammit, the song . . ."

Girlish laughter without innocence or delight faded in and out of the music. Fear took hold of Foreman and he hit it in anger.

"What the hell is going on?"

"There's gambling in the back . . ."

"What is this place?"

"El Tiburón . . ."

"Screw all sharks."

Leo's voice drifted out of the darkness. "I'll be around."

Someone held Foreman's hand. He jerked free, looked around. Shelly, very small, as if at the end of a long tunnel, pulling away.

"We should go . . ."

A tall girl in a lacy pink gown stood in front of him. Her eyes were great rounds and a smile was fixed on her mouth.

"Dance with me . . ."

Foreman danced through the darkness. Faint music came from unseen corners, and the shuffle of other dancers. The girl was big, her arms holding him tightly, bellyheat seeping through his clothes.

"They call me Charlene."

"They?"

"People. Men."

"What else do they call you?" He laughed, and knew it wasn't funny.

"Men have different tastes. Have you some special taste?"

"I'm queer," Foreman said.

"I don't believe it."

"Queer for My-T-Fine chocolate pudding with ice-cold sweet cream. Mother was a pusher and hooked me early."

The holiday smile hardened into a thin line. "Is it a joke?"

" 'Humor is the mistress of tears.' "

"I'm not sure I understand you."

"Me either. I suppose I'm looking for something and haven't a clue what the hell it is."

Charlene directed one ample thigh between Foreman's legs. "Thinking can spoil a man for other things. I have a room, let's go there. I'm sure I can divert you."

Foreman assessed her soberly—which was a laugh. "What do you have in mind?"

"So. Say what it is you want and Charlene will supply it. You and I together. Or would you prefer something more congenial, other girls? Your own pretty friend, perhaps? Watch, if you like, while Charlene does what she does so very well, or participate, as you prefer."

Foreman disengaged himself, stepped back. "Sonofabitch! A cat house."

"Please. There is no need for vulgarity in the public
rooms. Upstairs if that is your pleasure . . ."

Foreman stumbled away, hunting for Shelly. He called
her name. Louder. He tripped and fell, picked himself up
and went on. An open doorway led him into a book-lined
room. A gray-haired man was reading. He raised his head.
"Are you looking for something special?"

Foreman plunged back into the darkness. Again he went
down, feeling his way along the stone floor. Cool air
touched his cheek and he shivered. He was on the open
patio at the front of the house. He went back inside.

A sleek Mexican with large white teeth and a ready
smile sat with Shelly, talking urgently. He stood up at
Foreman's approach and offered his hand. *"Señor,* I am
Roque. I have been entertaining your wife."

"The lady isn't my wife," Foreman blurted out. "Are
you all right?" he said to Shelly.

"Paul, please, take me out of here. I'm frightened."

"There is nothing to fear here," Roque said. "Whatever
you wish will be supplied. I assure you . . ."

Foreman drove his fist low in Roque's belly. Air burst
out of him and he doubled over. Foreman hit him behind
the ear and he went down.

"C'mon," Foreman said, taking Shelly's hand. "The
party's over."

By the time they made it back over the hill and down
to the beach Foreman's anger seemed lost, his head
remarkably clear. At the surf line he splashed water on
his face, the back of his neck.

He stood up. "I'll take you back to your hotel now."

"Let's walk on the beach, please."

They moved along without touching, without speaking,
Shelly carrying her shoes in her hands. Foreman broke
the silence. "This town. Honky-tonk. Everywhere you
look, there's a hand out, begging or picking your pocket."

"I felt so awful back there. That man, the things he

said. I wanted to believe that kind of filth was behind me. I was wrong."

"Leo—"

"Why blame Leo? Being afraid is what I do best. Helpless, too, ever since I was young. I never had any friends. I don't have any now."

"I'd sign up."

"That would be nice," she said almost formally. "To have a friend before it, well, happens."

"What? What the hell are you talking about?" The skin across his shoulders grew cold.

"I've known it for a long time, I mean that I was going to die. I get hot flashes—at the most unexpected times. And headaches all the way down to my knees. And the weakness . . ."

He stopped walking and she turned back to face him. "Have you seen a doctor, Shelly?"

"Doctors say my blood isn't quite right, but they won't tell me what it is. Some say it's anemia, but they lie, you know. I guess they want to be kind. I understand but they can't fool me. Some days it's impossible for me to swallow my food and I have awful nightmares. I wake up sweating and crying . . . I went to a library and looked it up in a medical encyclopedia. The symptoms are unmistakable, Paul. Leukemia is what I have and it's going to kill me by New Year's Eve. I just know it. . . ."

They sat on the sand not far from the Hilton watching the moon-streaked bay, the white-capped night waves.

"*Love, Love* is very important to me," she said, voice low. "Harry's giving me a chance to do one really good thing. I want so much for it to be good, my part in it. You'll help me, won't you, Paul? I need help."

"Yes."

Foreman strained to sort out his reactions to Shelly's announcement. If she really had leukemia, how in hell could he even begin to comfort her? But why had the doctors told her anemia? That would be playing God with a vengeance. Unless that was, in fact, what she had— despite her more dramatic convictions, doubtless sincerely held, out of her deep need for attention, at least for sympathy, if not love. Either way, for real or imagined, she was an explosive situation. And he liked her.

"You're depressed," she said. "And it's my fault. Let's change the subject. Shall I tell you how Harry and I met?"

"How did you and Harry meet?"

"Well, I was living in Hollywood. I appeared in some pictures, three altogether, and I had the usual dreams of becoming a big star. But it wasn't right for me. My type was out of style in those days." She hesitated before going on. "I decided to go away, to forget about the movies. I went to San Francisco; actually, Sausalito. Have you ever been? It's very artistic, lots of painters and writers and poets. I did some modeling for a sculptor and for an art class. They gave me free painting lessons instead of money. I wasn't very good at it.

"One day I met Ceci, who had been in Vegas. She said the money was pretty good and it sounded okay so I went."

"And met Harry . . ."

She nodded. "I worked as a change girl for the slots and I made the mistake of playing them whenever I had time off. My money went right back into those cruddy machines.

"There were always lots of parties and I went to most of them. That's how I met Harry. He's the most dynamic man I ever knew, always doing something, always making plans. He's very ambitious. He was making nudies but he let me know right away that he was going to do something better. I could tell he really liked me because he at least respected me too much to put me into a nudie. He said that when the right picture came along, he'd use me. And he kept his word, Paul. He's the only man I've ever known who did. Harry changed my luck. I promised myself I'd be good for him and I've really tried.

"Not everybody likes Harry," she went on as if apologizing. "Sometimes he tries too hard and people misunderstand. He's been square with me, though.

"When he decided to make *Love, Love* he told me I was going to star in it. He even signed a personal manager's contract with me.

"Making the nude scene with Jim Sawyer was funny.

We were introduced only a few minutes before we began making love without any clothes on. We weren't actually making love, it was only acting.

"It took three days to shoot the sequence. It's very good, I think. Harry was very excited the first time we looked at the film. You'd've thought we were actually *doing* it, but Jim was never *inside* of me." She paused. "Seeing myself naked like that, it was hardly embarrassing at all. So you see, if *Love, Love* is good, it'll be like my legacy. Something beautiful to leave behind. That's important to me."

He cleared his throat, still wondering, and stood up. "It's late. Harry must be worried about you."

A small smile on her full lips. "That's nice, to have somebody who worries about you."

3

Under a translucent sky and a warming morning sun, a group of tourists gathered around the Monument to the Heroes on the Malecón opposite the *zócalo*. Curious, Charles Gavin took up a position nearby to listen to the tour guide.

"The bust in the center of the monument," the guide began in carefully enunciated English, "is, as you can readily see for yourselves, flanked on either side by a cannon. With such cannon was the Revolution fought and won.

"The bust in question is of Padre Miguel Hidalgo y Costilla, parish priest of the town of Dolores in the state of Guanajuato. A gentle man of supreme intelligence, Hidalgo issued the famous *Grito de Dolores*, the Cry of Dolores, which was a call for freedom. With it was inaugurated the Mexican Revolution on the night of September 15, 1810.

"To the right, we have the bust of Benito Juárez. Benito Juárez was a Zapotec shepherd from the hill country above Oaxaca and it was he as much as any man who forged liberalism and anti-clericalism into a single political force ..."

A man with a chicken neck leaned over and spoke loudly to his wife. "He means that Mexico is an atheist country."

"I thought they were all Catholics," she replied.

"Por favor," the guide said, his distress showing. "Not atheist. Mexican people believe very much in God, but for us it is better if the Church looks after our souls and not our pocketbooks. Since the Church in Mexico cannot own property, the priests do not become more concerned with land than with people, and that is a good thing, I think.

"So, back to Benito Juárez," the guide said. "Juárez was a very determined person. He made a promise to the woman he was in love with that he would one day become rich, successful, and famous. All three of these he became and he liberated my country from Napoleon III and Maximilian.

"The figure on the left is Vicente Guerrero, after whom this state is named. And he is another hero of the Revolution." The guide put his back to the monument. "I will tell you a little about Acapulco now. Not about the beautiful views and wonderful weather. Not about the pretty beaches and all the pretty girls—" He waited for a laugh, and got the routine stares. Tourists get tired. "No, I will tell you about the history of this place.

"First part, the original peoples. Would you believe it, we don't know very much about them. They were not like the Aztecs who built in stone. The tribes in this section of the country left little of themselves behind. But some artifacts which are about two thousand years old have been dug up. What do they tell us?"

He paused, unencouraged by group apathy, but pushed on. "They tell us that here existed a very high form of civilization. I do not want you to think that these people had jet airplanes and color television and drank Coca-Cola—no. These findings show Oriental influence and it is believed that these Indians had contact with the peoples of the Pacific islands also. Unfortunately, ladies and gentlemen, the Mexican government doesn't have a lot of money to spend on excavations and many traces of these ancient peoples have been covered over by the jungle.

"Second part, Hernán Cortés and the Spanish conquistadores. The Spaniards made use of the magnificent natural facilities offered by the Bay of Acapulco as early as the beginning of the sixteenth century. From here, the Spaniards explored the coast and they built a settlement in what is now Puerto Marqués inlet, which they thought would be an easier place to defend in case of attack, no? Also, they cut a trail across the mountains so that burros could take treasure to Mexico City and bring back supplies. Later pirates arrived, including Sir Francis Drake. He was a pirate to the Spaniards and a hero to the English. It goes that way today also, no!" Modest, grudging laughter—he hurried on. "The Spanish built a big fort in the bay but it was destroyed by an earthquake in 1776, same year as the American Revolution.

"Third part, the Mexican War of Independence. My people free themselves from Spain. *Viva Mexico!* After that, no more trade with China, and the jungle wiped out the burro trail. Acapulco stopped being important to anybody.

"Fourth part. Mexican people discover again how beautiful is Acapulco. Next *norteamericanos* find out. Better to be here warm and clean than in garbage strikes in New York City or Minnesota blizzards." A smattering of applause. "Today United States citizens like yourselves still come. Acapulco is Riviera of the West, no? Now we go inside the cathedral. Follow me, please . . ."

Charles went into the *zócalo* and settled onto a bench. A shoeshine boy appeared and Charles agreed to let him work on his shoes. An elderly homosexual left his table at the sidewalk cafe across the street and tried to engage Charles in conversation, was waved away. A second boy offered to sell him some Chiclets. He bought two packs. The shineboy finished and Charles admired his handiwork.

"Very pretty," someone said.

On the next bench, two American girls. Both young and pretty, with long, careless hair, jeans, and loose-fitting Mexican blouses.

"A mark of distinction," Charles said.

"That was obvious to us right away," the prettier of the two girls said. "You can sit with us, if you want."

They made room for him between them. Charles slumped down to the bottom of his spine and considered his shoes. "That's a very righteous shine. I mean, in New York a shine like that would go for maybe half a buck."

"You're a financier?" the second girl said.

"Not really."

"Then why so much talk about bread?"

"One time—"

"What else can you talk about?" the first girl said.

"You want to hear all about the history of Acapulco? I happen to be a recent authority."

The second girl smothered a grin behind her hand. Her friend scowled. "Maybe you're one of *them*." She hooked a finger back toward the Monument to the Heroes.

"Them," Charles said reflectively. "Us. And all this time I thought I was just me."

"I don't think much of him," the second girl said.

"Oh, he's okay," her friend said. "What's your name?"

"Charles."

"I'm Becky, for Rebecca, and she's Livy, for Olivia."

"Hi."

"You're new?" Livy said.

"We just got here yesterday."

"Who's we?"

"Theo and me. My father."

"Your *father!*"

Livy groaned and Becky put her face in her hands.

"Your father," Livy said again.

Charles bobbed his head up and down, up and down in that special way that so bothered Theo. "You're right, all right. Mine is a long, sad story. First part, Theo and Julia are divorced . . ."

"Big deal!" Livy snapped.

"An old story," Becky said.

"But wait—Theo wants to be my buddy, my mate for life."

Livy, hunched over, gave off a mournful wail. "Your story, my life."

"And mine," Becky said, not unkindly. "Only my folks were glad when I split. You know what my mother's thing was? Explaining *life* to me. But it was her life, her wasted, money-grubbing, suburban-fuckinglife."

"What do any of them know about life?" Livy said. "Theirs, yours, or mine?"

Charles didn't hear her. His eyes were on Becky. He decided she was one of the prettiest girls he'd ever seen, her face softly shaped, the eyes a faded green, her mouth on the edge of smiling. Her neck was long and graceful and when she moved, her breasts also moved freely under the Mexican blouse.

Livy's voice, like her round face, seemed dull, without life, Charles thought. Suddenly.

"They fucked up good," Livy said.

"How?" Charles said.

"How! We lived in a town in Indiana. A small, small town. My father never had the guts to get out where the action was, to find out what he was. So he stuck my mother and me away there too. I was pretty square then. Y'know, football games, proms, studying; all of it. I finished first in my class. *Numéro uno,* you should pardon my Spanish.

"I thought I was pretty good when I went up to the university. And you know what I found out? That I was dumb, is what. *Dumb.* Like the teachers in that itty-bitty high school I went to didn't know anything, so I never *learned* anything. Not really. Not that it was any better in college. Hotshot professors filling your head with their pedantic bullshit, never *looking* at you.

"One time I went up to one of them on campus and said how do you do, like I was being very proper, right?—He never even recognized me."

"Unreal," Becky said. "My folks collected paintings. Art, my father called it. They bought all kinds of things and maybe some of it was good. But they didn't *know*. They just *bought*—Like squares painted all one color and labeled 'Number 14' and 'Hard Edge' and 'Pop Art.' They just collected."

"What about faces?" Charles said. "Nobody does faces anymore."

"Are you putting me on?" Becky said.

"I mean it. I'll bet there isn't a single painter in all of the beautiful-for-spacious United States of America who does portraits. Well, is there? If it wasn't for mirrors, nobody'd know what a human face looks like."

"Well said, young man," added Livy.

"I mean, even us, we're sitting and rapping and looking around or at the ground or, Livy, you keep digging your fingers. Nobody looks at anybody else. More painters who do faces. That's the ticket."

"Well," Becky said.

"Used to be," Charles stated with growing authority, "that any hack with a brush and paints could do a face. No more. We've forgotten how."

Livy's firm round face puckered and ridged and she contemplated Charles briefly, almost balefully. "I'm not so sure about him." She stood up.

"I'm all right!"

"Maybe . . ."

Becky rose. "We're going anyway. There're these cats

who have some very high-grade grass."

"I'll come along," Charles said, not wanting to be alone.

"No," Livy said. "They see us with another boy and they're liable to get uptight."

"Maybe another time," Becky said.

"Where will I find you?" Charles said to Becky. "Where are you staying?"

Livy's grin was a challenge. "Look on the beaches . . ."

"A real groove," Becky said. "You can always panhandle a tourist for a few pesos and there's better food dumped in the garbage at the big hotels than poor blacks eat back home." She started away and stopped. "We're heading out to Sunset now. We'll be there for a while, the far end. Come see us, if you want . . ."

Marcella Gonzales Cortina's house was a modest affair by Acapulco standards, with only three bedrooms and a small swimming pool shaped like an amoeba. It boasted a large, high-ceilinged living room decorated with English antiques and original oil paintings. Thick walls kept out the sun's heat and clover-shaped windows filled with orange, green and yellow glass filtered out the glare.

When Marcella bought the house, her nearest neighbor had been more than half a mile away and friends had advised her against the purchase, pointing out that she would be too far removed from the center of activity. But money for Marcella had been a concern—perennial with her— and the price had been right.

Only a few improvements had been made in the Villa. Two inner walls had been ripped out to alter the proportions of the living room and a small bedroom had been transformed into a huge closet, busy with drawers and enclosed hanging space. The most significant alteration had been done in the bathroom. Though quite large, it had been designed for strictly utilitarian purposes; Marcella changed all that. She had installed a deep, oval sink, a black-marble shelf extending out from either side of it, and gold faucets. An enclosed shower with eight heads strategically located; the floors tiled yellow-and-black, each tile to Marcella's specifications; and from floor to ceiling, the walls were covered with highly polished mirrors. It was the bathtub that was Marcella's peculiar pride and the source of so much comfort. It had been constructed on two levels, the upper shelf shaped for ease of sitting. Marcella used the room for a variety of purposes: beautifying herself, of course, writing letters (the warm water provided one with a sense of comradeship, encouraging long, friendly missives), dining in leisurely comfort (not always alone), talking on the phone, making love (a mirror added a touch of visual spice, a most satisfying lagniappe).

Life for Marcella in Acapulco was full, stimulating, and gracious; and Marcella seldom looked back to what might have been. Born in Cuba to a Spanish father and a Cuban mother, she grew up on a large estate thirty miles from Havana. She received her early education from private tutors and later was sent to Eden Hall, a Sacred Heart institution, near Philadelphia, which though rather progressive did not offend her father's sense of propriety.

Over the years, Marcella developed a number of valuable skills; she was able to speak, write, and read five languages fluently, she became an expert driver of fast cars, she learned to fly a light plane, to flirt with discretion. When she decided she wanted to marry Federico Francisco Vadillo, she ignored the fact he was already married and seduced him, arranged for her father to offer him an excellent job in his cigar factory, and convinced Federico to leave his wife. Though Señor Cortina disapproved of divorce, he made no objection to the marriage, unable to stand in opposition to his daughter's extraordinary will and ferocious temper. Shortly after the marriage ceremony, Marcella prevailed upon her father to promote Federico to a more worthy position; he took over the management of the cigar factory.

Within a year of the marriage, Marcella was shopping for a suitable lover; Federico, an avid tennis player, lacked the stamina for sports, for business, and for Marcella too.

All that became somewhat academic when Castro marched into Havana with his bearded band. Not quite able to grasp the significance the change in governments represented, Federico tried to get Fidel to endorse the Cortina panatella. "A Cortina cigar—the revolutionary smoke!" were the words he intended to put into Fidel's mouth. Before Federico could discover whether or not his plan had been put directly to the Supreme Leader, an enthusiastic Fidelista decided to speed up the revolutionary process and deposited a very sharp knife into Federico's broad back.

The funeral was modest, it being the collective family wisdom that any ostentatious display might be misunderstood by the aroused masses. Two days after the funeral, Señor Cortina suffered a fatal embolism.

Assembling what spare cash her father kept around the house—half a million American dollars, plus another million in blue-chip securities—Marcella herded her weeping mother and two faithful servants into a hired motor launch for the trip to Florida and freedom. Halfway across, on Marcella's command, the servants clubbed the boat owner on the head and dumped him overboard, thereby saving one thousand dollars and a dozen boxes of fine Havana cigars.

Eight days after their arrival in Miami, Marcella's mother was struck by a taxi on Collins Avenue. She died on the way to the hospital. Marcella buried her in consecrated ground, gave each of the servants five hundred dollars and her blessings, and took a plane to New York.

In a Fifth Avenue shoe salon, she met a French nobleman who sold her six pairs of shoes and began to court her. He refined her French accent, took her to very bad, but cheap French restaurants—he had no taste for food—and made energetic love to her. After three months, Marcella agreed to marry him.

Less than two years later, under the shoe salesman's management, Marcella's fortune stood at only a little more than three hundred thousand dollars. The Frenchman, Marcella understood, was a luxury she could no longer afford.

She flew to Juárez for a Mexican divorce, then went on to Acapulco. The remainder of her funds invested in Mexican financial bonds, Marcella vowed to live on the nine per cent they netted. She spent carefully; made sure to receive full value for every peso. And when she took a Mexican lover, she doled out only small amounts of money to him each week, leaving him always in need. For seven years this policy had kept her in lovers until she tired of them. Life in Mexico was considerably cheaper.

On this particular day, Samantha came to visit. Marcella found that odd since Samantha generally summoned her friends to Villa Gloria when she required company. Obviously Samantha had something in mind, came seeking a favor. Marcella restrained her curiosity and greeted her guest effusively, offered chilled sangría. They sat opposite each other in the living room, separated by a small table of inlaid native woods while Samantha reported on her European trip and Marcella recited all the local happenings.

Samantha lifted her glass, put it back down without drinking. "There's something I want to talk to you about, Marcella."

"Anything, my dear—"

"How shall I begin? Very well. Marcella, I have sworn off every one of those parasites that insinuate themselves into the lives of women such as ourselves."

"How right you are!" Marcella wondered where this would lead. She cautioned herself to be on guard; to say nothing without considering it twice. She smiled encouragingly.

"How long must I pay?" Samantha said without self-pity. "Don't I deserve a man who will be a man, take care of me?"

Marcella waited. No stress showed on her face, the face of someone who worried not at all about events over which she had no control. She touched her reddish-brown hair with learned casualness and showed her even, white teeth in a small smile when Samantha failed to continue.

"You deserve the best," she said. "We both do."

Samantha twisted her mouth in a childlike grimace. "Bernard informs me that my financial situation is not what it might be."

A flush of satisfaction came to Marcella. She remembered the estate outside Havana, the losses that damn shoe salesman had caused her, and felt somehow revenged by Samantha's difficulty.

"Bernard knows about such things," she said.

"He says the market may remain depressed for some

time, matters may grow worse."

"I don't trust this administration," Marcella said. "Inflation has already diminished the value of the peso and who knows where it will stop. This talk of helping the peons. Nonsense! They don't want help. The poor Mexican simply hasn't any ambition to improve his lot. I know. It was the same in Cuba. Samantha, I foresee the day when we may be forced to leave this country."

"Oh, no!"

"I had to flee Cuba leaving all my belongings behind."

"Where would I go?"

Marcella patted her friend's hand. "It isn't happening yet."

Samantha brightened. "That's true and there's no point in anticipating such a horrible prospect, is there? We must live for the present, isn't that so, Marcella?" Marcella nodded solemnly. "Let me tell you what I've been doing."

Marcella listened attentively; this was the reason for Samantha's visit and it occurred to Marcella that she herself might stand to profit in some as yet unforeseen manner.

"Marcella—I have let go nearly half of my household staff!"

"How dreadful!"

"And the *Starfish* is up for charter."

"Bernard's suggestions?"

"He insists on certain stringencies. The Rolls and the Thunderbird are to be sold."

"Bernard *knows*."

"And no . . . more . . . parties . . ."

"No! Without Samantha Moore's entertainments Acapulco will be so dreary."

Samantha sat straight in her chair, hands folded primly, small breasts pushed forward, the nipples in shadowed outline under her soft blue blouse.

"Not just yet, Marcella. After a great deal of thought, of soul-searching, I've decided to allow myself one party each season. But no more."

"Ah."

"I've submitted the idea to Bernard for his approval . . ."

"Else why a financial wizard for a friend?"

"Exactly. He approves, however reluctantly. But there

are difficulties. Which is why I've come to you, dear friend. For your invaluable advice."

"Whatever I can do——"

"You must give me your opinion, your honest opinion."

"You shall have it."

"Be brutal."

"I shan't spare you."

"Good. I intend to launch the new season with a massive fête, lavish, spectacular, one that will draw my friends from all over the world. This party must be special, exciting, dramatic. I want people to anticipate it for days, remember it for months. Do you see where I'm going, Marcella?"

"I do indeed. How clever you are!"

"You really think so?"

"I can, however, foresee some problems."

Samantha's face visibly changed—lines and pulls at the corners of her mouth. Dr. Koenig's warning voice came back to her and she produced a more pleasing expression.

"What problems?"

"To make such an affair different it must be different."

"I believe I've considered that." She spoke sharply, then, more kindly. "What would you say to a masked ball?"

"Commonplace, by itself, I fear. No, Samantha, the key lies in choosing a theme for the party, a raison d'être."

"My dear, what?"

"The evening must be fully integrated, relevant, God help us, to our times. . . ."

Samantha chewed her lip. She had believed that a large party was the solution to her social problem; but Marcella was right; more was required. An idea emerged.

"I have it!" she cried.

"Yes?"

"An Indian party. Yes, a Mexican Indian costume party. Mixtec, Aztec, whatever. There will be native dancers and music——" She recognized the expression of doubt on Marcella's face and fell silent. "You don't think it's a good idea . . ."

"On the contrary, I do."

"But?"

"What we want is an uncommon idea, yes?"

"Yes." Samantha slumped back in her chair. "It is rather vulgar, I suppose."

"Limited is the word. What would you say to the Indian motif carried forward to a broader, deeper, more rewarding canvas, one alive with the past, present, and even the future?"

"Marcella! You make it sound so exciting!"

Marcella leaned forward, spoke in a low, intense voice. "Mexican history!"

Samantha didn't know what to say; she said nothing.

"Send out invitations on scrolls of parchment. They must be written in hand in the old style. Everyone must come as a character, actual or fictional, out of the glorious history of the Republic. Cortés, Montezuma, Zapata, anyone at all. Some people may wish to come collectively, presenting a historical *scene,* a tableau depicting a famous event . . ."

"Marcella!"

"Do you like my idea?"

"I . . . it's stupendous!"

Marcella squeezed her eyes shut and Samantha understood that she was *thinking.* "There was a gap in the circle but I have found the missing fragment." Her eyes opened. "The Home for Unmarried Mothers . . ."

"You do so many good deeds, Marcella, and I've done nothing. I've meant to volunteer."

"Here is your chance. Provide a sensible *social* purpose for your gala. Raise funds for The Home. Sell tickets to the party, Samantha."

"Sell . . . !"

"Of course. No one in Acapulco has ever done it before. Be the first. Price the tickets exorbitantly high. Let's say five hundred dollars a couple. Yes, that has a nice sound to it. That will bring in a goodly sum for the Unmarried Mothers and keep out the wrong sort of people. Of course, all the expenses of giving the party would be paid out of the money collected."

"Is that quite honorable?"

"Everybody does it, my dear."

Samantha took Marcella's hands in her own. "Dear, dear, brilliant friend. What would I ever do without you?"

"I've no idea. But with me you will have the party of

the season, Samantha, indeed, of the decade."

"The idea is simple," Foreman said, slurring his words. "The important thing is to use what Acapulco has to offer —the bay, the beaches, the ocean, the singular appearance of the streets and the shops, the houses, the contrast of rich and poor. And always those great craggy mountains looming up like portents."

"The more outdoor stuff we use," Bristol said happily, "the less we got to spend paying for interiors or building sets. You're thinking with me now. . . ."

Jim Sawyer said, "What about the script, or rather the lack of script?" He was a tall man with the handsome, flat expression of a career Marine on a recruiting poster. Thick arms and shoulders gave him a top-heavy appearance, as if his body were truncated, somehow deformed. "I like to work with a script. How else can I learn my lines? Develop my characterization? It makes me feel better. After all, I am an actor, not just a pretty face, if you know what I mean."

"What about that?" Bristol said, as if trying to be heard across the room. "Maybe you ought to knock out a script."

"No script," Foreman said tonelessly. "Dialogue will be supplied as needed. In the interest of spontaneity," he added. "I'll try to explain what I'm after in the picture. I've worked up personalities and background for each character. With that information, with a growing feeling for the character each of you portrays, none of us will reach for easy responses from the audience. Nobody will have a chance for the cheap effect. What I want is to grab the audience early on and bring it into the life of the picture, make it a participant in experience instead of a collection of onlookers. This is a love story, I hope. Love in all its varieties, including the ecstasy, the degradation, the madness, and the true sanity of it. The film needs the cadence of a heartbeat, the rhythm of a living person."

"You make it sound beautiful," Shelly said.

"Sorry to get carried away. I know all that sounds sort of pompous. What I really want is a love story—I mean a real one. That will do just fine."

"I'll do my best for you," Sawyer said, and meant it.

"Hold it!" Bristol snapped out like a drill instructor. "What are you talking about? Maybe you think you're Rembrandt and I'm your patron! Forget it. Give me a picture people will pay to see, a crowd pleaser."

"You said you wanted an artistic picture, Harry," Shelly said.

"Artistic *looking*. Give 'em a hard on, open their tear ducts, that's what I want."

"I just said a love story would be just fine," Foreman said, "but I'm not talking about kitsch."

"Save it for your speech to the New York film critics. I want a *Love Story*, too—low budget, with plenty of sex. Sock it to 'em. Pull 'em into the theaters."

"This project," Foreman said, holding his annoyance, "can be good *and* commercial."

Bristol shook his head. "Just remember I'm not interested in hollow victories. This picture has to make it for me. Set me up."

"Do it my way and you'll get everything you want. Depend on it."

"Bristol depends on Bristol. Come through and it'll be steady-Eddie with us two. Otherwise—"

"Let me explain, Harry. You see, I've changed the story line."

"I liked it the way it was."

"Listen, Harry. Shelly is on the run. As the wife of a successful industrialist, she's been turned into another business asset. One morning she wakes up and decides to cash in. She leaves, makes her way to Mexico, meets Sawyer. He is also on the run, but from himself. He's had a breakdown, is afraid he might kill someone. Maybe himself. The two of them learn to feel alive again through each other. They do simple things, concrete, that reveal them to the audience, that tell us who they are."

"Where's the sex?"

"That twenty minutes of yours, Harry. I can use almost all of it. In short takes, almost subliminal at first, then longer sequences."

"It sounds marvelous!" Shelly said.

"You shut up!" Bristol said.

"There'll be new love scenes, Harry," Foreman added hurriedly. "As it develops naturally out of the characters and the action. Film is visual, Harry. You said it yourself, a minimum of talk. Fluid movement backward and forward in time, soft lighting, slow dissolves for continuity, for the tempo of these two people's lives . . ." He swung around to the far corner of Bristol's hotel room, to where Gary McClintock stood against the wall. "Mac, afternoon, take your camera up into those mountains, get me a head-on shot of the sun setting."

"What the hell for?" Bristol wanted to know.

"I'm not sure yet," Foreman answered. "But I'll use it, it won't be wasted. This afternoon we begin shooting. First the beach scenes. Very simple. Long shots of Shelly sunning herself, walking, the meeting with Jim. But after today, I'm going to work the skin off you two." He glanced over at Bristol. Some of the color had returned to the flat face.

"One more thing," Bristol said.

"What's that?" Foreman asked.

"That place you took Shelly to last night—"

Foreman looked at Shelly; she avoided his eyes. He wondered if she ever *looked* at anyone.

"It was a mistake, Harry," he said.

"Sounds okay to me. I'll contact the management, maybe we can work it into the picture."

"I'll think about it, Harry."

"You do that."

Charles dozed at the edge of the pool in the hot sun. Unlike his father, Charles didn't tan easily. He had already discovered that the tropical sun was different from any he had ever known, brighter and more intense, threatening. And he had felt threatened ever since arriving in Acapulco, as if some secret part of himself were under attack.

The drone of his father's voice woke him. The voice of accomplishment. The voice of how-to.

Charles pushed himself onto his elbows. With two other men, both wearing business suits, Theo sat at an umbrella-shaded table. They were sipping cold drinks and poring over graphs, sales projections, advertising layouts. A cloud of determination seemed to waft up from them.

Theo had said that this afternoon belonged to him and Charles. He talked about swimming in the bay, taking a glassbottomed boat ride around the harbor. Inexplicably, Charles wanted to see the underwater statue of the Virgin of Guadalupe. What possessed people to sink a gold religious statue under the water? Looking at it, an answer might come. But not today. Maybe not any day. Unless Theo should suddenly rise and announce that the business conference was at an end, the rest of the day belonged to his son. Not likely, thank God.

Charles lay back down, mind wandering. He remembered the man he had met here at the pool —Paul Foreman, and he wondered if Paul Foreman was a father . . .

Shadowed behind dark glasses, Theo's eyes were alert, searching the faces of the two men opposite. Reaching for every advantage always, Theo had chosen to sit in the shade; neither of his employees dared to suggest that the angle of the umbrella be adjusted to protect them all from the sun. Sweat stood out on Marvin Williamson's bald pate and he mopped it repeatedly with his handkerchief. The other man, Jerry Baumer, didn't sweat as much but he found it impossible to keep from squirming in his chair. Baumer was a plump and ordinarily jovial man with a small red mouth and pink cheeks. He spoke in a thin, reedy voice that most people found vaguely unpleasant.

"This has been a most rewarding meet, Mr. G., enriching I would say. These get-togethers keep a man on his toes, so to speak. My batteries are recharged. A session like this, a tremendous learning experience. My input is tremendously increased, I would say."

"What I'm after is an increase in output, Jerry."

Baumer peeled his trousers away from his thighs. "Yes, sir. And I intend to see that you get it."

"We'll go over it once more," Theo said. "First to you, Marvin."

Under his bald head, Williamson was thin and worried, eyes seldom still behind steel-rimmed spectacles. He had a face older than its wearer and a soft, narrow body to match.

"The chemistry of our product, Mr. Gavin," he said,

pronouncing his words with prissy exactness, "well, it matches any now on the market. And we will bring each product in at an exceptionally low unit price . . ."

Theo cleared his throat. "No argument, Marvin. Economically it's now feasible to go into production. But I'm still not sure about the scents . . ."

"I see," Williamson said uneasily. He was Theo Gavin's chief chemist, and as such felt responsible for all the laboratory work. "Mr. Gavin, perhaps some criticism is in order. But I've done my best and—"

Theo waved him still. "I'm thinking about changing directions. Something simpler, less sweet, less overwhelming. We've got to move with the times. Women are less willing to accept passive roles, they're rejecting the old ways."

"Women's Lib and that sort of thing," Baumer put in.

"Something like that," Theo replied. "Let's get away from the heavy, sophisticated perfumes and soaps and so on. Let's get more of the outdoors into our product."

"How about this?" Baumer exclaimed, half-rising, the pudgy face excited. "The Natural Smell!"

Theo glared at Baumer, who lowered himself back into place.

"Smell is not the word. But natural is, that's our new concept, gentlemen. *Natural*."

"That's really terrific, Mr. G.," Baumer said. "The way you cut through, see things clearly. Right along I've had this feeling, a presentiment, that we'd missed the boat. But here in a couple of sentences, you clear it up. Natural, natural. That's the key. The Natural Woman. The Natural Look. It's a Natural! Hey! Maybe that's what we ought to call the line. . . . !" He looked searchingly at Theo.

"The advertising campaign," Theo said in a voice rich with disapproval. "It's very bad."

Baumer's small mouth opened and closed.

"There's a tremendous investment in this line, the lab work, the manufacturing costs, packaging. Plus an outlandishly large advertising budget. Sales must reflect investment within six months or we're in trouble." Theo fixed each man in turn. "And I don't intend to get into trouble."

"I promise you, Mr. G.," Baumer said, the thin voice flattening out abrasively. "Trust me."

"I trusted my father," Theo said. "One day he went out and never came back. Years later I met him by accident and he told me he'd been planning the whole thing for months before he did it. He laughed about it, like it was a big joke. My trust comes high. Very high."

Baumer cocked his head like a whipped puppy. "You really put things straight, Mr. G."

"Your agency gets fifteen percent off the top, Baumer. That will mean more than three hundred thousand dollars in the first year, much more afterward. You better produce."

"Yes, sir. As of now, we begin again. When I get back to L.A., I'll put the entire staff on one of our marathon brain-storming sessions. We'll worry it to *life!* I promise you an outstanding campaign."

Theo grunted and turned to Marvin Williamson. "From now on, the entire line is priced up. Double everything . . ."

Williamson took off his glasses, wiped them on his tie. Squinting, he located Theo. "Don't you think that's a little high? Don't you—"

"I think we'll do what I want done."

Williamson adjusted the glasses back on his nose; at once they began to mist over. "Aren't you afraid—?"

"You're afraid, Marvin. Which is why you work for me instead of the other way around. Gavin cosmetics are going to be right up there with Revlon and Rubinstein. We're going to convince the American woman, women everywhere, that they can't possibly really live, in a romantic sense, without our products. Jerry, next time we get together, I want a list of alternate names for the various products. Those you submitted originally won't do."

"Yes, sir."

Theo stood up. "Let's go up to the suite. I want to check the price list, item by item, and the packaging. That's another thing—the new color treatment, too harsh, garish. This is a class product, I want subtlety, good taste, sophistication . . ."

He went over to where Charles lay with his eyes closed. "Chuck, you asleep?"

Charles opened his eyes.

"Sorry about this afternoon, but business calls and all that. You understand. Tonight, though, a big one on the

town—you, me, Betty, and this friend of hers. Betty tells
me she's a fantastic-looking chick!" Pleased with his easy
use of what he imagined to be a word out of Charles's
vocabulary, he kneeled down and made his voice intimate. "Chuck, you just reach out, that's all you have to
do, and it's yours. Anything you want." He punched
Charles lightly on the shoulder. "You get my meaning?
Tonight will be a gas, right?"

Without replying, Charles closed his eyes again.

Eight kilometers outside of town, The Nest. Once a mon-
astery, later a prison, finally a factory where cheap tourist
souvenirs were produced. Currently it belonged to a syndi-
cate of wealthy Americans who resided part of the year
in Acapulco. They had rebuilt it, brought in an Italian de-
signer from New York to decorate it, transformed it into
a lavish and very expensive restaurant. Fresh, prime grade
U.S. beef was flown in daily from Texas and fresh fruits
and vegetables from California. A German baker prepared
rolls and breads on the premises, and a French pastry chef
was in charge of desserts. The master chef was an American, trained in Paris, Rome, and New York.

Intimacy was the theme of The Nest. And luxury. And,
on request, privacy. Dimly lit stone chambers served as
individual dining rooms, guests sprawling out on thick Oriental rugs and oversized pillows, eating off low, dark-wood
tables. Oil lamps flickered in the stone walls and an unseen
guitarist lamented love lost and found in Castilian Spanish.

Theo and Betty Simons sprawled out on one side of the
table; opposite them, Charles and Vera Mae. Vera Mae
was petite, a series of carefully molded curves in a bright-
yellow dress. Her face was something near a triangle set
in a sea of golden curls. All during dinner she had looked
up into Charles' eyes, as if expecting to find locked in them
the secret to her future.

Dinner over, they drank expresso and crème de menthe
and Theo explained the theory behind his new cosmetics
business.

"It's all a question of merchandising," he told them, the
two girls attentive. "The three P's. Packaging, pricing, pro-

motion. All very simple. Let me run a test—girls would you buy a cleansing cream or toilet water that was called 'The Natural Woman'?"

"Oh," Betty Simons said. "Isn't that clever. That's what most girls want, isn't it? To be beautiful and natural, not all painted up."

"I certainly do agree," Vera Mae drawled, as if afraid to release the words. " 'The Natural Woman.' Is it your idea, Theo?"

"Modestly," Theo said, "I accept the blame."

Charles stopped listening. Next to him, Vera Mae shifted, pressed closer, her breast coming to rest on his shoulder. Her scent drifted into his nostrils and it bothered him that he wanted to make love to her, that she could get to him at all, knowing it was all an act, that she had been bought and paid for by Theo.

"Let's have some dessert," Theo said, eyes rolling as if in search of an enemy.

"My honey doesn't need dessert," Vera Mae said, rubbing Charles' belly in slow circles. "I'm sweet enough for any boy."

Charles wanted to sit up but Vera Mae was a pliant obstruction; her body stretched lengthwise against him, one leg curled tightly over his thighs. She fingered the tender skin under his jawline.

"Wouldn't you like to give Vera Mae a kiss, Chuck?"

He made an extra effort and sat erect. Vera Mae fell back to the cushions. She gazed up at him. "Ah get the feelin' little ol' Chuckie doesn't turn on to me . . ." she announced to no one in particular.

"My name is Charles," he said.

"Be nice to the girl, Chuck," Theo said.

"Everybody be nice to everybody," Betty Simons said. She reached for Theo's hand, placed it on her breast. He took it away, speaking quietly but angrily to her. She glanced over at Charles and shrugged.

"Something bothering you, Chuck?" Theo said. "This is a party. You need to learn how to have a good time."

Charles felt squeezed, his eyes swollen. It was becoming difficult for him to breathe. He made it to his feet, eyes settling nowhere. "I have to go—"

"What do you mean!" Theo said. "We're having a party. This is *your* party."

"I'm not feeling so good."

"Poor baby," Vera Mae said. "Let me fix it for you."

"I'll be all right," Charles said, retreating. He tripped and fell backward onto the pillows, scrambling up in embarrassment. "Go on with your party, don't worry about me." He lurched toward the door and jerked it open, disappeared.

Behind him, Vera Mae uttered a long, low sigh. "Oh, damn! Ah did like that boy of yours, Theo Gavin. He was cute and I was primed for some real funnin' . . . Never did have a boy skeedaddle on me before."

"Don't let it get you down," Theo said, flexing his left bicep, kneading it steadily. "Both you girls have been well paid and I expect to get my money's worth, one way or another."

Squealing happily, Vera Mae crawled across the table to Theo. "I am simply wild about partying . . ."

He shuffled along the surf line, kicking the small waves at his feet back to the sea. He felt exhausted. His mind seemed incapable of a single thought. He stared. Up at the sky, a swelling, never-ending void. And at the damped-down sand underfoot. Stared into the darkness.

His legs ceased functioning and he stood with knees locked, letting the night air cool him. Splashing came from the dark sea and a girl's laugh. His eyes came into focus and two figures materialized, rising out of the moonless water. Charles blinked and his knees unlocked.

"Hi!" A female voice.

Charles squinted at the advancing figures.

"Hi!" A male voice.

He saw them climbing the gentle slope of sand. A boy and a girl, gleaming naked in the starlight.

"Charles," said a familiar voice.

"Becky . . . ?"

She stopped in front of him, face vibrant, happy. Her breasts trembled with each breath and the thick auburn wedge between her legs was matted down with sea water.

"Meet Stone," she said. "Livy and I picked Charles up this afternoon."

"Hi, Charles."

"Stone?"

"Stone for stoned, man. Drives the big people craz-eee
. . . outafucking-sight."

Becky shivered and hugged herself. "Come on, Charles,
we're camped up that way." She ran ahead, Stone right
behind her. Charles took a step and another, broke into
a run. Up-and-down, up-and down . . .

Five in all, three girls, two boys, huddled under blankets. A slow, hot fire burned in a shallow bowl scooped
out of the sand. Becky inched up to the flames, making
small warming noises.

"The fuzz come along looking for fires," Stone explained. "This way they can hardly see it. We fake 'em
out."

"Charles is new," Becky said.

"He came with his father," Livy, the round face sullen
and unattractive in the glow of the flames, said.

Charles sighed and looked at the others; no introduc-
tions were made.

"Come over here," Becky said, "and talk to me." He
obeyed gladly. Someone gave him a banana and he accepted it, surprised at his returned appetite. Someone else
passed a joint around.

"Very powerful magic," Stone said.

"Best grass in Mexico," Becky said.

"Bombs away!" someone said. No one laughed. When
the joint burned down, another was sent around the circle.
Soon Charles was warm and no longer weary. Why, he
puzzled, did he feel so much at home with strangers?

"What's going down?" a voice said.

"Where?"

"Anywhere, baby . . ."

"Dig the flame, blue and green and dancing yellow.
Very wild fire, sensual and true."

Time warped, sending Charles along a twisted trail back
to his childhood, catapulted him forward again. Pain and
pleasure mingled and he tried to sort out his emotions, to
link them with specific moments, incidents, people, places.

Time held still and Charles came to rest, peaceful and content at last. Eyes fluttering shut, he lay down. Someone draped a blanket over him but he didn't stir.

"Man, that's a loose cat."

"Be still."

"Well, all *right*."

Charles slept.

In the not so early morning, he woke. Another body clung to his, arms encircling his waist, bare toes scratching at his ankles.

Vera Mae . . . ? Startled, he tried to rise.

"Easy, baby," came a gentling whisper. "It's Becky. All right?"

He fell back. "All right."

She spoke to his ear. "All afternoon, all night, I kept wishing you'd show . . ."

He visualized her as he'd seen her earlier, coming naked out of the sea with Stone. Jealousy made him less than he wanted to be. "You and Stone," he said. "Were you thinking of me when you were skinny-dipping with him?"

"Shhh. That's nothing. Stone's always so bombed out he couldn't do it even if I wanted him to." She giggled.

He laughed too.

Her mouth came down on his mouth, to quiet him. "Everybody else is asleep, so it's all right."

He heaved himself around and they lay embracing, mouth to mouth. She licked his lips.

"I almost didn't get here," he said.

"But you did."

"I hitched and it took four rides. I thought I'd made a mistake, you were someplace else."

"You were so bushed."

"A real bummer with my father."

"See!"

He sighed.

She kissed him.

"I'm glad I found you," he said.

"Me too."

They lay that way for several minutes before they kissed again. She sucked on his tongue. "Ooh," she breathed into his mouth. "Right from the start, you turned me on, made me twitch. I told Livy . . ." She guided his hand under the rough wool serape she had on; she was naked. Her breast filled his hand.

"Anything," she murmured, fingers fumbling with his trousers. "Anything at all." And, so help me, he thought of his mother, of Julia asking him what he wanted for his birthday—"*Anything you want, dear. All you have to do is tell me and it's yours.*"

He stroked her hip, her strong buttocks, fingers dragging into the crevice and downward.

"You're great."

"You too," he said in a small voice. He wished it hadn't happened this way, with the others so near. At the same time wished they would all wake up, see him and Becky this way.

He kissed her again.

"Something's wrong," she said.

"Nothing." Theo and Betty Simons and Vera Mae . . . he shivered and was cold again.

"This is a groove," she said, coming up on her knees. She removed the serape and her breasts seemed immense white targets and the hairy patch had dried and lost its sheen.

"A groove," he said.

"Touch me here."

He reached obediently between her legs.

Breath burst out of her like a heavyweight hooking hard. She worked his trousers down to his knees. "How beautiful. Beautiful." She bent and kissed him, filled her mouth with him.

A passion stiff and revengeful, full of anger, took hold and he was ashamed. None of it was her fault; she was doing only what she felt was right and generous, *loving*. She was not Vera Mae and he was not Theo. Right? Right. . . . He touched her cheek, the back of her head.

"Come here," he said. "Lie next to me."

She did. There was a touch of silence and she began to shiver. "It's okay," she said. "It always happens. I get so excited I begin to shake. One thing—will you say my name? Just so I know you know it's me. Just say it once so I can tell you remember."

"Becky . . ."

"Ah!" She put her finger to her mouth. "This is so nice and friendly."

Foreman lay in his bed at the Señorial and commanded himself to sleep. He emptied his mind of all thoughts, images, fantasies, night terrors. Drained, by force of will, the body tension from his skin, muscles, joints. He stretched and flexed, closed and opened, wiggled and tugged. He lay limp and at ease, floating toward the near edge of oblivion.

A capricious nerve in his thigh leaped, and he was instantly alert and awake. His mind reached back to Jiquilisco and Jenny . . . *You never missed it until you didn't have it*. His hand, like a separate will, closed on his quivering penis, member, shaft—name it, he had it. He drew his hand away and swung out of bed. Dressing swiftly, he left the hotel, not allowing himself even to consider his destination, brain switched off.

Shoulders hunched, he strode without purpose up from the Costera into deserted streets and alleys, up grades and down again. His heart pounded and his lungs worked harder. Music echoed in his ears.

A cantina. Swinging doors and harsh yellow light and the sound of a jukebox and Tex Ritter wailing "High Noon." Foreman hooked his thumbs in his belt, curled his mouth in Western disdain, turned his eyes into icy globes that would strike terror into men's hearts and went inside.

For tourists only. Carefully designed and operated. Waiters in black with silver spangles, huge sombreros dangling down their backs, polished toy pistols on their hips. And sloe-eyed *señoritas* in tight crimson gowns as hostesses. Foreman stopped his Gary Cooper and went to the bar, ordered tequila. He belted it back, took some salt and lemon, had another. Fingers trembling, he lit a cigarette and tried not to consider his baser appetites.

He thought about *Love, Love*. And about Shelly. Her innocence; she was caught somewhere between a child and a woman, her eyes sad, a beautiful girl. In trouble. At this moment she would be in bed with Bristol. He'd be rooting around in that very desirable body with all the sensitivity of a hog in a sumphole. Foreman drank quickly and the barman refilled his glass. Better him, because, of course, Mr. Foreman was sensitive. You bet, at least that. Don't knock it, Mr. Foreman. It's not so bad. It lets you know when to make your move. . . .

At an unknown time in the near future you will self-destruct. Bad black thoughts, for Christssake . . .

Through the shifting gray cloud of cigarette smoke, slow-moving set-pieces. Fat men with smug eyes and damp lips, women studded with diamonds, and wrinkled brown cleavage pushing out of crusted gowns.

No different.

No different from . . .

FOREMAN! *Foreman.* Fore . . . man . . .

He closed down the echo chamber and concentrated on serious drinking. His burned-down cigarette scorched his fingers and he dropped it with a loud oath. A large man with a thick chest and a massive jaw, regaling his companions at a table close by, broke off his monologue long enough to cast a disapproving glance at Foreman. Foreman showed his teeth, clowning, and lit another cigarette. Glass of tequila in hand, he took up a position behind the big man's chair, poised in concentration.

"The trouble with Mexico," the big man was saying, "is that people still live in the seventeenth century. They have no drive, ambition."

"Oh, shit!" Foreman said affably.

The big man looked over his shoulder. "Beat it, fella." He turned back to his friends. "It's the Latin temperament, a racial characteristic, I suppose. All those mixed breeds."

"Oh, indeed shit!" Foreman said.

The big man shifted around, gave Foreman a longer look. "What's on your mind, fella?"

"Shit on what you say. Is what's on my mind."

"He's drunk, Duke," one of the women at the table said nervously.

"You've had one too many, fella," the big man said.

Foreman emptied his glass, set it on the table. "Too few in my considered opinion. Too few to take your damn bullshit."

"All right, fella. That's about enough."

"About enough is not necessarily enough. Or do you mean enough is too much? Or, enough is as good as a feast. I can't remember who said it right now but I know it wasn't me, things being what they are. On the other hand, it was *definitely* Will Shakespeare who wrote, 'Plenty as Blackberries,' which is a smart way to say Enough. You disagree?"

The big man shifted his chair away from Foreman, closer to the table. "The Mexican will never amount to anything because he is incapable of visualizing the positive results of hard work, of education, of thrift . . ."

"Mucho shit," Foreman said cheerfully. "What positive results ever came to the poor Mexican from the hard work he's done. Spaniards killed him. The French made him a slave. The *gringos* merely exploited him."

"Fella," the big man said, "go away."

"Shit and double shit . . ."

The big man moved with surprising speed, jerking up and around in a single, smooth maneuver, his lumpy right fist chopping at Foreman in a short, swift arc.

Foreman made no effort to avoid the blow. It landed on the side of his head and he went down. Someone screamed and chairs were flung aside. Foreman smiled a crooked smile, let out a belch, and passed out.

"Damn fool never even tried to fight back," the big man said.

"Don't sweat it, Duke. . . . He asked for it. You gave it to him. Everybody's happy."

Foreman's eyes opened into darkness. He was afraid. He had been bad, done something naughty with Evelyn McCarter who lived in the next house and been scolded for it, also spanked, sent to his room. And he had stayed there without supper, wishing to revenge himself on his mother, wishing she were dead. . . .

And so she had died. And Paulie had known, *known*, that he was responsible. He ached to tell someone, but he never quite got up the nerve to reveal his terrible secret.

He remembered he was no longer a child—and he understood the reality of his mother's death and knew that he had nothing to feel guilty about. He sat up and made an effort to locate himself. It came rushing at him out of the blackness—the tourist bar, the tequila, the big American with the quick fist. Foreman groaned and fell back.

A light went on. "Are you all right, luv?"

A figure came into focus. A woman stood looking down at him. Thin, nervous, her face in a fixed smile, and her hands never stopped fluttering.

"Oh, dear," she said. "You must feel awful. I've been there a thousand times myself. The coffee's on . . ."

Foreman sat up. His head felt misshapen, soggy. "Where—?"

"My apartment. You're all right here. The john's down the hall, if you require it," she ended properly.

He stumbled off in that direction, suddenly desperate, fumbling with his fly; and had to wait for the stream to fall. Finished, he bathed his eyes in cold water but avoided the mirror above the sink as if it were a window into hell. He went back inside.

She sat on the couch wearing a washed-out pink robe, a slender woman in her middle thirties. Her hand touched her dyed red hair and she smiled.

"I'm Hetty Parker."

He told her his name.

She filled two cups with steaming water from a clay pot. "I'm sorry, it's only instant."

"Instant's fine."

"Strong, I guess."

"Please."

He sat next to her on the couch, warming his hands on the cup.

"It would've been okay," she said. "I mean, you could have slept all night."

"Did you bring me here by yourself?"

She gave a proud nod. "You came around a little and I found a taxi. He helped me get you inside."

He drank some coffee. "Thanks."

"I couldn't leave you on the floor back there. This man, he was immense, he hit you when you weren't looking."

Foreman again saw the fist getting bigger, exploding against his temple.

"You had a few too many is all," she explained. "You didn't mean any harm. He shouldn't've hit you."

He finished the coffee and she refilled his cup.

"I saw you when you came in," she said shyly. "You're the kind of man women notice, you know."

"Oh."

"Oh, yes. It's your face. It's sort of shot to hell and intelligent at the same time, if you don't mind my saying so. It's a very special face."

He raised his eyes. She was clearly one of the walking wounded. He should talk . . .

"I live here," she said. "In Acapulco. I suppose that sounds funny."

"Why should it?"

"Well, some men would think so, a woman living alone in a strange country. I'm from Kansas City, Missouri, that is. After I got divorced from Milton, Kansas City turned sour for me. All our friends were really Milton's friends and I was never so lonely. A million people live in that town and not one of them wanted to know me. I was a Spanish teacher before I got married, so it was natural that I came to Mexico. . . ."

"Is it better for you here?" he said, feeling he had to say something. His head began to throb. "Do you have any aspirin?"

She stood up. "Oh, yes. I'm sorry. I should've thought. I'll get you some." She stopped and looked back from the doorway. "I'm lonely here too," she said, and disappeared. Foreman closed his eyes and tried to crawl deeper into the lidded darkness.

"Here we are!"

He opened his eyes. Hetty came into the room, leading a girl of about eight years by the hand. A pretty child with round cheeks, her face puffed with sleep. "Nancy, this is Mr. Foreman. This is my daughter, Nancy."

The child looked at Foreman, blinked, and turned away.

"I wanted Nancy to meet you," Hetty said. She handed him two aspirins.

"I'm sorry we woke you up, Nancy," he said.

Hetty sat on the couch, pulling the child along. "Nancy and I have been working on her Spanish so that she'll be truly bilingual when she grows up. But we speak English most of the time. Why is that, Nancy?"

"Because we're loyal Americans," the child answered obediently.

"We don't ever want to forget that, no matter where we live. Isn't she sweet? Talk to her, Paul. It's like talking to another adult."

"Put her back to bed," Foreman said.

"Oh, Nancy's used to staying up late, keeping her momma company. Aren't you, Nancy?"

Foreman tossed the aspirins back into his throat, washed them down with coffee. "I'm going," he announced.

"Oh, *no!* Not yet, please. Nancy's going back to bed now. Please, Paul, a minute more."

Foreman agreed to wait and she took the child into the other room. When she returned her eyes were bright and the heavy odor of freshly applied toilet water advanced before her.

"Isn't Nancy a marvel! I absolutely adore her. She wasn't at her best, of course, but there's so much perception and sensitivity in that child. Nancy has perfect pitch about people. Her judgment, I mean, is absolutely on the mark. She liked you, Paul, I could tell."

"I have to go," he said.

"Oh, please not yet! Don't you just hate it late at night, especially when you can't sleep? I do, so much. Being by myself in the dark. Sometimes I wake up afraid that something weird is in the room with me and I begin to shake and cry. Why don't I get us another drink? There's some gin left, I think . . ."

"I've had it."

She held thumb and forefinger an inch apart. "Just a short one," she said.

She brought two glasses and a bottle, filled them both, gave him one. "From the second you came into that bar, I could tell you were somebody special. Are you, Paul? Somebody special? I mean, are you famous, or like that?"

"Stop it, Hetty."

"I mean it. There's a fierceness in your eyes. I can see it."

"I know, you're very perceptive. Your whole family is. Look, I'm sorry, but I really—"

Her hand on his arm restrained him. "*I'm* sorry!" she said. "It is presumptuous and rude and I apologize to you. But I have to say this. There is a wonderful authority about you, a sense of command. You were in the military, weren't you?" She ended with a small-girl teasing expression.

He didn't want to remember. "The Marines."

"There! I just knew it. And you were an officer, am I correct?"

He answered carefully. "The only thing worse than leading men to slaughter is sending them there."

"Oh, yes. Oh, yes. I agree. Violence and killing, war, it's all very bad. I hate it so. But you must have been pure torment for the ladies in your dress blues. Handsome is as handsome does!"

"I never wore them."

"Another thing I have noticed," she said, shifting closer, "is the unusual quality of your voice. You possess a resonance, I would say, a *vibrance*. Women are excited by the sound of a real man's voice. Did you know that? But of course you did, a person of your obvious intelligence. I shouldn't tell you but I know you'll understand. Sitting here, your voice gets down into some deep part of me. I'm fluttering like a girl on her first date." She sucked in air and arranged his hand on her bellyrise. "There. There is where I feel it first. Would you believe, a woman of my age and backgound, that my heart is doing flip-flops? Oh, yes it is. Well, here, see for yourself." She moved his hand onto her breast. "Can you feel my heart throb? No? Press harder, squeeze me if you want . . ."

He took his hand away.

"I've shocked you," she said, speaking swiftly. "Please don't be. Perhaps you can't comprehend what it means to a woman like me to discover a man like you. I am like a prospector working the barren hills and making a rich and unexpected strike. Paul Foreman, you are pure gold."

She gave off a raw sex that wrapped itself around him until in reflex he began to respond.

"Here," she murmured, showing her breasts. They stood out like a young girl's and she moved her shoulders so they moved. "Aren't they nice? I was very careful when Nancy came, exercise and massage. I have always been very proud of my breasts. They may be my best feature."

"Your daughter," he said.

"She won't bother us, I promise you. I told her not to and she always obeys." She was standing, tossing aside her

robe, then back on the couch, hands roaming over his
body, her mouth wet and loose against his face and neck.
She fumbled with his belt, tugged at his trousers.

He kissed her and touched her breast and waited. Nothing.

"I understand," she said. "The first time. You're high-
strung. I am myself. Try to relax. It'll happen. You'll see.
I can help. I know what to do. See, see, you're beautiful
here, so beautiful. I know you'll be special. Oh, I love doing this to you, I love it . . ."

Her breathing was harsh and swift, body jerking with
spastic tension. Foreman allowed himself to fall back on
the couch, eyes closed. His mind reached back until Laura
came into view and the sounds he heard and the scent he
smelled were the sounds and the scents of Laura. Once
again those quick hands fluttered across his belly, his
drawn-tight scrotum, making him swell and grow hard,
until all of him was centered there. He exploded.

On the third day of filming, the memory of past failures
convinced Shelly she was going to ruin Harry Bristol's movie. Also Paul Foreman's. She forgot her lines, didn't follow Foreman's directions. One scene had to be shot five
times because of her, and when Bristol cursed at her she
started to cry and ran off.

Foreman went after her. Unless he could bring her
back, in every way, he saw the picture going down the
drain. Bristol had instinctively recognized the value of
Shelly's child-woman appearance, style. To Foreman, with
each day's work, she became more and more the essence
of the film.

He told her so. "You have it in you to be a star, Shelly.
One of the biggest. In the same way that Monroe was a
star, and Taylor; the biggest of them. There's a special
quality in you and it will expand on film and go out to
people, make them respond to you. That's the magic of
film. And it's real."

She searched his face, looking for any trace, any slightest suggestion of mockery. She found none.

"I've made a mistake with you. I've over-directed you.
So from now on you're free. Forget the words. Oh, sure,
I'll still supply the dialogue but if you lose it, okay, go on

your own. Say what you like. Do what you like. What you *feel*, Shelly. Make each scene your own. Forget the camera. That's Mac's problem. You work free, just let it out."

"I'll try."

"When you're ready, we'll do the last scene again."

"Whatever you say, Paul."

They went through the lengthy sequence without interruption and when it was over Foreman hugged Shelly and she was laughing and crying again, but this time with excitement. "I was stuttering," she said. "All kinds of crazy ideas kept going through my head. What I said—I kept forgetting the dialogue—was it all right?"

"Couldn't have been better."

"Oh, Paul! I wanted so much to do it right."

"It was right. . . ."

Nothing much had ever been right for her before. Her career, her marriage. Now there was only *Love, Love* and it had to be right. After all, she thought, it was her last chance, wasn't it? With Paul Foreman's help she might finally make it. She trusted Paul, and she trusted Harry. She had to.

"Dame un veinte, señorita . . ."

A small boy was standing in front of her, hand outstretched.

"Como?" she said.

"Un veinte," he repeated. *"Para un pan."*

The words trailed off, a parody of the old beggars one saw everywhere in Mexico. *"Para un pan . . ."* For a piece of bread . . . She searched through her purse, offered a five-peso note to the boy. He stared at it in disbelief, then turned and ran off, leaving the note in her still-extended hand.

A laugh drew her attention. The tall American was leaning against a waterfront piling, stroking his yellow beard.

"Remember Leo?"

"I don't think I want to talk to you."

He held out his hand. *"Un veinte, señorita, una caridad . . ."* He shook his head, eyes assessing her figure in tight yellow slacks and a brown blouse. "The way you look, you shouldn't walk along the Malecón by yourself. Never know what undesirable might accost you."

"Like you?"

His laugh was thin; straightening up, he came toward her. "The kid suckered you. Hustling tourists is a way of life for kids like that."

"That's what you do," she said, defiance in her voice.

"Isn't that what tourists are for? Then they go back to their home turf and brag about how they were taken."

She took a backward step. "You're not very nice."

"Don't be so uptight. Foreman, he's a movie director, he's loaded. El Tiburón pays me a small commission. A cat's got a right to live."

"You should've warned us about that place."

"Surprise is spice." He moved forward again. "Listen," he said quietly, intimately, "you must have some pesos on you. Let's have a couple of brews. I know a place. Then, after, I've got some grass . . ."

She walked away, trying to close him out of her senses —the suggestion in his voice, the way he made her feel about herself. She concentrated hard on the sheer physical act of walking, increasing her pace, and so failed to notice a solitary walker passing along.

Her concentration was brought back to the present by a speck of dust in her eye, and she saw another man. He seemed to be waiting for her. She shivered inside and looked for a way around. He was rather odd-looking, angles and thrusts, one shoulder seeming higher than it was meant to be, the other a bit foreshortened, sloping directly down from his neck. His head tilted forward so that he viewed the world from beneath a bony thrust of brow. Around his throat, a multicolored ascot. His cheeks were dark and rough, his features large and cleanly outlined.

"*Buenas tardes, señorita,*" he said. He directed her attention to an easel set up at the side of the walk, and a folding chair. "In only a few minutes," he said in English, "I can do your portrait. Charcoal, pastel, watercolor, whichever you prefer."

There was a Midwestern bite to his speech that calmed Shelly's fears. She gave him a careful smile.

"I don't think so."

"Only fifty pesos for the charcoal. Eighty for the pastel. A hundred for watercolor."

"No, thank you."

"Don't be hasty. I can be bargained with. Make me an offer."

"I don't think so."

He lifted the high shoulder. *"Mañana,* maybe. Or the day after. I'll be around here every day."

Something made her hesitate, some recognizable shadow in his eyes, something of herself? "All right," she said. "Do me in charcoal."

"Watercolor only takes a little bit longer. You'd be superb in color."

"Charcoal," she said firmly, surprising herself with her preference.

She sat in the chair and held her face according to his directions. He studied her briefly and then his hand attacked the drawing paper in broad, confident strokes. Lines and shadings materialized and out of them a face began to take shape.

"This will always remind you of Acapulco when you return to—where are you from?"

"Las Vegas was the last place."

"I have been peeled and stripped in Vegas more than once, dried out in the desert sun."

"You gamble?"

"It's a sure thing. A loser. An addict."

"I was that way, with the slots. Then I stopped."

His hand darted over the paper. "How long are you going to stay here?"

She hesitated. "Until the end of the month. And you?"

"As long as the tourists hold up. They'll be flocking in next week for the Christmas holidays."

"Have you always been an artist?"

"I've done other things. I taught art appreciation in Indianapolis to kids with big allowances. For them painting began with Andy Warhol and music with the Jefferson Airplane." He seemed pleased when Shelly laughed. "Laughter agrees with you. It does good things for your face."

The compliment, as always, embarrassed her. "Tell me more about yourself."

He told her that he had tried painting for a while, but

soon discovered that the world was loaded with painters, "many almost as bad as I was. Anyway, during my New York period I learned that my appreciation of art is much more highly developed than my ability to produce it."

"New York is too big for me, too crowded and fast."

"All true. But a fabulous place for educating yourself. For example, I learned about orgone boxes there."

"What's an orgone box?"

"For me, a definition of youthful. Actually, it was the theory of Wilhelm Reich, a disciple of Freud, that with human frustration, anger, and the rest, huge amounts of sexual energy were being sort of dissipated into the atmosphere. Reich decided that if a person put himself in a wooden box lined with metal, he would be able to reabsorb into his body a certain amount of that charged sexual air, orgone energy. I built such a box for myself and put it in a corner of my bedroom. I sat in it for one full sixty-minute hour each day."

"And?"

"And nothing. No bargain-basement box can fix me up," he said cheerfully.

"Who says you need fixing?"

"Beauty sees beauty everywhere." He stepped away from the easel. "Come and see yourself."

She did. "I love it!" she cried. "It's flattering, of course, but I love it anyway."

"It's okay."

"Will you sign it?"

He looked into her face and, satisfied, scrawled his name across the bottom of the drawing paper.

"Morrie Carlson," she said aloud. "I'm Shelly Hanes."

They shook hands solemnly.

She fumbled in her purse, handed him fifty pesos. "Are you sure that's enough?"

He looked at her. "If you're not pleased, we can set a lower price."

"Oh, no! I really do love it. But that expression on my face—as if I'm about to run away."

"Don't do that," he said. "Look, I'm dry. Let me buy you something to drink . . . and with it you get the rest of my thrilling autobiography."

"The drink and the autobiography, yes to both."

"*Señorita*," he said bowing. "Follow me . . ."

4

Filming still went slowly. In order to shore up Shelly's confidence, Foreman rehearsed her over and over, continued to allow her wide latitude in dialogue. It did very little good. Her scenes often went flat when she stumbled over words, even her own. Extra takes were called for every day.

Jim Sawyer was another problem; he turned a stolid, Midwestern face to the camera, alternately smiling or scowling—apparently the gamut of his repertoire of emotions. Foreman pleaded with him to forget his face, just say the words. Sawyer couldn't or wouldn't; five times Foreman was forced to cut away from him, intending to leave his voice on the sound track, to replace his face with something more dramatic, more interesting.

And the tourists. The streets and beaches, the shops, the restaurants, were crowded with visitors. Many of them considered the making of a movie a major source of their entertainment, and came to watch, to jabber among themselves. They got in the way of the film crew, made setups more difficult, the actors more self-conscious. Foreman, able to get less and less usable film each day, grew more irritable.

And Bristol, hovering around like a gloomy angel, making his suggestions, carping at the actors, urging more action.

"Too damned static," he complained. "This is a movie, make it move. Let's have more going on."

"More isn't necessarily better," Foreman told him. "Look, Harry, let's cut this out. I'm tired of the ogre producer versus sensitive director bit. To hell with it. Neither of us is that bad or that wonderful. But let's get it straight. I agreed to deliver a first cut. Until then, the picture is mine. Unless you decide to fire me."

"Did anybody say anything about firing anybody? All I want is for the picture to be good."

"Okay, back off and give me a fighting chance."

"No offense intended, Paul. This Mexico's got me down. My plumbing still doesn't work right. My guts are like jelly."

Foreman expressed appropriate concern for Bristol's digestive tract, and went back to work. The next morning Bristol returned to the attack.

"You got to give me more of Shelly in the picture. Shelly with no clothes on. Shelly making it with Sawyer. And work in one or two fights. Sawyer is good with his hands."

This time Foreman was waiting for him. "I've got just the scene, Harry. Sawyer's a free spirit, right? I'm putting in a sequence that begins when he promises to take Shelly swimming in the pool of a very plush villa belonging to some world-famous millionaire living here in Acapulco. The villa's unoccupied, closed down, but Shelly doesn't know it until they get there. Over the wall they go, and swim . . ."

"Nude!" Bristol exclaimed, like a delighted child.

"Right, Harry. Later, the night watchman shows up—"

"Perfect. That's the place for a good fight. Now you're thinking straight. What can I do? You want me to find the villa? Okay, you got it."

Bristol hurried away, returning before the lunch break. He took Foreman aside.

"Well, I did it. I think I found the perfect place."

"You work fast, Harry."

"Damn right. A thing's gotta be done, I do it. You wanna check it out this afternoon?"

"Good."

"Whose place you think I got? And I think the price will be right."

"Merle Oberon's house."

"She here! Maybe I could get to her for a bit in *Love, Love,* if I asked right? Nah, guess not."

"The villa, Harry?"

"Samantha Moore's place. How about that! One of the most famous women in the world."

"That's good, Harry."

"And one of the richest."

"Then why is she renting it out?"

A puzzled look on Bristol's face. "I never thought of that . . ."

Bernard Louis Font drove his silver-gray Jaguar with a pride near to arrogance. He sat in a carefully considered pose, one hand casually on the wheel, the opposite elbow in the open window, chin resting comfortably in his palm, forefinger laid along his fleshy Gallic nose.

"This area," he said, his English meticulously crafted, "is known as La Mira. Here the homes are all very beautiful, the people who occupy the homes are also very beautiful. So it goes, yes?" He gestured down toward the bay. "Below us is the Cantinflas villa. Of course you know him, the famous, very talented Mexican movie star. And beyond, yes, that house, that is where Dolores Del Rio lives. A fantastic woman! Still beautiful beyond compare, proud, gracious. I am an admirer. These days she dedicates herself to the theater. Villa Gloria is only a short distance more. It will be ideal for your purposes, Mr. Bristol." Bernard ended the travelogue with just the right amount of condescension.

Bristol allowed nothing to show in his manner. "We'll see. Maybe my director won't like the place. Whatever my director says, goes."

"Of course," Bernard said. He glanced into the rearview mirror. Foreman was slumped across the back seat, rangy body relaxed and indolent. The long, pale face was in repose, eyes closed. Was it possible that he was asleep? "Mr. Foreman . . . !"

Foreman raised his right hand.

"Villa Gloria is a showplace in Mexico, known throughout the republic. The Roman pool offers advantages no other pool in Acapulco can boast. The underwater room—"

Foreman lifted his hand in half salute, let it fall.

"Sounds okay," Bristol said. He visualized Shelly and Jim Sawyer in the water, bare-ass, coming closer and closer to the camera in that underwater room. Each movement showing teases of flesh, until Shelly swam slowly back up to the surface, revealing all of herself. Jesus!

He swung around to face the little Frenchman. A pudgy little man without any of the attributes Bristol associated with business acumen; as when he'd first met him, Bristol thought he looked soft, easy to manipulate. "Listen, Font," Bristol began, "if we like Villa Gloria, it might just be possible—and this is no guarantee, y'understand—it might be possible to work Samantha Moore into *Love, Love,* give her a chance at a comeback. How's that grab you?"

There was, Bernard reminded himself, an inevitable vulgarity in the Anglo-Saxon races that no civilizing process could overcome. It was, he supposed, something in the genes. DeGaulle had been right not to trust Churchill and Roosevelt. Still, this was business, and his voice remained pleasant.

"Miss Moore is a fulfilled woman, gentlemen. There are her friends, her gardens, her charities, and her travels. These are sufficient."

"Then why does she want to rent out her house?" Bristol said, looking back knowingly at Foreman, who ignored him.

Bernard remained cool. "My suggestion. A small amusement, I thought, a diversion. And the income would permit me to make certain advantageous tax deductions on the villa. Miss Moore agreed on that basis alone. In any case, all business transactions will be through me. Exclusively," he finished, a new edge in his voice, startling Bristol.

"Ah," he said, moments later. "We have arrived."

The Jaguar glided to a stop in a shallow driveway. In front of them, a pair of massive wooden doors, intricately carved and set into an ancient gray stone wall that reminded Foreman of the Pennsylvania State Prison. Bernard pressed the horn and soon an elderly man opened the gate. Recognizing Bernard, he waved him through.

A maid led them into the house and along a wide, cool corridor lined with green plants set in red-clay pots. Beyond a small cactus garden, a large stone dolphin spouted a stream of water into a fountain centered in a blue-and-yellow tiled patio. A dozen steps down, along a shaded arbor, past lemon trees and avocado trees and finally onto the veranda of the pool, the low rays of the westering sun glinting off the still water.

"Here, we begin," Bernard said, with the pride of vicarious ownership. *"La pièce de résistance!* The best first, eh! Consider. The pool is of ample size and the shape is varied. Bends and curves everywhere. Like a woman, yes!" Bernard rubbed his palms together, obviously pleased with himself.

"About the underwater room . . ." Foreman said.

"I will take you presently," Bernard said.

"That could be good," Bristol said. "Shooting from down there. What do you say to colored lights, Paul? Nobody's ever done anything like it since Esther Williams. A scene like that could mean—" He broke off aware of Bernard's growing interest.

Foreman circled the pool, looked up at the house. It rose up out of the rocky terrain in layers in much the same way *campesinos* terraced a hill to grow maize or beans, offering a stony, gray face to the sea. Portions of the structure, visible only from this angle, were painted a bright Mexican pink. Natural color softened the harsh fortresslike lines of the architecture: lush greenery and splashes of yellow mimosa, vermilion bougainvillea, periwinkle jacaranda.

Foreman tried to visualize Shelly and Sawyer, moving from level to level, working with the trees and gardens; abrupt cuts for time passage; their and hopefully the audience's sense of coming alive again in this uninhibited, natural setting.

"I'll want complete run of the house," he said in a matter-of-fact voice.

Bernard shook his head in sad refusal. "The pool, the entranceway, the approaches. This patio, naturally. The rest remains off-limits."

"At these prices?" Bristol said.

"I'm not sure this place will work for me unless I have complete freedom of movement," Foreman said. He moved to the edge of the veranda, looked out toward Roqueta Island. A narrow beach faced him across the water, and glass-bottomed boats that gave tourists a look at the tropical fish among the rocks close to shore.

He closed his eyes and looked at the dancing sunspots. Two nights before, while viewing the dailies, Foreman had been caught up in the action, by the performances that he'd helped Shelly and Jim Sawyer give. Just possibly this picture might really be something special. Maybe he was a director of real talent. He'd closed off such thoughts for some time. Now they somehow seemed less far-fetched, especially (incongruously?) measured against Villa Gloria, this ostentatious assemblage of tile and stone and greenery. Anyway, he felt more inclined to admit just how important *Love, Love* was to him. Face that, face more of the rest of the truth of his life. Progress . . .

He turned away from the sea. Across the Roman pool, Bernard was talking swiftly, hands carving the air in emphasis.

But Bristol was barely listening. His eyes roamed over the facades and walls, the gardens and walkways of Villa Gloria. For him it was a voluptuous summing-up—to own such a place, to display it in every detail to favored guests, to know it was *yours* . . .

He turned a hard face back to Bernard Louis Font. "Forget it," he said. "I can't tie my director's hands. Anyway, he doesn't like the place."

Bernard turned to Foreman, feeling distinctly uneasy. "But in all of Acapulco there is no house more beautiful, with such variety, such dramatic perspectives. Under your skillful direction Villa Gloria will become a special visual triumph. Let me show you the underwater room . . ."

"We're wasting time," Bristol said. "Let's go, Paul. There are other houses to see."

Foreman wore a mask. "Let's get to them." He was enjoying, in fact admired, Bristol's bargaining technique. In order to get what he wanted, Bristol was prepared to risk losing the house, which clearly was perfect for their needs.

Bernard's eyes went from one man to the other, measuring. He was sure the Americans wanted to make their picture at Villa Gloria, but at what price? He had promised Samantha to restrict their activities to the less-private portions of the house. Was this simply a ploy to keep down the asking price . . . ?

"It's warm," he said affably. "I will order some refreshments and we can discuss—"

"There's no point," Bristol said.

Bernard held back an oath. This directness of Americans. Was it any wonder they were so disliked around the world? No tact at all. And so much money . . .

"From your point of view, Mr. Foreman," Bernard said with full charm unleashed, "are there shortcomings? State them frankly. Corrections can be made, compensations—"

"*I'll* tell you," Bristol put in. "Your price is too high. And keeping us to the pool, it's not friendly. And where is Miss Samantha Moore? She doesn't think we're good enough for her? Maybe she doesn't really want us around."

"No, no! You mustn't think so. I assure you, sir, misunderstanding . . . all items are negotiable, all arrangements possible. Miss Moore, my word as a Frenchman, Miss Moore is honored by such distinguished company. Like yourself, Miss Moore is an American, a very democratic lady. Charming, delightful in all ways. She, like myself, will be pleased to have you produce this cinema at Villa Gloria—"

A sudden movement drew their attention to the terrace above the Roman pool. Behind the low stone wall and in front of the boiled-green leaves of a line of papaya trees, was Samantha Moore. She stood there in an embroidered white peasant blouse that rode low over one shoulder. She looked a romantic figure—solitary, at once vulnerable and commanding.

Foreman was impressed. She had managed a neatly framed visual cliché; and for her it worked.

"Bernard," she said, voice friendly and gay. "Won't you introduce me to your friends?"

The Jaguar drew up to the sidewalk in front of the Hilton, and Bristol and Foreman got out. They stood without talking until Bernard drove away, then Bristol began to laugh.

"You see me handle that character! He figured he had us faked out. No chance. Never hustle a hustler. You were great, Paul, just great. The way you gave me that opening about not being sure you liked the joint. That's when I socked it to him. You walking off and looking at the scenery like you didn't give a damn. Perfect . . . shook Frenchy up, I tell you. You know what I think? I think Miss Samantha Moore was up on that terrace all the time, listening in. Let me tell you something, she needs the dough bad, otherwise why would she be renting the place?"

"You know, I never thought of that," Foreman said, trying very hard not to smile.

"Believe me, I know. That Bernard, his price came down fast when it looked like the deal was going to blow. I think the dame is flat-out busted. Which gives me an idea. Her name still has some p.r. People remember who she is. She still gets into all the society columns, right. If I gave her billing . . ."

"Slow it, Harry."

"Put her in the picture. A bit. Anything."

"Doing what?"

"Find something. Make it up, if you have to. She'll come cheap and it'll sell tickets."

Foreman braced for battle, opened his mouth to speak, but before any words came out, Bristol looked suddenly stricken. "They're back! The goddammed runs are back!"

Foreman watched him stiff-walk off toward the hotel entrance, and tried hard not to feel too good. No luck.

Acapulco's municipal market was much like markets in other towns and villages in Mexico. Tourists and natives wandered among the stalls, bargaining, buying.

Men and women called out wares and prices, while children played games among the stalls. In the distance, church bells marked the half-hour and boys hawked copies of *Excelsior* and the *News*.

Everywhere the mixed scents of fresh and rotting fruit, of frying fish, of meat too long in the sun—and the odor of barbecue, of frying tacos, freshly baked tortillas. Neat pyramids of oranges and uncountable stalks of green and yellow bananas and counters covered with chiles, spices, herbs, mangoes, green coconuts, curative teas.

Foreman found real pleasure in these Mexican markets. He enjoyed wandering through them, enjoyed the good-natured exchanges with the vendors in that improvised combination of poor Spanish, poor English, and expressive sign language. He paused now to inspect a cotton Toluca shirt trimmed with blue-and-red stitching.

"What are you going to take, buyer," the shopkeeper

chanted in melodic Spanish. "What can I offer you?"

"Nothing," Foreman answered.

"Ah. What can I do for you? You like the shirt, I will make you a price. A little money. Make me an offer."

Foreman waggled a forefinger.

The shopkeeper smiled and shrugged. "Maybe tomorrow."

"Maybe tomorrow," Foreman repeated and moved on, only remotely aware of being physically jostled by Mexicans coming and going in the crowded lanes. During his first weeks in the country, the continuous body contact had annoyed him. People came too close and there was an insistent elbowing, an almost constant physical pressure, a push that managed to be just this side of an American shove. In time he became used to it, aware that the elbowing and shouldering was in fact cautious and gentle, without the hostility of Times Square or the Loop. Here the touching of flesh was more a wordless signal of another presence, an unspoken announcement of one's need to go on and the intended direction.

Foreman sauntered past a fortuneteller, along a line of stalls displaying pottery from other parts of the country. Ahead of him, a pair of young Americans. The boy lean and loose-gaited, long brown hair flowing with each of his ungainly strides; the girl pretty, well-shaped, barefoot.

Foreman came up behind them. *"Buenas tardes,* Charles," he said.

The tall boy turned, his brown eyes guarded. Recognition came slowly.

"Hullo," he managed, as if caught in some forbidden act. "I didn't expect to see you here."

"Nor anywhere else," Foreman said, smiling at the girl. Her prettiness was compromised for him by what seemed a self-conscious pelvic thrust, a disapproving turn of mouth. There was a kind of defiant, almost belligerent sexuality about young girls like this one that puzzled Foreman, as if they wanted disapproval and thereby could confirm the rightness, the superiority, of their own actions. It was, he felt, a pretty boring waste of energy. "I happen to like native markets," he added.

"For the bargains, I suppose," the girl said.

"Why don't we call it a draw before the match?" Foreman said, and held out his hand and introduced himself.

She looked at his hand and finally took it briefly. "I'm Becky."

"You two just looking, or shopping?"

Charles answered. "I want a serape."

"There are some Indians back up this street. Their serapes looked good to me."

"Not just any serape," Becky said. "There's a village north of here. San Juan del Mar. They do terrific work. Natural colors and none of those phony patterns."

Foreman stayed humble. "I'm no expert on serapes, but if you want to try the Indians—?"

"Sure," Charles said.

Becky shrugged and fell into step between them, eyes cast down.

Four Indians, hunkered down alongside two stacks of folded serapes, talking earnestly among themselves.

"*Buenas tardes,*" Foreman began. The Indians fell silent, studying the three Americans with professional interest. They stood up. "My friends," Foreman went on, his Spanish slow, "are looking for a very special kind of serape."

Sombreros came off and all the Indians began to smile. One man stepped forward. "Ah," he said in a soft, lyrical voice. "These are very special serapes. The workmanship is special. The colors are special. The designs are special. Your friends are very lucky, they have come to us. We have very special serapes." His smile widened and he glanced at his companions; they nodded approvingly.

The spokesman made a gesture and two of the men opened a large serape, spread it between them. A geometric pattern suggesting a Mondrian painting, done in orange, black, and red.

"A very special serape, *señor.*"

"That's for tourists," Becky said.

Foreman agreed. "No, no. My friends know exactly what it is they want. A serape made in the village of San Juan del Mar . . ."

"Ah . . ."

"Do you have any work from San Juan del Mar?"

"*Trabajo de San Juan del Mar,*" the spokesman said rapidly to his friends. He pointed at a short, dark man. "This is Soledad. He is from San Juan del Mar and so his work is naturally the work of San Juan del Mar." Logic triumphant.

Another serape was brought forth and displayed, front and back. Foreman, laughing loudly, shook his finger. The Indians laughed, too, without embarrassment.

"No," Foreman said. "The work we seek is simple and the colors are natural."

"Sí, sí. Aquí tiene colores naturales. Sí."

A third serape was broken out of the stacks, a bird design in black, brown, and white. Shaking his head, Foreman laughed again. The Indians exchanged sheepish looks and soon all of them were laughing. The attempted subterfuge had failed, but all were pleased by the quick thinking of their leader, pleased also with this interesting and amusing interlude in an otherwise ordinary day. The big American was friendly and sympathetic, though his Spanish was not good. And he had not yet gone, so a sale might still be made. Another serape was opened.

It was then that the shortest of the four men stepped forward, eyes fixed on Charles' wristwatch, which he wore fastened to a beltloop of his jeans.

"How much does a watch like that cost?" the Indian asked.

Foreman translated.

Charles brought his hand up to his forehead. "I don't know. My father gave it to me in celebration of my going out for football in high school. A mistake. A week later I was cut from the squad . . . I don't know, about two hundred bucks, I guess."

Foreman addressed the Indian. "It's worth a lot of money."

The Indian nodded sagely. "I will give your friend fifty pesos for the watch."

"Señor, the watch is very expensive, it is worth more than twenty good serapes."

The Indian examined Foreman's face and decided it was possible to bargain. "Very well, seventy-five pesos."

Foreman translated.

Charles said, "It was a gift."

"The watch was a gift," Foreman said in Spanish.

The Indian checked the watch closely. "Oh, but that must have been a long time ago. All that is forgotten. I will pay eighty pesos."

"No, *señor*," Foreman said. Charles and Becky began to move away.

"My final offer," the Indian called after them.

Foreman lifted his hand in salute and went after Charles and Becky. Behind him, the Indians were hunkered down again, talking seriously among themselves.

"Those Indians seemed to like you," Becky said to Foreman cautiously, as if afraid he might take advantage of any softness she showed toward him.

"They enjoy the exchange."

"But we didn't buy."

"The way they see it, if not today, then tomorrow. If not us, someone else. These markets are a miniature of Mexican customs. They're rewarding, if you don't expect Mexicans to act like Americans."

"Like my father," Charles said. "If you're not exactly the way he is, he figures you're some kind of nut pervert, or worse."

"Has he been to the markets?"

"Are you kidding! He makes it the other way. Acapulco gives him all the phonies he likes, all the brass-assed chicks. Wow. At his age, he could at least be a little more, well, you know, discreet."

"You mean, leave the girls alone?"

"Well, at least act his age."

"I have a hunch your father's not much older than I am, and I still like girls, if that's all right," Foreman said, grinning at Becky.

"Well," she said gravely, "you don't seem so old to me."

"You come across pretty straight," Charles said. "Like you care who you're talking to. You dug those Indians and they knew that. My father bullshits. He'd dismiss those Indians for the crime of being Indians, also for the bigger one of being poor."

"Maybe he's been there," Foreman said. "Maybe the memory is distinctly unkicky for him."

"Oh, come on," Charles said to him. "I was beginning to think you could play it straight. We're not complete jerks, you know. I never said poor is better, and I'm not conned by it, either. But to keep on living down your past, or whatever it is . . . that's plain dumb."

"And amen to that," Foreman said. "Well, at least you seem to feel *something* about your father, which is better than nothing. You're bothered, and if you're bothered enough, maybe you'll still make the effort to get together with him. Who knows, you and your father might still make it. Sorry about the speech . . ."

"No sweat. But me and my father? Maybe . . . but I doubt it. . . ."

Five minutes after separating from Charles and Becky, Foreman saw the tall girl with the wheat-colored hair for the first time. She stood with her legs firmly planted, bargaining with an aged woman over the price of a rebozo. The exchange was swift and good-natured and her generous mouth was mobile, alternately smiling and drawing down in exaggerated dissent. An impasse was reached and the girl made a gesture of finality and strode away, the loose-fitting cotton dress she wore failing to disguise the full ripeness of her body.

On impulse, Foreman hurried up to the old woman. He indicated the rebozo the girl had been interested in. "Give me your best price," he said.

"Sixty pesos, *señor*. The work is complicated . . ."

"Fifty," Foreman said, offering the money.

"Bueno. It has not been such a good day for business and now it is getting late."

The rebozo tucked under one arm, Foreman went after the tall girl. For a long interval, it seemed as if he had lost her. He retraced his steps, went down another market lane, seeking that singular wheat-colored hair. At last he spotted her, head above the crowd, and he tried to move more rapidly.

"Con permiso. Perdón."

He looked up and she was gone. Foreman searched the cross lanes, then continued straight on out of the market. No sign of her anywhere. He felt suddenly chilled. Startled by his reaction, he hurried up one street and down the next, doubled back, circled around. She was gone.

Feeling a growing sense of loss, he continued into the *zócalo* and swung up the Costera. At Sanborn's, he browsed through the paperback books without much interest. He started out. At the end of the store, at the drug counter, the wheat-colored hair. He picked his way forward but before he could reach her, she was out the nearest exit.

Foreman plunged after her. She was moving along the Costera in a free-swinging stride. He broke into a run, slowed down as he came up to her, matching her pace. He examined her profile with blunt curiosity. Her features were clearly defined, her brow wise and smooth, her eyes large. Her nose was straight and her skin glistened in the sunlight like Carrara marble.

Gradually, she became aware of his presence, glanced briefly at him, her expression cold, disdainful. She walked faster.

"Hey," he said. "Don't run away again."

She kept going.

"Be friendly," he said, catching up. He offered the rebozo. "I come bearing a gift."

She stopped abruptly, looked over the rebozo as if it were an alien and dangerous object. The tip of her tongue appeared in the corner of her mouth.

"It's for you," he said, feeling clumsy. "A present."

She shook her head. "I never saw you before."

"Look," he said, spreading his arms. "No tricks. N strings. Nothing up my sleeves. Back in the market . . . saw you, wanted to meet you. That's all . . ."

Her eyes measured him. Finally she laughed, pleased but apparently still suspicious. "You went to a lot of trouble. But no thanks. Goodbye, whoever you are."

She was on the move again.

He trailed after her. "I'm Paul Foreman. A name to inspire confidence, friendliness, ongoing relationships. Be a pal."

"I've got a pal," she said lightly, not looking at him.

"Not like me. Consider my qualifications for palship— fourth in my class at Yale, at least I would've been if I hadn't quit in my junior year. An excellent chess player, an outstanding swimmer at the shorter distances. I smoke too much, but I'll give it up. How's that grab you?"

"That should make your wife happy."

"Is that what's worrying you? I'm not married. Oh, I was, but she's a fading memory of no consequence."

"Not interested."

"Nor do I have a brood. I am free and forty, except for certain hangups, which is not so uncommon."

Her wide mouth seemed about to laugh again, but she kept on.

"Consider before you commit an act that may ruin both our lives. A girl your age should think of her future . . ."

Eyes straight ahead, she said, "And what is my age, Mr. Foreman?"

"You do care for me! Otherwise you'd never have remembered my name."

"My age?" she said sternly.

"That was only a device—feeble, I grant you—to get your attention. Don't you care that I care?"

"My age?"

"Thirty?"

She glared at him without slowing down.

"Twenty, then?"

"Twenty-six, and I don't look it."

"That's true. You don't look it. I'm blind, with very bad judgment. It's just that you have such mature poise—"

"And you've had lots of practice, I'm sure."

"No, no. No. Please don't lose us in a fit of girlish pique."

Brief laughter, still protective.

"Take the rebozo. Something to warm you, to remind you of this encounter."

"I can't do that," she said.

"I bought it for you," he said flatly.

"I'm sorry," she replied, hurried on.

He looked after her. Her hips swung in a fine, natural arc and her bottom was firm and promising under the cotton dress. *"I love you!"* he shouted after her. Passersby stared at him with curiosity and alarm, skirting past. If she heard, she gave no sign. She climbed into a battered jeep parked at the curb, backed out, handed a peso note to the *tamarindo,* and drove away without a glance in Foreman's direction.

He stared at the rebozo. Then retraced his steps. In Sanborn's he spoke to the drug clerk in Spanish.

"Señorita, I require your assistance in a very important matter."

"Yes, sir."

"There was a young woman, a few minutes ago. An American with hair long and yellow, skin like polished marble, very tall with a fine figure. Not that I paid much attention to her."

The clerk smiled.

Foreman showed her the rebozo. "She dropped this on her way out. I followed but it was too late."

"Ah, sí. If you like, I will keep it for her. She comes here once in a while."

Foreman put the rebozo behind his back. "Consider. What if the señorita wants to use it? What a tragedy! If you will tell me where she lives, I will deliver it myself. This same day."

The clerk raised her eyebrows, seemed amused by his display. "Señorita Biondi lives in the mountains. To go there would not be such a good thing, I think."

"The mountains?"

"Among the Chinchahua tribe. The Chinchahua are not friendly to strangers."

"The mountains can be cold, especially at night. A sturdy rebozo would come in handy. What is Señorita Biondi's Christian name?"

"Grace, señor." Foreman thanked her, started away. "Señor will go to the Chinchahua village?"

"Yes."

"With your permission, señor, a suggestion. Do not go unarmed . . ."

5

To Acapulco, by plane, mostly, also by car, by bus, and some by private yacht. They filled the hotels and the rooming houses, found space with friends or rented a cot with native families. They jammed the restaurants and the bars and the nightclubs. They lined the pools by day and the beaches, sizzling under coconut oil and iodine, willing themselves to brown. Others sprawled in the shade of thatched-roof cabanas and sipped pineapple juice spiked with rum and tequila and devoured platters of *camarónes a la plancha,* searching the passing parade for a celebrated face, a presence that would add glitter to their vacation.

On the bay, fronting Playa Condesa, waterskiers sliced great white-water circles and more daring vacationers floated high above, hanging from multicolored parachutes, attached by cables to speeding power boats. Farther out in the bay, sailfish darted about like skittering creatures, colored sails in contrast to the cloudless horizon.

The season had officially begun. Parties went on day and night, in private villas and at the more expensive restaurants and clubs. But these, it was generally conceded, were minor social happenings of no consequence and included none of the city's more favored residents.

The columnist for the *News* was forced to fill his weekly space with the names and activities of clothing manufacturers, executive secretaries, and retired military persons below the rank of general. The people who mattered had yet to appear or, having arrived, were barely settled in.

Sunday. Couples strolled along the Malencón looking at the boats, the lacy fish nets strung out to dry, shopping for jewelry and coconut soap in the small outdoor market opposite Sanborn's. Others remained dormant, indoors or out, recuperating from the previous night, looking ahead to the *comida,* and the activities of the night to come.

Not Harry Bristol. Since eight fifteen that morning, he had been studying and revising the budget for *Love, Love,* paring bits of production fat. Pickings were slim. On paper, the original budget had been tight, every dollar accounted for.

Production had changed all that, and Foreman was the villain, insisting on an extra take, experimenting with a different camera angle; various set-ups. Bristol swore, his stomach rumbling in answer. He popped an Entero-Vioforme in his mouth, washing it down with Coke. Purified or not, he was off Mexican water for life.

"Harry," Shelly said, coming out of the bedroom.

"What's the matter with you? Can't you see I'm working?"

She inspected the back of his neck. How peculiar that she'd never before noticed how thick it was, how out of proportion. Bulky men with bulging muscles had never appealed to her; yet here she was with Harry. It was something to think about, she told herself.

"Harry," she said. "It's Sunday."

"Three cheers for Sunday."

"We're in Acapulco, Harry."

"Tell me what I don't know."

His hair looked suddenly thinner on top. It occurred to her that for the first time she was *looking* at Harry and it seemed almost an act of disloyalty. She'd been that conditioned.

She touched his shoulder gently. "It's so beautiful outside, Harry. Let's do something, go somewhere."

"I'm doing something. I'm working. You go if you want. I don't mind."

She made a face at the back of Bristol's head and went back into the other room, took off her dress and replaced it with tight white shorts, a sleeveless turquoise blouse. Satisfied with her appearance, she sat on the bed.

What to do? Should she go to the pool, or perhaps to one of the beaches? Being alone in a public situation always bothered her. And especially in a bikini; she loved being attractive to men, yet at the same time felt afraid, vaguely ashamed even, when they gave her the appreciative stares she asked for.

She thought about Morrie Carlson. Since that first day, she had seen him twice. One night, with Harry's permission, she went with Morrie to watch the cliff divers from the bar at the Hotel Mirador. And one afternoon, Morrie had visited the site where they had been filming. Shelly had introduced him to Harry and Foreman, some of the other members of the company. That night Harry had been sarcastic about Morrie, mean about the shape of his body. Shelly hated him for doing that, and was surprised at having the courage to feel such emotions about Harry.

In the closet, behind some empty suitcases, was Morrie's drawing of Shelly, framed and under glass, wrapped in green-and-gold paper. This was to be her present to Harry for Christmas next week. Perhaps the gift would divert him from his work now, and she could persuade him to take her out. She carried the portrait into the other room.

"Harry," she began.

"Not now, I told you."

"This is for you, Harry."

He put down his pen, turned around slowly, eyed her with disapproval. "Those are some shorts," he said.

"You like them, Harry? They're new."

"Every swordsman on the beach'll be groping you."

"Would you be jealous?" she teased.

"Just don't wear them is all. If I want you putting out for somebody else, I'll tell you."

"All right, Harry," she said quickly. "I'll change them. But first I've got a present for you." She offered him the package.

He held it as if it were a dangerous weapon. "What's that?"

"A present, silly. Open it."

He undid the ribbon, stripped away the paper, studied the portrait. "It's you," he said finally.

"You like it?"

He looked at the portrait, then at Shelly, and back again. "It's okay."

"I thought it was pretty good."

"I got the real thing, what do I need a picture for? That guy Carlson did this?"

She nodded once.

"What's going on with you and him?"

"Don't Harry, please."

"I asked you a question."

"Nothing's going on. Morrie's my friend."

"*I'm* your friend! Whataya need another friend for when you got me?"

"It's not the same."

"Bet your sweet ass it isn't! You making it with that creep?"

"Oh, Harry. Don't call him that."

"Answer me!"

She sensed that this was a test. He didn't actually believe she was sleeping with Morrie Carlson, just wanted to hear her deny it.

"I won't!" she told him, almost stamping her foot. "I won't answer."

"The hell you won't."

She took a backward step.

"I haven't done anything wrong. What's more, you know it."

Bristol grunted with satisfaction. "I knew you didn't make it with him. Probably can't even get it up."

"That's very nice," she said.

"A dame like you," he muttered, staring at the picture. "I remember what you were when I found you. Practically a whore. If it wasn't for me, you'd be hustling it in Vegas."

She turned pale. "No," she managed, "I'm not like that."

"You gave me your word when we got together, you'd be straight."

"I *have* been, Harry. I really have."

Still staring at the picture, he said, "Tell the truth, this picture stinks. Really stinks. If he was any good, he wouldn't be doing this crap for peanuts." Without warning he sailed the picture against the wall, the glass shattering as it fell.

Shelly picked it up, pulled away the broken glass. "It's good, Harry," she said, wanting to believe it and not really able to. "It is good. And your opinion's no better than mine." She went into the bedroom and slammed the door behind her.

A few minutes later, Harry came after her. "Listen, I

shouldn't've heaved the picture that way. Let me have it, I'll get some more glass put in. On me. Maybe it's not so bad at that. I mean, what the hell, I kind of like it."

She gave him a cautious look. "You mean it?"

"Sure, I mean it."

"You're not sore anymore?"

"Nah."

Her smile came quickly. "Then let's go out, do something."

"Okay, okay." Then, suspiciously: "Like what?"

"You know those little boats on the bay, Harry," she said going to the window. "Come and see. They call them sail-fish. I've always wanted to try that, Harry. Could we, please?"

"Well, okay. But just remember that because I said I like the picture it isn't okay for you to hang around with that . . . that Morrie character. Remember who pays the bills around here."

She started to laugh. "I'll remember . . ."

"And take off those goddammed shorts!"

Samantha woke alone, and feeling afraid.

A bad dream, harsh black-and-white dream. She was a child again, living on a military post with her parents in one of those ranchstyle houses with thin walls the army provided for its field-grade officers.

There was a party, *her* party, but no one came. None of the children she had invited came. Not one of her friends. She'd sat at the head of a long, gaily decorated party table, by herself, tears on her thin face. And in that moment she knew she had no friends, not one.

Samantha pulled the sheet up to her neck, drew up her knees, hugging herself, just as she had when a child. Even now that dream seemed real, a present fact of life. And she was frightened as she was on that day so very long ago. Ever since then, when she gave a party there was the residual fear that no one would come, that she would be alone with her unattended festivities.

To be lonely was the worst condition. So painful. Yet she had been alone so often. Not one of her marriages had provided the closeness, the affection she craved; nor had any of her lovers given anything beyond a physical attentiveness, which peaked out soon after meeting and steadily diminished thereafter.

I deserve something better . . .

Cradling her head in her hands, Samantha tried to visualize each of her lovers, to place him in the proper order of appearance. It became difficult to juggle all the names and faces in her mind so she began to make notes, to list each one's characteristics, physical or otherwise, positive or negative.

How few good things there are to say . . .

Soon she had compiled a considerable catalogue. She was, she noted with some dismay, a promiscuous woman. Such a view of herself was unsettling and she slammed the notebook shut, deposited it out of sight in the drawer of her night table. She got out of bed.

Naked—Samantha was a firm believer in allowing one's skin to *breathe,*—she arranged herself on the Persian prayer rug given her by the Arab (he fancied it for making love) and began her yoga exercises. Breathing in and out with disciplined regularity, Samantha tried to exclude all corrupting thoughts from her consciousness. But certain exterior considerations continued to intrude and she gave up. This was no day for serious meditation.

In the oversized bathroom, she switched on the sauna, brushed her teeth with furious energy while waiting for it to reach the desired temperature. Once stretched out on the slatted wooden bench in the sauna, she allowed her eyes to flutter shut, urging her pores to open wide, and all destructive elements in her body to ooze away.

How weak and self-indulgent she had been at Bernard's the night before. All that champagne, all that too rich, too delicious food. Shame, Samantha. She made a mental commitment for five minutes extra in the sauna this morning.

What a peculiar evening it had been, taking unexpected turns. Of course, Bernard's little entertainments were frequently strange. Bernard had a faculty for surrounding himself with people concerned with the drearier sides of life—the sordid, in fact.

Last night was a perfect example. During the vichyssoise, one of the guests, a composer of Broadway musicals, had held forth on what he described as the world revolu-

tion of the young, the poor, the disenfranchised. What an
unattractive man he was, eyes small and glowing, chin
weak, his language much too flamboyant. Since it was
generally agreed that this composer's major talent was for
self-promotion and money-making, Samantha found his
revolutionary stance hypocritical. After all, few men had
been created equal; experience had taught her that.

During the entrée—a splendid chicken *chipotle*—the
composer maintained that everyone present, Bernard included, was too self-satisfied. All, it seemed, failed to
grasp the import of the new revolution, would fail to understand even at that cataclysmic moment when the
campesinos of the world shot them down like French
aristocrats.

An American called Gavin, darkly handsome with the
weathered look and big shoulders of an outdoorsman, had
answered. He pointed out that the aristocrats of France
were guillotined (that even he, a crude American *businessman*, knew that), and said that the composer was not only
wrong in his judgments about the future but was rude to
spread gloom over such a fine dinner party in the presence
of such a beautiful and charming collection of ladies.

Samantha applauded lightly and smiled at the American. He nodded his head in acknowledgment, but that was
all. Samantha's curiosity about Gavin rose steeply.

Over a dessert of immense strawberries in claret, the
composer launched another attack—the revolutionary nature of art. He proclaimed the changes in painting, the
novel, theater, motion pictures. He referred to oppressed
minorities, to homosexuals in films, the blacks, the poor.

Samantha was finally moved to speak, sounding more
Bourbon than she felt. "How depressing it all sounds. Myself, I never go to a film unless the star wears a mink
coat."

Marcella whooped. "Darling, how marvelous! What a
wit you are, Samantha!"

Her remark accomplished what had seemed impossible:
the composer grew sullen, finally silent. But it failed to
draw any further attention to her from Mr. Gavin. Dinner
over, he closeted himself with Bernard and was not seen
again until just before he left.

Too bad, she had thought at the time. Evidently he

was less interesting than he appeared. So many men were. Businessmen especially were often dullards—American businessmen most of all—devoted to the techniques of acquiring large amounts of capital, when everyone knew that all the joy was in the cultivated expenditure of money.

The gentle buzz of the timer interrupted, and Samantha stepped out of the sauna, slipped into a yellow robe. Downstairs, crossing the living room, she called out to the maid, continued on to the Roman pool. She dropped the robe on a chair, gazed briefly into the water vapors rising in the morning light, plunged in. She had completed four laps in the heated water by the time Trini appeared with coffee, sliced papaya, and the *News*.

She read the weather report. In Paris, it was forty-eight degrees, fifty-one in London, and only three degrees warmer in Rome. A snowstorm had closed all airports in the northeastern United States and eight inches of snow covered New York City, the temperature there thirteen degrees above zero. Samantha let the paper fall to the ground and raised her face to the sun, closed her eyes. All that chilly intelligence made being in Acapulco so much sweeter.

Presently Trini appeared again. "Flowers for the *señorita*."

"Who from?"

Trini extended the six dozen blood-red roses that were cradled in her arms. Samantha removed the card, read the careful script: "You made dinner a delightful and rewarding experience." It was signed Theo Gavin.

Theo. What a nice name. She'd never cared much for Ted or Teddy, and Theodore had such a prissy ring to it. Theo. It fit.

When she was alone, Samantha read the card once more. Gavin was once again a person of interest. Considerably so. How long since a man had been experienced and sophisticated enough not to display his interest in her immediately, and directly? Most men had almost no social finesse. Theo Gavin obviously was not among these.

Red roses. A rather ordinary choice, actually, the kind of bouquet a truck driver might send to a waitress, or a schoolboy to his girl. A reassuring thought—was she underestimating Gavin; perhaps the roses were a deliberate

ploy on his part not to appear too worldly, too clever, and
thereby too obviously interested. Of *course!* That had to
be it. He was an expert player, had cast his line into the
sea, meant to troll his line until she nibbled the bait.

Her finger came up to her chin and she smiled to herself. Gavin would be a pleasant change from all those
brown Mexicans—Kiko (the bastard!), and before him
the riding instructor, and before him that awful gigolo
(he had lasted only a very short time, of course), and the
matador (bullfighters so often seemed to confuse loving
and killing, and their ability to do either was constantly in
question).

A tall, strong American. Purposeful, proper, clean masculine. Time spent with such a man might be rewarding
in many ways. Gavin clearly possessed an appreciation of
the best things in life; would be able to afford them. A
new and startling idea surfaced; she entertained it willing-
ly, examined it from every perspective. Such a man might
very well be a permanent solution to all her present difficulties. She made her decision—she would invite Gavin to
her Christmas party, as a nonpaying guest, of course.

On the beach, Becky and Charles. Both seated, both hugging their knees, faces turned toward the sea, careful not
to look at each other.

"I'm going," Becky said for the third time. "You do
your own thing."

"A couple of days more and I'll go with you."

"Uhuh. No way. The fuzz busted Stone and two other
boys for *possession.* All he had on him was some *seeds* in
his pocket. They're liable to get seven years. This place is
unreal. I'm splitting. Oaxaca will be a ball." She stood up.
"I'm going for a swim . . ."

He watched her. She was a strong swimmer, much stronger than he was, and it bothered him that he wasn't able to
match her stroke for stroke (he couldn't keep up with
Theo either).

"You're a terrific swimmer," he told her when she came
back.

She rolled in the sand. "The trouble is, you never
learned to breathe right."

"That's what my father says."

She sat up.

"Give me two days," he said. "We'll hitch all the way."

"I promised Livy. Anyway, this town crawls with tourists. I've had it. There's a festival of the radishes in Oaxaca. I want to see it."

"Radishes and mushrooms. A vegetable trip . . ."

She didn't laugh. "What's the big deal with this crazy safari? You don't even like your father."

"I gave him my word I'd give it a chance."

"What about your father's word to you? Has he ever been straight with you?"

"That doesn't tell me what to do."

"Fathers," she said. "Maybe Stone is right—he said if his father doesn't die by the time he's twenty-one, he's going to kill him."

"That's head talk."

"Maybe. Anyway you don't owe your father anything."

Charles was beginning to feel exhausted. He didn't want to think about Theo but he had to. He wasn't sure what it was he wanted from Theo. Or from himself. Was it possible still to reclaim some kind of good relationship with Theo? With either of his parents. Had there, in fact, ever been anything worth saving in his family? He had no answers except one; he had to try. And if nothing came of it, okay, but it wouldn't be his fault. It would be *theirs*.

"You'll never make it with him," Becky said.

"Maybe not. But they just don't have a clue about what we live with. How we *feel*. Maybe if I try to—"

"Forget it. There's just no way. We try, but they're long out of it. Really, Charles, *forget* it."

"Maybe it'll be the same for us, with our kids."

"We're different."

"You believe all adults are the same?"

"Like out of a plastic mold, man."

"Paul Foreman's not like Theo."

"Never trust anyone over thirty."

"What happens when we get to thirty?"

"Never trust anyone over forty."

Both of them laughed and Charles put his arm around her.

"We're good," she told him aggressively. "We're good. Hold the thought."

"Is Stone good, talking about knocking off his father?"

"Maybe that's the way to go. Maybe kids should off all the old ones, take the power, the money, everything. Parents don't understand anything. They think today is still yesterday. You think I care about the *Depression!* That's all my old man used to talk about, how it was when he was growing up. Screw that! I live *now.*"

Charles felt as if he were going through a mysterious experience, a surreal trip in which nothing was what it seemed to be, no truth constant. He wanted to remember what life had been like when he was very young, early in his parents' marriage. Theo and Julia must have loved each other then, must have loved him. *What went wrong?*

"I want this last chance with Theo," he said aloud. "He's my father. Corn that up if you want."

"Wow. That man's trapped you. Goodbye, old Charles. See you when you're the full statistic—complete with two-and-a-half kids, PTA, and swapping wife. You'll go the whole route."

"Maybe I'll catch up with you," he said.

"No way. I'm going to Oaxaca. *Adios . . .*"

She walked rapidly away. He sat there for a long time, wondering if the world had ever made a bigger square.

Forty minutes out of Acapulco, Foreman decided he'd missed the turn-off. He put his foot on the brake, slowed the VW. Fate, he told himself, and an inadequate system of marking were combining to keep him from ever finding Grace Biondi. On the road to the front, a man astride a small, gray burro, moving without urgency. Foreman pulled up alongside.

"With your permission, sir," Foreman said in halting Spanish. "I look for the road that leads to the village of the Chinchahua. Can you give me directions?"

The man assessed Foreman from under a tattered sombrero. "You are going to the Chinchahua village?"

"With your assistance."

"You are going there in this automobile?"

"That is my intention."

"Ah, *señor,* the road is very bad with many curves and holes. That is a journey made better on a burro."

"I have only this car, *señor*."

"Yes," the Mexican said soberly. "It would be an honor if you could ride my burro. I will look after this automobile until your return."

"You think I will not be coming back?" Foreman said gravely.

"Well, *señor*, the Chinchahua are a fierce people. Still, who can say what God's will is on this or any other day."

But you're not giving odds on his being with me, Foreman said to himself. Aloud, he said, "Which way to the Chinchahua, *señor*?"

The Mexican rubbed his nose. "Straight ahead. There is the village of La Cuarenta y Ocho. Do not stop there. Soon after, you will see it, on the road. On the right side. A shrine to the dead. There is the road you want."

"Thank you, *señor*."

"It is nothing."

The shrine was a rococo affair in bright blue, pink, and white paint, with a glass-enclosed Virgin dedicated to a man who had died in a traffic accident at this place. Twenty feet beyond the shrine, a dirt road. The VW rattled across a dry driver bed, up a steep bank, and across a short, rocky plateau. Then onto a dusty track heading upland. Foreman shifted downgear and the VW responded, put-putting ferociously as it bounced up the grade.

At some points, the road was barely wide enough to accommodate the VW as it curled around rocky points in right-angle turns. Stunning vistas opened up, deep, green valleys and striated rock formations laced with color and studded with cave openings. Once Foreman barely outraced a small rock slide and minutes later he rounded a bend to discover the outer edge of the track had fallen away. A quick turn saved him from a similar end.

Rocks in the road and potholes sent the tiny car lurching from side to side and Foreman fought the wheel with both hands. An abrupt left took him higher, higher still, over a brown hump, dropping swiftly. A straight-away was lined with trees that might have been cypress, growing in close order like a tall, green fenceline.

Foreman blinked and hit the brake hard. The VW

skidded, the rear straining to catch up with the front. Two men stood in the center of the road, calmly watching. When the car stopped they moved toward it, their rifles pointed at Foreman.

He searched for a way around. The trees were too close to the road. He considered a quick U-turn, escape in the direction from which he'd come. A quick glance out the rear window revealed two more men, both armed. Foreman sighed and switched off the ignition. He stepped out into the cool green mountain air.

"Buenas tardes, señores!" he called out with what he hoped would pass for unafraid cheerfulness. He arranged a smile on his face and pressed on, despite the sudden dryness lining his mouth. He wiped his hands on his trouser legs and turned his palms up and out in a gesture of friendliness. He was pleased to see that his hands were trembling only slightly. *"Señores,* I am very glad to see you. I am lost and need help. I am on my way to the Chinchahua village to visit my friend, the Señorita Grace Biondi. She is an American, like myself. Can you direct me?"

Nothing. The four men stood straight and stiff in soiled white trousers and shirts, staring at Foreman. Behind thick black mustaches, somber and unrevealing faces. Suddenly Foreman felt as if he were an actor in an old movie about Mexican bandits. It was, he conceded silently, not a very good picture.

"My Spanish is poor," he said. "Forgive me. So if it's all right with you I'll just get back in the car and go on. It's been very nice talking to you gentlemen . . ."

He opened the door of the VW; the man nearest to him slammed it shut.

"We appear to have arrived at an impasse," Foreman said. He reached for his cigarettes. "Mind if I smoke?"

The man who slammed the door held out his hand. Foreman gave him the pack. "Help yourself," he said.

A second man stepped forward, rifle centered on Foreman's chest. "Señorita Biondi spoke of no visitors," he told his friends.

"Well," Foreman said. "You gentlemen must be Chinchahua! What a break for me. Why don't I give you a lift to the village? Climb in, don't be shy."

One of the men behind Foreman spoke. "I think it

would be good to shoot him now."

"Yes," another said. "Let him walk into the woods and kill him there. That way we don't have to carry the body."

"Agreed," another said.

"That's very funny," Foreman said. "But I'm not sure Señorita Biondi would understand such humor."

"Shoot him now."

"Now fellows let's stop this talk of shooting and killing. I know you're only teasing but it upsets me. Tell you what, let's make a deal. Take me to Señorita Biondi. If she says I'm not a friend, then you shoot me on the spot."

"We can always kill him," said the one who agreed earlier to let him walk before dying.

"And the automobile."

"*Sí*," Francisco said.

Foreman reached inside the car and four rifles were cocked immediately. He displayed the rebozo. "For the *señorita*," he said.

"Let's go."

The Chinchahua village contained about thirty or forty small houses made of wood and corrugated metal. Some had slatted roofs while others were covered with heavy black paper. A single dirt street ran through the center of the village ending in front of a small white church. In the street, the usual chickens, pigs and soccer-playing children. Spotting the newcomers, a dozen mangy hounds began to bark and howl, charging forward. Foreman's escorts delivered a series of well-placed kicks and the dogs retreated, sullen gratitude in their watery eyes.

People appeared in the street, collecting behind an old man with a white mustache, his face burned almost black by the mountain sun. He stood in the center of the street, staring at the oncoming men. They stopped six feet from the old man and one of the men spoke in a language Foreman had never heard before, deference in his voice. The old man listened, looking at Foreman out of dark-brown eyes set behind broad cheekbones.

"I'm an American," Foreman said in Spanish. "I came to visit Señorita Biondi."

"That's right!" a voice said from back in the crowd of villagers. A path opened and Grace Biondi came forward, her pale-blue eyes round with concern. She came up to Foreman and took his hand, shook it.

"The cavalry to the rescue," Foreman said in English.

"Be still. Lét me do all the talking." She switched to Spanish, talking to the old man. "He is a friend, Don Miguel. The mistake is mine, I failed to explain to him the customs of the Chinchahua . . ."

The old man studied Foreman. "Our enemies are clever. This could have been a trick to take us off guard, to place a spy in the village. One night while the people sleep . . ." He touched the machete that hung from his belt.

"I shall allow you to remain," the old man said to Foreman in Spanish. "It is only right that the Señorita meet with her own people. But you must act according to Chinchahua custom or you will be punished according to Chinchahua custom." He turned and walked away, moving with the easy stride of a much younger man.

The crowd broke into smaller groups as people returned to their homes. When they were alone, Grace Biondi swung around to Foreman.

"You were very close to being killed."

"That notion occurred to me."

"Why are you here?"

"I came to see you."

"Where's your car?"

"Those boys with the rifles flagged me down. One of them stayed with the car."

"I'll see about it later. Since we're supposed to be friends, we'd better act like it. Come with me. You'll stay a while for appearances, then you'll go."

She moved off and Foreman fell into step alongside. "You're not as tall as I remembered," he said.

"You must be a fool," she said. "There is no other rational explanation for your behavior."

"This is better. Just the right size. In every way."

"*Señor,* would you prefer Don Miguel's men?"

"Now, Grace, be kind."

"How did you find out my name? I never told it to you."

"I'm one of those enterprising Americans. There are ways. I don't suppose you remember my name?"

Midway along the street, she stopped. "I remember your name. Does that please you? I live here. Come inside. I'll feed you and then it's back to wherever you belong."

The hut had only one room, a corner of which served as a cooking area, smoke from a small cooking fire drifting out between the slats in the roof.

"I belong with you, Grace," Foreman said.

"Beans and tortillas for lunch." She stoked up the fire. "One of the women who has become my friend makes fresh tortillas for me every morning. They're quite good. I do the beans myself. *Muy picante, señor*. If chile isn't your style, you may go hungry in these parts."

"I'm an old Mexican hand."

She served the beans in clay bowls and they sat on three-legged stools, Foreman using the rebozo for a cushion. He spread some beans in a tortilla and ate rapidly, surprised at how hungry he was. Across from him, Grace Biondi chewed deliberately, eyes cast down. She was more beautiful than he'd remembered. Her skin was tawny, polished smooth, her features delicate yet strong, clearly defined. Her mouth a carefully sculpted line that fascinated him and excited his imagination.

"How did you find me?" she said, with a quick, searching glance.

"A secret. Let's talk about us. This is like some kind of a 1930 flick—hero comes crashing into the wilderness and is captured by a proud and primitive Indian tribe. Just as they are about to spread-eagle him to an anthill and a horrible death, a beautiful blond goddess appears to claim him for her own."

"I invited you only to lunch. Don't get carried away."

"You wouldn't talk that way if you'd seen the movie."

"Shall I tell you how *this* movie ends?"

"Don't bother."

"At the final fadeout the 'hero' goes riding down the mountain by himself, never again to be seen in these parts."

"Has it occurred to you that men are the true romantics?"

"Eat your lunch."

He cocked his head. "You're my first blond Italian . . ."

"What an interesting way to put it."

"Tell me the story of your life."

"Mother Irish; father Italian. Born New York, brought up in Philadelphia."

His eyes were drawn back to her mouth. Her lips were a deep-rose color. He wanted very much to kiss her. He brought out the rebozo. "This is for you," he said quietly.

"Oh . . ." She made a sound that suggested delight and regret at the same time. "It is lovely, isn't it? But I still can't accept it. We really don't know each other."

"You have an Italian father, an Irish mother. Born in New York, raised in Philadelphia . . . How do you do . . ."

She took the rebozo and pressed her face against it. "I love the natural smell of the wool."

"It's yours."

She hesitated. "Very well. I accept it, with pleasure. But nothing is changed. After lunch, you have to leave."

"En toute chose il faut considerer la fin," Foreman said. "In every affair it is necessary to consider the end." He devoted himself to the remainder of his beans, aware that she was examining him with what he hoped might accurately be called renewed interest.

After lunch they climbed along a winding path behind the village, crossing a narrow meadow where a herd of goats grazed under the watch of a young boy. He waved and Grace waved back, spoke to him in Chinchahua.

"You seem to get along pretty well with these people," Foreman commented.

"One either gets along well with the Chinchahua or not at all." She hesitated before going on. "The Chinchahua live a strictly communal life. The welfare of the tribe comes before the welfare of the individual. That's true of all the mountain people in this region. Each tribe is a unit, with very few people in each village. The Chinchahua are among the fiercest of the mountain people, with a real antagonism to strangers. The life or the death of any single person is only incidental, if it serves the general good, keeps the tribe alive."

"That's cutting pretty close to the bone, isn't it?"

"The Chinchahua exist close to the bone. Men, women and children, there are only sixty-seven of them. In a land of poor people, they are just about the poorest. And with little chance of improving their life. They can't shed the culture that shaped them and they can't make peace with an outside world that threatens them. They're one of the purest blood strains in the whole country, but they're like strangers, aliens in their own land. Outsiders. Outlaws. Yes," she said, as if answering a question, "they certainly would have shot you. Or any other intruder. Killing just isn't a moral problem for them. It makes sense. Experience has divided the world into two camps up here—Chinchahua and their enemies. Obviously you aren't a Chinchahua."

"Good guys and bad guys."

"They've made alliances with some other tribes, but these are delicate arrangements that have to be remade every six months or so. They're about basic survival things like water rights, use of the Acapulco road, that sort of thing. But the Chinchahua have learned not to depend on treaties."

"For example?"

"For example, years ago the Chinchahua made a treaty with the Huachucan. The Huachucan occupy an area that borders Chinchahua territory west of here, extending across the highway. For nearly half a year, the Chinchahua lived by the treaty, and kept an eye on the Huachucan. Gradually a trust developed and in time the barriers came down. Herds were taken to the better grazing lands farther from the village and no harm came to them. Women were allowed to go down the mountain to do their washing in the river. They were never bothered. Boys went hunting by themselves, nothing happened.

"Until one Sunday afternoon when a party of Huachucan attacked the largest Chinchahua herd, killed the boys, and slaughtered every goat and cow. An hour later, a Chinchahua woman had her throat cut while she was on her way back to the village from the river. The Chinchahua counterattacked and for nearly two months there was bloody war. A hundred Chinchahua men died and nobody knows how many Huachucan. The Chinchahua have trusted nobody ever since."

"When did all this happen?"

"As nearly as I can make out, about one hundred and fifty years ago."

Foreman whistled through his teeth. "These fellows are champion grudge-bearers."

"The Chinchahua have a saying—'A dead man may betray nobody.' "

They had settled down on a wide rock ledge, Grace dangling her legs over the side. Next to her, Foreman forced himself to peer down into the valley more than a thousand feet below. He leaned back on his elbows.

"I've been trying to figure out how you fit into this," he said.

She looked at him, then away, "I'm an anthropologist. I'd heard about the Indians in the mountains here and was curious. I visited a few of the villages but they all had their guards up, kept me away. The more they held out the more determined I became to know them. But it was hard. I went to the University in Mexico City, hoping to study Chinchahua history and language. Unfortunately, there is no written history and it's a rare outsider who speaks the language. But one of the university ethnologists put me onto an archaeologist who did speak Chinchahua and he tutored me. Then I came back. This time I was able to talk Don Miguel into letting me stay."

"What do you do?"

"I study. The Chinchahua have no alphabet, no written language, no written history. Legends and myths are passed along, one generation to the next. Some of their stories refer to men with black hair on their faces, men who gleamed in the sunlight. That no doubt means the conquistadores, bearded and wearing armor.

"Like the other peoples of Latin America, the Chinchahua made friends with the Spanish, trusted them, learned Christianity from them," she added, some irony evident in her voice. "But the Spanish betrayed them. At that time, the Chinchahua lived in the forests around Acapulco Bay. Later, to survive, they pulled back into the mountains."

"What about the other tribe."

"The Huachucan? Legend has it that two Chinchahua brothers fought over a young tribal beauty. One of them killed the other and ran off with the girl. That was the beginning of the Huachucan."

"Cain and Abel."

Grace made no reply and he gave her a long, searching

look, as if trying to see beneath the tawny skin. In profile, her features were finely etched, almost fragile. Yet he sensed a vein of strength running deep; and if at times she seemed defensive, there was no suggestion of subterranean angers waiting to explode.

"How long do you expect to stay up here?"

She smiled and shook her head. "My plan was to stay for three months. I've been here almost three times as long. But I'm beginning to think it's time to leave. I don't think it's my imagination, but I see changes in Don Miguel's mood. I think I'm beginning to be an embarrassment, to be a strain on him and the whole tribe. After all, I am an outsider, even if more knowledgeable than most. I hope I'm wrong because my work goes very well. On the other hand, I'm getting anxious to write up what I've learned—"

"Go on, please." She refused a cigarette and he lit one for himself.

"There's a theory that before Cortés, Oriental peoples landed in this portion of the Western Hemisphere. There are some indications of such a visit throughout South and Central America."

"So?"

"I suspect the Chinchahua may be a direct link to those early Oriental explorers."

"And you intend to prove it?"

"I guess so. But that would only be incidental to my real work. You see, I'm recording the Chinchahua language with the hope of creating a written alphabet. At the same time, I'm taping the history of the tribe."

"From the legends?"

"Yes. What I really hope to do is prove to the Chinchahua, to the Huachucan and the other mountain tribes that they are really different branches of the same family. Their languages are very similar, with many of the same roots. Maybe when they realize that they'll stop fighting with each other."

"A noble sentiment."

"One you don't share?"

"How is your alphabet coming?" he said, ignoring the question.

She shook her head. "It's been very difficult. For weeks I made no progress. Then suddenly it began to open up for me. I've made a number of breakthroughs. It's hard work, complicated by the suspicions of the tribal leaders, by the complexity of the language itself. Just imagine, in Chinchahua, there are seventeen verbs for 'run' and a dozen variables of the word 'sleep.' They have no word for 'retreat,' " she added.

"Do or die. Madison Avenue is loaded with that kind of hardnosed cat. My country right or wrong. Damn the torpedoes, full speed ahead. What else?" he said. "This is a lot of sweat for sixty-seven savages . . ."

She hesitated, decided to go on. "I want to publish a dictionary so that others can learn, go into the field, work in the different villages. When there's a written language, self-help manuals can be printed. The Chinchahua will be able to learn modern methods of farming, raising cattle, sanitation, basic medical care."

"Beautiful. But you left out one thing."

"What's that?"

"The Chinchahua can't read."

"But they can learn, can't they?" She pushed herself erect. "It's time to go back."

They walked for a few minutes without touching, an invisible barrier between them. Then he stumbled and went down on a polished stone slope, slipping and sliding, but unhurt. Unable to restrain herself, she laughed, waiting for him to stand again.

He rolled onto his back and stared up at her. "You look as good from this angle as any other."

Her mood changed quickly. "You mustn't talk to me that way."

"I want you to know how I feel."

"Please. Get up. We should get back to the village."

He stretched out his hand and she retreated a step, folding her arms.

"You just don't much care for me, I guess. Well, irresistible I'm not," he said with assumed petulance.

"I—you're a bright man, I think—"

"I know, but we're strangers. Look, so were the Chinchahua when you just met them. At least give us the same break you gave them."

He sat up. "What do you want to know about me? Ask me anything."

"Well. Do you like Acapulco?"

He put on a serious expression. "It's not so bad, but on the other hand it's terrible."

For a moment she didn't know how to react. Then she laughed. "You don't strike me as the tourist type. What *are* you doing there?"

"Only if you sit down."

She backed off another step. "Tell me as we go. We can walk slowly."

"Fair enough." He told her about *Love, Love,* how Bristol came to find him, how the project developed. "Bristol would like me to blueprint every scene, every frame, to bring the picture in under schedule, under budget."

"Can you work fast and still make the movie you want to make?"

"I keep telling myself I can. But every time I slow down to think there's Old Harry, pushing for more sex, more action. It's a movie so make it move!"

"Maybe he's right. Movies imply action, don't they?"

"Well, sure, but they also can have some thought content along the way. A movie is a pretty complicated thing. Lots of people are involved and every flick is a collaboration. But the director is the man in the slot, and finally it's his picture. It's my way of writing and, not to be too uptight about it, it's my signature. I'd like to sign something good."

"I understand that."

"You know, the camera is a rather special machine, like a neurotic mistress, in a way—you've got to handle it very carefully, and know what you're doing. Even then, it can beat you."

He threw up his hands. "Look, a guy like Bristol, he won't admit or even understand about a camera, and the beauty and larger-than-life truth you at least potentially can manage with it if you've got some talent. I'm no Bergman, but I'd at least like to be Paul Foreman, and to have this picture be the best of me. I hope that's not too damn self-important . . ."

They were back in the village, and at the end of the street, pointed back down the mountain, stood Foreman's red VW.

"I don't think so. And stop apologizing. Doing this picture may be a good thing, you'll at least have a chance to find out more about yourself."

He looked at her. "What makes you think *that's* what I want?"

"I wish someone like you would come up here," she said, letting it pass, "someone with a movie camera to make a permanent record of the Chinchahua in their daily life. Their festivals are incredibly beautiful and exotic. The music is simple but the dances are intricate and sensual. Each one tells a story." They were at the car and she broke off, smiled absently. "Thank you for the rebozo. It is lovely."

"There's more where that came from," Foreman said, wishing he could really let out the unaccustomed, unaccountable, instant feeling he had for her, damn near an instant obsession, if that were possible. And he wished even more that she would be able to respond . . .

The sailfish skimmed across the waters of the outer bay. Shelly, on the tiller, raised her head and laughed into the wind. Gulls circled against the high blue sky and a pelican plunged into the water, coming up with a fish in his great beak. Shelly felt exhilarated, weightless, as the boat whipped over the low swells.

Even the violent love-making Harry had put her through just before they'd come to the boat couldn't damp her high spirits. In fact, if she were to be really honest with herself (which was rare) she had enjoyed much of it— and always did. Harry was gross and didn't act like he gave a damn what she felt or what he was doing for her. And sometimes she could only fake it to keep him happy. But when he was at his best—his total natural, selfish best—he was a special kind of man, and a woman had to respond whether she liked it or not. This time Shelly had liked it much more than not.

Unpredictable breezes lifted the tiny craft, set it down roughly, spray raining up at Shelly and Bristol. They headed straight out to sea.

Bristol fought the boom as it sliced back and forth, in an effort to keep the sailfish upright.

"Oh, Harry!" she said. "Isn't it exciting!"

"Turn this damn thing around!"

"Are we far from shore, Harry?"

"A couple of miles at least. Go left and I'll try to straighten out the sail."

Shelly squinted into the nimbus of reflected light shadowing the waves. No other boats were to be seen, but far inshore a parachutist swung gracefully under a blue and white umbrella.

"Take her around!" Bristol shouted, and Shelly obeyed.

A gust of wind filled out the sail and the sailfish tipped like a great listing bird. Shelly pushed hard on the tiller. The boom swung swiftly from port to starboard, barely missing Bristol's ducking head.

"Watch out, dammit! You'll put us in the drink!"

A power boat came roaring out of the horizon, slicing across their bow. They were bumped roughly by the wake, the prow dipping water. Without warning, the wind shifted and the sail ballooned the other way, the boom swinging toward Bristol's back.

"Harry! Look out!" She lunged forward, reaching, but the boom went past, picking up speed, passing inches over Bristol. He looked up, pale and frightened. "What are you trying to do!" His eyes reached past her. "Oh, Jesus! Where's the rudder?"

She jerked around. The rudder was gone.

"There it is!" he shouted, voice muffled on the wind. "Off to the right!"

Her eyes darted across the swells, finally picking up the glistening brown angle of wood; the water between it and the sailfish widened swiftly.

"We've got to get it back," Harry yelled.

Shelly looked to the front. The sailfish, backed now by a steady breeze, was angling out of the bay toward the open sea.

"I can't do it!" Harry said. "I can't swim that far."

Shelly pulled off her jersey shirt, her slacks, dived into the water. She stroked to a point where she imagined the rudder would be, allowing for drift, breathing regularly, going with the swells. Twice she swallowed water but managed to keep going, making a conscious effort to kick with rhythm and power.

Lifted by a high swell, she spotted the rudder, changed course. Breathe and kick, she commanded herself, stroke. Breathe and kick . . . Abruptly the rudder came into view. Renewed she swam faster until her hand closed around

the slick handle. Sucking air, reveling in her victory, she
turned, looking for the sailfish. It was gone.

Her head swiveled wildly and she saw only green swells
spuming white. Gathering her strength, she lifted herself
higher, saw nothing, and fell back, her head going under.
Coughing, she struggled up to the surface, clearing her
lungs, fighting to regulate her breathing.

Calm . . .

Don't panic . . .

Somewhere out there Harry was trying to find her, to
get help. Time. Time for rescuers to come. Time was
what she needed. She fought to relax, to conserve energy. It was possible to float for hours, if you kept your
head.

She forced herself to think. First, which way to shore?
She looked up at the sun, hoping to see her position but
was only confused. She searched for a boat. None.

What next? Patience. She rolled onto her back and
breathed deeply, head back in the water, face lifted. Cradled by the swells, warmed by the sun, she drifted, terror
protecting itself with something like euphoria. *When this
was over, what a lovely tan she would have.* A giggle
trickled out of her; her head came forward and she swallowed water. Coughing and spitting, she came erect, fighting to stay above the surface.

The cawing of birds came through the noise of the sea.
Her head twisted around, eyes squinting into the glare. A
V of terns, winging low across the water. The birds, she
realized, were heading toward shore and she struck out to
follow. An unnatural weight made her right arm heavy.
All during this she had been holding on to the rudder.
She released it.

Alternating strokes, she found that swimming on her
side used the least amount of energy. Nevertheless her
weariness increased, arms and legs heavier now.

Breathe, kick, stroke. Breathe, kick, stroke. Concentrate. Each thrust of leg, each arm-pull brought her nearer to the beach.

Something slimy and cold brushed against her calf and
she jerked away. Shark! Arms and legs thrashing, she
willed herself through the water until it became impossible to go on. Panting, she made it onto her back, trying
to remain still; she remembered hearing that sharks tend

to attack moving objects.

Hanging in the water, back arched, legs and arms slack, sucking air into her burning lungs, she waited for her strength to return. A muscle in her thigh tightened and she flexed the limb, afraid it might cramp. Her body seemed to be floating higher now and her breathing was a controlled exercise—deep in, slow out. Calmness wrapped itself around her, a sense of ease and well-being. And in that tranquil interlude, she decided that this was where she was going to die.

Until now she'd been too involved in the struggle to live to consider dying. Now she knew the truth—Harry wasn't coming back. Saving himself was all that mattered and since that was a fact she had always known, she really didn't care. Even if Harry should find help, it would get to her too late.

And I looked, and behold a pale horse:
And his name that sat on him was Death . . .

The words took her back in time. Her father had been a gaunt man with a disapproving mouth. Each night the family gathered about him while he read from the Holy Book. Each night, readings that scared Shelly near to death . . .

Each night.

She was going to drown. Her death day was this day, with New Year's Eve two weeks off. Drowning was a better way than most. A soft fall into warm darkness. Easy . . .

Her head slumped, and she thrashed around, spitting water. She swam hard again until she once more tired, floated.

Why did she struggle so? She'd been so sure that when her death day came she would give herself over easily, glad to leave a world that had mostly given her pain. Still she knew no one had hurt her more than she had hurt herself. No one was to blame . . .

Oh, darling Barbara . . .

Her mind came abruptly back to the present. She wanted something less painful to concentrate on. Morrie Carlson. Morrie was the nicest man she'd ever known.

Wait. Once she had thought that about Lou Whitesell

and he had turned into the worst bastard of them all. Worse than Pete Millar? Or Davey, with the pretty eyes, or Frank or Big John Williston or Roy or Willis or Harry? Harry Bristol?

About Harry Bristol . . .

Every man she'd ever been with. Using, sucking life from her, making her make herself believe, for the moment, that it was fun, exciting. And Harry, deserting her, leaving her to die.

Soon, Barbara. Soon, darling . . .

A distant roaring, a fearsome clatter growing louder and closing fast.

Off to her right, a power boat bouncing across the waves, dragging an airborne chutist fifty feet above. He was shouting unheard, waving his arms frantically, pointing at Shelly. The second man in the boat was trying to decipher the wild semaphoring. He stood and looked out to see, struck the pilot on the shoulder twice. The boat swung back in a diminishing circle.

"No podemos parar, señorita," one of the men in the boat was shouting through cupped hands. *"El paracaídista caigará al agua. Espere un tantito más, sí?"* He made a gesture. *"Volveremos."*

The boat picked up speed and churned away. "No!" Shelly tried to scream, a choked protest coming out. Then the boat was out of sight and only the chutist remained, fading toward the horizon until he too disappeared.

She fell back in the water. She felt suspended, suddenly graceful in the way that ballet dancers are graceful, the way she had always wanted to be. A blinding glare shut out everything and she went slack, falling now in slow halfturns into the depths.

She was jerked back. A hard pull breaking the languid drop, and pain again.

A man was in the water with her, holding her waist, lifting; hands were pulling her into a speedboat. She gave them no help.

"Está bien," she heard a distant voice. *"Está bien, gracias a Dios. Unos momentos más y . . . Ah, bueno. Vamos a llevarla a la playa . . ."*

Shelly stopped hearing, stopped struggling, gave herself over to the green swirl, sank gratefully into a blackening emptiness . . .

6

McClintock began setting up late in the afternoon but not until dark was he able to properly test the lights. Adjustments were made and another test before Foreman was satisfied. The primary camera was placed at one end of the Roman pool; the second, a rented camera, in the underwater room, with a crew hired especially for the purpose.

The technical arrangements completed, Foreman took his actors aside. "There are two ways to approach this scene," he said, eyes going from one to the other. He saw nothing in Jim Sawyer's face, mostly because it was as empty as the man behind it. Shelly refused to meet Foreman's look. "Do we make a nudie or a scene that takes on some meaning?"

Jim Sawyer said, "In my opinion, I have been doing the best work of my career. I intend to continue doing so."

Foreman gazed out at the dark bay. Lights from yachts at anchor shimmered in the water. Sawyer was an incompetent actor and Foreman had limited the harm he could do by keeping his speeches at a minimum, but there was no point in discussing that now.

"I appreciate that, and I recognize your talent," Foreman said.

Sawyer stroked his hair affectionately. "Nice of you to say that."

"In this scene," Foreman said, "you're going to have to forget that you're naked. If you concentrate on your bodies you'll tighten up, the tension will show. Freedom, naturalness is what we're after."

"I read you loud and clear," Sawyer said. "Something like *Blow Up*, where David Hemmings rolls around with two chicks in the photographer's studio. That was a very profound moment for me."

"The point is, we are *not* making just a sex scene."

Sawyer laughed. "An awful lot of boobs and balls are going to be floating around for nothing."

"I'm after sensuality," Foreman said. "That's sex with some feeling in it, some true emotion. It comes from inside, not just a reflection of skin."

"You'll get it from me," Sawyer said.

"Shelly?"

"I'll try, Paul."

"You've got to concentrate on what you *are* in the picture, on what you as the character feel. This is an adventure story about a discovery. It's about two people who are beginning to find, through each other, what they're all about. This swimming scene, it's a love scene, a discovery of love. It's also fun, a lark, a romp. A kick!" He put his hand against Shelly's cheek in an affectionate gesture. "Now, concentrate. You've climbed the fence of this deserted villa, you're trespassing, breaking the law. Two kids having a ball, except that you're adults. At first you're both embarrassed by your nakedness, ashamed, maybe. Neither of you has ever done anything like this before. In the water, you get past your inhibitions about being naked and begin to find yourselves, your freedom. That's the moment of discovery I want to get on film." He gave them an encouraging smile. "Remember, have fun in the water . . ."

Shelly's mind raced back to the day before, to the terrifying loneliness she had felt in the waters of the bay, the awful, seductive pull of the water. She remembered how she had run away from her rescuers as soon as she could, not even thanking them, feeling like a cheat, and vaguely cheated.

"The cameras will follow wherever you go," Foreman was saying. "While you're in the water you'll just be with each other as human beings. Only after you climb out of the pool will you be conscious of the fact that all this time you've been naked, unprotected. At that point, when sex comes, it will be natural, healthy, open. It will be something worth the name 'love.' "

"I'm scared," Shelly said.

"Okay," Foreman told her. "Be scared. But don't hold back. Fear might even sharpen the quality of what I'm after."

"I'll do my best, Paul."

"Okay. Into the water, both of you. Swim around, get used to it. Work off the surface jitters. Don't go near each other. Let your bodies become the bodies of the people in the film."

Foreman went back to the camera and looked around. The crew was unusually quiet, standing in watchful poses. With all lights extinguished, Villa Gloria loomed up like a fortress in the dark. Behind the camera, Foreman saw Samantha Moore. In a flowing white lace gown, hair hanging across her shoulders, she appeared almost translucent, a creation of someone's imagination. Next to her, Harry Bristol—thick-bodied, gross, his face a flat, pale blob in the darkness. He was talking rapidly, hands working like a middleweight in close.

Farther back, standing alone, Bernard Louis Font, a watchful gnome.

And on the garden terrace, a line of faces, the servants. Foreman smiled to himself; no wonder they thought all foreigners were nuts.

He took a position alongside the camera. "Actors out of the pool, please," he said in a normal speaking voice. "No rehearsal. We'll do a take as soon as everybody is ready."

A wardrobe girl supplied towels and waited while the actors dried themselves. Make-up people repaired any damage done. Shelly put on yellow lace panties and a bra. She gazed across the length of the pool and nodded.

"All right, people," Foreman said. "Shelly and Jim have just come over the wall. You've stripped down. Jim to the skin, Shelly to her bra and panties. When Jim goes into the water, Shelly will, after some hesitation, decide to go after him. Take off the pants first, Shelly, then run toward the pool, discarding the bra as you go. Got that?"

"I think so."

"Jim. When you see Shelly in the water, go after her. Tentatively at first, then more aggressively but always with some restraint. Make this a sort of ritual mating dance. Step up the tempo as you go along. You'll be lit from above and below, filmed from both angles, so don't worry about the cameras.

"When you've run through the complete routine, Shelly will climb out of the pool and head straight toward the camera and on past. Jim, you follow.

"One more thing—expect to do the scene a number of times. Consider this initial take a run-through. Relax, do your best. Enjoy it. All right, everybody, this is a take. Actors in position, please. May I have the lights and quiet, please. Let's go to sound. Give me the cameras, Gary. All right. Action. . . ."

Bristol leaned forward, eyes straining to see past the nimbus of light reflecting off the surface of the pool. He saw Shelly pull the yellow panties off in one protective movement, graceful and childishly awkward at the same time. Then she was running, tossing the bra away.

A thick lusting in Bristol. That body, the familiar yet so strange flesh, that often seen and touched and smelled but never understood body . . . The heavy breasts moving as Shelly ran in a disjointed female run. The fine round of belly, firm above the near blackness of her still-mysterious patch.

Her flesh reminded Bristol of every woman he'd ever known—ripe female flesh. Shelly might have been his first wife, or his third; she was more spectacularly beautiful than either. Or his sister, or his mother, or Hilda Anderson who lived down the street when he had been fifteen. Hilda Anderson who had been the object of so many fantasies; Hilda Anderson, screwed in every position, done this way and that, each time better than the one before because he could play all the roles.

Bristol looked quickly at Samantha Moore. She was unlike any woman Bristol had ever had. The look of her— the delicate way she was put together, the fine features, the proud lift of her chin. What would it be like to be inside her? To smell her and taste her? Sweat broke across his shoulders and trickled into the hollow of his back.

Samantha Moore. Screwing her would be more than just getting laid. She was a *name,* well known around the world, her face familiar on three continents. For years Bristol had read about her in newspaper columns—about her marriages, the scandals, the divorces. She belonged to a world he had always wanted to be a part of. Screwing Samantha Moore would be . . . an *event.*

When *Love, Love* was in release, was a success, when

Harry Bristol was famous—no more unknown chicks putting out for a days' work. Goodbye to cheap broads. Only the best: stars, debutantes, socialites. Like Samantha . . .

He arranged his features in what was intended to be a pleasant expression. "Ever seen a picture made before, Miss Moore?"

She managed to look down at him. "Mr. Bristol, Danny Marty was my third husband. *The* Danny Marty. Danny Marty the movie star . . ."

"Sure," he said. The Samantha Moores of the world thought they shit roses. Screw that. Yes, indeed, screw it.

"Just my little joke," he said.

"I appeared in five *major* films myself."

Major, he thought. Five paste jobs. A few songs, library footage, some no-names—all put together in a few weeks on some unused sound stage. Tax losses for the studio. She hadn't amounted to much more than another face . . .

He said, "I've seen every one of your pictures. I always thought you were great."

"Mr. Bristol, they were despicable concoctions made by a greedy little man. My performances were, to be charitable, inept. Fortunately I realized that my future lay in other endeavors."

"Whatever you say. I'm still glad you're gonna be in my picture."

"Mr. Foreman made the part very appealing—a symbol of beauty and degradation! What woman could resist something like *that*? There I'll be, drifting on and off-camera . . . how delicious. I am drawn to contradictions."

Bristol nodded without hearing. Whatever she liked, he'd like to be it.

Bristol looked back at the pool. Shelly, breasts shining, broke out of the water, arms outstretched, naked to the waist. She fell back and went under.

She was a good swimmer, Bristol reminded himself. What a break! Otherwise—oh, Jesus, yesterday had scared him shitless. Water had always frightened him. And being on that lousy little boat alone in the ocean. Anything might have happened. One big wave and goodbye Harry Bristol.

Goddammit! Was it his fault he was a bad swimmer?

Otherwise he'd have gone after her, brought her back. What good would it have done for both of them to have drowned?

He'd explained it all to her last night. He'd used her top to signal for help, but no boat had stopped. And not until an hour later did a native fishing boat scoop him out of the water.

By that time, he pointed out logically, Shelly'd been rescued. As he knew she would be. He had confidence in her ability to take care of herself. Physically she could take care of herself very well.

He had tried to make love to her then and for the first time since they'd been together, she refused him. For the first time she'd said no and meant it. No, but without anger or even resentment. No, without accusing him of cowardice or desertion.

Damn well better not, he thought. One word and out she went. What was she? A nowhere dame going nowhere. He gave her this chance. She owed him, every day and twice on Sundays. One wrong word and back to the slots . . .

"Miss Hanes has a beautiful body," Samantha Moore was saying.

Bristol nodded and edged toward her.

Shelly was swimming toward them. Her face was animated and she seemed to be enjoying herself. Behind came Sawyer, closing the gap, but not too rapidly. Shelly made it out of the pool. She was laughing as she moved without restraint toward the camera, body shining under the powerful lights. She dashed past Foreman and McClintock into the waiting arms of the wardrobe girl who wrapped her in a long terry-cloth robe. Breathing hard, she looked inquiringly back to the camera.

"That was good, everybody," Foreman called. "Kill the lights, please."

"What did you think of it?" Bristol said to Samantha.

"It was quite lovely, very effective."

Bristol considered her carefully. "How would you like it if I tell Foreman to write something similar into the picture for you, Samantha?" he said, risking her first name.

"Mr. Bristol, you flatter me. But you needn't trouble yourself on my behalf."

"No trouble." He excused himself, went over to where Foreman, Shelly and Jim Sawyer stood in a tight huddle. "That was great," he broke in. "I can't wait to see the shots from underneath. There better be some closeups of the parts that count."

"It was good," Foreman said to the actors. "We'll take a short break and do it again."

"What for?" Bristol grumbled. "That was good, you said."

"Go away, Harry," Foreman said cheerfully.

"That looked okay to me. Why do you need another take? All this, the extra camera, the lights, the crew."

"Stay loose, Harry. This time, we're going to try something a little different."

"Experiment on your own time." He turned away, headed back to where he'd been standing. Samantha Moore was gone. He swore under his breath and looked around for someone to talk to; being alone in a crowd made Bristol uncomfortable.

Bristol looked at his watch again; nearly five A.M. What the hell did dames do in the john so long! It would be daylight soon. Damn Foreman! He'd kept the company working until nearly an hour ago, doing that one scene over and over.

"Shelly!" he yelled. "What the hell are you doing in there?" He looked at the watch again, put it on the night table. Tomorrow, first thing, he was gonna have a long talk with Mr. Paul Foreman, straighten him out. But good.

"Shelly!"

She came out of the bathroom and went to her side of the double bed, lay down, and pulled the sheet up to her chin, back turned to Bristol.

"You must be a water freak—the bay, all that pool time and now a shower?"

She made no reply.

He stared at her back. She excited him ways no other woman ever had. Part of it was feeling superior to her, even owning her—especially in bed. He touched her neck.

"Are you still sore about what happened in the bay? I told you how it was."

"I'm not sore."

"What do you call it, the way you're acting?"

"I'm disappointed is all."

He came up in a sitting position. "You blame me because I'm a rotten swimmer?"

"I don't blame you."

"I didn't say you should go in after that damned rudder, did I? Well, did I?"

"No, you didn't say that."

"Well, okay!" He lay back down and neither of them moved or spoke for a while. "You must be tired," he said finally.

"Yes."

"Me too. Still . . . being tired doesn't change it for me, except for the better. Isn't that funny? The more tired I am the more I want it. When I was a kid, I'd play ball all day, basketball. Rough games. All day, eight, nine hours at a time. I was pooped, all shot, exhausted. But I'd get horny. I've always been that way." He put his mouth against her bare shoulder and sucked at the smooth skin. "The way you taste. The minute I laid eyes on you, I wanted to taste you, really taste you . . ."

"Harry, I'm so tired."

"That sonofabitch Foreman! He's gonna hear about tonight. He promised me economy. Then tonight—eleven takes, three different set-ups. He thinks he's making *Ben Hur,* for Christ sake. I'm way over budget and New York's on my back. Eleven takes and he gives the company tomorrow off . . ."

"People are tired, Harry."

"I'm tired. But I don't take days off. I keep going."

"It's going to be a lovely movie, I think."

"Since when do you think? Ah, to hell with it. It's only business, right. What matters is that you're okay and we're back together. We're sort of a team, right. Believe me, yesterday really shook me up. Let me tell you—a guy gets to be my age and he's been around, he knows when he's got a good thing going. And you're the best." He cupped her breasts. "You don't find a body like this in every bed, believe me. The best I ever had . . ."

"Please, Harry. The way I feel, don't say anything you don't mean."

"Well, sure I mean it. You're the best. Watching you run around bare-ass tonight, all those horny bastards looking at your boobs, your box. You know what I thought—*that* belongs to me, I thought. Private property. Look but don't touch. I was glad they could see what really first-class merchandise you are. Listen, I was talking to Samantha. Next to you, she rates zero with me." He moved her onto her back, mouth on her breast as he did so.

There was no strength left in her and she made no protest when he reached roughly between her legs. He bit her breast and hurt her.

"You never had anybody like me," he muttered against her.

"Never," she replied automatically.

"All those guys, faggoty Hollywood types."

"Never a real man until you."

"I'm gonna give it to you tonight, a special ride. I'll charge you up!"

She closed her eyes. "You always know how to turn me on, Harry."

"In a minute you'll be flying—"

"Ah," she said, when time enough had passed for it to be believable.

"Good?"

"Ah, Harry."

"You really like it, don't you?"

She made small noises in the back of her throat.

"Tell me," he persisted.

"I . . . love . . . it."

"You never get enough, do you?"

"Never . . ."

She moaned and turned her head, twisted her hips in a rising tempo. This way it would end more quickly. She was so tired. So very tired . . .

7

"How nice," Grace said, looking at Coyuca Lagoon. "I've never been here before. Living in the mountains makes me feel closer to God. But there are days when I miss the sea. There's something warm and comforting about the water."

"Mother of us all," Foreman said.

They were sitting under a coconut palm, Grace's back against the trunk, Foreman sprawled out next to her. Her face was relaxed, reflective, and she looked even younger than she was.

"Whenever I visit the shore," she said, "I feel revived. Thank you for bringing me."

"My pleasure. This place is like a tropical island. And only a few miles away from the Acapulco carnival."

She laughed and raised her face to the sun. In a black tank suit, she presented a stunning figure, her proportions full yet subtle, lines long and strong. Foreman wanted very much to make love to her and, wanting, knew that to go too quickly would be a mistake.

He cleared his throat. "Tell me about that old man you were with this morning. Was he filling your head with more fanciful myths about the days before the conquistadores?"

The first pallor of day shaded the sky when Foreman had left Acapulco, less than an hour after he dismissed the *Love, Love* company. By the time he arrived at the Chinchahua village, the sun was above the ridge line and people were moving about. His presence caused no alarm. Grace would explain later that the approaches to the village were always guarded by armed men, that he had been sighted, identified, and permitted to drive on. "But don't take the Chinchahua for granted. They are not creatures of habit and they're bound to be curious about you.

They may tolerate you for a while, but they are likely to turn on you at any moment."

"And what about you?"

"The same," she said.

At first she had resisted his efforts to get her to spend the day with him, to go swimming. But he kept talking until the old man she was sitting with lurched to his feet, muttered something in Chinchahua that made Grace laugh, and left. "Joaquín says that when a young man and a young woman talk too much and too quickly there is no room for serious work. He promises to speak into my machine another time."

"In that case," Foreman had replied, "get your suit and let's go."

And she did.

Now he waited for her to tell him about Joaquín.

"Joaquín," she said, pronouncing the old Indian's name fondly. "What an amazing man he is! Joaquín is a *curandero*, you see."

"A curer?" Foreman translated.

"A healer. A medicine man."

"A witch doctor is what you mean?"

"Almost but not quite," she said with a playful smile. "Joaquín is a witch."

"Oh, come on. What's a nice girl like you doing fooling around with an old witch?"

She put her finger across her lips and considered him, the blue eyes contemplative. "I don't expect you to believe in Joaquín."

"Do you?"

"No, but in a way I wish I could. But we're from a different world. Joaquín's powers are very real to the Chinchahua. Indians all over Mexico believe in witches and react to witches' powers. Sometimes to the death."

"Psychosomatic—"

She silenced him with a gesture. "Will you admit that there aren't rational explanations for everything that happens in the world? Science can't explain all the phenomena of our lives. Diseases exist for which modern medicine has no cures. When a Chinchahua gets sick, as strong and as courageous as they are, he simply falls apart. 'The whole head is sick, and the whole heart is faint,' as the Bible says . . ."

He sat up. "How about—'Joy and Temperance and Repose/Slam the door on the doctor's nose.' "

"You're impossible," she said laughing. "You'll get no more out of me."

"Please go on. It's just that I've been corrupted by a cynical world that doesn't believe what it can't see."

"You mean it as a joke, but it's true. And it's too bad."

"Back to Joaquín. Did he get a masters degree in witchery at Johns Hopkins?"

"One is born a witch. In the Aztec empire, only those born under the sign of rain could practice the art. Texcatlipoca, the god of night, was the patron of the witches. Once he changed himself into a jaguar and chased another god out of the sky and got control of the universe . . ."

"That's what I call a god!"

"It was only temporary."

"A god with feet of clay," he amended.

She went on as if he hadn't spoken. "Anyone who had the power to change himself into an animal was called a *naqual.* In Spanish, that translates to *brujo.* In English, to witch. This morning Joaquín was talking about other witches he had known. Or heard about. His father, his grandfather, his grandfather's father, all were *curanderos.*"

Foreman kept his face straight. "Do you suppose these *curanderos* specialize, like American doctors?"

"As a matter of fact, they do. Joaquín's father was very good at curing the *ojo,* the evil eyes." She hesitated, continued more slowly. "A week after I arrived at the village, I saw Joaquín practice his art for the first time. A woman came to him complaining that an evil spirit rested on her husband each night while he slept and that her husband had been bewitched and made impotent."

"How was she to look at?"

"Be serious," she said. "The woman told Joaquín that before the casting of the spell her husband had thrown himself at her many times each night."

"That devil."

"The wife was convinced that her husband had been cursed by another woman."

"In other words, hubby was grazing in somebody else's pasture."

"The thought did occur to me."

"There's a deal to challenge any witch worth his potions. How did Joaquín handle it?"

"He produced charms. He spread some blue and red powder in a saucer and lit it. He told the woman to put a live horned toad in a jar and bury it under her house. A few days later, she returned to report that her husband was acting more kindly toward her but that his impotence lingered on. Joaquín told her to look near the shrine that stands on the hill at the entrance to the village and there she would find something. To show it to her husband."

"Ahah! An incriminating photograph taken during the last *curandero* convention in Miami Beach, right?"

"Wrong. The woman went up to the shrine and made the sign of the cross, asked for forgiveness for all sins, past, present, and future, and searched the ground. Nearby she found a sisal bag filled with dried chiles. She brought it to her husband and that night for the first time in months he made love to her."

"And they lived happily ever after?"

"No complaints so far. You're not convinced, are you?"

"Are you?"

She stood up, tugged her bathing suit into place. "I don't believe in witches but I believe that witchcraft exists and for some people it works. Joaquín *is* a witch and he does good for the Chinchahua. I think that sometimes it's better to believe in something than to believe in nothing at all. I'm going swimming!" She shouted, running toward the water.

Foreman watched her go, enjoying the easy rhythm of her body. She got to him in ways he could remember no other woman doing. Not even Laura. Laura was something else, he thought. Then he was on his feet, moving after Grace Biondi . . .

Foreman rented a small, awning-covered boat in which they drifted around the lagoon, the water broke occasionally by a fish's leap, the air hardly stirring. Foreman told her about himself, his checkered career in advertising, the theater, about the novel that had barely got underway, about his marriage.

"What's worse," he said, trying to end the autobiography on a light note, "being unhappily unmarried or unhappily married? I've been miserable and I've been sad, and believe neither is so good." He glanced sidelong at her. "Not funny, is it?"

"Not funny," she said. "Don't you think it's possible to be happy?"

"Speaking from experience, no. There are good moments now and then. Like now. I suppose that's what happiness really is—some good moments."

"I believe in something much more."

"How would you know?"

She avoided looking at him. "Why are you so defensive?"

"Come on!"

"All the jokes. You quote somebody instead of saying what *you* think. I've a feeling about you . . ."

"A feeling," he said. "With apologies to Women's Lib, isn't that just like a woman!"

"My father would agree with that. He also disapproved of education for a woman. He disapproved of my reading."

"And?"

"And I read anyway, more than father would've liked. At college, I took a literature course." She giggled. "Mr. Lynwood was the instructor. He'd say, 'I've read *Moby Dick* once a year for the last ten years for the enrichment of my spirit . . .'"

"That's heavy going."

"Oh, Mr. Lynwood was a fast reader. Also worker. Mr. Lynwood had an affair with Maureen Brennan one summer. And this is a *Catholic* women's college. Maureen's parents transferred her to Wellesley. Mr. Lynwood took up with Joanne Furillo. Word of his extracurricular activities reached the always-attentive nuns and Mr. Lynwood was asked to move on to some other grove of academe."

"Mr. Lynwood was a man of parts."

"Tell me about your novel," she said, trying hard not to smile.

"No novel. Just a few sketches."

"Will you finish it?"

"Maybe I don't have the guts."

"To look at yourself?"

"You play rough, lady."

"Sorry."

He touched her hand. "I'm no kid starting out. This movie is going to make it possible for me to put up or shut up. Necessary, in fact."

"Like Harry Bristol?"

"I'm not Bristol."

"Yes, but didn't he put up, pull it all together by himself? Nobody invited him to make a movie, he just did it."

"Hey. Hurray for Harry."

This was a low blow, she realized, even if a necessary one. Still, enough for now. She didn't want to lose him.

"Shall I tell you more about the Chinchahua?" she said with manufactured brightness.

"No," he said automatically. Then he laughed and the stiffness went out of him and he leaned back in the boat.

He took her hand and pressed the tips of her fingers to his mouth. She withdrew her hand, but slowly. "Did you always go to Catholic schools?" he said. "I mean, well, I'm an atheist."

She nodded. "I used to be an atheist myself. Anyway, I didn't believe."

"You believe in a lot of things. Witches, the old jazz about captain of your soul . . ."

"And in God," she said. "I came to Christianity by a considerable detour. My father hated the Church. My mother goes to Mass every day, sometimes twice. She keeps religious pictures all over the house. I can't bear that kind of thing and I reacted against it. But two years ago, when I was teaching school in Africa, I began to feel a need for something more . . . I started to look at the possibilities."

"And went back to the Church?"

"Not exactly. I learned about—no, I sensed—Jesus Christ. Please don't laugh at me. My world was suddenly different. For the first time, I felt truly alive. Remarkable changes took place—food tasted better and I took pleasure in breathing fresh air. I had another *reason* for myself, for doing whatever I did, for living.

"As for the Church. Well, the Church was founded by Jesus, something many churchmen seem to have forgotten. But the Church has turned into a bureaucracy loaded with property and stocks and bonds. It's like a museum.

"Here in Mexico, the Church is pre-Reformation and still shows many of the excesses that the Protestants revolted against—the cult of the saints and the Blessed Virgin, almost to the exclusion of God Himself."

"If you feel that way—"

"But within that same institutional Church is another Church, the *living* tradition of Christ. There are priests and nuns and bishops who are living for today. They show us the way by example. That Church, and those Christian men and women, are beginning to make the word Christian mean what Jesus meant. Their church is the one I belong to."

Foreman stared into the reflecting off the water. Grace Biondi was a lady not for conning. A challenge. A problem . . . To make matters worse, she was, no doubt, a virgin. She celebrated some damn metaphysical coupling with Jesus. What did she need with him? With any flesh and blood man . . .

"It's getting late," he said, turning the boat back to shore. "I want to get you back to the village before dark."

And after he left her, had gone back down the mountain, he vowed to keep a safe distance between them. But in the days that followed, instead of relief, it was as if something had been put aside, its whereabouts forgotten, something he wanted very much.

The *Starfish* plowed through the swells of the Pacific heading north, staying in view of shore. Owing to a very special, very expensive gyroscope, the vessel pitched only slightly and seemed never to roll. The gyroscope had been a gift from a former admiral of the United States Navy in charge of procurement for a West coast station; he had pleaded with Samantha to marry him, promising to divorce his wife. Samantha accepted the gyroscope but refused the admiral, having learned that the military mind was invariably a stultifying organ and best not associated with for very long.

Next to Samantha at the stern of the *Starfish*, lounging comfortably in a softly padded deck chair in the shade of a striped awning, was Theo Gavin. They sat quietly looking back at the wake of the *Starfish*, accepting drinks from a white-clad steward and nibbling tiny shrimp in a spicy pink sauce.

Samantha glanced over at Theo, and their eyes met. She developed a shy smile and looked away, mind turning over. She rather approved of Theo, his manly and proper appearance, thinking that neither word would have described any of her husbands. She wondered what it would be like to be married to Theo, what sort of children they might produce. Nonsense. Children were simply out of the question. Not that she'd ever been compelled to spawn any reproductions of herself. Not ever. Still, the idea was titillating. Theo Gavin would surely create fine-looking, strongly built sons, all lean and darkly powerful, with the kind of skin that would quickly tan. People who looked right, Samantha was convinced, were right.

"You must be proud of your son," she offered.

Theo munched thoughtfully on a tiny shrimp. The day's charter for the Sailfish was two hundred and fifty dollars, a hell of a lot; he intended to get every cent's worth out of it. He ate another shrimp.

"Samantha," he declared solemnly. "These are not good times in which to be a parent."

She sucked on her straw and the tequila-laced liquid spurted coolly against the back of her mouth. She waited for him to go on.

"Take Chuck. Bringing him to Acapulco, well, I wanted him to have a real holiday. Look, every father wants his son to be a man, to take life by the tail and swing it around his head. Circumstances have kept Chuck and me apart, more than I'd like. This was our chance to make up for lost time, to get closer. Samantha, believe me when I tell you I tried. As hard as I could."

"I know that, Theo."

"You're an understanding woman, Samantha. My ex-wife—she was against Chuck's coming on this trip. Pure spite."

"How awful!"

"A boy needs a man to identify with."

"There are so many non-men in this world."

"Sometimes I wonder—"

She touched the back of Theo's hand. "Don't blame yourself."

"Would I be a good father if I said the boy failed himself? Would that be fair?"

"Sooner or later we all must face the truth about ourselves."

Theo placed his hand on tops of hers.

She withdrew her hand.

"Have another shrimp, Theo."

Instead, he took her face between his hands and kissed her. Her thin lips were quiet and cool from the tequila drink, and he warned himself to be careful not to offend her. With her breeding and background—

"Ever since we met," he said, "I've wanted to kiss you. Can you understand how it is for a man like me to be with a woman like you?"

"I think I can, Theo."

"Have I offended you?"

She loosened his grip on her cheeks and attended her straw. "I'm an old-fashioned woman, Theo. Cheapness has never been my style."

"Will you forgive me?"

"When I give myself, it must be wholeheartedly, without reservation."

"Of course."

"I do like you, Theo. Each time we meet, I become more fond of you." She faced him. "My annual party is Christmas Eve. A fund raising affair for charity. I want you to attend, as my personal guest, of course."

He took her hand. "I'd be pleased if you'd let me contribute . . ."

"How sweet you are. And you must bring Chuck along. Perhaps he and I can become friends. It's a costume affair —dress as your favorite character in Mexican history."

"Chuck won't be coming, I'm afraid. He's disappeared. He's not a strong boy and not very experienced. I'm worried about him."

"Have you notified the embassy in Mexico City? They handle that sort of thing."

"I'll take care of it when we get back."

He looked sidelong at her. So beautiful, her precise and prideful features remote and cool. Inklings of possibilities came to him, and he tried to imagine what it would be like to be with Samantha Moore, to make love to her. To make her his wife, even.

What a prize *that* would be!

The sign on the door read "Bernard Louis Font, Associates." But no associates were in evidence. Only a middle-aged secretary and Bernard. He greeted Samantha and led her into his private office, seated her, and retreated behind the refectory table that served as a desk.

"Does my imagination play tricks, my dear," he began, "or are those lovely cheeks of yours flushed? A new love or an abundance of our Acapulco sunlight?"

"Some of both, perhaps."

"Bravo! Bravo to that."

"It may be too soon to speak of love, but Theo Gavin is an attractive man."

"And apparently a businessman of stature in the States, my informants tell me. He never hesitated when I quoted the charter rate for the *Starfish*."

"How odd that was, being entertained on my own yacht under rent to my escort."

"Business is business, my dear."

"Which is why I've come. Theo, Mr. Gavin has made me a small proposition."

Bernard's brows rose. "Such things are best settled by the principals, yes!" He laughed and Samantha smiled indulgently.

"A *business* proposition," she said.

Bernard laced his fingers together. "That interests me. Tell me everything."

"It seems that Theo is about to launch a new business, a very exclusive—"

"Exclusive," Bernard breathed, "means expensive. Go on."

"A line of toiletries and cosmetics. He had intended to cater to women but Theo's had a marvelous idea. He is convinced that the time is right for men in this area, to use more and better cosmetics. He is transforming the line from women to men."

"And why not? Must the male always reek of the men's room? To this I say emphatically *no*."

"Theo agrees."

"What would Samantha Moore's role be in all of this?"

"Theo intends to launch the new company with an extensive advertising and publicity campaign. The details are still to be worked out. Theo suggested that possibly I might become the spokeswoman for the new product, the symbol of femaleness—his phrase, Bernard—indicating with taste and discretion what it is a real woman desires in a man."

"Excellent!"

"You approve?"

"In concept, yes. Still, caution is in order. Such arrangements involve many details. Money, for example."

"Naturally neither of us spoke about money."

"Naturally. But a man personally and professionally interested in a woman would pay lavishly for her services. As your agent, I will reject the first offer. And then bargain intensively. This development could be important for you, my dear, as well as for Mr. Gavin."

"Bernard, you won't allow me to become involved in anything too sordid."

"Never."

"I depend on you, dear friend."

"Whatever is done will be done with delicacy. The utmost taste. You must be presented as what you are, the ultimate woman, the ultimate lady. There will be advertisements with your photographs. Who would be best—Avedon? Karsh? We shall see. And of course, a wardrobe. St. Laurent might be the one. Paris couturiers still possess special chic, I think. I suppose there will be a great deal of television. Lighting, make-up, camera work; all are required. That fellow Foreman who is directing *Love, Love*—what would you say to him? He's experienced in this sort of thing, I'm told."

She summoned up an image of Paul Foreman. "What an attractive thing he is. Sullen but perhaps violent. Still, I think not. Theo might resent a director who was too handsome."

"An excellent point. For the moment, the question remains open. I suggest that being a spokeswoman would demand your appearance at sales meetings, conventions, so on and so on. We will insist on first-class accommodations in travel and hotels, all expenses paid, naturally. Appearances should be so scheduled that you have proper rest periods and are never, never overexposed."

"Bernard, you are so clever."

"And back to the financial details. Ah, money. How delightful its prospect is! Have you considered an amount?"

"Not really."

"I shall begin conversation at fifty thousand dollars American per year, on a sliding scale over a five-year period."

"Bernard, do you think—"

"I think Mr. Gavin will pay for your services."

"Bernard," she said hesitantly, "would it be possible to spend winters at Villa Gloria? I do so love it here and to be away from all my dear, dear friends . . ."

"It will be written into the contract."

"One more thing, dear friend. Some suitable accommodations must be arranged between us, a percentage of whatever income I earn must go to you. You serve me so well and always at such little profit to you."

"Your continued friendship is my most tangible treasure."

"A token payment, Bernard."

His eyes clouded over.

"Five per cent, Bernard."

The cloud lifted. "Ten per cent would be proper, plus normal business expenses."

Her brows arched, fell back. "What a good friend you are."

He kissed her extended hand. *"Chérie . . ."*

Morrie Carlson lived in an unpretentious room in a green-and-white hotel set halfway up a hill, owned and operated by a Mexican family. A shallow terrace provided him with an unobstructed view of the bay along an artificial valley formed by two rising condominiums. With the sun dropping toward the horizon, Morrie sipped a Carta Blanca and described the difficulties in painting sunsets to Shelly Hanes.

His face, angular, the skin rough, seemed almost Romanesque in the fading, yellow light. Shelly enjoyed the ready flow of his talk, the easy male sound of him.

"I imagine it's a question of color perception," Morrie was saying. "It eludes me and for a painter that is fatal."

Shelly was confused whenever Morrie talked to her about art, its history. But with him, she felt comfortable and there was never any need to defend herself.

"People are my talent," he said. "Faces and bodies. Some day you'll have to pose for me. You've got a fine body."

She stiffened and her fingers tightened around the glass she held. Why was it men always brought the conversation around to the way she looked, to sex? The compliments, the questions, the comments on her breasts and legs; they were for one thing, she knew, to get her into bed. She wanted it to be different with Morrie.

He finished his beer. "What is it like to be beautiful, Shelly? I've always looked at beautiful people like they were freaks—they seem so unbelievable to me. What is it like?"

Her mind faded into the past.

"In high school," she said, "I was too plump, too clumsy to be even a cheerleader."

"Horses for courses," Morrie said. "Everybody does his own kind of cartwheels. Whatever your life's been like, you're a mysterious and haunting woman . . ."

She laughed. "Mysterious and haunting, that's almost as good as being the prettiest girl in school."

"You are beautiful."

She shook her head. "If it were true, I'd feel it."

"You're going to become a very important movie star."

"No. Even if what you say is true, there isn't time."

"You're not still strung out on that New Year's Eve death wish of yours! Forget it, Shelly. If you had been destined to die, you'd have gone under out in the bay."

A rush of terror and dark memory came flooding back. She shivered. "It was awful out there. The loneliness. That was the worst part of it, being alone. Harry shouldn't have left me alone, should he, Morrie?"

He didn't answer.

"I felt so . . ." She searched for the right word. "Betrayed," she said. "I thought about Barbara, and that's when I guess I was glad to die . . ."

"Barbara?"

"I wanted it to be good with Harry, for it to be more than . . . an accommodation. Men have always taken me out just to get laid. I was never smart enough or pretty enough to expect anything else. And later, when I was older, I kept hoping somebody would come along to make it different. I wanted so much to be with a man who at least would *talk* to me afterward, who would care what I thought. For a while, I thought it was going to be that way with Harry, but it's no different. Not really . . .

"Barbara was my baby, my daughter. I got caught, you see. His name was Rick and he was an actor. But I *wanted* Barbara and even if Rick hadn't married me, I would have had her.

"Rick was convinced he would be a big star, like Robert Mitchum or Bogart. But he never did make it. Maybe he was too pretty; he had soft, brown skin and big eyes. The trouble was Rick was more attracted to his face than to mine, more excited by his body than mine. In bed sometimes he would touch himself more than he touched me. He counted every calorie and exercised every day and measured his waistline every night.

"Rick was never around when I needed him. When Barbara came, he was on location, doing a bit part in a TV Western.

"What a beautiful baby she was! Fat and happy, always laughing. Rick never liked Barbara. How can a man not like his own baby? One day he took his things and walked out—Barbara was two years old. I had to do something to support us both so I began making the rounds of agents and producers again.

"From the first, it was the same. Men put their hands on me, saying if I did this they'd do that . . . Only even when I did what they wanted me to do it didn't work for me. There were some small parts but nothing very good, nothing that mattered.

"I kept trying. One day I got a call from this man. He said he was a producer and he thought he might have a good part for me in this picture he was planning. Morrie, I knew it was a hustle, I *knew* it!

"He said I should come to his office after six o'clock. I was so anxious for the job that I went along, let him keep me on the phone, let him talk me into coming to his office. I flirted with him and while I was flirting I heard the car brakes. Barbara, my baby, had wandered out into the street and been killed by an automobile while I was cockteasing some sonofabitch with no balls . . ."

She breathed in and out once. "I miss her so much, Morrie. So much that I wish I were dead too and with her in—" She didn't speak again for a long time. "I'll pose for you," she said. "Without clothes, if that's what you want."

"I want to *draw* you," he answered.

"Sometimes I'm very stupid. I know that now." She stood up. "I have to go now. Harry's going to be sore at me for staying out so late without telling him . . ."

8

At ten minutes before eleven, a French starlet arrived at Villa Gloria to celebrate Christmas Eve. Her ticket had been purchased by her producer who was hopeful that the starlet would attract a certain amount of attention to herself and also to his film, due shortly for worldwide release. The starlet came dressed as a Mexican peasant woman; one succulent breast was exposed and to it was pressed a curly-headed blond doll, as if suckling.

Soon after, a myopic Greek billionaire offered the starlet one hundred dollars for the privilege of substituting for the doll. The offer was accepted and the Greek presented his mouth to the starlet's nipple. Thirty seconds later, his wife appeared and severed the tenuous connection with an angry shove. The billionaire staggered backward in alarm and toppled into the Roman pool.

Laughing brightly, the starlet fled with the hundred dollars, the doll back at her breast.

By eleven o'clock, it was evident that the party was a great success. Villa Gloria vibrated with people who looked as though they had found their way in and never intended to find their way out. Groups and huddles and crowds, they formed in rooms and patios and gardens, sending up a raucous din.

Beyond the pool, a lavish display of food and drink drew the hungrier guests; waiters dressed as *charros* passed around trays of hors d'oeuvres and drinks.

A rock group blasted away from a protected position on the tiled terrace at the north end of the pool, a stone wall guarding their rear; inside the house, mariachis strolled from room to room, strumming Mexican ballads.

By the time Foreman appeared, the Greek billionaire had left with his wife and people had forgotten about his unexpected bath. Foreman located the bar and began drinking Scotch straight. The long face was closed, the pale eyes turned inward, the cascade of sound closed out. After three quick drinks, he carried a water tumbler half-full of Scotch to an empty corner and surveyed the activity around him.

"Hello!" a cheerful voice said nearby. "You must be that marvelous Paul Foreman Samantha's told me about."

His head came around to confront a handsome woman with a brilliant smile and brindled brown hair that broke across her shoulders. Tanned breasts swelled out of a peasant blouse and a black skirt embroidered in silver and gold encased opulent hips. She gave Foreman her hand.

"Samantha is convinced you are a genius. Are you a genius? I've always adored being with men who are. My theory is that a genius in one area is at the very least superior in another. Oh, but I'm being rude. I'm Marcella, Samantha's very dear, very best friend. Picasso and Casals, for example. We know that Picasso, until very few years ago, was quite vigorous, or so I'm told. Genius!" Her laugh climbed the scale in easy flights.

Foreman filled his mouth with Scotch, swallowed.

Marcella was impressed and said so. "I've always been in awe of American men. What enormous amounts of whisky your countrymen consume. Frenchmen drink a great deal, too, but somehow it isn't the same. The French being what they are, I mean. I am from Cuba, myself. Anti-Castro, needless to say, and I have a natural affinity for rum." Her eyes flickered across the frayed army shirt he wore, along his faded jeans. "Oh, but what *are* you? What have you come as? Your costume, I mean."

"I don't wear costumes. I don't like costume parties."

"Oh, dear. That's because you've never learned to make a fool of yourself."

He allowed himself a short grin. "You talk a lot, Marcella. You're also something of a dish."

She thanked him automatically, head swiveling, eyes tracking through the crowd.

Foreman followed her glance. "Did you lose something?"

"Oh, I hope not."

"Is it valuable?"

"Dear, yes. At least for the moment. It's my favorite

Mexican toy, and it's *very* handy. You'll know when you
see it because it's the prettiest thing around. It's called
Agustín. Oh, there it is! Agustín! Darling!" She went
plunging into a mass of people toward a short, slender
youth who might have been seventeen years old.

Foreman emptied his glass and went after some more
Scotch.

"So I made an appointment with this fellow to visit his
workshop and looked over his *tapetes*. When I arrived he
wasn't there. I asked when he'd be back and was told *un
momento más*, in a little while. Three and one-half hours
later he showed up. *Un momento más* . . . now I ask you,
how can that kind of thing go on in a country that wants
to become a part of the twentieth century?"

Louise Peters wore a crimson-red lace blouse that revealed
her breasts in a filigree pattern of light and shadow. Bernard Louis Font found it almost impossible to take his
eyes away from one audacious nipple that stared tantaliz-
ingly out at him.

"We're here on holiday," Louise said, looking down at
Bernard, who was dressed as the Emperor Maximilian.
"A very special holiday, for a very special reason."

Bernard lifted his eyes reluctantly. "Ah?" he said, making it sound very French.

"It's my husband. Jason, is his name. You must meet
him, Bernard. I'm sure you two men would find much in
common."

Bernard returned his attention to her nipple. "Perhaps
some time."

"Jason's going into politics, you see. In New York City.
It's all been arranged. These matters are resolved behind
closed doors, as you surely know. Jason's only twenty-six
and he's going to be the party nominee for Congress from
our district. Naturally, he'll be elected. Jason's very attractive and he's for all the right things."

Bernard wet his lips. "What things are they?"

"Why, the people, of course. The poor, the disadvantaged. Black Panthers and people like that."

"Ah," Bernard said, eyes wandering back to her breasts.
"I have never been a populist, you understand, but I am
sympathetic."

"Then you'd like to meet Jason?"

"In good time. Meanwhile, allow me to show you the
maze . . ."

He was internationally known. The Swedish conductor of
a major American symphony orchestra. He rode into
Villa Gloria on the back of a huge white stallion, wearing white homespun, a black sombrero, two pistols and
crossed ammunition belts. Behind him on foot, came a
dozen companions, similarly attired, herding some goats
and two cows in front of them, firing blanks in their rifles
and singing *"La Cucaracha."*

"Zapata!" one of them cried.

"Emiliano Zapata!"

"Land for the peasants!"

"Mexico for the Mexicans!"

"All power to the peons!" the conductor shouted, firing
his pistols in the air.

Shelly discovered Foreman out on the terrace, looking at
the night. She lurched toward him, calling, "My director!"
and coming to a stop inches away. "I'm so glad to see you,
my director."

"I believe you are slightly crocked, Shell."

"I should hope so. Wasn't it nice of Samantha to invite
us to her party for free?"

"A highly selective invitation. The director, producer,
and the two stars. Has Sawyer taken off his clothes yet?
Like he said, it's so natural for him. A real swinger."

"I saw him leave with a pretty young boy."

"Beautiful."

She giggled. "Do I impress you as being drunk? Because I think I am. Two drinks set me off. Three and the
word 'no' departs from my mind forever." She squinted at
him. "You're not going to, are you?"

"Not going to what?"

"Drag me off to your bed. Are you?"

He only smiled.

"You're not going to. I can tell. That's all right. I think you're a nice man, Paul Foreman. But of course, I am not a very good judge, having met very few nice men."

"Nice guys finish last or thereabouts, a famous philosopher once said. Leo, I believe, was his name."

"The philosopher was right." A closed-in feeling took hold, made her seem and feel suddenly older. "Harry wants you. Harry is sore, which is nothing new. Harry is nearly always sore. You better see what he wants."

"No hurry."

She wavered and fell forward, ended up against him, peering up into his face. "A man who doesn't scare so much, that's beautiful. No hurry for Harry." She giggled again, stopped abruptly. "Everything scares me. Let me tell you what I am going to do. I am going to go to midnight Mass, is what. Isn't that a kick! Me in church! Come with me, Paul."

"I can't do that, Shelly."

"Sure." She shoved herself away from him. "Well, maybe among all these heathen I can find one believer. Just one . . ."

He watched her go and watching thought about Grace Biondi. Grace would go to Mass, too, in that little church the Chinchahua had erected behind the village. She would pray for the poor Indians and the poor blacks and the poor . . . *everything*.

Grace Biondi was good. She reeked of good.

"Grace Biondi's goodness is a distinct pain in the ass!" Foreman said aloud.

Nobody paid any attention.

"Imagine!" the woman said, eyes glowing with memory. "I was walking at my husband's side when it happened."

"On the street!"

"In the open. In front of a sidewalk café. In full view of hundreds of people. You might've thought we were in Rome. This little Mexican came up behind me and put his hand on my bottom, took a leisurely feel. I could hardly believe it. When he had enough, he moved on."

"What did you do?"

"Nothing, of course. If Seymour had known, he might have killed the little creep."

"*Como México no hay dos . . .*"

"The men of this country are . . . fantastic!"

" 'The strange, soft flame of courage in the black Mexican eyes . . .' Lawrence said that."

"How incredibly *right.*"

"It's the land, this savage land."

"So masculine—the boys are so, so endowed . . ."

"All the church spires."

"The cactus standing straight up."

"It's all so very—"

"Mexican?"

"*Macho,* my dear."

Samantha presented herself as the Empress Carlotta, wearing full-length black velvet, the neckline a deep V, with a fitted bodice, blond hair piled in layers of curls descending down the back of her neck.

She spent the first few hours greeting each guest, making sure the servants fulfilled the demands of the celebrants. Exhilarated, charged by the sound, the laughter, by all the good talk, by the beautiful people, her cheeks grew flushed and her eyes shone as she guided Theo Gavin through the villa, ending on the patio that ran along outside her private apartment. They gazed down on the Roman pool. Sound drifted up in muted waves and she sipped champagne and perceived private visions of a full, rich life.

"This is an incredible house," Theo said.

"I love it. This view, this place. Life here is so rewarding. I never want to leave for very long."

"To live among all this beauty, you're very lucky."

"You're so understanding, Theo."

"I try, Samantha."

Next to her, he felt swollen and clumsy, too big, with

no place to put his hands. He reacted to her strangely, affected as no other woman had ever affected him. A quick side glance showed her to be remote, an alien creature, unattainable, and therefore to be attained at any cost. What a prize! The ultimate trophy!

"Samantha . . ." He dried his hands on his trousers. "Our working together means a lot to me."

"If only I can provide what you require."

"You can and you will. We'll need to spend a great deal of time together. I hope you don't mind."

"You must have so many more important duties to attend to."

"Nothing more important than being with you."

"What a delight to anticipate."

"Personal attention is what I give all my enterprises. And it is what I shall apply to the cosmetic line. For the product to succeed, there must be suitable promotion. Inevitably, and if for no other reason, you will be the object of a great deal of my attention."

"No other reasons?" She watched his face.

From any other woman he would have taken it as a deliberate provocation, a sexual gambit. But not with Samantha. Too subtle, too refined. He wanted to feel her mouth under his, to touch that golden skin, to revel in that physical perfection. What was it she had said on the *Starfish* that afternoon?—"I'm an old-fashioned woman." He respected her attitude. After all, getting laid was no trick, not these days. Come to think about it, he'd never had any trouble finding someone to accommodate him, not since he was sixteen.

His handsome, uneven features, his muscular aggressiveness, that inner drive he possessed; all drew attention to him after that. Women went to him, young ones, older ones, single and married; some of them even offered money. Of course, he never accepted any.

With men it was different. Once in a while a man would offer him gifts and cash, though Theo had responded to neither. Not until he was eighteen with Hillary. Hillary, blond and slight, with a wicked smile and a quick tongue, and a repertoire of sex stories that excited Theo's interest. Just for curiosity's sake, he had told himself. Once. Only once. And through the years, whenever he had allowed a man, Theo had done what he did that first time with Hillary. He thought about a woman he knew. Any woman. That way he could be sure he wasn't queer . . .

"I understand there will be contracts to sign," Samantha said, breaking into his thoughts.

"They're being drawn now."

"Such things confuse me."

"Everything will be worked out between Bernard and myself." Like Hillary, he told himself in passing, Samantha was delicately boned, with that perpetually tanned skin, the same wide, unblinking eyes, the same clean lines of face and body.

The faint scent of her perfume drifted into his nostrils and he moved a step nearer. She lifted her chin. Theo hesitated, then kissed her. Time held still and he started to worry that she would pull away, be angry. He was a fool to take this chance! There was so much to lose . . . But when she made no move to separate her lips from his, he let his breath out slowly and encircled her waist.

Her body became less rigid, her lips parted and Theo tentatively placed the tip of his tongue against her square white teeth, as if afraid she would bite. Nothing happened. Encouraged, he stroked her arms and as if in response her fingers came to rest on the back of his neck. He shivered and pulled her to him.

He never knew exactly when it happened, but her thigh had insinuated itself between his legs and he swelled in response. He reached for her bottom. Pleasant little rounds, though a bit less firm than he had imagined; he patted them each in turn, then caressed them appreciatively.

He waited, but there was no sign of displeasure. He breathed more rapidly and groped his way between her legs. She hung to his neck for balance.

The heavy skirt she wore was a formidable barrier and he wasn't sure whether he was touching the precious private places of Samantha Moore or one of the many folds in that damned skirt. He said her name. She said his. He told her that she was beautiful, desirable, the most exciting woman he'd ever met.

"Please, Theo, don't judge me."

He breathed faster, struggling to lift the long skirt with one hand. The fabric bunched up in his fingers. With his other hand, he located, at last, bare flesh. He sighed; she gave a small cry.

"I want you more than I've ever wanted anybody, Samantha."

"To do this—are we right, Theo? It should be special between us."

"This is special," he said, plucking at her panties.

"How kind you are to say so."

A thought intruded. "Don't indulge me, Samantha. Just because you're going to work for me—"

"Theo! What a terrible thing to say. Even if the contracts weren't almost signed, I'd still want to hold you, to be close to you."

"I hope you mean that."

"More than I've ever meant anything."

She put her face against his hard chest and her hand came to rest on his bulging trousers. "Does this convince you? My touching you this way?"

His fingers worked under the panties, found her out. She gasped and rose up on her toes, wiggled her small bottom—she stopped, stepped away, contact broken. "Oh, Theo, you're so much man . . . *all* man. But it's been so long for me since my divorce. What if I can't please you?"

How could he tell her the pleasure, triumph, joy *those* words gave him. He directed her hand back to his penis. She gave him a reassuring squeeze, and drew away.

"Theo . . ."

"Let's go to the bedroom."

"I can hardly breathe."

"For a few minutes."

"My guests, the party . . ."

"I'm going to explode."

"Poor darling." She touched him again. "I'll be missed downstairs."

He was sweating. There was so much to lose . . . "Whatever you want, Samantha."

"Believe me, this is as difficult for me as for you. But I do want it to be perfect."

"Soon," he said. "Or I'll go crazy."

"Soon."

"You go first," he told her.

"Oh?"

"I'll have to wait until I'm myself again."

"Of course, my sweet."

"Lack of organization causes a nation to fail in its goals," stated the German riding master. "Only through organization can a people be completely mobilized and directed toward the ultimate good of the state. This country is totally disorganized. Too much *mañana* and not enough right now . . ." A titled young Englishwoman came up behind the German riding master and pushed him into the Roman pool. She melted into the crowd, laughing.

"I barely touched the other machine," the Italian count, wearing only a buckskin loincloth and an Aztec calendar dangling from a chain around his neck, told the middle-aged Hungarian actress. "Immediately a crowd of disreputable looking persons collected and the filthiest children imaginable began crawling over my new Maserati. I was revolted. At last the police arrived and I expected they would extricate me from this absurd situation. Instead they arrested *me*. For two days I was allowed no phone calls, forced to languish in a dank, noisome cell, forced to buy my own meals which were inedible. Finally I bribed one of the guards and he contacted my embassy and I was freed. Mexico, I tell you, has all the disadvantages of every other nation and none of the advantages."

"But darling, how can you say that with me here . . . Surely I am an asset, natural if not national," said the Hungarian actress, and led him briskly off toward the bedrooms . . .

"Well, it isn't that I'm so fond of Mexico. But read the papers. The news from up north gets worse every day. Strikes, campus unrest, murders, bombings, inflation, taxes, the stock market, blackouts, police strikes, war alerts. I just couldn't bear to live in that atmosphere any longer. Surely not during the winter . . ."

She was a slender girl with hollow cheeks and a petulant mouth. She wore a white suit of lights and when she spoke it was rapidly, with no change of voice or expression.

"I've been sending Christmas cards," she told her listeners. "Religious cards, mostly, to my own address in Boston. And in each and every one, I've placed some of the best Acapulco Gold you ever saw. The finest pot, and it all goes back stamped *Feliz Año* by the Mexican postal authorities. What a screech!"

Bristol discovered Foreman leaning on the low stone wall that circled the bayside of the Roman pool.

"What do you see out there?"

Foreman didn't answer. His face was drawn, a reflection of the unaccountable anger that always seemed to flow just under his skin. He was worried; not so much that he might hurt himself but that he might hurt someone else.

Tonight, for example. The pressure had been steadily building, as he reviewed his wonderful satisfying heroic life. And the party, its staged gaiety, had made it worse. He'd gone off by himself to drink more Scotch and wait for his emotions to cool off. He recognized that he was measurably drunk and getting drunker; and with it he was increasingly aware of the threat he presented to himself, and everyone else.

Now Bristol.

He turned toward the producer. "Do you believe in witches, Harry?" "Come on."

"Angels? Devils? Do you think there's a God in heaven, in each of us?"

"Crap."

"That's what I thought you'd say. The thing is, Harry, we think alike about such matters and that scares the hell out of me."

"Didn't Shelly tell you I wanted to talk to you?"

"You talk, I'll listen."

"Okay. You were supposed to make a fast, low-budget flick. Instead you're pissing dough away like this is *Cleopatra* and I've got the Bank of America at my back. What's taking so damned long? You're not even halfway through yet."

"You said you wanted a good film. I'm trying to make it for you."

"You gave the company off tomorrow. What for?"

"It's Christmas."

"What's that to you? Or to me. I want 'em to have off, I'll give 'em off. Another thing, for the money I'm paying the Moore dame, she should have words to say. Let her earn her way."

"Samantha's going to contribute something special, what I want from her."

Bristol tried for the words he needed and failed. Something about Foreman kept him off balance, at a distance. As now, the edge had somehow passed over to the other man. Bristol grew defensive, frustrated.

But Foreman just wasn't producing. And Bristol thought he knew why. Foreman seemed bloodless, never raised his voice to the actors, avoided disputes, refused to argue with them.

Bristol marked him down as a weakling, a coward. And yet he really couldn't control him . . . A couple of good right hands in the mouth would straighten him out. If *Love, Love* weren't so important—

"Okay, Foreman, now hear this. All shooting has got to be finished by the afternoon of December thirty-one. I intend to celebrate New Year's Eve free and clear."

"That's it?"

"You bet your ass that's it!"

Foreman emptied his glass and placed it very carefully on the low wall and walked away.

"Hey! I'm not finished with you."

Foreman stopped without turning.

"Since nothing's happening here tomorrow. I'm flying up to New York. I want some action out of that distributor of mine. When I get back, things better be hopping around here."

"Your last word?"

"You got it, loud and clear."

"Then excuse me. I feel naked without a glass in my hand."

Bernard escorted the French starlet with the nursing doll around Villa Gloria. On the third floor, his hand at her back, he moved her into one of the guest bedrooms, closed the door behind them.

"Too dark," she said at once.

"Don't be afraid," Bernard said, groping his way toward her.

"Baby doesn't like the dark."

Bernard took the doll out of her hand, put it aside. "The moment I saw you—" he began.

She laughed softly. "All night long, no man has looked at my face."

"You could become another Bardot."

"Ah, if only it were so . . ."

"An American company is making a film here. The producer is a friend—" His eyes adjusted to the dark and he was able to make out her naked breast, a generous pale circle with a dark aureole at its center. He moved closer. "You are magnificent."

"Where's baby?" she asked plaintively.

His cheek came to rest against the soft white mound and his mouth sought out the nipple, lips closing insistently.

"Ah, baby," she cooed.

He sucked harder and pulled at her skirt. She held his head in place and made maternal sounds of approval.

The titled young Englishwoman drank champagne swiftly and attempted to seduce the sturdy daughter of an Australian diplomat. She failed to see the German riding master come up behind her. He lifted her bodily and carried her over to the Roman pool, dropped her in. She came up coughing and swearing, mascara streaking her cheeks, still holding onto the champagne glass.

"Mexico's a great country, Mr. President," the Washington political columnist said. "But there are many aspects of life here which I, as an American, cannot understand or, forgive me, quite approve."

"Ah," the ex-president of the republic said, distaste showing through his smile.

The United States ambassador cleared his throat apprehensively. "Many areas of life in the United States leave something to be desired, it must be conceded." He laughed uneasily.

The columnist ignored him. "Here's one example," he said to the ex-president. "This morning I watched a pair of street dogs attack a fine-looking animal, obviously someone's house pet. They almost killed the poor creature, yet no one lifted a finger to chase them away. That could never happen in my country."

"Ah," the ex-president said. "That is readily explained. "You Americans, forgive me, treat your animals often better than your children. To you, animals are pets. To us, they are food . . ."

"Any luck?" Jason Peters said to his wife. He was an upright man with the washed, open face of the American heartland. "My explorations have produced a few leads, but nothing definite," he added.

"Patience and fortitude," Louise Peters answered. "I met a cute little Frenchman who took me into the maze and tried to bite my right tit."

"And?"

"That's it. He was a pudgy little man with a soft face and a body to match. Not at all my type."

"Are you ready to receive my report?"

She brought her heels together, braced her shoulders, breasts thrusting. "All ears, luv." Louise gazed proudly at Jason. It pleased her to be his wife, pleased her to bear his name, pleased her that they were going to have such a stimulating existence. First a congressman. Then Jason would become a senator and after that governor. It would not have surprised Louise if Jason were to become President of the United States before his forty-fifth birthday. After all, Jack Kennedy had done it. And Jason's family had at least as much money as the Kennedys.

"I met a fantastic-looking creature," Jason was saying. "She is an actress making a movie here. Shelly Hanes is her name and she is absolutely superb, Louise. Beautiful and extremely feminine. Make you want to crawl right inside of her."

"Sounds marvelous."

"One small drawback—she was putting away the booze pretty good."

"I loathe a drunken woman."

"Drinking, not drunk," Jason corrected. "But she didn't respond to my little hints."

"Shall I take over?"

"A small strategy should be worked out."

Louise clapped her hands happily. "Lovely! What orders, commander?"

"Shelly has a friend named Bristol. A bulldog sort of man with a great deal of animal vitality . . ."

"Makes me twitch to hear that."

Jason patted her cheek. "Why don't you talk to Bristol? Let him get to know you. But not too fast, darling."

"My impulsiveness."

"I love you for it. But some control is in order. Bristol is another generation and we don't want to scare him off."

"Not another word, luv. Discretion is my middle name."

"There he is, Harry Bristol, the one in blue . . ."

"He does look a bit bulldoggish. Oh, Jason, you're so clever. What a marvelous campaigner you'll be!"

"Samantha!" Marcella began. "This is a perfectly fabulous affair. The talk of the season. The standard by which all other parties will be measured."

"Marcella, how good of you to say it."

She leaned closer. "I mean it. But that isn't what I want

to talk about . . . it's about Agustín, well, not exactly about Agustín. He's such a dear boy, so helpful. I mentioned that you were alone and Agustín told me about this simply exquisite friend of his who takes tourists scuba diving, or something like that. His name is Julio and he's at large, so to speak. Agustín offered to bring him around, if you'd like to meet him."

"How generous of you to think of me."

"Agustín . . ."

"Thank Agustín for me. But the timing isn't at all propitious. You see, I've been a busy little bee myself."

"And you've located a plaything all your own?"

"Another time, perhaps—"

The titled young Englishman, fiancé of the titled young Englishwoman, tapped the German riding master on the shoulder. The German came about crisply. The Englishman said, "Angela asked me to do this," and hit the riding master in the mouth. He went backwards and regained his balance, spit blood.

He followed the young Englishman, now sauntering away, tapped him on the shoulder. The Englishman came about with graceful indolence and received a blow in the pit of his stomach. Bending forward, he threw up. The German kicked him in the face. The Englishman toppled onto his side, blood appearing on his lips. The German marched away. A group of young Englishmen carried their friend away, calling for a doctor.

Of the two doctors in attendance, one had passed out in the Mexican garden some time before, and the other was locked in the maid's bathroom with one of his patients.

The Swedish symphony conductor rode the white stallion at a gallop across the tile terrace and into the Roman pool. The stallion swam to the shallow end and stood there shaking. The conductor, burdened by the pistols and ammunition belts he wore, sank to the bottom. It required two strong men to drag him to the surface, where artificial respiration was performed and bets were made as to whether or not the conductor would survive.

"What are you?"

The girl was tall and leggy, with the sort of face found often at Vassar graduation exercises. If there was nothing wrong with her face, there was nothing memorable about it either. It was a face that went well with McMullen blouses and Shetland sweaters. She spoke from between clenched teeth and there was a suggestion of impatience in her voice, as if to receive a prompt response was her birthright.

"What's your guess?" Foreman said. This girl was almost as tall as Grace Biondi but her body lacked Grace's natural, unself-conscious pride.

"Aren't you going to tell me?"

"Is there any reason why I should?"

The girl shook her head in a small motion of annoyance. "Why are we talking only in questions?"

"Because we've got no answers?"

"Ask me the right question and I'll give you a dandy answer," she said.

"What am I?"

She inspected Foreman's shirt and jeans at length. "An American hippie in Mexico."

"Wrong."

"A peon?"

"Still wrong."

"Give me another guess."

Foreman drained his glass and handed it to her, walked away.

"Hey!" she called after him. "We haven't finished the game."

Foreman kept going. At the bar, he helped himself to a full bottle of Scotch, answered the barman's objection with one of his terrible smiles. In the domed reception foyer, he heard his name called.

Shelly Hanes came toward him. "Change your mind," she said.

"About what?"

"Midnight Mass. Come with me."

"No way. But I'll give you a lift back to your hotel."

"I'm going to Mass."

"Get Bristol to go with you."

"Harry in church! Oh, that's funny." She went toward the door and Foreman followed. Outside, he maneuvered her to the red VW. "Get in," he said, "I'll take you to the cathedral."

"Paul Niceguy. Thanks but no thanks. I want to be with somebody at Mass. Take me to my friend."

"Name it."

She bumped her head getting into the Volkswagen and sat curled up, rubbing her brow. Foreman got behind the wheel.

"Where to?" he said.

"On the hill. With a terrific view. Every place in this town has a terrific view. Have you noticed that?"

"I noticed. What's the name of the street?"

"When we get there, I'll know."

Foreman drove around for nearly thirty minutes before Shelly said, "This is it!" He stopped the car and she opened the door.

"You're sure?"

"Thanks for the ride, Paul Niceguy." She kissed him and ducked low getting out. "Not this time," she said triumphantly to the beetle, and hurried into the hotel.

Past the deserted reception desk, up the stairs that led to Morrie Carlson's room. She knocked on a door. No answer. She knocked again, squinted at the brass numbers on the door. Wrong room. She went on until she came to his room. She knocked and said his name. From inside, a cautious stirring. She placed her ear to the panel and listened. "Morrie," she whispered, thinking he might be asleep. "Morrie . . ." The door opened and Morrie peered out at her, face drawn, eyes pouched, his cheeks stubbled.

"Morrie! I missed you! All night I missed you!" She launched herself at him and her momentum carried them both back into the room. Laughing giddily, she spun free. "I drank a lot, Morrie. More than I should. Christmas Eve, Morrie. Merry Christmas! I'm going to

Mass. Come with me, Morrie, please come with me. It'll be beautiful, good for both of us."

"Go away, Shelly," he said, voice heavy and flat.

"It's important," she insisted. "I don't know why, but it is."

He took her by the shoulders, fingers rough. "Dammit! Pay attention. You shouldn't be here. Can't you see, I'm not alone."

She made an effort and objects began to shift into distant focus at the end of tunnel eyes. On the bed, a woman. Naked, sitting with drawn-up knees.

"Invite your friend to stay," the woman said coolly. "Two for the price of one."

"Shut up!" Morrie said. He moved Shelly toward the door. "Go to your hotel, go to bed. Sleep it off." She was back in the corridor, the strength going out of her knees. She almost fell. She leaned against the wall until she was able to make her way out of the hotel.

Going down the hillside, it was difficult to keep her balance. Twice she stumbled, managed not to fall, moving ahead blindly. Without knowing how she did it, she found her way into the *zócalo,* to the cathedral. The tall, wooden front doors were locked. Hugging the wall, she circled around to the side entrance. The doors were locked here too. She banged against them with both fists.

"I want to go to Mass!"

"Is something the matter, *señorita?*"

She raised her head. A man in a rumpled uniform stood at the edge of the sidewalk, a wary expression on his brown face. "I want to go to Mass . . ."

"*Señorita,*" he said patiently. "It is three o'clock in the morning. Better if you go back to your hotel, no? You want me to help you?"

"No, I'm all right. I'm all right."

"I don't think so, *señorita.*"

She sucked on her lower lip. "I'm fine. Very good. I can take care of myself."

He shrugged and went away. Shelly made her way across the *zócalo,* across the Costera to the beach. She tripped and went down to one knee, came up hurriedly, going on. A shoe came off, she didn't seem to notice. She went faster, until her knees gave way and she sprawled

face down on the sand. She lay still, waiting for it all to
end.

The VW carried Foreman away from Acapulco with all
the speed its four-cylinder engine could muster. It coughed
and snorted and banged as it mounted the first ridge,
began the twisting run toward La Cuarenta y Ocho. Huddled over the wheel, staring into the twin cones of light
that seemed to drag the car deeper into the night, Foreman strained to clear away the blurred edges of his vision.
A rabbit appeared in the road. Foreman hit the brake
and swerved, wheels dipping into the soft shoulder. The
rabbit scampered for safety and Foreman hit the acceler-
ator.

He unscrewed the cap of the bottle of Scotch with one
hand and drank. The bite of the liquor jarred him back
toward full wakefulness and he took a second drink.

Time passed unmarked on the night air as if life existed
nowhere but in that tiny vehicle. Visions and swirling
brilliances illuminated the dark alleys of his mind, remind-
ers of failures, blunted ambitions. He disconnected all cir-
cuits, preferring his present solitariness. He gripped the
wheel with furious concentration, the journey from no
place to nowhere demanding all his attention.

Except he was going somewhere, and something was
wrong. He'd come too far!

He rode the brake and the VW shuddered to a halt.
And stalled. Refused to start again. He cursed the battery
and tried again. The motor sputtered, refused to start. He
labeled the internal combustion engine, along with the
telephone, as infernal torture machines.

"One more time," he said aloud.

The motor raced to life. Foreman complimented the
little car as a faithful friend, the product of superior en-
gineering skill and quality control. He shipped it around
and headed back in the direction he'd come from.

Before long, the shrine, and the turn-off into the mountains. He made the corner without slowing, barely avoid-
ing the ditch, sped across the plateau and higher.

He drove without consideration of hazards, skidding
and sliding, fish-tailing around corners, speeding along a

short straightaway. A developing exhilaration caused him to drive faster and suddenly the beetle went lurching to one side, scraping against the rock and dirt wall; it bounced once or twice, kept going.

On a steep grade the car began to labor, putt-putting erratically, shuddering in protest. It struggled to the crest and coasted down the opposite side, coming to an exhausted halt in a deep ravine.

Foreman swore and went through the starting procedure. Nothing happened. He addressed the little car in gentle tones, inquiring about its physical health, its emotional condition. He stroked the dashboard lovingly and switched on the ignition. The engine groaned and squeaked, went silent.

Foreman punched the dashboard and cursed. The car made no response. Foreman changed his strategy, spoke in seductive tones. He offered vows of loving care and regular oil changes. Nothing.

Disgusted, he located a flashlight and went around to the back to study the engine. The flashlight refused to light. He heaved it into the night and struck a match. In the flickering light, the motor appeared to be fastidiously assembled, a totally incomprehensible arrangement of gadgets and things. Before the match burned out, he was able to identify the carburetor. With this accomplishment behind him, he climbed back in the driver's seat and drank some more Scotch.

Fortified, he made it over to the side of the road and relieved himself. Pleased by his competence, he tucked himself into the tiny rear seat of the car, took another drink, and began to sing:

> "On the road to Mandalay,
> Where the flying fishes play
> And the dawn comes up like thunder
> Out of China cross the bay . . ."

He explored the shadowed alleys of his besotted brain for the next verse and failed to find it. Taking swift comfort in another mouthful of Scotch, he corked the bottle, put it tenderly aside. He folded his arms and allowed his eyes to flutter shut. "Help!" he shouted into the night, and went happily to sleep.

9

Charles was rocking steadily to a not-unpleasant humming. Gradually he came awake, but still rocking. His eyes opened reluctantly and he looked around. He was in a station wagon heading south over the mountains toward Oaxaca.

Behind the wheel, an immense man with pink cheeks and curly red hair, graying at the sides. Big, fleshy hands held the wheel effortlessly, the station wagon seeming an obedient extension of his great bulk and strength.

"You sleep pretty good," the big man said.

Charles rubbed his eyes. "Guess I'm not very good company, sacking out like that."

The big man laughed, a full sound. "I'm a great believer in sleep. Fellow told me when I got into the army—'Run a mile, rest a mile.' It works for me." The pink face sobered. "You were dreaming."

"Oh?"

"Not a good dream." For the first time, the man at the wheel looked at Charles. His features were blunt, hacked out by a heavy hand, the nose short and strong, the lips full and ready to smile, the eyes steady and bright under a ridge of bone trimmed with faded brows. "You made a noise—like you were upset."

"I don't remember dreams," Charles said, hoping to end the conversation.

The big man grinned and studied the road ahead. "Same for me, once upon a time. But I set my mind to it, trained myself to remember. Lay in bed each morning until I did remember. Had some dandy dreams, worth remembering." Charles said nothing and they drove in silence for a few minutes. "Never did get to introduce ourselves," the big man said. "Seems to me you were asleep sixty seconds after I picked you up."

"I'm Charles Gavin."

"Mailman's my name."

"You're making an automobile tour of Mexico?" Charles said.

Mailman's laugh seemed to erupt. "Try again, Charles. Two guesses per customer. And the customer is always right."

"You're a salesman?"

"Used to be. Maybe I still am."

Charles saw an opportunity to keep the conversation away from himself and took it. "What do you sell these days?"

Again that oversized laugh. "Hope, you might say, is my stock in trade."

Charles assessed the big man cautiously. "Are you some kind of a missionary?"

"Never actually thought of it that way. Maybe so. A missionary without God, or a church. Hope is my prayer and work the litany. Pride, I guess, completes my Trinity."

At first Charles had seen Mailman as an extension of the station wagon; a ride, nothing more. Then as a stranger, another member of *that* generation serving up nothing but disappointments and failures. Now he wasn't so sure.

"Why are you going to Oaxaca, Charles? What will you do there?"

Charles grew defensive. "Look around, I guess."

"A good town," Mailman said. "There's a university, people are friendly. Crowded this time of year. You have friends there?"

Charles nodded once and looked out the side window. Mailman grinned. "I live outside the city, place called El Rancho. Everybody knows it. You need a place to crash, a good meal, look me up. West of town . . ."

Neither of them spoke again until Charles stepped out of the station wagon in front of the Señorial Hotel in the *zócalo*. He thanked Mailman for the ride. The big man waved one fleshy hand and drove away without a backward glance.

It was two days before Christmas when Charles arrived in

Oaxaca. Workmen were erecting stalls that would be oc-
cupied by competitors in the Festival of Radishes, by
gambling games, shooting galleries, and vendors of
buñuelos.

Under the arcades facing the plaza, the café tables
were filled with foreigners reporting to each other on their
adventures at Mitla or Monte Albán or in the marketplace; Mexicans reading, sipping expresso; and others
who simply examined the passersby.

A brown-skinned boy with a brilliant smile tried to get
Charles to buy an onyx elephant. A girl went past hawk-
ing Chiclets and an old woman made a determined effort
to sell him a Mitla rebozo. He resisted them all.

Remembering that Becky had said that everyone
showed up in the *zócalo* sooner or later, Charles joined
the *paseo* circling the square, searching the faces on the
benches. Twice around and he gave up, settled into an
empty place on one of the iron benches next to a black
boy about his own age.

"Just hit town?" the black boy said.

Charles nodded. "It shows?"

"It's the look. 'I got no place, no friends in sight.'
Right?"

"So right. You know a chick named Becky? Or one
called Livy?"

"I hope."

"Uhuh. But this town gets them all. They'll show."

"Faith, baby," the black boy said. "You want a bed, try
the León. León is from Chicago. Tell him Andy sent you.
He's a brother."

The entrance to the Hotel León was on a sidestreet, a
narrow entrance that opened into a gloomy lobby. Behind
the registration desk, an enormous black man with a
shaved skull. León.

Charles introduced himself, said Andy had sent him,
and did León have an empty bed.

"A million and one kids are scattered around town and
lots of 'em are crashing here. There's five in 102 and I
guess one more can't hurt. Five pesos a night. In advance."

Charles paid and asked León if he'd met Becky.

León shook his massive head. "Hang around the
zócalo, maybe she'll show. Watch out for the fuzz. They
are smart and tough and with that hair and rucksack,

the way you're dressed, they've already spotted you."

"I'm not looking to get hassled."

Charles deposited his rucksack on an empty cot in Room 102 and went back into the streets. Church bells were announcing the hour when he arrived back in the *zócalo;* he found space on a bench facing the street, settled down to wait. Datsuns, Volkswagens, an occasional American car circled the plaza in a lazy ritual convoy, horns sounding at the slightest delay. Motorcycles roared in and out of traffic, going nowhere; and the whistles of the khaki-clad traffic police signaled each change of lights.

The afternoon wore on and the tempo of life in the *zócalo* quickened. A balloon vendor strolled under his floating inventory, multicolored devil balloons, black octopus balloons, balloons made to resemble pink-and-white gnomes with triangular red hats. One shining globe broke free, sped off toward distant white-and-gray clouds scudding above the dusty mountains behind the city.

Darkness came rapidly. Bored and growing hungry, Charles left the bench. At a nearby stand, he ordered a *buñuelo.* A flat, round pastry, it came crumpled into a cheap clay bowl, drenched in a sweet honey syrup, cost two pesos, and was delicious; Charles ordered a second. By custom, once you'd eaten the *buñuelo,* you smashed the clay bowl on the pavement. Charles asked a young Mexican why.

Fíjese," he said with a shrug. "I cannot tell you."

"You make a wish before you break the bowl," another boy said. "It is a tradition."

An old lady nearby laughed and, overhearing them, said, "You break the bowl for the pleasure of breaking it."

Charles slammed down his bowl; it didn't break. A shaking of heads from the onlookers. He smashed it underfoot and earned a smattering of applause.

Back in the *zócalo,* the flow of pedestrian traffic had grown heavier. A woman sold hand-embroidered napkins, her inventory piled in a head-basket, an infant dangling from her rebozo. Young Americans in huaraches and homespun shirts; Mexican youths in tight trousers and machine-made shirts, their girls in miniskirts. Tourists taking pictures. *Campesinos* gazing stolidly at an elaborate crèche set up behind the bandstand. A vendor of *costa-*

ricas, those paper-thin wafers, struck his triangle to announce his wares.

On the bandstand, uniformed musicians played a Schubert serenade. Finished, they went into a John Philip Sousa march; at the first notes, Charles withdrew to a sidewalk cafe across the street. He ordered chocolate cake and coffee and felt very American for doing so. The cake was excellent, the coffee bad.

He was considering a second piece of cake when he heard his name. Running toward him from out of the crowd in the *zócalo* was Becky. She gave him a long, noisy kiss and then both of them began to talk at once. Laughing, they broke off.

"I guess I quit on you," she said.

"Never sell a Charles Gavin short. I said I'd come."

"Hi, Charles!" He looked around and saw Livy. "Glad you made it," she said with no special enthusiasm.

"Hi, Livy."

"So this is the dude you were going on about." The words came out of a short wiry youth with a small mouth and a head that sprouted curls of electric hair. He appraised Charles gloomily.

"Meet Happy," Livy said.

"Hello, Happy."

Happy grunted.

"Happy's replaced Stone," Livy said.

"A definite improvement," Becky said. "I think."

Charles grinned at Becky. "Man, am I glad to see you. I was about to raise the white flag. All day looking and waiting and no Becky."

"You must be loaded," Happy said, picking at the crumbs left on Charles' plate.

"Not exactly. But I can spring for a little something."

Happy sat down. "I'll have what you had." Charles called the waiter.

His mouth full of cake, Happy said he had spent time in Hashbury, the East Village, on a commune in Vermont. "None of it worked," he said. "I got special cravings."

"For what?"

"Warm weather, also Utopia."

"Where you figure that is?" Charles said.

"Inside your head, or no place, man. You just find the

right combination, open the lock."

"Happy's tripped on everything going," Livy said. "Pot, acid, opium . . ."

"All very groovy but not the ultimate. Tonight . . ."

"Magic mushrooms," Livy said confidentially.

"There's a guy," Becky said. "He's going to put us onto the mushrooms."

Magic mushrooms. Charles had heard of them, felt excited.

"The mushrooms will open up the real world," Happy was saying. "Turn loose all the great urges killed by the straights. There'll be magical vistas, soaring insights, truth . . ."

Charles remembered the crash pad on Houston Street. Even on his own, in a cloud of pot smoke, he had found no alternative to Theo's world—and when the private detective his parents had hired found him and forced him back to Julia's apartment, he wasn't quite as sore as he acted. He also acted indifferent to the idea of the Acapulco trip, but he had been anxious to go, to split and find something better.

"Pot . . . acid . . . now mushrooms. I don't see nirvana yet," Charles said.

"Who's your friend?" Happy grumbled.

"Don't be square, Charles," Livy said. "We'll really fly."

Becky took Charles by the hand. "You're coming with us. That's right, isn't it?"

"I suppose . . ."

"Sure," she said. "It's settled. I'd given up on you, sweet thing, and that saddened me. I figured Big Daddy pulled you back to straight country."

Charles made a face.

"Once more into the breach for hearth and home. What went wrong?"

"Everything and nothing. Same thing, I guess. Look, I'd like to drop it, okay?"

"Sure, no point in hacking it to pieces," Becky said. "We're not into their scene and that's all that matters."

"When is the mushroom man going to show?" Livy asked.

"Around midnight."

"What do we do until then?"

Happy glared at her. "Wait . . ."

They waited. And drank more coffee. And talked.

"How'd you get to Oaxaca?" Becky asked Charles.

"Hitched."

"All the way from Acapulco?"

"It wasn't so bad. I made it to Mexico City in one jump. A couple of schoolteachers from Detroit took me as far as Puebla and from there I got a ride on top of a load of peanuts to some Indian village. A family put me up for the night and in the morning they fed me tortillas and beans and gave me a couple of bananas and an orange for the trip. That's when Mailman picked me up."

"Who?" Livy said.

"Mailman. An odd guy. For a minute I kind of liked him, like he was somebody special. Then he started asking questions and I backed off."

"I know about Mailman," Happy said. "He runs some kind of a school, like for social workers, to help the poor Mexicans. Big joke. If you want to help poor people, you lay lots of bread on 'em so they stop being poor."

"Right on!" Livy said.

"Maybe," Charles said, "but what's so criminal about trying to help people?"

"Shit," Happy said. "I'll bet Mailman's raking in lots of government bread, some kind of a Federal handout."

Charles remembered the booming laughter, the sound of a man who didn't seem to be afraid. Charles opened his mouth to speak, shut it. Happy was probably right; Mailman was probably just another version of that great philanthropist Theo; his line just sounded better.

"Happy," Livy said. "Dig what's coming our way."

A Mexican of medium height in white pants, a colored shirt and a sombrero. Across one shoulder, a dozen serapes. "Serapes," he offered to the tourists at the sidewalk tables. "Very pretty serapes. Very beautiful." He paused in front of Happy. "Serape, *señor?*"

"Why not?" Happy said. "Show us what you've got."

The Mexican examined one face after another, his eyes steady. He showed his serapes without haste.

"This one," he said. "This is Chacmool, rain god of the

Mayans. Very pretty, very good luck. And this one. The birds are very good, the colors natural. Very much work and only two hundred and seventy pesos."

"Too much *dinero*," Happy said.

"*Señor*, the work, the colors."

"Not exactly my style," Happy said. He leaned forward, voice growing confidential. "You get the information I asked you about?"

The Mexican began to refold the serapes. "*Señor*, I have exactly what would please you. Not far away is a small room where I keep other serapes. Very beautiful work. If you would come there, I will show you. Make your choice. Some small, some large. All very beautiful. And the price is not so very many dollars. You will come?"

"Sure," Happy said, standing. "We'll all come."

In a dark, quiet street not far from the *zócalo*, they stopped in front of an old wooden door. The Mexican ushered them into a narrow courtyard which widened abruptly. On one side, apartments; on the other, a high stone wall. They followed the Mexican to the last doorway, went inside; he turned on a light. The room was small, the ceiling low. A single, bare light bulb swung in a small arc at the end of its cord. Stacked on a wooden bench along one wall, piles of serapes.

"My work," the Mexican said without modesty. "I design them. I sell them. It is very difficult work. To make a good serape takes eight, maybe nine days."

"You do it all by yourself?" Charles asked.

"My family, they help. Prepare the wool, the dyes. But it is my work alone. Would you like to see some of my work?"

Happy said, "Let's talk about mushrooms."

The Mexican nodded amiably. "Everything is arranged."

"Well, great!" Happy said. "You're going to take us."

"In the morning, *señor*, very early. My friend will be here. He is going to visit his family. He will take you to where the mushrooms are."

Happy scowled. "How much is all this help going to cost?"

"*Señor*, this is not an easy thing."

"How much?"

"One hundred pesos, *señor*."

"You're putting me on!" Happy said. "I'll give you ten."

"*Señor*. There is danger. The police are angry with people who do what I am doing for you. There are severe penalties. Seventy-five pesos and another twenty-five for my friend."

"Shit," Happy said.

"Pay the man," Becky said. "We expected it."

"I don't like to be taken, is all. Forty and ten is my final offer."

"No, no. The price you offer is not worth the danger."

"You dudes really got a good thing going," Happy said.

"*Señor*, there are tourists in the *zócalo*. I can sell many serapes at this time of year."

"Okay, fifty and twenty," Happy said.

"*Señor*, you make a hard bargain. *Bueno*. I agree. Fifty and twenty."

"Okay," Happy said, looking at the others. "Remember, we split four ways."

In Happy's camper side by side, sharing the blankets, burning the last of the grass, seldom talking.

The camper was parked outside of the city in a wooded area and only the sound of crickets intruded on their privacy.

"Big day tomorrow," Happy said.

"Big day," Livy echoed.

"I told you chicks I'd put you onto them mushrooms."

"You're beautiful, Happy," Livy said.

They finished the last joint and lay quietly in the blackness.

Charles felt detached, secretly a little crazy, and less turned on than he'd have imagined. On his right, Becky, her naked thigh pressed against him. On his left, Livy, also naked. They were paired; he and Becky, Livy and Happy. He touched Becky's hip and she stirred, rolled onto her side. His arms went around her, hands resting on her fine bottom. They kissed. After a while, he began to respond.

Soft wet sounds filled the air and Charles was unable to

close out Livy's small cries at his back. He forced himself to concentrate on Becky only. He stroked her belly, went lower, and she spread to his touch. He located one breast.

"Listen, people," Happy began. "The time has come to speak of other things—"

Becky giggled and Charles held himself very still, aware of his shriveling passion.

Livy leaned against Charles, her tiny breasts hot on his skin. Her hands reached around him.

"Knock it off, Livy," he said thickly.

"Happy and me," she murmured, "have decided that it's time to switch."

"Livy," Becky said, laughing. "A little self-control, girl."

"Fuck it. I want to have some fun."

"Thanks for working Becky up," Happy said to Charles. "I'll finish the job."

"Big talk," Becky said.

"Big sword."

Charles kept his voice low. "Let's just leave things the way they are."

"No way," Happy said.

"You get me, Charles," Livy said brightly.

Charles said, "I want Becky, and she wants me."

"Oh, Charles," Becky said, "of course I do."

"What's that got to do with anything?" Happy said glumly. "Get hip, man. We're changing partners. It's just for tonight. Livy'll give you enough ride."

Livy bent over Charles, mouth working toward his penis. He pushed her away.

"I told you—" he began.

"And I told you," Happy said. "Dammit, maybe you think this is the first time around for us?"

"What?"

"That's right, Charles," Becky said. "The three of us have been making it ever since we got together. No big thing, honey, love is free and beautiful."

"Sure," Charles said. "But tonight—"

"Try me later, Charles."

Charles fell back, aware of Happy crawling over him, falling on top of Becky. In a tight, demanding voice, he was telling Becky what to do and she was doing it. Charles made an effort to close it all out, then Livy was at him

again and her insistent flesh made it easier for him not to
hear, to convince himself that everything was as good as
it was supposed to be . . .

Once in the middle of the night, he woke and discovered
hands stroking his body, a voice whispering in his ear. He
told himself that finally he and Becky were together. But
in the blackness, he couldn't be sure even of that.

Out of Oaxaca the next morning up into the rugged and
barren mountains, speeding past immense organ cactus
that reached toward the sky like some pagan erection to
a forgotten deity. No one in the camper talked much, sudden starts that went nowhere, questions that remained un-
answered. Charles stared out at the passing landscape, displaying no interest in anything said, trying not to remember about the night before.

By the time they left the main highway, the sun was
higher and the air grew warmer. On a track of loose stone
and dirt, they twisted and looped around sharp corners,
climbing all the while.

Next to Charles, Becky spoke. "I hope the trip is worth
it all. This road frightens me."

From the sound of her voice, Charles knew that like
himself, she was afraid of what lay ahead; all of them
were. On the front seat, Livy sat beside Happy, hugging
herself tightly. Next to her, the mestizo who was their
guide. A small man with an arched brow and quick eyes,
he hadn't spoken since they started out, except to give
brief directions.

They went on. Skidding on loose rocks, lurching over
potholes, leaving clouds of dust behind, following the road
as it doubled back in long hairpin turns, dipping with the
abruptness of a roller coaster. As they climbed higher, the
air became thinner, crisper, and Charles was forced to
gulp rapidly in order to satisfy his need for oxygen.

All around them mountains. A dark stack casting ominous navy-blue shadows. High on the slopes, herds of
goats and untended burros strolled along the road.

The camper swerved, rolled. Charles turned his mind
ahead, to the mushrooms, to experiences beyond his ability to imagine. He ached to call it off and knew that he

would not; he had to find out. The mushrooms had become a symbol, a madstone, a voodoo charm; and in surrendering to its ancient spell he hoped to come finally to what was the truth of himself. The mushrooms, he hoped, were going to make him understand. Everything. He hoped . . . he was afraid . . .

Dusk had settled over the mountains by the time they reached the village. A collection of red-soil-brick huts with slanted wooden roofs. Chickens and pigs roamed between the houses and a pack of emaciated dogs howled ferociously as the camper ground to a halt. Children materialized out of the houses, faces blank, looking older than their years.

They climbed down out of the camper, stretched, and looked around; the guide chased the dogs away. A man wearing work pants and a sweater came forward, addressed the guide in a language none of them understood. The guide answered briefly, then hurried away.

"Welcome to our village," the man in the sweater said, his English tinged with an almost Oriental accent. He had a round, bland, remarkably well-preserved face. "I am Don Alvaro. I have been informed of your reason for coming. The mushrooms," he sighed. "That is not so easily arranged."

Happy stepped forward. "We came all this way, we paid . . ."

Don Alvaro looked into Happy's tight face. "Oh, there are mushrooms in these hills. But there are also soldiers. Army patrols are dispatched regularly in behalf of the authorities in Mexico City. They search for the poppy fields, for fields where marijuana is cultivated, for the mushrooms. It is known that our people like to help young foreigners who come seeking the power of the mushrooms, and the officials disapprove. They would imprison our people, if they could catch them."

Charles spoke. "In Oaxaca, they promised we'd be supplied with mushrooms."

"In Oaxaca," Don Alvaro said in a soft voice. "In Oaxaca, promises are easy to make. So it is in all cities, yes. But it is in these mountains that the promises must be fulfilled and that is not always so easy. I have lived in cities. In Mexico and in your country, too. In San Antonio, Texas, where I attended high school and learned to

speak your language and to read. I have always enjoyed
reading. Perhaps you have brought books with you. Here
it is exceedingly difficult to get books."

"What the hell!" Happy exploded. "Did we come up
here to hold a literary discussion?"

"Shut up, Happy," Charles said. "I've got an old copy of
Mother Night you can have."

"Good! An old book is new for one who has not read
it."

"You can have my copy of Franz Fanon," Becky said.

"Okay," Happy said. "Seminar's over, let's get to the
mushrooms."

Don Alvaro ignored him. "Soon it will be dark. You
must be tired. I will have you taken to where you may
rest and clean yourselves. Here the facilities are primitive
but they serve. Later we shall talk again." He moved into
the darkness.

Soon two women appeared, gesturing and chattering in
their own shrill language.

"They want us to follow them," Livy said.

They were led to a hut lit by a single candle. Straw
mats were scattered on the floor and a wooden stand stood
against one wall. The women left and when they came
back each of them carried a clay pot filled with water. By
the time the Americans had finished cleaning themselves,
the women were back with bowls of soup thick with
maíz de teja and chunks of chicken and warm tortillas.

"*Pozole,*" the women said almost together—like a harmony. "*Pozole.*"

The soup was highly seasoned and filling and they ate
rapidly and without talking. They were almost finished
when Don Alvaro appeared.

"I hope you feel stronger now. Please, follow me." At
the door, he paused, his manner conspiratorial. "I find it
may be possible to provide what you came looking for."

Don Alvaro looked at each of them solemnly. "Certain
men of the village dared to go up onto the mountain, to
locate the mushrooms and pick them. At this season of
the year, mushrooms are difficult to find. Also, they must
be prepared for use. There is a very great risk to us all."

Happy swore. "Sure, sure. How much?"

Don Alvaro measured him, but when he spoke, he directed himself to Charles. "On behalf of those who have

no English, I speak to you. They ask a price for their services, for the risks." Don Alvaro spread his hands. "One hundred and fifty pesos for each one."

"That's robbery!" Happy said. "I won't pay."

"Keep quiet, Happy," Charles said. He nodded gravely; Don Alvaro expected them to bargain, but with good form. "*Señor,*" he began. "We are, as you can see, all young people. We are also poor."

"It is known that all Americans are rich. It is known."

"Not us. The price you ask is too high. We cannot afford to pay it. It is possible that we may have to forget the mushrooms and in the morning return to Oaxaca without them."

Charles' mild threat amused Don Alvaro. "As you wish," he said, turning away.

"We are able to pay thirty pesos for each one," Charles said after him.

That drew an expression of regret. "Would you ask me to go to my people with such an offer? They would lose respect, select another to represent them."

"Two hundred for the four of us. It is our limit." Charles sat down on one of the straw mats, legs folded under him.

"Yes," Becky added. "Even that is too much."

Don Alvaro refused to acknowledge her presence. "I will tell you," he said after a while. "I will make you a very good price, but it is a final price. One hundred and twenty pesos for each person."

Charles closed his eyes. "Our final price cannot possibly be more than sixty for each."

"*Ay!*"

Charles stared at the near wall.

"That is your final price?" Don Alvaro said.

Charles jerked his head yes.

"I see, I see," Don Alvaro said, shaking his head. He spoke with obvious reluctance. "Well, it is easy to see that none of you is rich. We will come closer together. You can have the mushrooms for ninety pesos each." He put his eyes on Charles and waited.

Charles folded his arms across his chest. He was enjoying this, understanding as he did that to the Mexican form was at least as important as substance. He remembered Paul Foreman bargaining in the Acapulco market for a serape; how pleased the Indians had been with the experience even though there had been no sale.

"My friends will be angry with me," he said. "Still, I want to be fair. Seventy-five and, it causes me great pain. My friends will be poor for a long time."

"Yes, it is sad. Eighty-five. I can go no lower."

"Seventy-five, and that is too much."

Don Alvaro looked away, mouth thinning out. There was only the sound of their breathing in the hut.

"Very well," Charles said, coming to his feet. "We will split the difference. Eighty is our final offer. As we say in America, take it or leave it."

"You *Yanquis,* such difficult people to deal with. My people will feel cheated. I must have an extra peso from each, to show that I bargained hard . . ."

"*Bueno,*" Charles said. "Eighty-one."

Charles and Don Alvaro shook hands. The Mexican motioned for them to follow and they all left the hut, trooped along the dusty street without speaking. Somewhere a dog barked and another answered. A rooster crowed. A child cried in its sleep. A path led them up a slope to a low, flat-roofed hut.

Inside, one large room, the only light coming from the unsteady flame of a crude oil lamp. An old man kneeled on a straw mat, his face small and wrinkled, his large ears jutting out from a round head. He was muttering unintelligibly as they entered, not looking up. To his right, and slightly to the rear, a slender boy, duplicating the old man's position.

"The old man is Feliciano," Don Alvaro said, in a voice full of respect. "He is a *curandero,* a healer. He is a witch for good, using his powers only to fight evil. The mushrooms are new to *norteamericanos,* but to my people they are very old, a part of our lives. Feliciano uses mushrooms to cure certain sicknesses."

Don Alvaro spoke to the boy and he got up, brought a bowl filled with mushrooms, displayed it.

Don Alvaro said. "Three kinds of mushrooms grow in these mountains. Elsewhere others may be found. The magic is in the mushrooms, not in where they are eaten, or in what position. When they are used for curing, the mushroom dream allows the *curandero* to diagnose the sickness, and to cure it."

"What about when there is no sickness?" Charles asked.

"The mushrooms perform in many ways. It is possible that they will bring you close to people who are far away. Reconcile you with your enemies. If you have lost something, the mushrooms may help you to find it. They may take you to a beautiful place, by a beautiful way . . ."

"Right on, baby," Happy said.

". . . Mushrooms are magic, and who can say what magic they may produce in a particular man. Or woman," he added.

"Let's get to it," Happy said.

"Whenever the *curandero* is ready," Charles said, nodding in the direction of the old man.

Don Alvaro addressed Feliciano and he mumbled a few words to his young assistant. The boy went to the far corner of the room and came back with a stone brazier filled with glowing coals, placing it on the ground before the old man. Making a second trip, he brought four crude clay bowls. Each contained four mushrooms, two large, two smaller.

"A portion for each person," Don Alvaro said.

Feliciano murmured a melodic incantation and passed his gnarled brown hands over the brazier, dispatching curls of smoke in every direction. A few more moments and he poured a milky liquid over the mushrooms.

"Please make yourselves comfortable on the mats," Don Alvaro said.

Happy leaned forward. "What's he putting on the mushrooms?"

"A simple liquid that will cause harm to no one. It slows the power of the mushrooms, which is often too strong for Americans unaccustomed to it. Another time you may be able to accept the full magic."

Staring at the sand-colored, umbrella-shaped caps, Charles imagined they had begun to shimmer with the strength of their own magic; he flashed backwards in time to his own childhood, visualized Lewis Carroll's Alice shrinking and growing larger according to which mushrooms she ate. What would it be like to be a shrunken man in a world of normal beings? Or a giant among pygmies? He shivered.

Feliciano stopped chanting. He poured some liquid into the brazier and almost at once the sweet bite of incense floated on the air. Charles felt transported in time, in the presence of Aztec medicine men and antique mysteries.

The boy stood in front of Charles, passed the brazier back and forth in front of him.

"Wash your hands in the smoke," Don Alvaro instructed. Charles did and the boy moved on. When all of them had completed the ritual, the brazier was set down in front of the old man. He lifted each bowl over it in turn, voice rising and falling atonally, then offered them to the Americans.

"Take a bowl, each one," Don Alvaro said.

Charles stared down at the bowl in his hand. Four mushrooms. Four travelers on the magic journey. Four was a square number, cornered, balanced; did it represent some mystical combination?

"Eat," came a distant command, soft at the edges. "Enter the magic world. And fear nothing . . ."

Charles filled his lungs and lifted the mushroom to his lips. It was fleshy and tough and the stems were slimy. He forced himself to chew, to swallow everything. And when it was finally done, he was breathing hard. He put the bowl aside.

They sat still. Waiting. Not speaking, vaguely uncomfortable, expecting a dramatic change.

A low, undulating whistle came out of Feliciano, a heavy, penetrating sound. Soon it was transformed into a mournful chant, the chant and the whistle alternating. Suddenly an awful chest-wracking cough, a deep animal grunt as if the old *curandero* was himself possessed by some god-imposed illness. He lifted his face and began to speak, a shrill Spanish plea to unseen beings in the smoky air around his head.

"Oh, holy Virgin Mother protect these travelers on the magic road: Keep them from harm, Master. Let all the saints know that these are innocents and mean no evil, seek no gain except to come nearer to the Heavenly Father . . ."

The boy began to sing. Almost a parody of a human voice, low and nasal, and Don Alvaro joined in. In counterpoint, Feliciano was importuning a roster of saints and spirits and ancient gods for protection, guidance, succor.

It went on. And on. For uncounted minutes until time was stopped. Charles felt his brain begin to shimmer, float free. It was funny and he laughed. Except for his floating brain, everything was normal, as it should be. Abruptly, nothing was the same.

Flowing streamers of delicate hues and blends swam gently on the screen of his mind, familiar and safe. The tempo of movement increased and the shadings became more vivid, flashing brightly. His tongue was thick and slow.

But he wasn't afraid. He was bathing in a sea of rapidly changing color, screaming pinks and heavy reds and ponderous blacks and browns. He peered into a sea-green gem and was drawn down in a lazy, winding fall, all parts of his body loose and in harmony, lineaments oscillating into strange shapes, profiles, the green boiling up and darkening until it was almost black. Swarms of fish bubbling and hissing angrily darted at him, gaping mouths and glazed eyes, wide and somehow mocking. He thrashed about in a futile attempt to rise up out of the green . . .

"Where are you?" a voice in apparent anguish called out.

"Touch me—"

"Please—"

A hand was on Charles's hand and he fell back. His breathing returned to normal. How long had he been trapped in the green? A microsecond? Or light years? Stars twinkled in the blackest sky he had ever seen. Long-dead constellations, stars. Yesterday's stars, lighttails.

How strange!

Charles was suspended in an amniotic pool, sleepy and warm. He drifted afloat in comfort, an unborn and so undying existence. And all-knowing . . .

Across low flats a tide of churning whitewater, flooding the land. Charles was on his feet, running toward high ground. Atop a bald peak, he spun around in time to see the waters foaming up, falling back reluctantly. Soon land came back into view and mountains loomed up where before there had been none. A lush valley of shining rivers and rocks and forests and springs and beaches and all kinds of living creatures moving about, unafraid. And, of course, he knew this was the beginning . . .

Laughter and the sense of ecstasy—sheer delight—end suddenly, "My head, my head! It's being crushed!"

Charles tried to speak. His tongue traveled slowly

around the circle of his open mouth, he made no sound. Nausea, a voice he didn't know close at hand, words that sounded strange but he understood them—not the language, just the meaning . . .

Color came back. Broken slashes and demitints. Crystal patterns. Unfolding shapes. Pigments joined in gaudy streams so that he had to shield his eyes against the glare. A harsh overlay brightened the landscape and the color formed irregular striations, the flow constant, one level laminated fiercely against the next, the whole growing tighter, thinner, altered swiftly into a single gleaming cutting edge, swinging crazily, bouncing off a huge, gray boulder, shattering into scythes that hacked and sliced the sun out of a glaring, empty sky.

The muscles supporting Charles's spine went slack and he fell backward, smiling into space, seduced by the harmonies of Sirens. He wanted to make love to them all, to prove the truth to Theo—but he was too warm, too satisfied to make the effort. It was strange. It was funny, and nearby someone laughed with Charles.

A young boy appeared in the distance. It was himself, very small, trying to shut out the loud, angry talk of the big people that came from behind a closed door. Not wanting to see them together . . . not wanting to be with them . . . Now the boy was gone and a giant was in his place. No, that's not what he wanted . . .

He rolled over and buried his face in his arms and the nausea returned. He tried to sit up and found it too difficult, unable to coordinate his movements.

Someone spoke. Charles answered. Real conversation, free and open, the truth? The rhythms of speech became hypnotic. Lights glittered like jeweled points. Laughter, happiness . . ."

And nausea again, as though from a secret disease that had to be found and exorcised. Then he'd be all right again . . .

A face, full of rage, materialized in front of him. He masked his eyes, afraid to look at that face. Afraid to say its name.

The face shattered into glittering shards that formed sunlit stream. The water frolicked and was transformed into strings of glistening stones that went flying through the air. Tearing loose of their moorings, the stones glowed darkly and came at Charles like runaway meteors. He became exhausted dodging them, looking for a hiding place and not finding one. He ran. His lungs burned and his legs wobbled and gave way. He fell forward, chest heaving. He began to choke, to suffocate, to die . . . ?

No, because he was able to breathe again. He laughed because there was no danger, no real threat.

He could be anybody he wanted. Do anything ever done. He became successively John Wayne and Humphrey Bogart and Errol Flynn, excelling in derring-do with gorgeous ease, panache.

And he knew that this was crazy because it was an awful lie and he'd be punished for it, was *being* punished right now . . . in the dark . . .

Terror finally began to drain away, leaving the echo of that face, a challenge he hated and couldn't avoid. He slept and woke, shaken. He fell asleep again. When he woke again he could keep his eyes open and in focus, and he was beginning to piece some of it together as a pallid light leaked under the closed door and he raised up and looked around. Feliciano was gone. The boy, Don Alvaro, Becky, Livy, Happy—all gone. He was alone in the hut. Alone, like so often before . . .

He felt restless. There was something to be done, something *he* had to do. Like something mislaid that he couldn't for the moment find.

He rested, then tested his legs and was pleased to discover that they functioned reasonably well. He went outside.

The morning mountain air stung his cheeks and made his eyes tear. He pushed his hands into his pockets and made his way down the hillside to the village. The camper was parked at the end of the dirt street.

A family of pigs rooted in the ditch. Chickens pecked and squawked. Some boys kicked a soccer ball back and forth. A man crouched in front of his house and washed his feet in a puddle of water, his wife looking on with evident approval.

Charles felt the blood throbbing. He was cold and there was pressure in his bladder and the pain of hunger in his belly. Sensations of life, of being alive. There was still a chance . . .

10

A massive vise clamped down on Shelly's head. She moaned and sat up, one eye pried open. The glare was too much. She blinked and tried again. The waters of Acapulco Bay gave off offending pinpoints of early-morning light. She held her head and rocked back and forth, waiting for the pain behind her eyeballs to subside.

The events of the night before came rushing back like successive accusations—the party, the drinking, the visit to Morrie Carlson's hotel room. The cathedral . . .

And after that? She had gone to the beach, had run until her strength gave out, had lain on the sand breathless and crying and feeling very sorry for herself. She was ashamed.

She felt the long, first rays of the sun on her back and the penetrating warmth revived her. She realized that the beaches would soon be thronging with people, people she didn't want to see, be seen by. She forced herself to stand and headed back to the hotel.

She arrived back at the room prepared to face Harry's wrath and was almost disappointed to find him gone. A brusquely worded note told her that he had taken the early plane to Mexico City, and from there to New York. He intended to return the next day. Relieved, she stripped off her clothes, swallowed some aspirin, and crawled into bed.

When she woke the afternoon sun was streaming into the room. She lay very still, willing sleep to take her again; it refused. After a while she managed to make it into the bathroom. After a shower, she pulled on a pair of slacks and a blouse, tied her hair at the nape of her neck with a colored ribbon and went out.

Beyond Colonel Sander's Kentucky Fried Chicken, a coffeeshop. She sat in a booth and drank coffee and made herself eat some buttered toast. Feeling stronger, she left. Outside, she hailed a cab, went to Morrie's hotel. He wasn't there. She waited in the lobby. Nearly an hour passed before Morrie returned. He was pale, his eyes dull, his cheeks unshaven. He walked past her without speaking, going directly to his room. She went after him.

Once inside, he took off his jacket. Shelly gasped. "My God, Morrie, what happened?" The right side of his shirt was stained with blood.

Without answering, he began to fumble with the buttons of the shirt. But his fingers refused to function properly.

"Let me do it," Shelly said. She worked swiftly, carefully peeling the shirt away from his body. Newly crusted blood was in a vertical streak along his side, nearly six inches long.

"Have you seen a doctor?" she said, surprised at her control, coolness.

"No doctor."

"Sit down." He obeyed. "I'll get some water."

In the bathroom, she soaked a towel in warm water, returned to him. Working slowly, she cleaned away the dried blood.

"There's some seepage," she said.

"I'm okay."

"You're lucky. It didn't reach the bone."

"Nobody dies from a cut like that."

"Oh, you're a tough guy," she said. "A knife wound doesn't bother you at all."

He stood up and went into the bedroom, studied himself in the mirror.

"It bothers me," she called, going after him.

For the first time, Shelly was aware of how twisted his body was. The right shoulder was locked into place at an impossible angle. He looked thin, not really the strong man she'd thought. He turned back, holding a roll of tape and some bandages.

"I'll do it," she said.

He handed them over. She worked the edges of the wound together and pressed a bandage to it, then drew the tape tightly into place. She stepped back and assessed her work.

"I still think you should see a doctor."

"You've done the job. I'll survive."

"Damn fool," she said softly.

"Probably. I'm going to shave. Why don't you talk to me?"

She sat on the toilet and watched him. "I don't remember much about my father," she said, "but I can remember him shaving. He used a straight-edged razor and I thought it was terrific how he could pass a knife over his skin without hurting himself."

"How old were you then?"

"My father left just after my fourth birthday. I never saw him again."

"My old man took off right after this happened to me." He indicated his deformed shoulder. "I fell down some stairs when I was about two or so, fractured a couple of vertebrae. Matter of fact, ruined a budding athletic career," he added wryly. "Hell, I might have been a major-league shortstop or something. Failing that I turned to painting. My mother, a practical lady, suggested I might do better selling pencils. An unhappy lady, as you may have gathered. I suppose she came to mistake me for her dear departed husband. Maybe he was the smart one . . ."

Shaved clean, he washed and dried himself. He went back into the bedroom and she followed. "Actually, I'm not an artist, I'm a gambler. I think I told you, I'm an addict. Hooked the way skin-poppers are hooked on horse. Mine is also an expensive habit. Those drawings I do support the habit. When I get a bankroll, I find some action. Don't misunderstand, I don't always lose. Once in a while I win, and nothing is worse for a gambling man. Winning is the bait, and when I win, drink, and booze and cards are a bad mix. Two nights ago I won and started sucking on a bottle of tequila like it was mother's milk. Maybe it is. When I get drunk enough, I go out after a woman. Any woman will do. I get money, mainly so I can buy one. But by now I'm usually too drunk to make out. In the mornings, I tell myself that if I'd've been sober I'd've been a real man. Must watch that little booze problem—"

"Please . . ."

He ignored her. "That woman you found me with is a whore. Nice, very accommodating, but a whore all the same. She works hard at her trade and she's good at it. But I'm a bust every shot. So afterward I curse her and pay her, and send her away. Then I go out and find some more gambling action. Start the circle all over again.

"This time I really lost heavily, all the money I had, and more that I didn't have. So I cheated, and screwed that up. I tried to run but this body is not made for foot-racing.

"One fellow took a particularly dim view of my action and decided to teach me a lesson. He cut me and would've again if the other players hadn't stopped him. Last night, you see, I was a triple loser . . ."

Neither of them spoke for a while. Shelly watched him and wondered how a man of such intelligence and ability could be so obviously hurting himself and not seem to be able to stop it. And then she realized she could be describing herself—the last part, at least.

"You're the only beautiful woman I've ever known," he began absently. "Looking at your face gives real pleasure. Makes me feel good. I've never made love to a beautiful woman. Not even a pretty one. What woman would want me unless she were paid to perform?"

She took his hand and kissed it. "Morrie, don't."

"Let me tell you, the story of the Ugly Duckling is a rotten joke . . . and please excuse the wash of self-pity. I usually do better than this."

She pressed his hand to her breast.

"Listen . . . you don't—"

"Morrie. Come on . . ."

Touching each other, they made it to the bed. He looked at her, hardly believing what was happening, hoping that this time . . . and with it, beginning as always to be afraid . . . She was close to him, a good rich womanly smell about her. His hands began to sweat.

"Shelly, listen to me—"

She put her cheek against his. "Please, Morrie, don't say anything bad."

"You don't owe me anything."

Her lips closed around the lobe of his ear, teeth working. "This is for me," she said. "Before it was always for somebody else. This is for me. And for you, if you want."

He didn't speak. He couldn't.

She shifted around, her mouth settling over his. Her tongue explored the warm lining of his cheeks and her hands fluttered across his bare chest, carefully staying away from his wound.

They lay face to face. He became bold enough to touch her breast.

She opened her mouth on his shoulder, licking the skin, enjoying the strong male taste. She had never before felt this tenderness, the passion slow in coming to the surface, slow to overflow. With Harry—she felt no guilt, or pleasure in betraying him—with Harry, there was never tenderness.

She pulled away and looked at Morrie. "I love you," she said.

He closed his eyes, still afraid to speak, afraid this incredible scene would dissolve to reality.

She kissed each eye in turn. Their mouths came together in a lingering exchange of breath and touch and taste. His hands took more chances in their explorations and she was less afraid of reaching for him. They shifted and without knowing how it happened, without knowing who helped whom, they found themselves naked. He helped himself now to the lush feast she offered. No part of her was left untouched.

She responded. Hands and mouth caressing him, taking pleasure in his body. Finally with a short breath, he forced her onto her back, coming between her thighs, mouth fastened to hers. She reached and guided and urged him to become a part of her, to fill the inner void. He pressed forward, slid into the hot, dark dampness and went slack.

He fell away from her, cursing.

She held him and petted him, began again. She whispered her need for him, told him again that she loved him —and meant it.

She tried and he helped until again they came to that point where he lay between her legs, and this time she refused to let him stop. She told him that she was giving herself and that he was being less honest. He had no right to deprive her of his love, his manhood. No right at all to punish her this way. She made *demands,* and was shocked by her own courage and openness. She repeated the demands until he kissed her, silencing her.

And soon his body began to respond. Without strain he slid into her, their bodies moving in gentle but then more demanding rhythms. They told each other about their love and pleasure . . .

It happened. Not the end, but a beginning, a promise.

They lay quietly, thinking not too far into the future . . .

11

Sweat broke across Foreman's brow, rolling down his cheek, forming a tiny pool in the crook of his neck. Still asleep, he brushed impatiently at the annoyance. As if in response, a second bead traveled the same route.

"Too damned hot!"

He sat upright, eyes open but unseeing, staring into the glare of morning sunlight on the dust-caked windshield of the Volkswagen. He blinked, and blobs of brown beyond the glare shifted and dissolved until he was able to identify eyes and noses and mouths. Faces. Indian faces. Chinchahua faces, prideful, wary, eyes set deep behind prominent cheekbones, shaded under straw sombreros. Foreman tried to arrange a friendly expression. Apparently he failed because the nearest Chinchahua promptly pushed the muzzle of his rifle against Foreman's cheek. At that instant an army of vicious little people invaded his head, began hacking away at the tender interior of his skull.

"Practical jokes are the lowest form of humor, man," he muttered. Then, in Spanish, he said, "Too much drinking makes for a soft head."

The rifle remained firm against his cheek.

Foreman began to sweat more. "Friends, surely you remember me! I've been among you before."

The man with the rifle pushed harder.

"Dammit," Foreman yelled, "that hurts! And like I said, you know me. A friend, or at least a friend of a friend. Remember . . . ?"

Very delicately, Foreman directed the rifle away from his cheek. He lifted the corners of his mouth in what he hoped could pass for a smile rather than evidence of a gas pain, opened the door of the VW and climbed out. He managed one forward step before the rifle was brought down across his shoulders, pitching him into the dirt. A heavy foot settled across the back of his neck.

"I definitely surrender," Foreman said. "Take me to your ethnologist . . ."

The pressure on his neck increased.

"Okay," he warned. "I'll give you one more chance—"

The foot held steady.

Foreman gathered his strength and heaved himself in the direction of the Indian. Caught by surprise, the man went down heavily. Foreman came up, fist swinging.

"Don't hit him!"

Foreman held back. He looked up to see Grace Biondi hurrying forward. "You idiot, put your hand down and help him up. For God's sake, be quick." She spoke rapidly to the Chinchahua on the ground. "I told him you were only playing some kind of American game, that you like wrestling. Never mind, just apologize."

Foreman stood up, offered the Indian his hand. The man came erect without help, retrieved his rifle.

"Sorry I didn't break your neck," Foreman said, displaying his teeth.

"In Spanish, you fool," Grace said. "And for our sakes make him believe it."

"Perdón mi, señor," Foreman said, feeling no remorse. Then, in English, "Next time I'll stick that damn gun up your ass and blow your brains out." Big man in English, especially among the non-English speaking . . .

The Chinchahua assessed Foreman, then walked away, his friends close behind.

"What insanity brought you up here during the night?" Grace said.

"Right now I can't remember," he said, aware again of the little people industriously chipping away at the inside of his head. "At the time, it seemed like a good idea."

"You shouldn't have come."

"Oh, yes, I remember—I came to see you. Can't think why."

"You were very close to being shot."

"Death would be welcome. My head is about to split open. I may pass over before your very eyes."

"Hilarious." She gave him a long, searching look, sniffed. "You're drunk!"

"Wrong tense. *Was* drunk, have been drunk, will be

drunk again. At the moment, hung over. Christ, am I hung over."

"Please, I know I'm square, but don't use His name in vain."

He grimaced. "Christmas. Bah! Humbug!"

She said it with a smile. "Pagan."

"Christian," he shot back. "Hey, this is some name-calling."

"Anyway, as a Christian I can't leave you to suffer. Come along and I'll see that you get some treatment suitable to your condition."

"Whither thou goest I goest."

"Occasionally you go to excellent sources. But you may as well get it right—'Whither thou goest, I *shall* go.' Ruth said it to Naomi."

"That Ruth, a girl with a knack for turning a phrase."

Grace started up the hill, Foreman hurrying to keep up. She looked back, trying not to laugh. "For a man who looks as debauched as you do, you seem to be in pretty good shape."

"My shape's not so good. If you'll excuse me, I think I will throw up now." He ran for the trees and, once out of sight, did so. Weak and even paler than usual, he returned to where Grace was waiting. "Christmas comes but once a year, for which I'm grateful."

She continued up the hill.

"Hey, don't leave me! Remember, charity is a Christian virtue too." On unsteady legs, he went after her, caught up. But he was breathing very hard.

Four aspirins from her kit and a quart of bitter black coffee later, the little people inside Foreman's head had about completed their retreat. His nervous system stabilized and his skull, though tender, seemed intact. But there were moments when his eyes operated independently of each other; he managed to locate Grace Biondi on the far side of her one-room house.

"You still haven't told me," she said, "what suicidal impulse brought you here in the middle of the night."

"It's time you knew the whole truth," he said. "I am gripped by a black passion—"

"Be serious."

"My wheels are in a state of disrepair. I barely escaped from a band of Indians bent on savaging me. My head is mushy, very sensitive to pain, insult and abrasive noises of any kind. I happen to be exceedingly serious."

"I give up. You're a hopeless case."

"In the seventh grade, I had a teacher named Fitz-patrick. *She* was a witch. Miss Fitzpatrick was indefati-gable, never letting go when she was after a particular response from a particular student. It didn't matter that she terrified those children, that none of them had the answer in question. Miss Fitzpatrick insisted, she probed, she wheedled and coaxed, intimidated us all in a primal whine that resulted in an unpleasant clacking of the fourth and fifth vertebrae. I hated Miss Fitzpatrick in those days, I hate her retroactively. I will always hate her."

"And I remind you of Miss Fitzpatrick?"

"Only in your abnormally developed persistence. Oth-erwise you're a jewel and quite a bit prettier than Miss Fitzpatrick."

"Foreman," she said, "I've thought about you—"

"Good. And now you are witness to a man being de-molished from the inside out."

"You'll survive."

She wanted to touch him. "What do you want of me?" she asked.

"You."

"I don't think so. A man like you, you're not for me. Grief and pain go with you. Any woman who lets herself get involved with you is in trouble."

He surveyed her. "Think of it not as an involvement but a stimulating sexual adventure. I believe it was Goethe who said—'Women are silver dishes into which we put golden apples.' "

Slow pink color climbed up her tawny cheeks.

"My God!" he said "You blush!"

"Oh, keep quiet . . ."

"Not since I pressed too close to Kathy Smith at the sophomore dance in high school and was stirred to cer-tain involuntary responses, have I seen a blush."

"Finish your coffee and go back to Acapulco. What-ever you're looking for, you're more likely to find there."

"I remind you that my car is in a state of total collapse."

She went to the door and called out. A young girl appeared in the street and Grace spoke briefly to her. The girl ran off.

"Serefina will speak to Rafael," Grace explained. "Rafael is an excellent mechanic. He keeps all of the village's vehicles in running order. He'll fix your car."

"Grace Biondi, you disappoint me."

"How so?"

"Here you are devoting your life to work among the primitives, but you display no sympathy for a countryman in distress. Shame. Didn't I rush up here on my one day off to discuss your work, to explore with you the possibility of doing a documentary film on the Chinchahua? Nevertheless I am treated in cavalier fashion."

"Why should I believe you—?"

"Why would I lie?"

She considered that. "Well," she said. "Rafael is a good mechanic, but he isn't very fast. No harm is talking, I suppose," and in saying knew she didn't quite believe it, and didn't even care.

"Exactly. Tell me, what's a nice girl like you doing in a place like this?"

"Oh, you just aren't a serious man."

"Wrong! All I'm trying to do is understand you. Can one separate the doctor from his instruments?"

A vertical line appeared between her blue eyes. "What does that mean?"

"About this alphabet you're working out—couldn't it be done visually? On film, a man might say a word, a phrase, then it could be shown in animation. Broken down into individual sounds and letters . . ."

"You should hear something I've recorded," she said, going to the other side of the hut. She kneeled and rummaged through a cardboard carton. Foreman studied the matched rounds of her bottom straining under khaki trousers. Without question, her buttocks compared favorably with any he had seen during a long and not undistinguished—in that area, at least—career.

"Listen to this," she said, coming back with tape machine and cassette. "Luis is the speaker. He's very old, ninety or more. No one knows for sure." She switched

on the playback and her voice came out speaking Chinchahua. Then Luis, thin, grating, rising and falling in uneven patterns. "Listen closely," she said, "and you'll make
out certain repetitions. There—*aji*, listen for it. Depending on which vowel is stressed, also whether or not the *j*
is pronounced *je*—" she made a harsh sound in the back
of her throat. "There, Luis used it then. He is saying
came as against come or went or go. It can mean all of
those and more. One solid week before I figured that out.
It was invaluable, though, because that made other parts
of the puzzle fall into place. Chinchahua is not a varied,
colorful language like English, where so many words are
interchangeable or sound alike and have different mean-
ings . . ."

"Like to, two, and too?"

"Or their and there. Emphasis plays a larger role in
Chinchahua, pronunciation nuances that govern meaning."

"You seem to be making a great deal of progress," he
said, intrigued by the movements of her mouth.

"I've established fourteen letters, but I still can't figure
out some usages. I'm guessing that there are another six
or seven letters that correspond to some of ours. Plus
some formations that are unknown to us. That's why the
tapes—this way I can study patterns over and over and
get an oral history of the Chinchahua at the same time.
This tape—Luis is talking about a company of strange
gods that came here many years ago . . ."

"Gods?"

"Gods," she said, hitting the off button on the tape
machine. "Do you know the story of Quetzalcoatl?" Foreman rested his chin in his hands and gazed into her eyes.
"You definitely aren't a serious man," she said.

"Tell me about Quetzalcoatl."

"The beautiful bird from the south. But they also say
he came also from the east. Some tribes believe he was a
man born more than a thousand years ago who lived to
be about forty, maybe a shipwrecked sailor. Others insist
he was a missionary who walked across Mexico. Quetzalcoatl was the morning star, the god of fertility, the wind
god. He was the god of light and good and in this sense
you might say that he prepared the way for the coming
of monotheism to Mexico . . ."

"In other words, believing in him made it easier for the Spaniards to impose their religious beliefs on the Indians?"

"That's not how I'd say it, but I won't argue it. Some people think Quetzalcoatl was actually an invention of the early missionaries, who did indeed use devious means to bring the natives into the fold."

"What's the connection between Quetzalcoatl and Luis' story?"

"On the tape, Luis mentioned an ancient prophecy. The *brujos* spoke of a white-bearded Quetzalcoatl who would rise up out of the sea in the east and would be wearing a cross."

"And out of the eastern sea came old Hernán Cortés."

"Yes, and his expedition carried crosses."

"The Aztecs were a set-up for Cortés."

Grace smiled wistfully. "His arrival must have looked like the ancient prophecy come to life to Montezuma and his people. After all, one doesn't stand against a living god." She smiled again.

"I have something to say to you," Foreman said solemnly.

"Yes?"

"You should smile more often. It becomes you."

For an interval, she said nothing. "Back to Luis. On this tape he also refers to a group of pale gods that climbed out of the sea, huge creatures with red beards and white beards and shining skins."

"What do you make of that?"

"Remember, Luis is repeating a story that has passed down for generations . . ."

"With certain dramatic refinements along the way, I would guess."

"Maybe not. The oral tradition is strong and accuracy is often caught by the immediacy, even more than in writing. Father to son, old to young, generation to generation. I've matched stories and found them to be almost alike in all details, sometimes to the word."

"About those bearded gods?"

"I think Luis could be talking about the Vikings."

"On Mexico's west coast?"

"The Vikings were sea-going people. Adventurers. There are rumors of Vikings in this country long before Cortés."

"Okay. What happened to them?"

"Nobody knows."

"Not even Luis?"

"Luis mentioned a fort that the red-bearded gods erected along the waterfront. But it was washed away in a great storm."

"So much for red-bearded gods with shining skins," Foreman said.

She stood up and looked at him. "Foreman, you have the conceit of a man without convictions."

"Now what brought that on?"

"Oh, just trying to match wits. I realize I'm hopelessly outclassed. Well, Rafael will have your car fixed by now. You'll want to start back."

"My head," Foreman protested, clasping it in both hands. "I must rest . . ."

Grace led Foreman up the slope south of the village. Over one shoulder, in an expanding sisal bag, he carried their lunch.

They followed a dirt path that took them through a shallow valley, then climbed steeply until they crossed a field vibrant with yellow wild-flowers and the persistent thrum of thousands of bees at work. Grace laughed when Foreman flinched at the bees, waved him on.

"Don't bother them, they won't bother you," she said. "The Chichahua guarantee the technique."

"Do the bees underwrite the guarantee?" he answered, going after her with no enthusiasm.

Beyond the field, a wooded area, undersized pine trees standing well apart from each other as if, in unspoken agreement, each might receive its just share of sunlight and nourishment. The forest floor was a resilient cushion of fallen needles, and there was an exhilarating deep, green smell all around. A hundred feet farther on they started up again. On the rough open hillside the smells were different, the residual odor of goat a permanent stain on the mountain air.

The path climbed around rock corners, slicing between high, gray walls in which grotesquely shaped dwarf trees and wildflowers grew out of crevices. They walked without speaking, Foreman needing all his stamina to keep up with the tall girl, the muscles of his legs beginning to complain. The path widened abruptly, and Grace stopped on a ledge nearly ten feet across. Water spurted out of a rupture in the rock facing like a shining stretch of rope.

"It's very good water," Grace said, bending to drink. "The best in Mexico, according to the Chinchahua."

"They're lucky to have fresh water."

"Except that the stream runs dry before it reaches the village and it's too far for the women to come each morning. The goatherds use it, when they work the hills up above."

"If this were a Hollywood movie there'd be a rock basin here and we could go swimming."

"To the sound of a hundred violins," she added.

"And one romantic harp."

She sat down on the ledge, feet dangling over the side. "By chance is there a swimming scene in your movie?"

"Absolutely." He took his place beside her. The valley fell away far below in dusty, quiet shadows. "The actors have a ball in a heated swimming pool. Naked, of course."

"Of course."

A quick look told him nothing, except that she had a lovely profile. He leaned back on his elbows. "Do you feel it?"

"What?"

"That we're the only ones left in the world, and that no other place exists. Just this mountain, this spring, and us."

"What a frightening idea! Do you get many like it?"

Foreman decided to hell with it, and kissed her. Her lips were pliant, cool from the spring water, but passive; he put the tip of his tongue against them. She drew away.

"Another dumb idea," I guess.

"Do you have to be so defensive? You apparently think I'm a naïve child. I'm not. I'm a grown woman and I'll come around in my own time, if that's what I want to do."

He raised his hands. "Peace?"

"I haven't been making war." She removed the food from the sisal bag—milk cheese, tortillas, some oranges. She sliced off some cheese, wrapped it in a tortilla, and gave it to Foreman.

"May I ask a question about your movie?" she said.

"Fire away."

"Why naked actors?"

"It gets at the truth."

"What truth is that?"

"The truth about people. About their bodies and what they do with them."

She began to peel an orange. "I've seen some of it. But it looks to me like they're using their bodies more as, well, weapons—"

"Come on!"

". . . It made me, I admit, uncomfortable."

"Ashamed, you mean."

"Embarrassed, I'd say. For me and the other people in the theater, because in a way all of us were up on that screen too. If a person takes pride in himself, in his body, he doesn't especially want it to be a public spectacle. All that rolling around doesn't mean anything to me. It demeans sex and love, makes it the same for everybody, nothing special for anybody."

"Look, art is supposed to start with experience—"

"I agree."

"To do that a metaphor comes in dandy. Sex can serve very well as that metaphor. It's not the only one, but in the right context it's a damn useful and effective one."

"Why not *love?*"

"Who says no? And when did they take sex out of love?"

"Never, for me. But lately they seem to have taken love out of sex."

There was no good answer except to kiss her again. She made no move away and after a moment she shivered, her lips parted slightly. Foreman wondered if he was letting loose too much; himself, and her. He pulled away and concentrated on his lunch.

"You frighten me," she said softly.

"And you frighten me," he wanted to answer, but didn't.

"We don't know much about each other," she said.

He ticked it off on his fingers. "You have an Italian father, Irish mother. You're Catholic . . ."

"I prefer Christian . . ."

". . . No run-of-the-mill Sunday churchgoer and forget it type. You taught in Africa, you're startlingly beautiful and incredibly perverse."

"Why perverse? Is it because I haven't surrendered to your charms quickly enough to satisfy you?"

"Did I say that?"

"You're accustomed to speed. You travel fast in whatever direction the road happens to go."

"That's not exactly flattering to either of us."

"Where do you want to go?"

"Look, did we come up here to discuss what's wrong with Paul Foreman? You're so damned anxious to leave clothes on people, leave my psyche buttoned up too."

"I have reached a crucial conclusion," she said, soberly assessing him.

He was sure she was about to send him away. He braced himself.

"You have never known a woman exactly like me."

He let his breath out. "I concede the point."

Her blue eyes gleamed. "I've never known a man like you. That first time, in the market, and when you visited me here—you're so aggressive, so obviously sexual . . . so, damn it, attractive." He reached for her but she avoided his hands, shook her head. "I decided you were too much for me. I'm not a very experienced woman, you see. But today I began to see other qualities in you. Gentleness, sensitivity, compassion, too, I think. Why do you try so hard to hide it all?"

"What else do you think you see?"

"A very unhappy man. Also a man afraid to let anyone get too close."

"Oh, hell—" he started angrily, then broke off. He spoke again after a while. "Maybe you're right. Right now I sure as hell do feel . . . exposed."

"And it frightens you?"

He nodded.

They watched the sun fall behind the western range, shadows racing toward them like reaching fingers. The air was cooler now and Grace shivered again, hugged herself.

"I want you to know," she said quietly, "that I am not a virgin. I wouldn't want to deceive you. There was a man. I thought I loved him. It was a mistake. Not that he was a bad person, but he was too complicated, too de-

vious for me. I couldn't cope with him at that time in my
life. I was too young, I had no idea what I wanted. There
was no way I could give Arthur what he needed, and
wanted."

"How long ago was Arthur?"

"Almost three years." Then, very quietly. "There's been
no one since." She lowered her head.

He was beginning to understand. He stood up and offered his hand. "It's late and getting cold. Let's go back."
He pulled her to her feet, and they were together, mouths
fused. The good female smell of her seeped into him,
made him weak with desire, and fear.

In easy stages they went down together and his hands
traveled hesitantly over her body, less so as he went on
exploring. They spoke in throaty noises, lips never part-
ing, and when his hand discovered her bare breasts he
shifted closer, as if to insinuate himself under the warm,
lush flesh.

He wanted to strip away the clothing that kept them
apart, to lock himself inside her body, to roll with her
down the long hill. But an instinctive alarm system
alerted him to the dangers. Go easy, leave her the op-
tions. Sentiments he had never had before.

He kissed and caressed her and somehow her breasts
were exposed to the fading sunlight. Superb, slightly flattened mounds that peaked in crimson nipples, turned
slightly away from each other. He touched each one,
kissed each one. He went back to her mouth, warming
one breast with his hand.

"You're magnificent . . ."

She stared up at him. "Please, don't say anything you
don't mean . . ."

"You're beautiful, everything . . . the way you taste,
and smell . . ."

His lips closed over one nipple. Grace sighed. When he
touched her bare thigh, she shuddered, held still.

He said her name and looked at her. She had closed
her eyes and her face was neither relaxed nor strained,
more the look of time suspended.

"Tell me to stop," he said, "and I will."

Her lips moved soundlessly.

"You want this? You want me to make love to you?
Grace?"

"Yes."

With unsteady fingers, he undressed her; hurriedly removed his own clothes.

She lay still, the long late sun rays glinting off her strong, well-made body, golden hairs shining. She belonged in this high solitude, a perfect complement to the wind, the sheer cliffs, the hardy trees, and rock grass.

Foreman embraced her, head resting against her throat, breathing in the rich, full scent of her. They lay still for a long time.

"Have you changed your mind?" she said finally.

"I want you to be ready, sure."

"Please," she said. "Oh, please, please . . ."

He arranged his mouth on hers and she clung fiercely to him, he swelled again against the heat of her bare stomach. His movements were deliberate, controlled so as not to shock or frighten her.

It was not easy. And strangely that pleased him. Her flesh gave way reluctantly to the intrusion and there were still some restraints. Finally there was pain and with it a jubilant eruption and a wild, free sound broke out of her. He was transformed into something dark and melting and went tumbling into the sweet, golden depths of Grace Biondi . . .

Not speaking or touching, they went back down the mountain, through the village, past the rows of adobe huts from which the smoke of cooking fires drifted. Foreman reached for her hand but she held back.

"The Chinchahua," she explained sheepishly, "are very proper. Men and women don't touch each other in public."

"Suppose they knew what we've been doing—?"

She rolled her eyes in mock despair. "They'd stone me as a *puta*."

"You're putting me on."

"Not much. At the very least, they'd insist that I leave."

"The primitive mind at work. Apparently it's no different here than in the States."

Before she could answer, a squat, bowlegged man appeared out of the darkness, speaking in Spanish too swift for Foreman to understand. His message delivered, he moved away, shaking his head and laughing.

"That was Rafael," Grace said. "Your car is ready to go."

"Rafael inspires little confidence in his mechanical ability."

"Oh," she said, a slight edge to her voice. "Rafael said you ran out of gas."

Foreman swore.

"Rafael put in enough to get you back to Acapulco."

Foreman stopped walking, took Grace's hand. "Come back with me."

"To Acapulco? I can't. There's my work—"

"To hell with that," he said. "Stay with me until the picture is finished. Another week—"

"I couldn't do that."

"You don't want to."

"I mean that I wouldn't feel right *living* with you. Try to understand how I feel."

"Maybe you wish we hadn't made love."

"I'm not a specialist in guilts, but I have my doubts. Don't you?"

"You really are a live one!"

"I'm sorry you're angry. I'm not angry with you."

"Dammit, do you expect me to keep hauling ass up this lousy mountain every day, getting my face shoved in the dirt by a bunch of savages? What about *my* work?" He kicked at a pebble and missed. "Ah, shit! To tell you the truth, having a rifle pointed at me spoils my disposition."

She tried not to smile. "Your disposition certainly can stand some improving."

"Very funny. You could make a list of things you don't like about me. My disposition, my morals, the way I look, maybe the way I make love . . ."

"Stop it."

"Another thing, my name is Paul. You never say it. Not even up there. Say it, say my name. Paul. Say it, dammit."

"Paul."

"Oh, Jesus," he said. "Come with me, will you? I don't know why I want you to, but I do. Is that crazy? It must be. Come for a couple of days. Until my nerves calm down and I can work out some way to get back up here again."

"I won't go with you, but I'll be here when you come, Paul."

"They win again. The Popes. A line of cats who never knew what it was to feel the clutch of a woman's thighs. They didn't understand *anything*."

"Come soon, Paul. Please."

He took a couple of long strides toward the VW. "Just remember, on those lonely nights when you're cutting up with your diphthongs and glottal stops, you think about me. Turn off that damned tape recorder for ten seconds and think of me."

She watched him go down the hill toward the car, his shoulders high and tight, his head forward, all very manly. And strong, and all very much into his private misery. She wanted to go after him. But she didn't think she could. Not yet . . .

12

It was nearly three in the afternoon when Samantha opened her eyes. She at once felt sorry for herself. Sleep had failed to bring her to a state of well-being and a vague craving stirred uneasy rhythms in her.

She rolled onto her back and began to breathe deeply. She tensed every muscle in her body, staring at the ceiling, allowing no thought to enter her mind, charging her spirit for the day ahead. She exhaled very slowly. The exercise was designed to increase circulation and at the same time firm up her flesh; she was convinced also that it energized the brain tissue. Or so the masseuse at Dr. Koenig's clinic had told her. This daily ritual completed, she touched the signal button on the night table, went into the bathroom.

She showered, hot and cold, dried herself briskly before slipping into a long, pink robe with white lace ruffles at throat and wrists. On the patio, she seated herself at the round table topped with mottled, gray Italian marble, turned her face to the afternoon sun. Christmas in Acapulco was a disturbing time; even after all these years, she associated Christmas with snow, warm clothes, the exchange of gifts. Here, among her friends, the day had almost no impact.

"*Buenas tardes, señorita.*" It was Trini carrying a breakfast tray.

"*Buenas tardes,* Trini."

The girl placed a bowl of fresh sliced fruit in front of Samantha, a pot of coffee, an assortment of vitamin and iron pills.

"*Gracias,* Trini."

"*De nada, señorita.*"

"*Oh, Trini, el teléfono, por favor.*"

The maid brought a gold-trimmed French phone from

inside the bedroom, the white cord trailing behind.

Alone, Samantha chewed carefully on small sections of papaya and watermelon and orange slices, her thoughts ranging afield. So much was happening, so much that was good. Substantial rewards were possible, in so many different ways; she would let nothing stand in the way.

Last night's party. What a great success it was! One could judge such things almost intuitively. The sound of the guests, the expressions on their faces, the bright tone of the evening. The party would be a conversation piece for weeks to come. Samantha Moore would be envied and admired, invited everywhere.

The party had been more than just a social achievement. The evening had crystalized much for Samantha, had opened up new and exciting possibilities to insure her future.

Theo Gavin. Less than ten feet from where she was sitting, they had stood. Kissing, hands exploring like a pair of over-sexed adolescents. Men were such fools, especially American men. Especially American businessmen. It was conceit that betrayed them, as if success in business insured some special wisdom about the rest of human behavior. Such self-deception would make Theo Gavin an easy mark for a brainy woman of experience and ambition.

How typically American of him to allow her to establish the sexual pace of their relationship, to settle for a crumb when she had no choice but to provide the entire loaf, had he so demanded. No Mexican would have so settled, no European. Except possibly a German, Germans being what they were.

Poor Theo. All that misguided aggressiveness, the wasted strength, the misplaced manhood. What confidence he displayed when he was unsure, frightened.

She understood that he craved her for reasons locked in the subterranean parts of his character. What a simple and obvious man he was, how easy he would be to deal with, to manipulate and deceive. A tiny laugh broke out of her. What a surprise it would be if he knew how much she wanted and needed what he was going to provide. But that was something he would never learn. She was the bait and Theo the hungry fish . . . But this time the bait would swallow the fish . . .

She tried to recall the touch of his hands against her skin. Odd that she should find such a handsome and carefully kept man dimly repellent.

She warned herself not to be overconfident, to take too much for granted. Anyone as successful as Theo Gavin would also be clever, perhaps ruthless. She would have to use his strength against him, make him work for what he wanted, force him to wear himself out, to be grateful for her small favors.

Still, the deep craving. It traveled along the nerve ends. Her mouth became parched and her flesh felt thin and taut on her bones. She tried very hard to turn her mind to other things; failing, she picked up the phone and dialed.

Marcella almost laughed aloud when she learned the purpose of Samantha's call. The request was so familiar to her own way of life. She agreed at once to make the necessary arrangements . . .

His name was Julio. He had angular features and his hair was thick and curly, worn long. His eyes were truly black, neither afraid nor hostile. His white shirt was open at the throat and he wore gray trousers that Samantha thought were vulgarly tight. But then, he was recently off the *campo* . . .

He stood in front of Samantha and waited for her to speak. She sat on the deep couch in the study off the main foyer of Villa Gloria and assessed him. Marcella had called him exquisite. He was. His shoulders were powerful without being offensively thick, his brown arms were sinewy and well shaped, and he held himself with easy confidence.

He had greeted her politely, without a suggestion of obsequiousness in voice or manner. And now he waited, which was only proper, for her to tell him what to do.

She smiled at him. "The Señorita Marcella says you are a teacher of scuba diving, Julio," she said in precise Spanish.

"*Sí, señora.*"

"*Señorita,*" she corrected. "No more a *señora*. You are very young, Julio."

"Seventeen years, *señorita*."

"You live with your family?"

"No, *señorita*. They are back in the mountains. I share a room with Agustín, my cousin."

"How friendly," she commented. "Would you like a drink, Julio. A rum and Coca-Cola, perhaps?"

"I do not drink, *señorita*."

"The swimming and diving?"

"*Sí, señorita*."

"A *refresco*, then?"

"No, thank you."

She looked across the broad chest, down to where the pants bulged, back to his face. "You appear to be in fine condition, Julio."

"Thank you, *señorita*."

"For how long can you remain underwater?"

"For many minutes, I think."

"Take a deep breath for me, Julio."

He did. The white shirt expanded, the buttons straining his belly sucked in.

She sighed and placed her hand at the base of her throat. "Lovely. What a fine swimmer you must be."

"It is my trade," he said.

Among other talents, she thought. She got up slowly. "Look at me, Julio."

He did.

"What do you think?"

"*Señorita?*"

"Do you find me attractive?"

"The *señorita* is beautiful."

She inspected his boyish face, on a level with her own. She touched his cheek, smooth and cool. Her hand dropped to his shoulder. Rock-hard. "Julio, you are not afraid of a woman like me?"

He seemed to strut in place. "I am afraid of no one."

"*Muy macho*," she said softly.

He remained impassive.

She removed her hand. "You're not here to talk. Come along, to where we can be private and comfortable." At the head of the stairs, she turned back. "By the way, Julio—did Señorita Marcella discuss money?"

He met her eyes. "Agustín spoke to me about money, *señorita*. He said that you were very rich but I was not to take advantage of you. Whatever price you think is correct, *señorita.*"

"Of course."

In the bedroom, she faced him. "Shut the door and lock it." He obeyed. "Now take off your clothes." He began to undress. She watched closely, enjoying the play of muscle beneath the satiny skin as he bent and twisted. When he was naked, he straightened up.

"Seventeen years old," she murmured. "Walk for me, Julio. Across the room and back again. I want to watch."

He padded across the carpet without self-consciousness, returning at a deliberate pace. She motioned for him to repeat the short journey and while he did she took off her clothes.

"Look at me," she ordered.

He paused and looked.

"Does my body please you, Julio?"

"*Sí, señorita.*"

"There are many young girls in Acapulco—"

"*Sí*. But none so beautiful as the *señorita.*"

It was a lie, of course, but a perfectly acceptable one. To expect the truth in these circumstances would have been self-deceiving, a luxury Samantha did not permit herself. "Tell me about your girl friend, Julio."

He hesitated. "There is one . . ."

"A Mexican girl?"

The suggestion startled him. "*Señorita,* no! A foreigner, from Canada."

"And you make love to her regularly?"

"When there is time. My work—"

She silenced him with a raised hand. "What preferences do you have, Julio? Do you like any one way with a woman better than any other?"

He considered the question. "*Señorita,*" he said gravely, "I am at your service."

Samantha sat on the edge of the bed, eyes fixed on his fat brown member, relaxed now. She made a small gesture and he moved casually forward. She cradled the limp flesh in the palm of her hand, enjoying the contrast of skin colors. She kissed him, watched him begin to respond. She kissed him again.

"Ah," she said. "The dear thing is coming to life."

"*Señorita?*"

"Shut up, dammit. Just stand there. Do what you're paid to do but don't talk to me . . ." Her head came forward, taking as much of him as she was able, fingers digging into his hard buttocks, pleasure and need sounding back in her throat . . .

Theo Gavin was not a man to waste time. He placed both long-distance calls at once; and while he waited, he studied the new projection. There was a handful of minor faults—tests to be made, production schedules altered, budgets adjusted—and each of them was correctable; his enthusiasm stayed high.

The phone rang. The call to Julia had come through first. Too bad, he'd have preferred the other; but he was prepared to deal with her. He greeted her politely, asked about her health. She ignored the question.

"What's wrong?" she demanded.

The bitter, angry sound reminded Theo he was well rid of her. Still, no matter how much he disliked her, he confessed to a certain lingering attraction, at least some pleasant memories.

"It's about Chuck," he said, trying to be kind.

"What did you do to him?"

Always the accusation. From the start of their marriage, it had been that way. But they were no longer married—how poorly Julia compared with Samantha!—and he had no intention of being bullied by her.

"I did nothing, Julia. With a boy like Chuck, there's no chance to do anything."

"What are you talking about?"

He told her that their son had run away.

She screamed at him over the long-distance wire. "I give the boy to you for a few weeks and you lose him in a strange country."

"I didn't lose him. Try to understand, he ran away. He did the same in New York."

"Absolutely no similarity. Mexico is not New York. Here he's among his own kind, people he understands, places he knows. What if he's sick with no one to help him? Theo, if anything happens to Charles I will hold you personally responsible."

Theo forced himself to speak in a relaxed tone. "Nothing's going to happen to the boy. And blaming me won't help the situation. Keep your head, Julia. I want you to know that I did my best for Chuck. I took him swimming, spent my evenings with him, introduced him around, But Chuck is simply unreachable . . ."

"What have you done to find him?"

"Everything that can be done is being done," he told her. "The American embassy has been alerted, they have certain procedures in these matters. And the police. Also, the English-language newspaper is running a notice for me. I've also placed a large advertisement. These things take time—"

"That's not good enough. Hire some private detectives. Two, three, a whole agency if necessary. Find Charles, Theo; send him back so I can take care of him."

"You've certainly been a marvel at it so far."

"You bastard," she said. "Maybe if Charles had had a real father, and I'd had a real man—"

"Julia . . ."

"Notify me the minute you hear anything. Theo. And hire those detectives. For once, do something *right*." She hung up.

Julia, he thought, looking at the dead instrument in his hand. Thank God for a woman like Samantha. Style, breeding, an appreciation for a man's accomplishments. What a pleasure it was going to be—

The phone rang again. It was Jerry Baumer, calling from Los Angeles. The advertising executive came on with his usual blast of energy. "How's Mexico treating you, Mr. G.? Would've gotten back to you sooner, but—"

"Let's talk business, Jerry. First Samantha Moore."

"A beautiful concept. And switching the line to cosmetics for men, just beautiful."

"That's all changed, Baumer."

"You're not going to use Moore after all? Well, I must tell you I've had reservations from the start. I'm drafting a detailed memo which—"

"Baumer, be quiet and listen. We're going back to the original idea. The women's line and that's final. And Samantha Moore is a definite, an integral part of the team. I called to give you the keynote for the entire campaign . . ."

"Mr. G., I'm waiting."

"The new name for the line—SAMANTHA! Nothing else. Just that name with an exclamation point. How does that grab you?" There was silence on the wire. "Dammit," Theo said, "I've been cut off."

"Mr. G.," Baumer said. "Superb. *Superb*. The way you cut through to the heart of the matter—SAMANTHA! A real money label. How . . . how great!"

"You like the idea?"

"I *love* it, Mr. G. Absolutely love it. Every time Samantha is on TV or does an interview, the product will be plugged automatically. Her name *is* the plug."

"That thought occurred to me," Theo said.

"Of course," Baumer said, unflagging. "Samantha is SAMANTHA! What a great copy line! Let me make a note . . ."

"Build the campaign around the name, Baumer. Begin today. I want both coasts at work on it. Ads, publicity, a tour for Miss Moore. Get her on Johnny Carson, for sure."

"Johnny runs a tough operation. But I tell you this, if Samantha doesn't make Johnny Carson I'll return my fee to you." He laughed heartily. "And everybody knows it's against my religion to give back money."

"Maybe I'll hold you to that. Get on it right away. When the contracts are signed, I'll give you the word and then we go."

"Go is the word, Mr. G.!"

Theo hung up without saying goodbye, and congratulated himself. SAMANTHA! What a fantastic name for a line of cosmetics! It had an important sound, looked right, expensive and sophisticated. This was Big Casino. No more short-term highs and quick let downs. People thought Theo was rich, that all his enterprises were solid gold; all front. Oh, he managed to keep himself in Cuban cigars and handmade Italian shoes at a hundred twenty-five dollars a pair, but he wasn't rich. Not the way he needed to be.

Front was important, he reminded himself. The ability to make people believe you were doing better than you were. Take Samantha. If she should find out he was operating this close to the line, the whole deal might collapse.

But she didn't know the truth, would never find it out. Not as long as Theo Gavin kept the balls in the air and his feet on the ground. Just hang in there, he told himself. Keep punching and you've got to make it. This time, definitely. No doubt about it. None at all.

"There's something about the ocean, it sort of draws me to it," Shelly said.

Next to her, Morrie looked out at the water. They walked along the beach, paying no attention to the other people. It was night and the stars lit the beach and the water with a diffused glow that washed away everything unpleasant.

"Old salts, sailors, and fishermen—they're with you, they keep going back to it—"

She stopped, staring ahead. "That man, I think I know him." At the surf line, a tall, bearded man, staring out at the bay, body hunched as if poised to strike. "Can we go back, please, Morrie?"

"Whatever you want. I'll take you to your hotel."

"Oh, no! she said, her voice going small "Can we go to your room?"

"My pleasure."

Halfway back, he asked her about the man on the beach.

She hesitated. "His name is Leo. He's some kind of a hippie, I guess. But I always thought of hippies as kind people, loving. Leo isn't. Foreman met him somewhere and he took us to a place in *La Zona* one night, El Tiburón."

"I know it. Your friend Leo was probably shilling for the joint. Steering people there and collecting a percentage of the take."

"I didn't like being there. And seeing Leo just now made all the old bad feelings come back."

He put his arm around her and they made the rest of the walk without speaking. Back in his room, he offered her a drink. She refused.

"Please," she said. "Please, can we go to bed, Morrie? I want to be close to you with nothing separating us. All right?"

He kissed her hand. "Nothing could be more all right."

They undressed and got into bed from opposite sides, bodies reaching, fitting easily together. After a while, she began to tremble.

"Easy," he murmured. "Nothing can hurt you here. My God, you've made me feel like a man. Nobody else ever did that for me."

"Oh, Morrie, believe me, you're a man, all right."

"Were you thinking of that guy on the beach again? Is that why you shivered?"

"No. I was remembering that New Year's is only a week away."

"Nothing's going to happen to you."

"I know," she said, "but the feeling keeps coming back."

"New Year's Eve will come and go and so will your damn feeling. Forget about it."

"You're right."

He kissed her on the mouth, and a moment later she responded. And in the delicious release of their new-found expertise, the cold fear of New Year's melted away to nothingness . . .

Charles sat with his elbows on his knees, head in his hands, the ruck-sack on the ground between his feet. The morning sun had just begun to touch the tops of the tall trees that lined the *zócalo*. Beyond the bandstand, a man swept the walks with a huge palm leaf, in a wide swinging motion. Otherwise the plaza was empty and still.

Next to Charles on the bench, Becky hugged herself under her poncho. Her pretty face was drawn and weary, the eyes veiled, her mouth a disapproving line. To Charles, this silent interval was like the opening scene of a well-rehearsed play in which he had performed before. He seemed to know all the parts, all the lines; only the setting was different.

"I don't get you. I really don't," Becky said. "You come all this way, then split so soon. It makes no sense. What are you running away from?"

"I don't know," Charles said. "I'm not so sure I'm running. I think it's more like I'm just moving on."

"Happy says you're chickening out."

"On what?"

"On yourself, on us. What scared you, Charles? The mushroom trip, was it so bad for you?"

"Bad and good at the same time," he said. "Mostly good, at least that's what I think about it now. Once during the trip I had hold of something really true and important—at least for me." He snapped his fingers. "Then suddenly it left me. Flew away like a big old bird, gone. I wanted it back very much and when I couldn't find it, I went way down."

"You think you'll find it back *there?*"

"Maybe."

"Back there, that's all bullshit."

"A lot of it is, I know it."

"Then stay with us. With me. Oaxaca is a groove. The weather, the kids. In a little while we'll put together bread enough for another try at the mushrooms—"

"I don't think I can, Becky."

"I wish I knew where your head is."

Charles grinned. "Me too."

"Happy says you're strung out on your father. I said you're not. Now I'm not so sure."

"Maybe Happy's right."

"But that scene won't ever work for you."

"And this one . . . ?"

"Oh, come on!"

"No, seriously, Becky. Are our lives so much better? We're pretty messed up, you know . . ."

"We're not in *that* mess, *their* mess."

"Then into what? A bunch of heads scratching for bread so we can turn on. They drink, we burn pot. They screw each other's wives, we screw each other—"

"Wow, are you wrong! We *love* each other, free and like friends. We don't need a guy with a collar or a piece of paper for a house in Dumbdale to make it person to person."

"You bet. And how do you explain that Livy cries when she makes it and you can't look at me the morning after. We roll from blanket to blanket telling ourselves that we've invented a new way, when mostly it turns out to be another bummer."

Charles stood, heaved up his rucksack, shook his head. "It's better if I go."

"You're blowin' a good thing," Becky said.

Charles shrugged. "Maybe so. But I've got to find out for myself. Stay loose, Becky."

"You too, luv."

Charles waved goodbye and moved off, leaving Becky alone on the bench. Once he looked back, and was struck at how small she looked, as though he was already seeing her from a great distance.

13

Foreman worked the company long hours during the next two days, filming day and night in, for him, a highly organized fashion that should have satisfied Harry Bristol, but didn't. He complained frequently that Foreman was moving too deliberately, exposing too much film, taking too much time to set up his camera.

"Goddammit!" Bristol said when Foreman spent one entire morning scouting for new locations, "you're running a whole week late. The backer's screaming bloody murder. If this thing isn't completed, he won't spring for any extra dough and I'll be left with an unfinished movie and egg on my face."

Who'd know the difference? he thought, and said, "I'm doing my best for you, Harry. Different backgrounds will lend more color and visual excitement to the story. Working with a limited number of characters, it's important to keep the picture from getting static."

"As long as you wind it up in time," Bristol said, anger draining out of the battered face. Foreman understood that the producer had not surrendered, had only stepped back to survey the terrain before launching another attack. "Okay," he went on, the puffy eyes deceptively calm and watchful, "fill me in."

Foreman spoke with professional detachment. "After the big argument between Shelley and Sawyer, she goes off alone, into the hills behind Acapulco. Up there it's starkly beautiful and her softness will contrast nicely with the rugged cliffs. Very upset by what's happened, she speeds along a bad road, trying to release. What she doesn't know is that Sawyer is coming after her. We'll cut back and forth to work in tempo and mood with the action, use a split screen."

Bristol admitted he liked it.

"Every picture ought to have a chase. Keeps things moving. But I hear it can be dangerous up in those hills. The mountain people are some kind of tough hillbilly types—"

Foreman closed out Bristol's voice, thinking about his last meeting with the Chinchahua; he could almost feel that rifle against his face.

"We'll keep to safe areas," he assured Bristol, but was pleased he'd shaken him a little.

"What's this going to do to my budget?"

Foreman ignored the question. "When Sawyer gets Shelly, she'll already have had the accident. She'll be un-hurt but shaken, frightened. Then a big reconciliation scene—"

"Can they go at each other again right there in the car? Or maybe in the middle of the road? Hey, I once made it with a school teacher on a road in Florida. She was worried about snakes and wouldn't go in the bushes. Maybe you can use that—"

Foreman started back toward the camera, Bristol hur-rying to catch up. "One more thing, this flick has gotta be done by the end of the month. We're into the overcall now and my man in New York says no more dough. Do this right for me, Foreman, and you'll have it made. There'll be other pictures at better dough. You'll be home free." He took Foreman's arm, swung him around, voice low and grating. "I'll tell you again, if that rough cut isn't delivered by the second of January, New York takes possession. It's in the contract. I'll be outside with holes in my shoes, and you'll be there with me."

Foreman freed his arm. "That's how I began Harry."

That afternoon, Foreman announced the change in sched-ule. "Day after tomorrow, we assemble in front of the Hilton at seven A.M. One full day of shooting in the moun-tains, meals and purified water for all. Trucks will carry the equipment and there'll be buses for the cast and crew. Any questions?"

Samantha stepped forward. "Will it be all right if I use

my own car, Paul? At that ungodly hour, I don't think I could tolerate a bus ride."

"As long as you're there when I need you."

That night, Foreman, Bristol, and Gary McClintock gathered in the producer's suite to block out the rest of the week's shooting. They went over Foreman's scenario, scheduling the remaining scenes to get a maximum amount of usable footage at minimum expense.

"I've made a change in the reconciliation scene," Foreman said.

"What for?" Bristol said.

"So that the lead-in can happen on the mountain," Foreman said. "A slow dissolve will take us back to the beach immediately afterward. It will save nearly four hours of work."

"Well. That's more like it."

"After tomorrow, all the secondary people can be released. I'll still need Samantha for a couple of inserts. Otherwise, just Jim and Shelly. The last day will be all Shelly. I've worked out a dream sequence—Gary, I'll want the camera to move in very close, getting behind her eyes. Then, a fantasy in which she *sees* herself diving off those high cliffs . . ."

"Simple to do," McClintock said. "There's stock footage on the divers. The lab can do the rest."

"No good. I want Shelly appearing out of the landscape, folding out of a stony background from a fetal position, nude—"

"You're getting to me now!" Bristol said.

"Day or night?" McClintock wanted to know.

"Day. No sound necessary."

McClintock tugged at his nose. "A single take should do it."

"You never told me how you're going to end the picture," Bristol said.

"Something like this," Foreman said. "Shelly goes into a long, slow dive *in her fantasy*. The audience watches. Then a fast zoom in and we see her naked body spread-eagled on the rocks below, the sea splashing up around her. The camera freezes, impaling Shelly on the lens like a dead butterfly. Slowly it lifts, pans across the bay following the graceful swing of a parachutist over the water—"

"Sounds okay," Bristol said, "providing you just get it done on time . . ."

Samantha signed each of the six copies of the contract in the flowing, self-conscious script that had won penmanship prizes in high school. Next, Theo signed them in a carefully produced scrawl. He handed them on to Bernard who placed them on the tile-topped table in front of Marcella, indicating where she was to put her signature as witness.

"There!" Bernard exclaimed. "It is done! I offer congratulations."

The maid brought champagne and Bernard poured. "To a long and profitable relationship!" he toasted.

Theo smiled at Samantha. "I drink gladly to that."

She sipped her champagne, eyes lowered.

"This is excellent champagne," Marcella said.

"Twenty-five dollars U.S. per bottle," Theo announced. "Part of my stock in trade. My style . . ."

Bernard swirled the champagne in his glass. "There is a certain *je ne sais quoi* about American businessmen which I find uniquely attractive. A Frenchman in this situation would be concerned with culture and beauty. A Japanese might bob and nod and find it impossible to be negative about anything. A German—well, what can you say about Germans—he would organize the celebration and issue orders."

"And an American?" Samantha said delicately.

"Je ne sais quoi," Theo said, amused at his own flat, Yankee pronunciation.

"Exactly," Bernard said.

"I understand you have a son," Marcella said, making conversation.

Theo smiled his paternal sad smile. "I'm afraid we have very little going, as his generation would say. You know kids these days, looking for the end of the rainbow without knowing or even caring that it's only an illusion."

Oh my God, Marcella thought, and immediately applauded. "Very well put."

"Pragmatic," Bernard murmured almost to himself. "That is the word for the American businessman."

"Theo is pragmatic," Samantha said. "That's one of the qualities I so appreciate in him. So many men one meets are either idlers or frauds. What a relief to be associated with a man who knows what he wants and goes after it to make sure it works."

Theo looked into one face after another. "Well. That is nice of you to say, Samantha. I appreciate that. Now's as good a time as any, I guess. There are a couple more surprises to come."

"I just love surprises!" Marcella said.

"Surprises," Bernard said balefully. He placed his fingers to his mouth.

Theo cleared his throat. "To begin. I've given considerable thought to what's wrong with the cosmetics business as a business. My conclusion—the time has come to present the women of the world with a superior product, a product that not only promises her a more rewarding beauty in the future but brings her very practical immediate benefits."

"A splendid notion," Bernard said tonelessly.

Theo appraised him coldly.

"I'm afraid I don't quite follow, Mr. Gavin," Marcella said. "Isn't that exactly what the industry does now?"

"Call me Theo, Marcella."

"Theo."

He smiled at Samantha. "I ask you, what does the average woman look like at night when she gets into the marriage bed? A grease-smeared mess, with curlers or pins in her hair. An animated cadaver risen from her grave."

"What eloquence!" Bernard said, drinking more champagne. "What imagery!"

Theo nodded. "What does all this do for the love life of the average couple? No man can work up much of an interest in that creature next to him. What does he do? He puts his back to her, goes to sleep."

"And has an affair with his secretary," Bernard added.

"How sordid," Samantha commented.

"Something should be done," Marcella said. "I've always thought so."

"Something must be done at once," Bernard said. He helped himself to more champagne.

"In my travels," Samantha said, "I shall recommend perfume to all women before bedtime. The American marital bed must be put back in use."

"Bravo!" Bernard called.

Marcella smiled sweetly in Theo's direction. "I'll wager you have a fantastic solution up your sleeve."

"Yes, I think I do. The time has come to allow the ladies their bedtime skin bracer but to keep them smelling luscious and seductive."

"Luscious and seductive," Bernard murmured.

"But natural," Theo added.

"How?"

"Yes, how?"

"Natural is the key word. That means new scents, an entirely new cosmetic chemistry. Peaches, strawberries, fresh lemon . . ."

"Stupendous!" Marcella said.

"Innovative!" Samantha said.

"Is it pragmatic?" Bernard wanted to know.

"You better believe it," Theo said. "And there is a guaranteed fortune in the idea. I can feel it. Think of it, an entire line—creams, lotions, deodorants, perfumes, soaps, all made out of natural products. *Organic cosmetics!"*

"An idea whose time has come," Bernard spoke to his glass.

"Exactly," Theo said. "Fruits, flowers, no additives. No more than will be necessary, anyway. I've put my chemists at work. They've already come up with a special formula that will improve the complexion of every woman everywhere."

"That's unbelievable," Marcella breathed.

"Can you tell us?" Samantha said, leaning forward.

"Your secret shall stay in this room," Bernard declared cheerfully.

Theo spoke in a low, strong voice. "A rare Indian tea combined with the juice of rose leaves. Apply it at night as liberally as you want and it stays invisible, yet smells like some exotic Oriental garden."

"Astounding!"

"Brilliant!"

"Indeed," Bernard said, brain functioning sluggishly, straining to isolate a single elusive idea that refused to hold still long enough for him to examine it. He grew annoyed with himself for drinking too much champagne.

"We go into production right after New Year's. I know it will be a big seller."

"How exciting!"

"I'm not stopping there. There will be an entire catalogue of other preparations. I've ordered a mouthwash developed and toothpaste—"

"My admiration for you, Theo," Samantha said, touching his hand lightly, briefly, "increases the more I listen to you."

"And there's more to come, my dear. I've put my agents to work scouting up a proper location in New York for a beauty salon. It must be on Fifth Avenue, of course. I intend it to be the most unique, and expensive, salon in the U.S.A."

"Why not the world?" Bernard interrupted.

"Bernard's right. The most expensive salon in the world, and therefore the most exclusive. The salon will use only my products, of course, and we'll draw a famous clientele who, by their presence, and at no cost, will implicitly endorse the cosmetic line. And—" he paused for effect, "—once the operation is self-sufficient, I intend to franchise the name. There's a fortune to be made in franchises, you know."

"Superb!"

"Extraordinary!"

Bernard caught sight of the idea he was after and pounced on it, examined it through the glittering champagne mist and liked what he saw. "Is there any stock still available in the company, Theo?"

If Theo heard, he gave no sign. Again he examined each of the faces in the room, as if putting them to a private test. "And so," he said deliberately, "I come to the final item on today's agenda."

Marcella shifted forward in her chair. All this talk of business and profits stimulated her. And there was Gavin himself; she had underestimated him, made him out to be just another fatuous American businessman, shallow and dull. How wrong she had been! He was attractive and imaginative, and so *masculine* . . . a rough diamond, as Samantha had said, but, indeed, a diamond, and one whose market value was likely to increase dramatically. And soon.

Theo stood up, all eyes on him. His rugged face serious.

"Are you ready for this?" He paused, eyes fixed on Samantha. "The entire line, every last product, is going to have a very special name, a name that everyone will know and recognize, remember. That name is—SAMANTHA!"

For an extended silent interval, there was only the uneven sound of Bernard's breathing.

"Oh, Theo," Samantha sighed.

"Brilliant," Marcella said. "Brilliant, absolutely brilliant."

"Ah," Bernard said, struggling mightily to clear away the champagne mist.

"SAMANTHA!" Theo said again. "All in capital letters. With an exclamation point. It will make you world-famous, Samantha."

"Samantha is world-famous," Bernard said. His brain was clearing rapidly.

"Of course," Theo said, with a perfunctory nod.

Samantha manufactured a modest smile.

"There's one small matter," Bernard said. "A minor problem, but a problem nonetheless."

Theo felt the muscles across his middle tighten. "What problem, Bernard?"

Samantha lifted her brows.

Marcella grew watchful.

Bernard's pudgy face remained innocent. "The contract we signed doesn't address itself to the commercial use of Samantha's very own name. That strikes me as being somewhat inequitable. I suggest that an adjustment is in order." Bernard leaned back, fingers intertwined, pleased with himself.

"I'll tell you, Bernard," Theo said, voice reaching out as if to bridge an immense gap. "Don't push me. That could be a mistake."

"A small percentage of the profits is all I had in mind," Bernard said quickly, realizing that Theo was all business behind the occasional buffoon. "A flat fee for the use of the name and a certain amount for each item sold . . ."

Theo put his hands flat on the table. "The deal is made. There'll be no more talk of percentages and profit-sharing. None." Theo breathed in deeply and looked at Samantha. Then softened his tone. "In a year or two, when we have an accurate picture of the situation—"

"I'm sure Theo is right, Bernard," Samantha said quick-

ly, anxious to dissipate Theo's anger before it set in place.
The deal was a good one and she intended to improve it
considerably in the not too distant future, by marrying
Theo Gavin. But that was a private matter, of no concern
to Bernard. "Let me tell you all about my good news!"
she said.

"Oh, yes," Marcella said.

"Paul Foreman has put me into another scene in his
movie. Day after tomorrow we're going up into the Sierras
at some ungodly early hour to film it. It's even possible
my reputation as a film actress may be resurrected indeed,
refurbished, before this is over. Anyway, it should be great
fun."

"Those mountains can be dangerous," Theo grumbled.
"Maybe I'll go along, to protect my interests, business and
personal . . ." He smiled.

"Dear Theo, what a romantic you are!"

Bristol picked up the phone and recognized Louise Peters's
voice at once. He imagined her as she had been at Samantha Moore's Christmas party. Walking sex. No crap.
Right on the line . . .

"Are you surprised, my calling this way?" Louise said
coquettishly. "We've been thinking about you, Jason and
I."

Jason Peters, Bristol remembered, was one of those
slight, effete-looking men you often saw along Madison
Avenue. He hardly figured to be man enough for Louise
Peters and this call was clearly a signal of that fact.

Bristol grinned into the phone. "I've been thinking
about you. *Just* you."

"How sweet of you to say so. I was afraid you'd forgotten us."

"I remember . . ." Bristol hesitated—Shelly was in the
shower and couldn't hear. "I remember the top you wore."
He made himself laugh with throaty pleasure. *"Almost*
wore."

She giggled. "Why, Harry, you are a dirty old man."

"I keep trying."

"How nice! I'm glad to discover that there is at least
one real man left."

"If you have any doubts—"

She broke in swiftly. "Tell me about Shelly. What a beautiful woman she is."

Bristol swore silently. For a moment, things had appeared to be going his way. Why bring Shelly into this? "She's okay," he said gruffly.

"Jason was very impressed with her. He insists that she's the most attractive, most sensual woman he's seen in many a moon. I agree with him."

"Yeah." Bristol began to get bored.

"You're a fortunate man, to have a friend like Shelly."

"I suppose so," he said.

"We want very much to see you and Shelly," Louise said, voice growing intimate. "Won't you come to a small dinner party. You and Shelly. The four of us, it will be so much fun, so interesting. There's so much we don't know about you, Harry, and about Shelly."

He almost refused the invitation, decided against it. "When?" he said bluntly.

"Thursday at eight. Suite 2014 at El Camino. We'll have a ball—"

For more than an hour after leaving Becky, Charles stood on the Puebla road watching the cars flash past. Drivers eyed him with distrust and increased their speed. Or made the peace sign as they went by. Or ignored him altogether. He sat down on his rucksack and pretended indifference; that failed to work.

"Nobody loves me!" he howled to the high, blue sky, and laughed at himself. He stood up, lifted the rucksack to his shoulders, began to walk. Perhaps a display of purpose and energy would evoke a sympathetic response from some motorist.

He thought of Becky and of Julia, Theo. They were so much alike in their need to stake some claim to being special, with better answers. Yet sameness was what he was finding out in people. He was looking for the real difference that could bring a new kind of life, but was he after something that didn't exist? Never had?

He breathed in the warm, still air. Even without an-

swers, life would be pretty good if you didn't sweat it.
And the answers might still come.

He walked faster, only now noticing the car rolling silently behind him. It drew up alongside.

Fuzz. Mexican fuzz out of Zapata by Villa with certain
additions from Diego Rivera.

Charles produced his smile of innocence—practiced for
just such occasions. He lifted both hands in a gesture
meant to welcome their presence, make clear he was unarmed, unaggressive, and intended no harm to the native
population.

"Buenas días," he said, calling forth all of his very
limited Spanish. *"Viva la revolución: Viva Echeverría!
Voy a Puebla,"* he ended, pointing to himself.

The two faces in the car seemed unimpressed. The
prowl car stopped. The two men climbed out with that
bored and muscular awkwardness police everywhere seem
to affect. Their uniforms were starched and frayed and
one of them had a large, round belly and untied shoelaces.
They planted themselves in Charles's path.

"Don't I know you from somewhere?" Charles said, re-
calling a line from *Treasure of the Sierra Madre*. Mexico,
he decided, was one flick after another. He smiled to let
them know that he was making a friendly, small joke.

The one with the large belly stepped forward.

"What is in the bag?" he said.

"A blanket, some extra socks. Books."

"Dirty books?" the other said.

"I can't define porno," Charles said, "but I know it when
I see it," and immediately decided his smart-ass small joke
would be on him. He was right.

"Show us what is in the bag," Big-belly said.

Charles dropped the rucksack to the ground. Fast-draw
went through it, straightened up. "Look what I found," he
said, showing no surprise at all. He held up a small glass-
ine envelope containing some brown shreds laced with
green seeds.

"You're not going to believe me," Charles said amiably.
"But I never saw that before."

"It was in your bag," Big-belly said.

"It was in your bag," Fast-draw repeated.

Charles nodded thoughtfully. "That's funny. When I

left the *zócalo* that wasn't in the rucksack."

Big-belly was affronted for his partner. "I think he called you a liar."

"Did you call me a liar?"

Charles took a backward step. Fast-draw put his hand on the butt of his revolver. Charles held still.

"I don't think you're a liar," he said. "To the contrary. And you'll please understand that I never use the stuff on the open road."

"You admit it, then?"

"I deny it."

"That's marijuana you were transporting for illicit purposes."

Charles kept smiling. "Why do I get the impression I'm being framed?"

"We know how to take care of pushers around here . . ."

"Pusher!"

Fast-draw tossed the rucksack into the prowl car. Big-belly sent Charles after the rucksack. Seconds later, siren wailing, they were headed back into Oaxaca.

Charles sat up and leaned forward. "You know, the American ambassador won't like this—"

"Don't talk to the driver, *gringo,*" Big-belly grunted, shoving Charles backwards with his huge hand.

"This fucking Mexico," Charles said. "It's almost like real life . . ."

Agustín handled the power boat with practiced skill, slicing diagonally across the wake of a large yacht heading into the harbor. Behind him, Julio kept his eyes on the redheaded girl as she rode the waves with confidence. Julio was impressed with the athletic ability of American women; most of them were tall and supple and like this one seemingly tireless. Julio had also developed an appreciation for American women in bed; there too they were active and skillful. But the young ones never seemed to have much money and money was constantly on Julio's mind. Money made him think of Samantha Moore again.

"She is a movie star also," he shouted to Agustín over the roar of the outboard motor.

"*Sí*. She makes a movie now with an American company. Señorita Marcella tells me about it whenever I am with her."

"Ay! What it would be like, to be a movie star. That would be good, no."

"Stupid! You are Huachucan and I tell you there are no Huachucan movie stars."

"Ah," Julio said, "but am I not also Mexican? Pedro Armendariz, Aguilar, Cantinflas; they are all movie stars and they are Mexican too. What a life! One would be rich and sleep only with other movie stars."

"Stupid. Be satisfied that you have a rich *gringa* for a patron. Be clean and strong and she will invite you to sleep in her bed many times and you will be paid well for what you do for free anyway."

"Ay! I would like to help myself to some of her money."

"These *gringos*, they keep very little money in their houses. They deal with banks and places in America. Señorita Marcella has told me."

"The ones who make the movies, they have plenty of money, no."

"Yes."

"Why can't we get some of it from them?"

"And how do we do such a thing? Please Señor American Movie Company, Julio and Agustín, two poor Huachucan, would like some of your gold. Give us a little bit, a charity . . . Ay, Julio, stupid!"

The power boat described a wide arc as Agustín steered inshore toward the Ski and Scuba Club. "I am thirsty," he said. "Why do you not carry sidral in the boat?"

"Tell me again, Agustín, what the Señorita Marcella said to you."

"Only that tomorrow Señorita Samantha goes up into the mountains for the making of the movie. They go in the morning to do what it is that they do. That is all."

"I have been thinking about this, Agustín. I am making a plan."

"You are always making a plan."

"But never one like this plan."

"And never a plan that works."

Julio looked across the water at the redheaded girl. Her long legs wavered and she went down, skis floating free. "This plan will work," he said.

Agustín said nothing, but privately held slight hope for any plan Julio might concoct.

Julio tapped him on the shoulder. "The *gringa* is in the water. Turn back—"

Grace lay in the darkness of Foreman's room. Light from the street came through the shutters and made a yellow ladder across the ceiling. Outside a motorcycle went past and there was a burst of girlish laughter, an exchange of happy voices.

Next to her, Foreman breathed deeply. But she knew he wasn't asleep. She wanted to talk but was afraid of antagonizing him. There was a defensive remoteness about him; and though he had been inside her only minutes ago, they were still strangers.

After their last meeting, she had been left feeling as if some foreign element had insinuated itself under her skin, a constant irritant. What drew him to her, she wondered, and what did he want? Adding to her confusion was the double edge to his words whenever he spoke. An undertone of bitterness, however much he tried to sound light.

Still, she wanted to keep seeing him. The last afternoon on the mountain, she had wanted so much to draw him inside her body, to open herself to him, to be part of him. But afterward she felt she'd failed, and she'd been left anxious, on edge.

He was so evidently a man women liked and would give themselves to.

Why should he think differently about her? Hadn't she come to him this time practically begging for his attention? All the way down from the Chinchahua village she had warned herself to turn around, to go back. But her need for him had been too great. And when she had offered herself to him, she was mostly afraid he might not want her.

Even now, her womb drenched with his semen, she wasn't convinced he'd been glad to see her. Oh, he had accepted her into his bed quickly enough, made love to her with an exciting—almost violent—energy that at first was a little frightening. But it had been mostly physical, as if he were afraid to reveal any other side of himself.

Nor had she been so much different. Up to now she had believed that she was a fairly controlled woman, not dominated by the whims of her emotions or the occasional demands of her flesh. No longer. Foreman had brought out desires and responses in her she hadn't known were there, had confused her, made her a stranger she didn't really know. She felt flawed and exposed, as if something were wrong with her, something missing—and she didn't know what to do about it.

"I should go," she said.

"It's late. The Chinchahua would be shocked if you came sneaking in at this hour."

She wanted to be angry with him and couldn't. She wondered if she'd been a disappointment to him.

"You'll be more comfortable alone, you'll sleep better." The words sounded false in her ears and she knew she was really hoping he'd say she had pleased him, and ask her to stay.

"You're funny," was all he said.

"I'm glad I amuse you."

He lit a cigarette and in the glare of the match he looked like a pale rock carving. A spasm rippled along her spine.

He said, "You've traveled around by yourself, been on your own. You give the impression you're some kind of free spirit. You're not."

"You seem to know a great deal about me."

"I'm beginning to learn. What was he like?"

"Who?"

"Your seducer."

She had to stifle a giggle. "That sounds odd, such an old-fashioned word."

"I'm just an old-fashioned boy. Anyway, what made you go to bed with him?"

She hesitated. Foreman had asked the question as if the answer was his right. It wasn't. Arthur was part of her private existence and what had happened between them belonged only to her. It wasn't Foreman's business and yet she wanted to tell him.

"Why do you want to know?" she said, and knew that she was not being the Grace Biondi she wanted to be.

He puffed on his cigarette, his face impassive in the

brief glow. "You don't have to tell me."

"Maybe it was time," she said quickly. "Nature abhors a vacuum, after all."

"Don't be flip. It's not your style."

She *was* being flip, acting a part. She didn't like Foreman always answering a direct question with an evasive attempt at easy humor. And now it was she who was doing it, and it wasn't much more attractive. After a moment, she said quietly, "For a long while I thought being a virgin was important, a sort of badge of honor. I suppose I even hoped it showed, and I suspect it did. In time I came to understand something more about honor—and myself. I decided to stop being a virgin. It isn't something one manages alone."

He laughed.

"But why Arthur?"

"Arthur was attractive and we seemed to think alike, to want the same things. Or at least in the beginning I thought we did."

"And later?"

"Later I wasn't sure about anything."

"Were you sorry?"

"About losing my virginity? Oh, no. Besides, in a way, it's almost as if it never happened. There are no visible scars."

"All scars aren't visible . . . What about me? Why me?"

"I'm not sure," she said quickly.

"I'm sorry. Maybe I shouldn't have said that."

She came up on her elbow. "Is it wrong, not to be sure? . . . I don't know why you, you." She paused, went on. "There are also some things about you that I dislike. You confuse me."

"We live in confusing times."

"Are you really as cynical as you pretend to be?"

"Tell me more about you and Arthur, what separated you?" he said, ignoring her question.

She spoke swiftly, as if pleased at the chance to tell him. "There was so much going on, his work and mine. We didn't get to see each other as often as we'd have liked. And when we were together, we didn't talk very much. All we did was make love."

"Some women wouldn't complain."

She considered that, then lowered her head to the pillow and went on. "Arthur wanted to marry me. I guess he may have loved me."

"Why didn't you marry him?"

She remembered Arthur as a tall man with a thick waist and long, strong arms; she remembered he sweated a lot all that summer they were together. Amazingly, that was about all that was left of the memory.

"Arthur was pretty self-centered," she said. "His own comforts and pleasures were, well, the most important to him."

"You mean Arthur was a bust in the sack."

"Is that what I said?"

"He didn't satisfy you."

In her inexperience, she had considered Arthur's unconcern for satisfaction a natural male characteristic, to be tolerated, but she was also put on edge by it, and began to think up reasons to avoid their bedroom. At first she had doubted her own sexual adequacy, had decided the failure was her own. But after a while, she came to blame Arthur, resented his selfishness. Not until long after they'd separated did she understand, and also learn they were both responsible.

"It wasn't all his fault," she said to Foreman. "I certainly wasn't much help. In the end, I suppose I wasn't very good for him. And maybe not for you," she ended softly.

"Why don't you let me decide that. For a starter, may I say I think you're one hell of a woman?"

"You're not just saying that?"

"I promise you, everything will get better."

"Everything?"

"Everything," he said. "Including bed."

"Oh. I think I like that."

"What a carnal animal you are."

"How can you be sure?"

"Take it from an old lech."

"Braggart . . ." And then, "I feel I should tell you that I am absolutely terrified of you."

"Fear helps keep a girl in her place. After all, this is Mexico."

"Am I going to have to carry firewood on my head?"

"And walk three steps behind me at all times."

"Will that make me a good lover?"

"Some things you can learn . . ."

"What things?" she said after a while.

He took a last drag on the cigarette and ground it out, moved up against her. Their mouths came together in the darkness and his hand found her breasts. Her breath was warm and sweet in his mouth. His passion rose quickly but he held back for her. There was, he reminded himself, no end of time . . .

14

Mailman was leaning against the station wagon outside the Oaxaca jail, talking to two policemen. The massive red-headed man said something in Spanish that made the Mexicans laugh and he slapped his thigh in delight, the fleshy face crinkling up and growing pinker. When Charles emerged from the city jail, squinting against the bright sunlight, Mailman was the first person he saw.

The policeman glanced at Charles without interest, made a final remark to Mailman, and drifted away. He straightened up, wide and tall, looking down at Charles with friendly curiosity.

"Hello, Charles, remember me?"

The boy looked up into Mailman's lively blue eyes. "Did you spring me?"

"I maintain an open pipeline with the police around here. Sometimes it pays off. You're lucky, Mexican jails are no bargain."

"I was framed."

"Would you believe it, I believe you. Get in the wagon and let's go."

"Go where?"

Mailman assessed him gravely. "Well, look at you. With your head shaved, you resemble a plucked chicken. Surely you can use a decent meal, a shower."

Charles passed his hand over his bald pate. "Isn't that cruel and inhuman punishment? What makes some people so uptight about *hair?*"

"What makes hair so *important* to some other people?"

"Mr. Mailman," Charles said, climbing into the station wagon next to the big man, "I'm not sure I understand you."

That booming laugh filled the wagon. "Charles, you

don't even know me. Why the hell should you understand me!"

Charles slumped in on himself as they rode out of the city. Soon they were speeding across a flat, dusty landscape. "Up ahead," Mailman said finally, "that's my ranch." He looked over at Charles and grinned. "We'll put a sombrero on that head of yours. The sun around here can be wicked . . ."

A hot shower, a *comida* of bean soup, rice, broiled meat, caramel custard, and black coffee made Charles feel better. Mailman supplied him with clean clothes and a sombrero, suggested a tour of El Rancho in a jeep, vintage World War II.

They left the main house and drove over to a complex of new and old buildings. Men and women were at work everywhere. Mailman stopped the jeep and waved a hand.

"Blacksmith shop," he said. "Over there, our motor pool. We work over all kinds of engines, cars, teach our people to keep everything mechanical going, from a Model T to a road grader. The low building, that's a slaughterhouse. If a man wants to eat in some parts of Latin America he'd better know how to kill a chicken or a hog properly, how to butcher it. The hospital is beyond it. Every one who leaves here can deliver a baby head first or ass first, doesn't matter. Also set a broken leg, identify a rabid dog *before* it bites a child, perform an emergency appendectomy, if necessary."

"I don't get it," Charles said. "A guy I met said you were some kind of a social worker, a do-gooder. Is that what you're running here, a school for social workers?"

Mailman roared in amusement. "Social work is what they teach at Columbia University. Social workers are good for doing paper work, for getting between the poor of the world and what they need. You asked me once if I was a missionary—maybe in a way I am, or try to be."

"I remember what you said—something about without God or a church."

Mailman threw back his head and stretched. His forearms, jutting out of rolled sleeves, were thick and corded, covered with sun-bleached hair. "I guess that sort of covers it." He peered at Charles. "You believe in God, Charles?"

"I think so. When I was on the mushrooms, it was like His face I saw—"

"You can see a lot things on a mushroom trip."

"Are you an atheist?"

"Depends on what time of my life you're asking about. When I was in business, running with the boys, all of us very shrewd and getting very rich, I was sure there was a God who looked favorably on me and my kind. Hell, how else could we overlook what we'd done and justify what we had. Whenever old Andy Carnegie thought they were trying to put the squeeze on him, he'd say 'God gave me my money.' Me too." He laughed loudly. "Oh yes, I was a God-fearing, go-to-church-on-Sunday man."

"Not now?"

"I've seen kids with swollen bellies and rotten teeth dying of malnutrition. I've watched women with no husband and no money deliver their own kids—numbers ten, eleven, fifteen. And then watched them die of exhaustion before they were forty. I've listened to politicians in tinted glasses making glorious speeches about patriotism to peasants who are poor and sick, and then go back to their haciendas and do nothing to help their people. Believe in God, hell, no, I don't."

"What if you're wrong?"

Mailman poked a forefinger against Charles's shoulder for emphasis. "What if I'm right? What if getting born is purely the result of raunchiness and screwing and we're all standing around with our thumbs up our asses waiting to die? What if—listen, kid, this is it. There ain't nothing else."

"Then why bother? Why do you do what you do?"

"To stay out of trouble, I guess." He said it with a straight face.

The jeep rolled past a corral containing half a dozen horses.

"Look at 'em," Mailman bellowed. "Like the *campesinos*. Underfed, undersized. No pep, no life in 'em. It's the land. It needs a good steady drink of water. Irrigation is the answer. The government makes a stab at it, but never seems to accomplish anything."

"Maybe it can't be done."

"Shit on that shit. Look at the Israelis, the way they attacked the desert and defeated it. You know why, because they *wanted* to make a good life for themselves. It can be done here too. Work, intelligent planning."

"You sound like my father, like a businessman blueprinting a campaign of self-improvement."

"That's it exactly!" Mailman bellowed happily. "The same techniques apply here. It's the return that's different. Here the profit is in human lives."

"If you really wanted to help poor people, you'd lay a lot of bread on them." Even as he spoke, he realized that he was parroting Happy and disliked himself for it.

"Kid, let me straighten you out. Number one—every nickel I have has gone into this ranch, building it up, supporting the people who come here to study and to work. I train people to go out into the field, to get things done, to teach by example. Well, that costs money, lots of it. Number two—and you're not going to like this one —put a great deal of money in the hands of the poor and it will end up where it always ends up, in the pockets of the rich."

"That's still my father talking," Charles said. "The poor are too dumb to know what to do with money."

"I don't know about that. But poor people because they're poor have no experience with money. They don't *know* how to use it, how to make it work for them. It's something you have to learn. Swindlers and cheats live off poor people, not the rich, Charles. Phony advertising fools poor, uneducated people worst of all."

"I still think that if enough money"—

Mailman snorted. *"Thinking* is what you haven't done."

Charles felt intimidated, without being put down. He wanted to learn.

"If money isn't the answer, what is?"

"Hard work."

"The old Puritan ethic?"

"Hey Charles, spare me the schoolboy shit."

"Okay. You lay it on me and I'll listen with schoolboy respect. I don't imagine you'll consider that shit."

Mailman laughed. "That's our potting shed on the next hill. Making clay pots is basic to the peasant all over South America. It's important that our people can do it. We also teach them the uses of power, Charles. How to meet opposing power at its weakest point, how to exploit it, turn it to advantage. When our people leave here they know how to use modern agricultural methods to increase the yield. They speak the language of the people in the area they're going to. They know how to make the Indians value themselves more highly, to put a fair price on their labor. We teach poor people that the rich aren't necessarily wiser than they are or better, just richer . . ."

"Fine talk," Charles said. "I've heard it before, the liberal cocktail party line. You're just trying to make the poor people into consumers, get them to join your dumb human race."

Mailman grinned maliciously. "And you'd prefer they starve in a pure, uncorrupted, natural state? How romantic—"

"You don't understand. Changes have got to be made; other systems tried that—"

Mailman laughed, and Charles wanted to hit him.

"Systems become arbitrary, make us—as you may have heard—sooner or later slaves to them. I'm trying to be in the business of people, individuals. Systems finally are all failures, except to the degree that they let people stand against them. Systems and their machines—the twin gods of this world you're supposed to be trying to bring down. I'm sort of an expert on machines, by the way. I made my fortune designing them, then selling them all through Latin America. Until I finally got so rich even I had time to look at what I was doing, and what they were doing to the people they were supposed to make happy, wealthy, and wise. You make people feel like punch holes on a card, you got something to answer for."

"And what are you doing now," Charles said, feeling somewhat cornered, "trying to turn back the clock?"

"I don't know. For a while, maybe. But mostly, just trying to get it to run on time—for everybody."

The general room of El Rancho was a long, beamed

chamber decorated with dark wood, colonial furniture, and brightly colored upholstery. At both ends of the room, massive open fireplaces. Out of stereo speakers hung in the corners of the room, the muted intonations of James Taylor singing "Fire and Rain."

Mailman and Charles faced each other across a small carved table, drinking coffee, listening, occasionally speaking. Charles had begun to feel as if he belonged at El Rancho, as if he'd been there for a very long time. Somehow the place, and the people, seemed to reflect Mailman's presence; there was an air of confidence without smugness, of purpose, and good spirits.

"I like James Taylor," Mailman said. "No self-pity in that voice."

"The Beatles?" Charles asked.

"Big talents, right. But they faked us all out. All that love and tenderness when all four of them were into being superstars."

"I believed in them."

"And now?"

"They don't go down so easy any more."

"Not all the phonies are over thirty."

Charles grinned. "One for your side."

"Kids keep showing up at El Rancho rapping about what's wrong with the world, saying how they intend to put it right. Anything goes."

"Don't you have to throw the creeps out any way you can?"

"What happens afterwards?"

"We make a straight new world."

"You mean, it'll be Woodstock all over?"

"Right."

"What if it's Altamont instead? Mick Jagger hiring Hell's Angels to bodyguard him, then standing around while they stomp a black cat to death?"

"Maybe I'll go back to the mushrooms."

"Drugs are a way out, not in."

"What else do you suggest? I don't want to be like my father, always hustling after the buck."

"Are those the only alternatives you can see? Money and drugs. There could be another way."

"How do I find it?"

"Look in the right places," Mailman said, seeming to lose interest.

In the morning, after breakfast, Mailman led Charles to the jeep. His rucksack was in the back seat. A slight Mexican sat behind the wheel.

"Cesar will drive you back to Oaxaca," Mailman said.

Charles looked pale. "I was awake most of the night, thinking, believe it or not. And I think I'd like to stay here, go out in the field and help people——"

"First help yourself," Mailman said coldly. And then more easily, "I'm saying you have to find how to be the best Charles Gavin it's in you to be."

"How do I do that?"

Mailman smiled and Charles was forced to smile back. "You tell you . . ."

15

The men squatted around the fire that burned steadily in the center of the meeting hut. Smoke drifted up to the ceiling and gathered there in lazy layers, and a gray mist filled the hut. The men didn't seem to mind. They sat without moving or speaking, angular faces impassive, staring into the flames as if trying to comprehend its secrets. With two exceptions, they were all members of the elders' council of the Huachucan.

One man stirred, came to his feet. He was stocky and powerfully constructed, with thick shoulders and wrists. His face was bony, the eyes set far apart, his nose curved and thin. He assessed the men in the circle, all of whom he had known for as long as he had lived; or as long as they had lived. He had worked with them, hunted and gotten drunk on pulque with them, fought with them against enemies and had plotted other schemes to make money with them. They were good men; they were Huachucan.

"I have fixed my mind on the plan," Esteban said in a slow, resonant voice. "The plan will work, I think, but I am not yet convinced that this is a thing we should do."

He returned to his place in the circle and sat down. All the elders were not for this plan. And some who were for it would be of little use if it was put into action. The job meant risks to those who executed it and afterward there would be even greater risks. When a job took time, as this one would, the greatest danger always came later. Time sometimes made brave men afraid and wise men stupid.

Esteban was certain he would be able to control those men who remained with him, those who remained in the village. Huachucan custom and tradition would be at work to help him in that task; but what of the two who would be elsewhere? They were the frayed sections of the rope; and under pressure, a rope always broke at its weakest point. He brought his eyes around to the youngest men in the circle, to Agustín and Julio.

In some ways, they did not even look Huachucan. They had the short, strong, quick bodies of the tribe's men, but their faces were untouched by the hardships of life in these mountains. Their cheeks were too smooth, their eyes too large, their mouths too soft.

Esteban did not trust Agustín and Julio. They laughed too much; but they were young. They boasted of their sexual prowess; what Huachucan did not? They were clever; Esteban was even cleverer. They made money too easily; but they gave much of it to Esteban each month for tribal use. They lived away from the village; once a year, on the Night of the Dead, they returned to renew the Huachucan blood oath. They were weak; yet when war with the Llangayan had broken out, Agustín and Julio had returned to fight and had fought well.

Still, they were different, and Esteban could not completely believe in them.

And the plan. It was their plan. It could make the tribe rich; and that was good. But it could also fail, bring trouble down upon the tribe; and that was bad. Esteban thought back on decisions of other, earlier chiefs in similar situations; he weighed their actions and considered the results until he was convinced he was able to speak in wisdom, allowing neither cowardice nor courage to play a role in his thinking.

"I have studied the plan," Esteban pronounced, giving slow emphasis to his words. "It is a thing we should do."

"It is a fine plan!" Julio said, unable to contain himself. "It will work, I am sure of it."

All eyes were on the floor of the hut. Esteban finally spoke again. "It is good to learn that the one who brought the plan believes in it."

It was the moment Julio had anticipated. He understood the challenge, and the threat in Esteban's last words. It was the Huachucan way. And Julio had prepared himself to meet the test, to confront Esteban and the elders directly.

"I brought the plan before the elders' council for their wisdom. I did not come as a child. I presented it to you as a man who first considered it with disfavor and disbelief—" An approving murmur went up from the circle. "—I myself stood apart from myself and searched the plan from the side and the front and the back. I tore at it with my brain until it was almost destroyed—" There was a nodding of heads. "I repaired it and replaced the parts that were made badly. I submitted it to my cousin Agustín and demanded that he attack it and I answered each attack. Then I attacked and Agustín defended. The plan will work," he finished, lowering his eyes.

Guillermo, a younger member of the council, spoke. "We must know about the police."

"There will be two of them," Julio answered not looking up.

"How can we be sure?" Esteban said.

Agustín answered. He spoke more modestly than his cousin. "We used the telephone to speak to police headquarters. We pretended that we were of the movie company. In English, I said, 'Is it possible to employ more policemen when the movie is made on the mountain tomorrow? For safety's sake?' The official who answered became angry and shouted that there were many tourists in the city and they needed the protection of the police. 'Two' he said. 'Two are too many for such nonsense . . .'"

"That is how we are sure about the police," Julio said.

"Two is nothing," Guillermo commented.

"Let us talk of afterward," Esteban said.

"Afterward," Julio boasted, "we shall all be very rich."

"Afterward," Esteban said without expression, "the soldiers will come. Many soldiers. This *gringa* is rich and very important."

"No, no," Julio protested quickly. "The movie company will buy her back. In Acapulco they speak of such things. *Gringos* have been stolen in other countries and they are bought back for great sums of money. *Gringos* always pay for their own people. It is how they are."

"And the soldiers?" Esteban persisted.

"Such matters take time," Julio replied confidently. "Before the soldiers can reach the village, we will have our money, it will be hidden away, and no one will know what the Huachucan have done."

Esteban looked at the floor. One million pesos! What

woman was worth so much? It made no sense to him, but he had never been able to understand foreigners. "Do any of the elders wish to speak to the plan?" When no one answered, he went on. "Then I shall speak. We will do the plan, but carefully. The village must be protected. I have made changes in the plan. Ten men are too many . . ."

"What if there is a mistake about the police?" one of the elders asked.

"Ten will be too few to fight well and too many to run fast. Only a handful of men will be needed," Esteban said. "Those who remain in the village will be told nothing of the plan. Nor the women. Nor the children. If the soldiers or the police come after those who do the job, they will be led into the mountains, away from the village. If there must be fighting, it will be done at the high arroyo. There the soldiers can be trapped. But the members of the plan will not return to the village until the money is paid and it is all over and safe."

An approving sound went up from the circle.

"I will choose the members of the plan now."

"We will go along," Julio said excitedly. "You will need us to show you which woman it is . . ."

The weakness always showed, Esteban told himself with grim satisfaction. It came out in stupidity, in impulsiveness, the flaw inevitably making itself known. He addressed Julio. "You will describe this woman to the members of the plan so that there will be no mistake. You will describe her so that each member of the plan can recognize her at once. And when you have finished, Agustín will describe her. And then you will describe her again. And then Agustín. And then you. But you will not come with us. You and Agustín will return to Acapulco tonight. There you will make certain that many people see you. You will talk to this one and to that one and in that way no one will believe that there is any connection between you and what is going to happen. When it has been done, I will send word to you and you will do as I tell you . . ."

"*Así es!*" the elders agreed. "That is how it should be!"

"Now," Esteban said, getting to his feet, looking into Julio's face. "Tell us where these *gringos* will come from, where they will go, what their purpose is in coming. All you know you will tell us. Say it slowly. Nothing must be left. Begin!"

Julio began to talk, choosing his words very carefully . . .

Equipment vans, buses, a few private cars; they assembled
near the Diana opposite the Hilton. Samantha appeared
fifteen minutes late, accompanied by Theo Gavin who,
she explained to Foreman, had never seen a movie being
made. Ten more minutes passed without the arrival of the
police escort. In the lobby of the Hilton, Foreman located a telephone, got through to police headquarters. He
asked about the escort.

"*Sí, señor*," he was told. "The escort will definitely be
with you. Surely they have arrived . . ."

"Surely they have *not* arrived. When can I expect
them?"

"Very soon, *señor. Ahoritita* . . ."

Foreman hung up. *Ahoritita*, right now . . . That might
mean any time before sundown. He went back to the convoy and told Bristol what he'd learned.

"To hell with the cops," Bristol shot back. "Let's get
going."

Foreman looked at him, shrugged.

Minutes later they rolled out of town.

Foreman called for a take.

The company was established on a dirt road that
pointed directly west before cornering abruptly. On the
right, a sharp drop to the valley a thousand feet straight
down. On the other side of the road, a high rock wall.

On the road, McClintock checked cables, the position-
ing of lights and reflectors, the camera car.

Foreman went over to Shelly, seated behind the wheel
of a red convertible.

"You all right?"

"I think so."

"We've rehearsed it enough. You shouldn't have any
trouble. Keep your speed between thirty and thirty-five.
It'll seem faster on film. Later we'll put in sound." He
reached down and tested the safety belt that held her in

the seat. "Stay loose," he said, and went back to the camera car.

The scene was pure action. Shelly, near panic, was trying to get away from Jim Sawyer. The drive up the mountain was a jolting, unnerving, desperate ride. The car swerved and bounced, in and out of her control. On this narrow road, she sped straight into the blinding late sun. Straining to see, afraid that she was about to go over the edge, she peered into the orange glare and saw a vision of the white-clad woman that had been recurring in her mind. Screaming in silent terror, she wrenched the wheel, sending the car crashing into the stony side of the road.

"Cut!" Foreman cried, and immediately ordered a second take. "For insurance," he explained before Bristol could object. "The lab work is going to be complicated."

They did the scene again and again it went off without difficulty. Satisfied, Foreman congratulated Shelly and called for the next set-up.

In the shade of an equipment truck, seated on folding canvas chairs, Samantha Moore and Theo Gavin, holding hands. She disengaged herself and stood up.

"My scene, darling," she said. "It shouldn't take long."

"You'll be great."

"Theo, what a dear you are."

She joined Foreman and they went up the hill to where the road turned.

"Stay out of sight behind the bend," Foreman instructed her. "When you hear my whistle, step to the outer edge of the road. Along that line of rock markers McClintock put down."

"I see them."

"That will put you in a direct line with the sun." He looked up at it briefly. It had that special intensity that comes just before setting. "Another ten minutes and we'll be ready to go. Yesterday McClintock shot the sun alone, from this angle. Later, we'll match the two shots so that you'll seem ghostlike in the picture. Your 'presence' saves Shelly from going over the side . . ."

"I understand."

"Just hold your position until I end the scene. When the camera car makes the run up the hill toward you, keep your eyes on the driver. In the film, it will seem that you're looking at Shelly, warning her . . ."

He went back down the road and Samantha continued around the corner and out of sight. Back at the camera car, Foreman raised his voice. "Okay, people, we're going to run it through . . ."

Guillermo was angry. "It is some kind of a trap. Julio has led us into a trap."

Esteban made a hand gesture that silenced the other man. "Julio is Huachucan. He does not betray his people."

From where the five Indians lay on their stomachs in the tall brown mountain grass, the land dropped away steeply to the dirt road, nearly half a mile below. They had been waiting in this place since before sunrise, had watched the *gringos* arrive, had watched them make their movie. All was as Julio had said. And the tall blond *gringa* in the white dress; that too was as Julio had said it would be.

"I too do not like the plan anymore," a man named Tomás muttered. "Julio said there would be two police. There are none. Perhaps the police came last night, are scattered through the hills, hiding, waiting for us to act so they can shoot us all."

"I do not like it either," another man added.

"To like or dislike is nothing," Esteban said. "To understand is important."

None of the men replied; they were as afraid of Esteban's sharp tongue as they were of his heavy fists. A man became chief of the Huachucan only when no one remained to challenge for the position. The selection process was violent and left painful scars on the defeated candidates.

"Guillermo," Esteban said. "Go to where the horses are and see that all is as it should be."

Five minutes passed and Guillermo returned. "The horses are quiet. Chico has them blindfolded and ready for us."

Esteban motioned to the road below. "See, the woman comes this way!"

In a flowing white gown and long, golden hair shining

under the sun, Samantha resembled nothing these Huachucan had ever seen.

"*Ay, chihuahua!*" Tomás breathed. "That is some
gringa!"

The other men laughed and Esteban silenced them with
an upraised hand. "See, she comes by herself around the
bend in the road, where her people cannot see her. If we
were down there, this would be the moment to take her.
The others would never know she was gone."

"*Hola!*" Tomás said. "The police—"

Down the road, behind the equipment trucks, a police
car drew up and two officers climbed out.

"You see," Esteban said. "It is exactly as Julio told us it
would be. No tricks, no traps. A good plan." He watched
with interest as the camera crew went through their rehearsal, watched as Samantha stepped into the road when
Foreman blew his whistle. And when it was over, he saw
how everyone, including the blond woman, went back to
where they had begun. In that moment, Esteban understood what the people below were doing.

"Now!" he said. "We go down now. Ramos, tell Chico
to bring the horses to the flat place. The rest come with
me. Quickly!"

"Okay, people, Foreman announced. "This is a take. Action!"

The camera car eased forward, picking up speed as it
went up the hill. Foreman raised the whistle to his mouth,
blew a long blast. Samantha didn't appear.

"What's going on!" he shouted. "Stop the dammed
car!" He jumped down to the ground, ran up the incline,
calling out to Samantha. Behind him came McClintock.

"Come on, Samantha!" Foreman yelled. "Didn't you
hear the signal? We're going to lose the sun . . ." He went
around the corner and stopped. "Samantha! Where the
hell are you? This is no time to play goddamn hide-and-
seek . . ."

McClintock came up alongside. "What's wrong?" Movement higher on the hill caught his eye. He pointed. "Paul!
Up there!"

"What the hell!"

Nearly a hundred yards away, four men were, unbelievably, dragging Samantha Moore away.

"What in goddammhell is this! Where's the broad? Jesus H. Christ, we got a picture to make." It was Bristol, struggling to catch his breath, the prizefighter's face flushed and angry. Behind him, Theo Gavin and the two policemen. They were smiling cheerfully.

"Look up there," McClintock said.

Bristol swore. "This supposed to be a joke?"

"I would say," Foreman said slowly, "only if you think it's funny, that Samantha's just been kidnapped."

"You gotta be crazy!" Bristol shouted. He looked up the mountain. "Police! They've heisted my star! Do something, for Christ sakes!"

The policemen went for their guns. Dust kicked up around them, the crackle of rifles, and bullets ricocheting off the rocky hillside. The policemen scurried for cover, the others close behind.

"They are shooting at us!" one of the officers said in a voice of injured innocence.

"We've got to do something," Theo declared. "Damn, if I only had a gun."

The policemen holstered their weapons.

"Let's go after them," Theo said.

The officers moved away from him, as if he'd been declared contagious. One of them said, "It would be good for us to tell what has happened here to our chief. He is a man who likes to know what is going on." They hurried back down the road toward their car.

Foreman followed them.

"Where are *you* going?" Theo yelled after him.

"Where are you going?" Bristol echoed.

"Back to Acapulco," Foreman answered. "If we wait for the Keystone cops to do anything right, we'll never find Samantha."

Bristol swore and went after Foreman, Theo at his side. "Why?" Theo said. "Why would they take Samantha?"

"For money," Bristol said. "What the hell else! But if they wait for me to spring for a ransom they'll wait till hell freezes over. She ain't that important to the picture."

"Ransom," Theo said to no one in particular. "I wonder

what it'll cost to get her back . . ."

The police chief was a stout man with a luxurious mustache and a golden smile. He listened with evident interest to the Americans' report of the kidnapping, surprised at how nearly it jibed with the report made by his own men. Of course, he understood that his men had exaggerated their zeal to follow after the kidnappers, but that was to be expected.

The Americans finished and the police chief arranged his jowly face in an expression of official concern. He explained that the State of Guerrero was indeed a violent state, perhaps the most violent in all the republic. Only the other day, on the road to Zihuatanego a retired business executive was shot from a passing car; and a week before that foreign-trained guerrillas robbed a bank in a small town to the south; and there were always murders and shoot-outs among feuding families and Indian tribes. *Ay, chihuahua! How uncivilized people were!*

Such disregard for law and order, the police chief continued, leaves a very poor impression on the tourists, might one day drive them away from Acapulco. That would be the final indignity. Therefore, the chief informed his listeners, he considered the kidnapping of Samantha Moore a terrible blow to justice, an affront to the republic and an insult to his personal authority. To steal a rich Mexican was understandable—it kept matters in the family, in a manner of speaking—but to violate the person of such a respected and beautiful resident American was quite a different matter, in every way unacceptable.

"Unfortunately, *señores*," he went on, "at this time there is little I am able to do. Little, that is, which is visible to the untrained eye. However, my informants are already at work and soon pertinent information will come speeding back to me. By this time tomorrow I shall know the identity of the criminals who have perpetrated this horrible crime. I shall learn where they are hiding the Señorita Samantha Moore and then I shall act with unspeakable swiftness, with terrible revenge. That is," he went on, "if the army will cooperate. I cannot, of course, go into those mountains with only a few poorly trained, poorly armed men. That would be foolish, no?"

Fifteen minutes later word came that the chief's request for military help had been answered and an hour later an impeccably garbed major arrived swinging a riding crop against his highly polished boots.

"I am Major Sebastian de Aragón y Gonzaga," he announced. "Under my personal command are sixty finely trained men, all excellent riders with superb mounts. We are ready to begin the search."

"I shall go with you," the police chief said.

"So will I," Theo said. "I want to be there with a rifle in my hands when they're found. If they've harmed Samantha—"

"Bravo!" the major said.

"Qué macho!" the chief said.

Bristol motioned to Foreman and they went outside. On the sidewalk, the producer faced his director. "Those Mexican bastards are after my dough," he said unpleasantly.

"It's not personal, Harry. They'll take anybody's."

"Well, they're not getting any of mine. The dame is nothing to me. Besides, she's got dough of her own. That house is worth a fortune . . . You know, maybe there's something in this for me anyway . . . Maybe Samantha is going to be worth a little extra something to the picture after all. I'm going to call New York, see what they say. I got a notion we can make something out of this . . ."

Theo went back to his hotel and put through a call to Jerry Baumer, told him what happened, not wasting time with details. When he finished, Baumer said, "This is terrible! What can I do to help?"

"In the morning, the army is going after the kidnappers. At dawn, Baumer. It may be rough up there. A shoot-out, bloodshed."

"My God, that *is* terrible!"

"Baumer, make notes on everything I say."

"Notes?"

"Listen to me, man, a small war is going to attract a great deal of attention."

"What if the kidnappers kill Miss Moore?"

"I'm aware of the risks involved. The key to success in any enterprise is to keep one's head. To know what has to be done and to do it."

". . . know what has to be done and do it," Baumer repeated.

"Don't overlook anything."

"Depend on me." Baumer's enthusiasm was on the rise.

"First, *I* will accompany the soldiers tomorrow. I will be riding a horse right up in front of the column. It will be a large dapple gray. I've already made arrangements to rent him. Also, I will be armed—pistol, rifle, lots of ammunition."

"Mr. G., I wouldn't have the guts."

"That's not news, Baumer. Get this down, I am an expert horseman, an experienced big game hunter—I once bagged a record-sized jaguar with a single shot from a standing position. The cat was on the run at the time. He weighed in at close to three hundred and fifty pounds."

"That's good?"

"It's a record."

"Yes, sir."

"Check the company biography for additional information about me. You'll find vital statistics, photographs at different stages of my life, a rundown on my athletic record at college and since. Everything for a feature story. Check with the people at *Time*. They might want to do a cover story on me . . ."

"The last of the Renaissance men," Baumer said.

"Not bad. The important thing is to get every newspaper and wire service on this story at once. Samantha Moore is the key to it all. Her name is the product and the product is Samantha!"

"Oh, that is a good line. Let me get it down verbatim. Can you repeat it, please?"

Theo did, waited until Baumer had finished writing. "I don't know how this will turn out, Jerry, insofar as Miss Moore is concerned, but our responsibility is to the company as well. I wouldn't want anyone to point a finger at us for being heartless. We don't want to be called exploiters. It's up to you to find the appropriate way to take advantage of the situation."

"Will do, Mr. G."

"Be sure to emphasize the fact that I am *organizing* the rescue mission, that I will lead it. Get your full staff on this at once. And I want you down here before dawn tomorrow. Bring along photographers, reporters, anyone you can round up. Charter a private jet, if necessary."

"I'll be there in a few hours."

"This is the kick-off of our campaign, Jerry. I want worldwide press attention for the product, for SAMANTHA!"

"SAMANTHA!" Baumer intoned. "It'll be famous by the end of the week, I promise you."

"I'll hold you to that," Theo said, and hung up. His palms were damp. All weariness was gone. Every detail was dropping into place, the perfect fit, the perfect promotion. Theo could hardly wait for morning to come, to go up into those mountains, to rescue Samantha.

SAMANTHA! . . .

16

Marcella lay on her back, trying to shut out the intrusive ringing, to concentrate on the delicious reprise of herself and Agustín provided in her dream. Complaining, she reached blindly for the telephone. Next to her, Agustín stirred but went right on sleeping.

"Bueno," Marcella said, anxious to return to the dream.

"Listen, *gringa,"* a roughly accented voice said in English.

Marcella protested reflexively. "I'm a Cuban."

"I will say what I have to say only one time and then I am finished."

"Who is this?"

"I will talk about Señorita Moore. She is safe for the moment. She has been fed and given a place of her own to sleep. No one troubles her. Yet . . . You are her friend so we make this offer to you. By nightfall the day after tomorrow, one million pesos must be paid to us, otherwise the *señorita* will be killed. Pay the money and she will be set free without harm."

Marcella sat up and switched on the night lamp. "You'd better not do anything to Samantha—"

"Collect the money," the voice said, almost plaintively. "Señorita Moore is rich and all her friends are rich. Later she will return to all of you what has been borrowed, no. That way everybody will be satisfied."

"You're mad! Samantha hasn't got that kind of money."

"Do not think we are fools. A rich *gringa,* a movie star. Please, do this thing as I have told you or the *señorita* will be dead soon." He hung up.

Marcella shook her head. "Oh, why did they call me?" she muttered. "What am I supposed to do now?" She looked down at Agustín, the smooth face untroubled, his

breathing easy. She hated to wake the poor boy. Still, he
was a man and might have some idea how to properly
handle this crazy business. Damn, why didn't they phone
someone else? She touched Agustín's shoulder. "Come on,
lover, wake up."

Without opening his eyes, Agustín pushed one hand between her fleshy thighs. "Oh, what a lovely toy you are!
But this is *serious*, baby."

"Que pasa?"

"They called me. The people who took Samantha. Just
now. They want a million pesos for her. As if I had it.
Even if I did, I wouldn't put up that much for my own
mother. Especially not for my mother, the bitch."

Agustín took a firmer hold on her crotch. "Let the
gringos pay for her," he said.

"What *gringos*, Lover?"

"She is a movie star, no?"

She removed his hand, so as to be able to think more
clearly.

"A million pesos is not so much for a friend," he said.
"The *señorita* must have many rich friends." Agustín
closed his eyes.

Marcella considered what he'd said. "Bernard!" she
said aloud. "That *Frenchman* has every centavo he's ever
made." She called him; he wasn't at home. She dialed his
office number. He answered.

"Bernard, *darling*," she began. "Marcella here. What an
ungodly hour for you to be working. It's about Samantha . . ."

"I am awaiting a communiqué from the kidnappers."

"They called me."

"You? Why you?"

She repeated the conversation. By the time she was
finished, his breathing over the wire was loud and de-
cidedly unpleasant.

"One million," he said. "I can assure you that Samantha does not have that amount in cash. There is the *Starfish* to sell and some property overlooking Puerto Mar-
ques and Villa Gloria, of course . . ."

"Samantha would rather die than sell the house."

"Yes. Besides, it would all take too much time. We
have less than forty-eight hours."

"Bernard," Marcella said, "surely you have funds available . . ."

"I!" He sounded horrified. "My assets, such as they are, are not liquid. We must go to another for large sums. Essentially I am a poor man . . . I have it! Why not the American?"

"Bristol! What a marvelous idea! Those movie people always—"

"No, no, that one functions on a shoestring. Gavin is the man. Surely he can obtain such monies quickly. A phone call to his bankers in the States—"

"Bernard," Marcella said, stroking Agustín's cheek. "There is genius in you. But shouldn't the police be informed?"

"The police!" Bernard said, voice breaking in dismay. "You must be mad! The police will steal the ransom for themselves and get Samantha murdered in the bargain. No, no, the money and its payment must be done quietly, privately. When did the kidnappers say they would contact us again?"

"They didn't say. Oh, dear, do you mean they're going to call me again? I hope not. I'm simply not emotionally equipped for so much excitement."

"Let me know when they call. Before anyone else is notified. Is that clear, Marcella?"

"Yes, Bernard."

She returned the phone to its cradle. "What a night!" she said aloud. "I'm shattered, every nerve raw. I shan't be able to sleep a single wink. Agustín, dear Agustín, wake up. Be a dear and rub me down. My flesh tingles with upset. Yes, baby, there. All over. Don't miss a single place. Oh, oh, my that is . . . good, very good. Not so hard. Yes, yes, perfect, that way. Ah, Agustín, what a beautiful toy you are . . ."

First light washed over Acapulco as the army troops assembled on the Costera, augmented by a dozen heavily-armed blue-clad policemen. With a great deal of shouting and swearing, the horses were loaded into vans for the trip up into the foothills. This done, the soldiers took their places in open trucks. Two photographers, flown down from Los Angeles by Jerry Baumer during the night, took pictures of everything.

Theo, in polished boots and breeches, a pistol strapped to his waist, a rifle in the saddle holster, a sombrero on his head, sat stiffly on the dapple gray until the photographers were finished with him. He dismounted gracefully, turned the horse over to a policeman for loading and went over to where Jerry Baumer stood watching with Paul Foreman, Harry Bristol and Bernard Louis Font.

"You were great, Mr. G.," Baumer enthused. "That sombrero, a fine touch!

Theo shifted the pistol to a more comfortable position, wished he'd gotten a lighter weapon, a .38 perhaps. "We'll be moving out soon. I'll be in the command car with the major. Have one of the photographers up front all the time."

"Depend on it, sir. I've told Herman what we want and he's a good boy, he'll deliver."

"Matters here are in your hands, Jerry. Bernard is following through for me on the money arrangements. The funds should be in the Banco de Comercio by noon. However—"

"Not a cent gets paid," Baumer put in, "until we get the okay from you."

"Exactly. If the soldiers don't slow me up too much, I'll track those bastards down by afternoon, get them in my sights and . . ." He looked over at Foreman. "You ought to come along, Paul. Bring your camera crew. This should be exciting, you could work this into your story . . ."

"Thanks, Gavin, but I've seen this picture before. Except I can't remember who played your part."

"Suit yourself." Theo tossed off a salute and marched down the line of vehicles to the head of the column.

"Magnificent," Bernard said.

"A real man," Baumer said.

"A schmuck," Bristol said, turning away.

Foreman thought about the Chinchahua, each man a deadly shot, each one at home in those rugged mountains. Don Miguel would expect the cavalry and by now would have placed his men into strategic positions. Once the soldiers came within range, they would be slaughtered. Helpless targets in a shooting gallery. And Grace would be trapped between the two forces . . .

"Let's go," Bristol ordered.

"What?" Foreman said.

"Time to get to work. We've got a picture to finish."

Foreman's eyes moved from face to face. "I think I can help."

"What the hell are you talking about! Cowboys and Indians is Gavin's number. You're making my movie."

"There's still Samantha's final scene," Bernard said with some emotion. "We have a contract—"

"Shove the contract," Bristol told him. "Foreman, round up the crew and get to work. Shoot around Moore."

In the pallid light, Foreman's long face was gray, his eyes shadowed in the deep hollows. But before he could reply, Jerry Baumer spoke.

"By the middle of the afternoon, Mr. Bristol, the entire world is going to know what's happening down here. The word is going out over the wires right now. There's a network TV crew on the way down from Houston. More reporters, the works. People will resent it when they learn that you cut Samantha Moore out of your movie just when her life is in jeopardy. They'll say you're cruel, without concern for people. They'll say—"

"What the hell can I do about it? I got my own problems."

"Poor Samantha," Bernard said. "At this very moment, she may be dead."

"That's crap! Those kidnappers want dough and the going price for corpses is piss-poor."

"Ah," Bernard answered. "But if she were dead and we didn't know. We'd have to pay anyway."

"That's exactly right," Baumer said. "Mr. G. is not the sort of human being to take chances with the life of his fellow man. Or woman."

"Harry," Foreman said, "if I were in your shoes I'd consider my next move very carefully. Don't make any mistakes. A bad press could ruin you. If I were you, Harry, I'd cancel today's shooting."

"The budget . . ." Bristol mumbled, searching for a sympathetic face.

He found Jerry Baumer's. "Think of the publicity that's going to accrue to your production. The world will know about your film, that Samantha is starring in it . . ."

"She's not starring," Bristol corrected grumpily.

"Well, she should be!" Baumer said. "Why not rewrite her part, build it up, give her top billing?"

"Precisely!" Bernard cried happily.

"By nightfall," Baumer continued, "Acapulco will be the communications capital of the world. Millions of words and pictures will go out . . ."

"All about Samantha," Bernard put in.

"Millions of words," Baumer repeated.

"If I could be sure of a plug in every story . . ."

Baumer smiled indulgently. "I'm in a position practically to guarantee that."

"The ball's in your court, Harry," Foreman said.

Bristol exhaled. "Okay, Foreman, you got your day off. But don't let it go to your head. Win too many battles with me and you'll be out on your ass . . ."

Foreman, already hurrying to where the VW was parked, gave no sign that he'd heard.

Grace Biondi crouched over the tape recorder in the center of a double circle of dancing boys. They moved counterclockwise in a deliberate shuffle, kicking up yellow dust and chanting to the god of the wind in high nasal voices. Outside the circle, a dozen young girls clapped hands on the off-beat. Others rattled bean-filled gourds or clicked two pieces of wood against each other in counterpoint.

Grace directed the microphone at the singers, intent on capturing every syllable. She seemed to ignore the impatient honking of a car horn in the background. It persisted and she almost smiled, glad of the interruption. She turned off the recorder and dismissed the children, telling them that they would continue another time. Turning, she saw Foreman coming toward her in that characteristic stoop, peering out at the world from under his brows.

"You spoiled my recording session," she said without complaint.

"I'm about to spoil the rest of your day." He kissed her on the mouth.

"Don't! The Chinchahua . . ."

"The Chinchahua operate out of a very interesting double standard."

"What do you mean?"

"Let's talk in private."

She led him into the cool dimness of her hut and he promptly kissed her again, hands coming to rest on her firm bottom. "Jesus, you feel good to me."

"Don't speak about my friend that way." She laughed at the puzzled expression on his face. "Jesus . . ."

He grinned and slapped her bottom, released her. "Samantha Moore was kidnapped yesterday afternoon. We were doing a scene about ten miles north of here. A handful of Chinchahua snatched her and dragged her off into the hills. Pancho Villa strikes back!"

"That's not a very good joke, Paul."

"No joke. I saw it happen."

She looked at him carefully. "How can you be sure they were Chinchahua? If the Chinchahua did it, I'd know."

"Sure. Don Miguel would come to you first thing. *Perdón, señorita,* we've pulled off a snatch. Just thought you'd like to know. Come on, Grace!"

"Did you recognize them?"

"When you've seen one Chinchahua you've seen them all."

"What proof is there?"

"Nothing that'll stand up in court. But I can put together one fine circumstantial case. One that will satisfy me, at least."

"Try it on me."

"Okay. Begin with this—the Chinchahua have had their eyes on me since I started coming up here. They're a damned shrewd bunch, I give them that. It wouldn't have been difficult for them to find out that I was making a movie. You might have told them—"

She turned away.

"You *did,*" he said.

"I'm sorry."

"A natural thing to do. The point is, they began to see the possibilities. An American movie. A rich American movie star. Samantha *looks* like a movie star, she looks rich, she lives in a villa that smells like money. They probably sent a couple of people down into Acapulco to check her out. They must've figured this job would set the village up for life. And when I took the company into the mountains to shoot, it was easy for them to make their move . . ."

Startled by what he was suggesting, and afraid that it was true, Grace looked for some convincing argument to use against him. "How could they have known where you'd be and when?"

"No problem. We weren't hiding our plans from anybody. Wherever we set up we attracted attention—tourists, natives. When I decided to do the mountain sequence, I gave the company a day and a half advance notice. Time enough for word to get out to the KGB in Moscow and back."

In the half light, she took a backward step, watching him. "At least we can let the Chinchahua defend themselves."

"Are you crazy! I came to get you out of here before the shooting starts."

"What shooting?"

"The army is on the way. By now they're at the turnoff, unloading their horses. They'll be up here before very long."

Without a word, she ducked out of the hut. Foreman hurried after her. He caught up, took her arm. "What are you going to do?"

She shook him off, kept going. "I'm going to talk to Don Miguel."

"You expect him to confess everything? He's just liable to have both of us killed, along with Samantha."

"Go away, if you're afraid."

"Oh, that's beautiful. I come up here to save your skin and get insulted for my trouble."

She stopped, eyes steady on him. "I won't run away from this."

"Okay. I guess we'll talk to Don Miguel."

The chief was inside his hut, sitting on a three-legged stool, an infant playing in the dirt at his feet. There was no expression on his sun-blackened face and he studied his unexpected visitors out of eyes set back under folds of wrinkled skin.

"Don Miguel, forgive us for coming without notice," Grace began. "But something has happened and my friend has come as a friend to the Chinchahua to warn them . . ."

Don Miguel said nothing.

Grace spoke again. "As you know, Don Miguel, Señor Foreman is making a motion picture in Acapulco. Yesterday the picture making was done in the mountains, perhaps fifteen kilometers from here. Some men took one of the American women who acts in the movie. They stole her and are demanding a great deal of money before they will send her back. They ask for one million pesos."

Don Miguel's face showed nothing. "You spoke of a warning . . ."

"These men, whoever they are, will be found out. Señor Foreman has come to say that the soldiers are already on their way into the mountains. This will mean trouble—"

Don Miguel went to the door and called out. Soon the men of the tribe were gathering in the street. He spoke to them rapidly and they scattered. Back inside, Don Miguel said something to his wife. She dug under a pile of tapetes in the corner of the room and brought out a rifle, handed it to him. He draped a cartridge belt across his shoulders.

"I thank your friend for the warning," he said.

"Don Miguel," Grace said. "Listen to me, please."

His eyes were icy. "When the soldiers come we shall be ready for them. The Chinchahua will remember this warning and we have to you, señor, a debt of friendship."

"Christ!" Foreman burst out in English. "He's got it all wrong! Tell him how it is."

Grace took a deep breath. "Don Miguel, the soldiers believe the Chinchahua stole the American woman."

Don Miguel studied the faces of the two Americans. "How could this be? Had a Chinchahua done this thing, would I not know of it? Yet I do not know of it and so it could not have been done. The soldiers come anyway. They will not ask if we have done the stealing. They will not believe if they are told. The have a lust for killing but Chinchahua blood is never spilled easily. This is no time for talking, you and the señor will remain here. Not one soldier will reach the village, I swear it." Don Miguel went into the street, Foreman after him. The entire population of the village was milling about, each man carrying a rifle. All talk ended at the sight of Don Miguel.

"Soldiers are on the way," he shouted in the Chincha-hua language. "As in the past, we will hold the high points and when they reach the second high valley we will shoot them."

"This is ridiculous," Foreman said; then, in Spanish, "Don Miguel, if the Chinchahua didn't steal the American woman, who did?"

Don Miguel shrugged.

"Where did it happen?" Grace said to Foreman. He described the location in detail.

"Ah," Don Miguel said. "Huachucan."

"Are you certain, Don Miguel?"

"Who else would dare such an act in these mountains? The place you speak of is close to their lands, though it is still our territory. Once again the Huachucan have broken the peace. After the soldiers, we will attend to them."

"Don Miguel," Grace said. "Isn't it foolish to begin a war with the army when you have done nothing wrong?"

"They are coming," he replied, as if that answered all arguments.

"Even if you are able to kill all of them, the government will have to send more soldiers, more guns. Sooner or later they will destroy the Chinchahua and the village."

"What else is there to do except fight?" Don Miguel asked without emotion.

"Avoid a fight."

Señorita, no man does that."

"Yes, the men will die and leave the women and children to suffer. They will mourn their dead and the children will go hungry until they also die. Why punish the innocent?"

"What can I do? The soldiers will be here soon. The Huachucan have broken the peace."

Grace spoke quickly. "Empty the village. Send all your people into the hills. The soldiers will not go after them . . ."

"That is so. The soldiers are less cowardly than the police, but not so brave that they dare to leave the roads." Behind him, the men laughed and raised their rifles into the air.

"Señor Foreman and I will remain here," Grace went on. "We will explain to the soldiers that the Chinchahua had nothing to do with this affair."

"They will not believe you."

"Let me try."

"The soldiers will destroy the village, they will kill our goats and burn our fields."

"Not after I talk to them."

"The Chinchahua are men and will not hide with the women. You ask more of me than I can ask my people to do."

"There is something the Chinchahua can do. You can try to find out if the Huachucan really did steal the American woman. If they did—"

"Ah!" Don Miguel breathed.

"If you can locate the American woman, we will then know how to deal with the situation. War is not always the best answer to a problem—"

Don Miguel answered quietly. "War brings sorrow but it also brings peace. Talk has only brought more killings to the Chinchahua, more sorrow."

"Try a new way," Foreman said. "If it doesn't work, you can always shoot somebody."

Don Miguel considered Foreman's words. "Very well. If there is to be killing, it will come later. For now, we shall do it the way you have said. But if the soldiers damage our village, not one of them will return to Acapulco alive." He barked out some orders and four of the younger men sprinted toward the high ground. "My scouts will locate the woman and then we will talk again." He marched out of the village toward the craggy eastern peaks, all his people trailing behind. Ten minutes later they were out of sight and the only sound left was the sibilance of wind spurts kicking up dust clouds along the empty street.

Grace and Foreman sat on a grassy knoll behind the village in the shade of a purple-blooming jacaranda tree. They ate orange slices and waited for the soldiers.

"The army won't be here for at least an hour," Foreman said.

Grace laughed. "Maybe more. They can't be anxious to confront the Chinchahua."

"In that case . . ." He kissed her. She turned her face away.

"Please, don't . . ."

He chewed on her earlobe.

"Aren't you worried about Miss Moore? This range is likely to erupt into bloody warfare at any minute . . ."

"Not making love to you isn't going to keep the peace."

"You are obsessed with sex."

"Maniacally." He put his tongue to her lips. "I've always been partial to the taste of orange. An excellent way to get my basic Vitamin C."

"Mother warned me against men like you."

"Mother was a prig."

"What about your mother? Your father? You never talk about them. I take it you haven't fond memories of your parents."

"To hell with them. Let's discuss your mouth." He pulled her chin around. "I pronounce yours to be one of the more sensational mouths in operation. That is a mouth made for any number of pleasure-giving activities."

She moved away. "I want to know about you. For example, when you were a boy, did you like school?"

"A drag." He placed his hand on her belly-rise. "It is my intention to violate every area of your body. You have a supremely female body, you know."

She sighed, produced a bored expression. "One hears that sort of thing so often . . ."

"I'll bet your seducer never told you."

"Well, Arthur didn't talk much."

"How sad. Then you never heard about your breasts, for example. Let me tell you, outasight!" He leaned over and pushed the tip of his tongue into her ear.

She rolled away, laughing. "You're impossible!"

"Improbable," he corrected, getting on top of her. "You're crazy about me, aren't you? Come on, admit it." He nibbled her ear. "I intend to devour you."

"Cannibal."

"In my neighborhood, young Catholic meat rated very high."

"Oh, have you had a lot of experience with Catholic girls?"

"Only when the moon is full and my blood runs hot." He shifted his attention to her throat. "Love is *le mot juste* for what I feel."

"Lust," she corrected. "We barely know each other."

"We will."

"Aren't you interested at all in what I think or feel or want out of life?"

"Tell me your secrets."

"You really don't care."

He raised his head, masquerading hurt. "You're not so hard to figure out. St. Anne's primary school. St. Theresa's high school. St. Ignatius's college. Luckily I arrived on the scene in time to rescue you from the propaganda those nuns laid on you." He lowered his head between her breasts. "Oh, cushions of love and delight, to thee both I pledge my troth . . . or something like that . . ." He caressed one breast and she dropped her hand on his, as if to hold him in place.

"My parents," she said absently, "didn't believe in parochial education. I went to secular public schools."

"Congratulations are in order . . ." He began to undo the buttons of her blouse.

"Don't do that . . ."

He worked faster.

"You've had so much experience . . ."

"Stud to the world." He drew the blouse aside, undid her bra. Her nipples rose to his touch.

She said his name and her head fell back. He removed her skirt, her panties, undressed himself.

They kissed and touched each other.

She said, "It's so—odd, being completely naked out of doors."

" 'The nakedness of women is the work of God.' "

"You don't believe in God."

"But William Blake does."

"I see."

"You must learn how to submit gracefully." He moved a leg across her thighs and rested his cheek on her breasts. After a while he sat up and looked at her with clinical concern. "There's something the matter," he said.

"What?" she came into a sitting position. "What's wrong?"

"The right boob is bigger than the left."

"That's absurd! I'm in quite good balance, thank you."

He hefted one breast, then the other. "Clearly out of whack. When you walk, is there a tendency to list?"

"Horrible man! Without trying, I could hate you."

"Judge for yourself."

In turn, she examined each breast. "Oh! Oh, dear. The *right* one is bigger."

"Of course."

"Does that offend you?"

"I wouldn't have it any other way. Matter of fact, I happen to dig distortion."

She ruffled his hair. "I do please you?"

"Very much."

"There's so much I don't know."

"Well, I'll demonstrate. You do what I do. And if you don't get it right the first time, you'll do it over again until you do."

"Promise?"

He embraced her, mouth on hers. After a while she moved under him, gaining confidence, twisting to make herself more easily available to his hands. She pressed up to meet him as his finger explored her damp center. Her body began to quiver and small pleading sounds came out of her.

She held to him, old fears and restraints dropping away. Her flesh demanded more and her hands went out to touch him. *There* . . . and gradually her fingers searched his body as his had done to her, trying to imagine what she would most like if she were a man.

Sensation piled on sensation, and a thickening tension boiled up in her belly. Her head moved about, eyes fixed and unseeing, blood swelling in her veins. She trembled without control, everything forgotten except the craving that had focused between her legs.

She bit his shoulder and never knew she was guiding his erect passions into place. He plunged forward, forcing her back to the ground, lifting and tugging, struggling to go deeper. Spread now, she responded fully, nails at his back. They came together in conflicting tempos, soon resolved, their bellies making a soft wet slapping sound.

A dizziness rippled through her, a strange faintness. She tried to hang on to consciousness, to save herself.

Nothing helped. Soon she was off into a spinning void, a twister.

At once, all cravings, sensations, down to a single hot eye. Colors mingled and features bled into each other, lines converging. Tendons and muscles, cells and nerves, marrow and blood, fused for an endless, unbearable moment in time, breaking loose in a succession of waves that filled every place in her with total pleasure. She slumped, complete as never before, and weeping gratefully, hanging tightly to Foreman's slack body, determined to keep him.

"Hurrah," she muttered presently, "for our side . . ."

They lay under the jacaranda tree, fully clothed now, dozing in each other's arms. He stirred, his eyes opened; she woke, studied his profile in wonder and approval. They kissed.

"I love you," he said casually.

She didn't answer.

He kissed her again. "Say that you love me."

She hesitated. "I don't think I'm ready to say it."

"Why not?"

"I'm not sure."

"I'm sure, why aren't you?"

"You're quicker than I am. You have quicker reflexes, a quicker mind."

"It's true, I'm much smarter."

"Quicker isn't necessarily smarter."

He sat up and lit a cigarette, mood sobering rapidly. "Caution depresses me," he muttered. "Where the hell is the army?" He sucked on the cigaret. "I love you, it's only right that you love me back."

"Love with a stranger? Indeed!"

"You just had sex with that stranger."

"Sex with a stranger, yes. But love? Give me a chance, Paul, not just for my sake but so I can be more, give more."

He stared down toward the deserted village. "I'm not complaining. Besides, you give much more, you'll be inside out. However, I concede the objective evidence for my case isn't exactly persuasive."

"Please don't run yourself down. It's not very persuasive either."

He pulled around to face her. "To me, it is. I've always
believed a man has a sort of obligation to fulfill his best
self, that to do less was suicidal, not to mention cheap."

"You're very good at what you do?"

He shook his head. "I've never done anything I'm
proud of."

"This picture . . ."

"Yes, this picture. I tried to con myself into believing I
could make it a special film, but it won't wash. This is
Bristol's flick, it was from the first, it always will be. I've
known it all along but wouldn't admit it. I'm beginning to
think I'm not even a good craftsman. A hack, in fact."

"I don't believe that."

"Believe it. I made clever, witty TV commercials and I
made a clever, witty little movie called *Last Man Down*.
Bristol liked it and came after me. That was it, the ultimate judgment on me. I should've known it. I've been
trying to make Bristol the heavy of the piece. He's no
beauty, but he isn't my personal devil either. I needed a
scapegoat for my own shortcomings. Hell, I've become his
alter ego."

She touched his hand. "I suggest you forgive yourself,
Paul. It's pretty good therapy. There's plenty of time for
you, and besides, maybe the picture you're making is better than you think."

"Bristol will take care of that. He'll shovel in every
scene I leave out, every irrelevant frame in his twenty
minutes of sex."

He touched her cheek and grinned. "There I go again.
Evil ol' Harry. Wonderful frustrated genius Paulie.
Enough. I've made you, and that's a real accomplish-
ment. I got to learn to appreciate my basic talents more."

She kissed him on the mouth.

He stood up and pointed. "Down there, the soldiers.
With Theo Gavin out front, like Custer just before Little
Big Horn."

"I hope Don Miguel is right and the soldiers don't leave
the road."

"Shall we welcome them?"

They were halfway down the hill when Grace stopped.

"Paul? Do you think people can tell by looking at me
. . . ? Do you think it shows . . . ?"

He looped an arm across her shoulders and laughed,
continued toward the village.

"Paul, I think I'm very happy."

"You aren't very decisive."

"It . . . making love was so . . ."

"Naturally."

"Paul?"

"Yes."

"Can we do it again soon?"

He was still laughing when the soldiers rode into the
village. Foreman lifted a hand in greeting to Theo Gavin,
who reined in the dapple gray and glared at Foreman and
Grace.

"What are *you* doing here, Foreman?"

"Someone had to meet you, it seemed the neighborly
thing to do."

The Army major spoke in scrupulous English. *"Señor,*
where are the Chinchahua? Who is this woman? Is this
some kind of a trick?" Behind him, the troopers peered
nervously up at the high peaks and fingered their rifles.

"Oh, yes," Foreman said, "the Chinchahua. They send
their apologies but a prior engagement—"

The officer snapped off orders and a dozen horsemen
swept through the village. At the far end, they dismounted, returned on foot, rifles ready, inspecting each
hut wearily. A second command sent soldiers out to the
flanks, facing the high ground.

"The Chinchahua are not to be trusted," the major declared.

"That's what they said about you," Foreman put in.

"You told them!" Theo accused Foreman.

"Give the man a gold star. I did, indeed. Also, I inquired as to whether or not they had stolen our million-
peso lady. They had not."

"And you believed them?"

"I did. So why don't you and your task force just take
off? Grace and I will mind the village."

Theo peered out at the rugged terrain. "I intend to find
Samantha, to punish the criminals who did this thing. Depend on it."

"Bully for you, Teddy. Pull it off and the President may even phone you, just like he does winning football coaches. You're sort of the coach of this outfit, aren't you?"

"You don't seem to realize the seriousness of the situation, Foreman," Theo said. He turned his horse around. "We're wasting time, major. Let's go on."

The major spoke carefully. "Where would you like to go, Señor Gavin?"

"Up into the mountains, of course. Let's track the Chinchahua down, force the truth out of them."

"I wouldn't suggest that," Foreman said.

"Keep out of this!" Theo snapped. "This is a job for men who aren't *afraid* to fight."

"And die," Foreman added.

"Major!" Theo said.

"*Señor,*" the officer said with weary patience. "Up there are only goat trails, or no trails at all. We will surely lose our way, especially since soon it will be dark. Logic compels me to point out that the Chinchahua know this ground and we do not. Also, they probably are watching us at this very moment and we do not know where they are."

"Bravo, major!" Foreman said.

Theo glared at him. "We might still be able to find them."

The major raised his brows. "Such good fortune would be the death of us all. There would be a massacre. My duty is to my men and their families. I suggest that we return to Acapulco. There we will arrange for fresh horses and cool drinks. Who knows, perhaps additional word has come from the kidnappers and a change in plan is in order. In any case, this gentleman says that the Chinchahua did not take Miss Moore and I have no reason to doubt him at the moment. *Muchachos!*" he said. "We go back!" The troopers cheered and promptly formed a neat double rank, facing away from the village. Theo, his back straight, hurried to the head of the line, led the detachment back down out of the mountain.

Less than an hour later, the Chinchahua returned to the village. First the women and children, the old people,

then the men carrying their weapons with the casual re-
gard of those for whom guns were a natural extension of
their bodies. Don Miguel and the Elders were the last to
arrive. Grace and Foreman moved out to meet them. In
the blue-tinted light, Don Miguel's face revealed nothing.

"The woman was stolen by Huachucan. They hold her
in a shepherd's hut beyond the long ridge, on the eastern
slope. Their horses are hobbled and the guards are close
to the hut, so clearly they expect no trouble. The Huachucan are arrogant and this time their arrogance will
cost them in blood. We attack in the morning."

"Attack!" Foreman said to Grace in English. "What
the hell is he talking about? If they hit that hut, the first
one killed will be Samantha."

Grace translated and Don Miguel nodded solemnly.
"Our lands have been violated. The Huachucan have committed this act on our territory and brought the Army to
our village. We must act. There is no other way."

"The hell there isn't!" Foreman shouted, when Grace
translated. "The idea is to get Samantha back alive. Okay,
the bad guys shouldn't have come over to this side of
town. But they did and so far nobody's been hurt. Let's
keep it that way. I don't know which is worse, this band
of bloodthirsty aborigines or that Gilbert and Sullivan
army Gavin brought up here. Unless we do something,
Samantha's a dead pigeon."

Grace arranged a stiff smile on her mouth, spoke in a
grim voice. "Stop yelling. Don Miguel is not a fool. Insult
him by tone or word and we'll all be sorry. Now make a
genuine apology in Spanish for losing your temper."

"The hell I will."

"And make him believe it."

Foreman faced Don Miguel and spread his hands. *"Per-
dóname, Don Miguel. Yo soy un gringo estúpido. Perdón."*

"Sí," the chief agreed gravely. *"Tiene razón."*

"Would it be possible to talk to the Huachucan?" Grace
wanted to know.

Don Miguel answered slowly. "The Huachucan will
shoot any Chinchahua they see. Especially with night
coming. Talk between us can do no good."

"Will the Huachucan shoot me?" Grace said.

The question surprised Don Miguel; he would never allow a woman to do men's work. "They will not talk to you."

Grace understood. "What if my friend comes with me?"

Don Miguel measured Foreman. "Perhaps with a man at your side. But this one speaks poor Spanish and his thoughts show in his face."

"I will talk for us," Grace said.

"Perhaps the Huachucan will not kill you, but I doubt it."

"I wish to try."

"Very well. I will send two men to guide you to a place near where they hold the woman. But you must go to the shepherd's hut by yourself. And if you are not killed, you will have to find your way back alone. I risk no lives for such foolishness."

"Can we leave at once?"

"Go now," Don Miguel said.

Behind them, the sky glowed crimson and blue and pink. But the slope below was cloaked in lengthening shadows and the shepherd's hut was almost invisible in a grove of leafy trees. A curl of smoke drifted out from under the thatched roof, filtering lazily through the leaves.

"How do we get down there without getting shot?" Foreman said, thinking as he said it that he probably deserved to be shot for letting her talk him into this crazy mission in the first place. He and Grace were alone, the guides having climbed back over the long ridge which they had earlier crossed. He had an almost certain conviction that he wasn't going to live through the night; and he wanted very much to continue living.

Grace touched his arm. "We've got two choices . . ."

"Right. We can run away from here or we can walk. Running is faster."

"Stop it. One of us can stay up here while the other one goes down to talk to the Huachucan. That way if anything goes wrong—"

"That's the worst idea I've heard in a long time. What's the second choice?"

"We go down together."

"I'm beginning to feel threatened."

She kissed his cheek. "Be brave. I depend on you."

"What if they decide to shoot us while we are on this evening's stroll?"

"We'll have to be very quiet."

"No, ma'am. Just the reverse. Let's make some noise. Let them know we're coming. Nobody appreciates company dropping in unexpectedly, especially at dinner time. All right, let's go." He started down the slope, calling as he went. *"Hola! Huachucan! Hola,* down there. *No tiren!* Hold your fire, men. *Somos amigos! Muy amigos!* Keep your fingers off the triggers. *Somos amigos con mucho dinero, muchachos!* Did you get that?—*mucho dinero!"*

Four men with rifles drifted into view, faces vacant under their sombreros. Foreman stopped a dozen paces away, arms raised.

"Well, *buenas tardes,* men. Or is it *noches?* Anyway, *buenas, buenas."* Grace came up alongside him. "Say hello to the boys, dear. Say something quick."

She spoke in a conversational manner. "My friend and I are here to talk about the Señorita Moore. We have come to buy her back. But to do business in the dark when rifles are pointed at you is not such a good thing. Is there one among you who speaks for the Huachucan or have we come to the wrong place?"

One of the men cursed and raised his rifle. But before he could use it, another one ordered him away, then motioned to Foreman and Grace. "Go inside the hut," he ordered.

They did. Inside, smoke and the sweet-sour smell of spoiled fruit mingled. Five more Huachucan were present, short, strong men with thick features and heavy bones. Huddled in one corner, Samantha Moore. She raised her head and wailed in relief at the sight of Foreman.

"Oh, please, Paul, for *God's* sake get me away from here."

"Have you been hurt, Samantha?"

"Goddamn right, I have—"

"I think she's all right," Grace said to Foreman, then to Samantha. "Just stay where you are. And don't talk. Not a word. This is going to take some time." Her eyes went around the room. "They won't tell us which one is the chief. Naming him would be the same as a betrayal. We have to pick him out."

"What a fun game," Foreman said.

"Make a choice."

"The one by the fire. He looks right. You can almost smell the qualities of leadership. Reminds me of a West Pointer I once knew."

"I think you're right." Grace took a single stride closer to the fire. "*Señor, jefe*," she began. The squatting man kept his head down. "We are here to discuss the woman. No soldiers have come with us. We are unarmed."

The squatting man lifted his head "Your man cannot speak for himself?"

"My man has less Spanish than I."

"I know you. You are the woman of the Chinchahua."

Grace flushed at the implied insult. "I am a friend of all Mexican people. I study the Chinchahua language. And you are Don Esteban, chief of the Huachucan. Three times I tried to speak with you and three times I was turned away."

Esteban gave no sign that he understood what she was talking about. His attention was entirely on the present. None of them had expected this to happen, for this man and this woman to appear. Nor had he. All of the business was to be dealt with by Julio and Agustín over the telephone. The plan, which had gone so well up to now, had suddenly come apart. Esteban wondered how these two had discovered this place, but pride prevented him from asking.

"You are here," he said, "but you were not asked to come. You are not of our tribe, therefore you are enemies. The Huachucan give death to their enemies. Still, we are men of intelligence and we will listen to you first."

Grace fought down her fear. "You stole this woman from the American movie company. My man is the chief of that company. He has come to take her back."

"To come is one thing," Esteban said. "To take from Huachucan is another."

Grace realized she had blundered. She tried to recover. "Don Esteban is wise and he knows that the American woman is puny and not strong enough to do a day's work. Still, as the Huachucan would do, we wish to reclaim our own. It is clear that the woman can be of no value to the Huachucan and so we wish to relieve you of the burden. But we do not desire that you go unrewarded for keeping her without harm. It is fair that a certain payment should be made."

No one spoke. Mention of money had come round faster than the Huachucan had anticipated. They would have preferred more sparring, a matching of wits, the building of an argument with slow precision before the actual bargaining began.

Esteban stood up and folded his arms. "A price has been asked," he said.

The Indians avoided looking at Grace, waited for her to respond. She spoke casually to Foreman. "I'll mention a figure to you in English. Object and make it strong, to back up my position."

"Go."

"The asking price is a million. Suppose I offer twenty-five thousand?"

"No!" Foreman said, voice heavy with disgust. "No woman is worth that much. But what worries me is that glory nut, Gavin. He's liable to show up here any minute with his soldiers and get us all killed if this isn't settled by daylight. So pay the two dollars, as the old joke goes."

"That's enough, thank you. Don't overdo it." She directed her attention to Esteban. "My man says to take a woman as you have taken this one is banditry and insists she must be returned freely. He promises to say nothing to the authorities . . . However, he is a reasonable man and to please everyone he offers a payment for services. Twenty-five thousand pesos."

Esteban raised his hands in despair. "The price is one million pesos."

"*Aah*," the listening Huachucan sighed in admiration of their leader.

"No woman is worth such an amount," Grace said. "Perhaps my man will double his offer, but that is all."

Esteban stared into space. "The foreigner is of the American cinema, no. And she has many rich friends. They can pay. Nine hundred and fifty thousand pesos."

"Seventy-five thousand," Grace said.

"We are too far apart. We will kill the *gringa*."

"Dead women bring no money to anyone."

"What's all this about killing?" Foreman said in English.

Grace jerked her head in assent, said to Esteban, "My man wearies of so much talk. He orders me to make a final offer. One hundred thousand pesos."

"I will make you a final offer," Esteban returned. "Eight hundred thousand."

"No!" Foreman said. "Tell him to keep the woman."

"*Please . . .*" Samantha said, dying every second they talked.

"Shut up!" Foreman snapped. "Tell him what I said," he said to Grace.

She repeated it in Spanish.

Esteban glared at Foreman, spoke with soft menace in his voice. "To do business through a woman is not a man's way. Nor am I a seller of souvenirs in the market. I am chief of the Huachucan."

Aah . . .

"*Dos cientos miles,*" Foreman said crisply.

"Seven hundred thousand," Esteban said. "It is true the *gringa* is neither strong nor a worker. But there are few women with hair that color and she still is young enough to pleasure some men. You have my final offer."

Grace shook her head.

Esteban folded his arms, face immobile.

Foreman took Grace by the elbow, steered her toward the door. "We are going!" he announced loudly.

"Six hundred thousand," the chief said. "My final offer."

Foreman calculated rapidly. "That's forty-eight thousand U.S. bucks, right? What the hell do I care about Gavin's money? The sonofabitch will write it off as a tax loss or a promotion expense. Tell the chief he can have half a million if he provides us with safe transport back to Acapulco."

"You're sure Mr. Gavin will go for that much?" Grace said.

"Oh, yes!" Samantha cried. "I know he will."

Grace faced Esteban squarely. "Our final offer. Five hundred thousand pesos, a great deal of money for only one woman. We will talk no more about it." She moved her hands in a slicing motion, horizontal to the ground.

Esteban examined her face, looked at Foreman. *"Bueno,"* he said. *"Bueno."*

"Bueno," Grace said.

"Bueno," Foreman echoed, offering his hand. Esteban shook it once, turned to his followers, a broad smile creasing his walnut face.

Aah . . .

17

El Playamar was a sprawling complex of buildings constructed in the colonial style, more like an old hacienda than a modern hotel. Built only two years before, it had been set down on a hillside, insuring that every room, suite, and private bungalow, was provided with a clear view of the sea. Luxury guided the thinking of the owners of El Playamar, luxury and profits. In order to attract guests who could afford to pay exorbitant rates, the owners tried to foresee every possible desire, arranging the hotel accordingly. They installed ten swimming pools around the property—heated, cooled, curative, salt water —and fourteen clay tennis courts, a private golf course, an indoor gymnasium, an outdoor gymnasium, eight hot rooms—dry and steam—a solarium, horseback riding, skeet-shooting, shuffleboards, squash courts, a game room, transportation to all beaches, boating, and daily classes in bridge, modern dance and yoga, and marathon sensitivity groups every weekend.

At El Playamar, it was possible to dine at any hour of the day or night, and bar service was continuous. You could have your clothes cleaned at four in the morning, or be supplied with a sixteen millimeter movie projector and the latest major releases. Medical and dental attention was always available.

"It's a simply marvelous hotel," Louise Peters enthused to Harry Bristol and Shelly over brandy and coffee. Two bus boys cleared away the remains of dinner and withdrew, smiling and bobbing obsequiously.

The four of them were settled comfortably in the spacious sitting room of Louise and Jason's private bungalow, the lights low, soft music coming from concealed speakers; a wall of glass doors opened onto a discreetly lighted garden of vines and exotic red-and-white flowers.

"Friends in New York," Jason explained in his most sincere manner, "recommended us to El Playamar. The Hartwells, perhaps you know them. They knew we appreciate privacy and assured us El Playamar could provide it. As you see, they were right."

"Each bungalow," Louise took over, "was put up with the good life in mind. The walls are thick enough to exclude the heat of the day, the chill of the night, and all sound."

"And high enough to turn away prying eyes," Jason added.

"One could entertain a hundred people and no one outside would ever suspect . . ."

"Not that we would, of course. Blatant displays aren't our style . . ."

"Intimacy is what we try for . . ."

"Intimacy and naturalness . . ."

"In all things . . ."

"A conscious rejection of the encumbrances of civilization . . ."

"Rejection of the rubbish . . ."

"Clothes, for one . . ."

"Jason and I are sunworshippers. Literally."

"We pay daily homage to the Sun God, when possible . . ."

"Don't you just love to get tan *all* over?"

"Don't put it down to vanity. Oh, no. Vitamin D comes from the sun in its purest form."

"That's okay," Bristol said, "when people have good-looking bodies." He patted his thick, hard middle. "But I'm no spring chicken . . ."

Louise inspected him openly. "I'd say you take pretty good care of your body."

"I watch what I eat."

"I'll bet you exercise. You have the look of a strong man to me."

"I used to bench press two hundred twenty pounds easy. But these days I move around so much . . ."

"And Shelly," Louise broke in, shifting around to face her. "Shelly looks absolutely superb. How do you keep your figure and that lovely complexion? I envy you so."

"You'll never see a better shape," Bristol said. "Stripped down, she's sensational."

"Harry . . ."

"Don't be modest, dear," Louise said, mouth curved absently.

"Look," Bristol went on, "I know about bodies. In my business, you have to."

"Earlier," Jason said, leaning toward Shelly, his smooth face ingenuous, eyes vacant and steady, "Harry was telling us about that nude swimming scene you did at Villa Gloria . . ."

Shelly wet her mouth. From the moment she and Harry had arrived at the bungalow, she'd felt uneasy, as if she didn't belong. Harry said they were going to a party and she had been prepared to deal with a number of people. In this small group, she felt tense, and resented the increased attention directed her way as the strange evening wore on.

"I've never seen anyone naked in a movie," Jason said. "That is, no one personally known to me."

"Is it a blue movie?" Louise said brightly.

"The real thing, you mean?" Bristol said. "Nah. It *looks* real but that's all. You seen any stag reels, Louise?"

Louise kept her eyes on Shelly as she answered him. "They're so kicky. All that exposed flesh, but mostly tired flesh, hardly up to the job at hand, as it were."

"I've got some great stuff back in the States," Bristol said. "Maybe we can arrange a filming—"

Shelly finished the brandy in her glass, wished someone would change the subject.

"I've wondered what it would be like being an actress," Louise offered.

Jason laughed. "First thing you have to know is how to take off your clothes."

Louise clapped. "You're right, darling! Acting is often secondary."

"Don't you agree, Shelly?" Jason said. He went over to her, refilled her glass.

Shelly lifted it to her mouth, murmured something to the rim.

"What?" Bristol demanded. His laugh was abrupt, harsh. "Most chicks can't get their shoes off without falling over. I've auditioned a thousand of them."

"I wonder how I would do?" Louise asked no one in particular.

"Brilliantly, darling," Jason answered. "Are we about to learn of your secret ambition?"

"You should've told me," Bristol said, hunching forward. "I'd've put you in the picture."

"Dear Harry—"

"Would Louise be right?" Jason said thoughtfully. "The personality, the face, the body? Shelly, what do you think?"

She drank some more brandy, finding it impossible to raise her head, to look at anyone.

Bristol answered the question. "Louise would be sensational."

She laughed, her head going back, breasts pushing forward in clear outline under the delicate green blouse she wore. Bristol hawked his throat clear. "Naturally, you'd have to audition, like everybody else."

"Could you do that, darling?" Jason said. "Take off your clothes before strangers?"

"That would be a test," she said.

Jason smiled mirthlessly, eyes sliding over to Shelly. "I suppose, with practice, one can develop a faculty for it."

"Where does one get to practice?" Louise said. "One doesn't go around undressing in front of strange men."

They all laughed. Except Shelly. She concentrated on the brandy in her glass, on delivering it to her mouth, on swallowing, allowing the sting to subside, repeating the process. The laughter was a dim background noise, along with an indistinct blend of voices. Out of that insistent thrum a single voice grew louder, clearer—*"Why don't you come around at the end of the work day? When things quiet down. That way we won't be rushed or interrupted . . ."* And she had continued to listen, not daring to end the conversation, unable to turn away from any opportunity that might further her career. *"How did you get my name?"* she had asked, not even listening to his reply, knowing the answer. An agent or a producer or a director had given him her phone number, had told him that Shelly Hanes was available, on call, easy . . . And she was . . . *"Can I depend on you?"* the man on the telephone had asked. And she had promised to be at his office within the hour. And then the piercing shrill of the braking car, of horrified screams, of Barbara, Barbara . . . She had finished the conversation politely, wandered out to the street to find out what had happened . . .

"Shelly!" Bristol's abrasive voice dissolved the memory, and she obediently raised her eyes. "Louise asked you a question."

"How did it feel," Louise repeated, "the first time you stripped in front of a stranger?"

Shelly reached back through the brandy vapor. But the first time was lost in a rush of faceless men and cheap wooden desks and dusty carpets and those awful fake leather couches that stuck to your skin . . .

"I've always been a believer in getting expert instruction," Jason was saying. "Why don't we find someone to teach Louise how to get undressed properly?"

"But who?" Louise said, eyes wide.

"What about it, Shelly?" Bristol offered.

Shelly swallowed more brandy.

"Shelly," Louise murmured. "Would you?"

"Sure," Bristol burst out.

"First lesson coming up," Jason said.

Louise came to her feet, pirouetting, ending up with her legs apart under her long, sea-green skirt. "What do I do first?"

"Tell her," Bristol said to Shelly. "Go on, tell her."

Shelly roused herself. "They . . . always your legs. That's always first."

"Do I just show them?" Louise asked her audience.

"Sure," Bristol said.

"Go on, darling," Jason urged. He moved deliberately, sitting on the arm of Shelly's chair, smiling down at her.

Louise slowly lifted the long, green skirt.

Jason shifted around impatiently. "Too much skirt," he said. "Why not just take it off?"

"Whatever you say, darling." She undid the waist fastenings, let it fall, stepping out of it gracefully, turning slowly.

"Terrific," Bristol said. "Great legs . . ." The blouse she wore ended at her hips and below it a triangle of yellow lace. He became aware of himself, of the bulge in his crotch. "Listen . . ." he muttered.

"Take the blouse off," Jason said.

Louise obeyed. Her breasts were larger than Bristol had imagined, round globes that sagged only slightly, bobbling as she moved to display herself. Facing Shelly, she paused.

"Would a producer be interested in me at this point?" she asked in a low voice.

"Would Louise get the job?" Jason said to Shelly, fingers playing across the back of her neck.

Bristol swallowed. "Jobs are highly competitive."

Louise giggled and turned around.

"Harry wants to see the rest of you, darling," Jason said.

Without a word, Louise pulled off her panties, displaying herself to Bristol front and back. "How," she said after a moment, "do I compare to Shelly?"

"A contest!" Jason said. "Let's have a contest."

"Stand up," Bristol commanded Shelly. She didn't move. Bristol crossed rapidly to where she sat. "Stand up, I said!" He took hold of her arm, jerked roughly.

She made it to her feet. Someone took the glass from her hand and she felt deprived, a thing of value lost forever. And she was suddenly tired, her body cumbersome, her legs weak. She shivered.

Words spoken to her had no meaning, no effect. And then hands were at her, undoing the fastenings of the skirt she wore. She was being turned, examined, touched.

"The body of a young girl."

"Where do we go from here?" Jason asked.

Louise was laughing. "You go to Shelly, darling. What a delicious dessert she'll make for you. Meanwhile, Harry and I can get to know each other. Later . . ."

Bristol was at Louise before she'd finished speaking, hands reaching.

"Gently, honey, gently. When I'm properly ready you can get as rough as you like, but now—"

Bristol took one breast into his mouth.

After a moment, Louise detached herself from him. "That's just fine, Harry. But poor Jason. He's not having any fun at all . . ."

Bristol turned around to see Shelly backing away, skirt raised protectively.

"What the hell are you doing!" Bristol yelled. "You been here before. Take off those fucking things and don't ruin this for me."

She continued to back away. The worst of it was that part of her was drawn to them, to what they all wanted of her—attracted and repelled at the same time.

"No, Harry, please, don't make me."

His hand flashed out, landing on her cheek. She stumbled and almost fell."

"I don't want to."

"Dumb bitch. As if one more screwing makes any difference. You lost count years ago. You been putting out for the cripple, you'll put out now. Take those damned things off . . ."

She began to unbutton her blouse. "Oh, you bastard. You bastard—" She whirled suddenly and ran for the door, was out of the bungalow before anyone could stop her. Bristol swore and went after her, came back alone. "She's gone," he said. "No sight of her. How do you figure a broad like that? She used to be okay."

"Dear me," Louise said. "Well," she went on cheerfully, "there's still the two of you and the one of me. I do believe I'm built to accommodate you both. Let's try, Shall we?"

Shelly ran. Blindly toward the ocean. Twice she fell, losing her shoes, but kept on. She lunged past night-time revelers and failed to see them, or hear their taunting laughter, or respond to their crude invitations.

She made it to the beach, stumbling across the sand to where the soft water broke in silent wavelets. Gasping, she went to her knees, head low.

When she was able, she went into the water until it reached her waist, bathed her wrists and splashed her face, turned back to the sand.

She was ashamed, deeply ashamed. Mostly because she knew she was responsible for what had happened, for what had always happened to her. Harry Bristol. He was the same as every man she'd ever known. She'd made herself available to everyone, takers and users, had asked for the brutality and abuse. Had often even craved it. . . .

She began moving without direction along the darkened strand. She was a big liar, especially to herself. There had been no chance with Harry. And not with his movie. Not with anything. It would soon be New Year's Eve, it would at least be ended then. . . .

Why wait?

Into the ocean, the water rising until it was around her chin. A swell broke over her and she swallowed, choked and coughed, arms thrashing. She swam, managed to find her way back to shore. Shivering and cold, yet suddenly refreshed, she began to laugh, her mind functioning clearly. What a crazy idea. She was *not* going to die. She was not seriously ill. A little anemia was all that was wrong with her, some chemical thing that caused the sudden flushes, the weak times. Nothing more than that. Admit it. You're going to live.

She twirled around until her feet crossed and she went down. Crying and laughing. Okay, she'd gone all the way to the bottom. Like the man said, there was no place to go but up.

And Morrie. When they were together she felt good, complete. They would help each other.

She was running now. Exhilarated by the possibilities. She ran on, going faster, until her lungs burned and her legs wobbled. Gasping, she pitched forward, waiting for strength to return. She knew it would soon. Just as she knew everything was going to begin to be all right.

She lifted her head and screamed.

A hand slammed down across her mouth, smothering the sound. She tried to bite the hand. No use. She went slack and lay still.

"That's it," a hard male voice said. "Screaming's going to bring the fuzz and we don't want that. I'll let you go if you promise to be good—"

She managed a nod and he released her. Her eyes rolled upward and she struggled to remember—the long bony face, the yellow mustache, the sparse beard.

Leo . . .

"Hey, baby, remember me?"

She sat up, shaking but less afraid. At least she knew Leo. "I'm cold," she muttered.

Leo put his hand on her shoulder. "You're wet. Take off your clothes, everything. You can have my serape."

"I want to go back to my hotel."

"You're lucky I found you. Come on, I know a place where you can get warm." He took hold of her arm.

She pulled free, scuttling crablike along the sand. "Let me alone!!"

"Hey, stay cool. You can't run around the way you are. Somebody might find you and—"

She made it up to her feet, broke into a run. He was after her from a quick start, reaching. The blouse ripped away in his hands and she fell. She rolled, trying to regain her footing, but he was too fast. His hands found her breasts and he began mouthing obscenities against her throat.

". . . the smell of you . . . other chicks made me think of . . . pulling off, seeing you . . . now give out . . . now I'm going to get . . ."

She fought. Punching and kicking, in silent fury as if to conserve her strength, driving him back with the unexpected fierceness of her attack. Free of him, she ran again. He closed in and she changed direction.

A low tackle brought her down, the fight knocked out of her. He turned her face up and tore her panties away, face moving down between her thighs. Her hand swung and she raked his cheek. He got up on his knees and hit her in the stomach. She retched and brought her knees up. He avoided them and swore, punched her again. And again. Kept on punching . . .

18

At nine fifteen the following morning, Theo Gavin delivered half a million pesos to Paul Foreman. Foreman promptly drove up into the mountains, made his way to the shack where Samantha Moore was being held. He delivered the money to Esteban and the two men shook hands, gravely thanked each other.

Less than one hour later, Samantha was back inside Villa Gloria and minutes after that she was naked and sweating out the collected filth of her experience in a private sauna. This done, she showered, then floated on a rubber raft in the Roman pool, emerging only when Bernard materialized with a physician, the chief of police, and the local stringer for United Press International, each in his own way anxious to examine the victim. Samantha made them wait until she was properly dressed and made up. But that didn't take too long.

SAMANTHA! HOSPITALITY SUITE
Press Only

So read the neatly lettered sign on the door. Inside, one of the Hotel Royalton's luxury suites had been transformed into working and drinking headquarters for members of the world press corps. Banks of telephones had been quickly hooked up, after certain appropriate amenities had been observed toward an executive of Teléfonos de Mexico, and four of his subordinates. A trio of bilingual secretaries was on 24-hour call, red-jacketed waiters stood by to serve food and drinks; messengers waited in the hallway; and feminine companionship could be had on request.

When the news came that Samantha was safely back at

Villa Gloria a mild, alcoholic cheer went up. Two European writers placed calls to their offices; an Australian reporter asked Jerry Baumer to arrange an interview with Samantha; the rest went back to their drinking.

In his own suite, Theo Gavin was talking to Bernard Louis Font. "How is Samantha? What did they do to her?"

"Do?" Bernard said, clearly surprised. "Oh, I see! Let me assure you, Theo, not a hand was laid on her, as I understand it. It makes one wonder, does it not? About these savages, I mean. Obviously they possess very little appreciation for the more beautiful things of life."

"Let me talk to Samantha."

"Impossible, dear friend. The physician attends her currently and then it will be the police chief's turn. Poor Samantha, the ordeal has exhausted her. She is spent and afraid for her life."

"But it's over. I paid the ransom, half a million pesos."

"And how wonderfully generous of you. And how fortunate that you at least had such a sum available. I, of course, would have done likewise, had my financial condition been otherwise. However, if I may be allowed a correction—it is not over. The police chief talks of assembling an armed force powerful enough to sweep the mountains from village to village until the bandits can be apprehended. He insists that Samantha should identify them."

"Good! I'd like to get my hands on those people."

"Dear Theo, try to grasp the essence of the situation. Such a procedure can lead only to additional distress for our Samantha. Should the kidnappers be identified and imprisoned, their relatives, friends, fellow tribesmen, would surely be angry and resentful, desire revenge. Paul Foreman understands this and insists he can remember no face clearly."

"And the girl, that Grace whatever her name was?"

"She is gone. Back to the Chinchahua, perhaps. One cannot be sure."

"Well, why can't Samantha claim she doesn't remember what they looked like?"

"Dear Samantha is a fragile creature. She wishes to terminate the entire affair. At once. Only in that way can she be assured of a normal way of life, tranquility—"

Theo broke in. "But if the law wants her to—"

"A suggestion, if I may."

Caution spread through Theo. "Make it."

"This police chief, he has a sincere fondness for money. A few thousand pesos discreetly offered would insure an end to all stress and difficulty, sordidness could finally be put aside . . ."

"How many thousands?" Theo said, his irritation clear.

"Ten should be sufficient."

Theo calculated rapidly. That was only another eight hundred dollars; Baumer could work it into his entertainment budget. "All right," he said into the phone. "I'm on my way out there. Keep the chief away from Samantha."

He hung up and called the Hospitality Suite, told Jerry Baumer that he wanted to see him. Minutes later, the advertising man arrived, talking excitedly.

"We've really hit the jackpot, Mr. G. This is really going to pay off. I've got interviews set up and calls in to every network TV show that uses guests and—"

Theo cut him off. "How many pesos have you got on you?"

"About twenty-five thousand. Cash comes in handy. Especially with the girls. They insist on being paid—"

"Give me ten." Baumer counted it out instantly. "I'm on my way to Villa Gloria. Samantha needs me. Anything important comes up, contact me there."

"Yes, sir."

Theo went to the door and opened it. A tall youth, his head covered with a crop of short, new hair, stood with his hand poised to knock. Theo stared at him, without recognition.

"Hello, father," Charles said.

The ransom was paid. Samantha had been delivered back to Villa Gloria. And Foreman and Grace went off by themselves to sit on a deserted section of beach. For a long time, neither of them spoke. Finally Foreman took her hand.

"Stay here with me," he said. "A few more days and

this masterpiece will be wrapped up. We can pile into the VW and take off."

"You make it sound so easy."

"It is easy. Just say you'll stay."

"My work with the Chinchahua is finished, I think. They let me live with them and cooperated with me as long as I didn't upset their lives. All that's been changed. I brought you into the village and they'll connect that with the army's intrusion and the Huachucan's violation of their tribal lands. I'm sure Don Miguel will tell me to leave."

"Great," Foreman said. "Pack your things and move in with me."

"I couldn't do that."

"Because we're not married?"

"That sounds pretty square, I guess."

"What if I said I'd marry you?"

"The answer would still be no."

"I see," he said.

"I don't think you do. I need to feel certain you love me—"

"I do love you. Maybe it's more that you're not convinced you love me."

She took a deep breath. "I'll admit this—I'm just not sure what I feel at this moment. What there's been between us has been like nothing I've ever known. You made me aware of my body, my feelings. But it's all happened so fast. Love is partly sex, but it's got to be a sustained commitment, and neither of us has made that kind of commitment yet. That takes time, and effort."

"All right. I want us to take the time, to make the effort. Stay with me, give us a chance."

She shook her head.

"It's not that simple, Paul. There's still my work. It's finished here, but I should go back to Mexico City, to the University. My tapes have to be transcribed, the results evaluated. It may be possible to complete the Chinchahua alphabet with what I've got. The results have to be written up, gotten in shape for publication. That will open the way for other people to make practical application of my work, go further in helping the Chinchahua, all the tribes."

"Has it ever occurred to you that those Indians don't want to be helped? They might prefer to be left alone."

"Maybe so, but the Chinchahua, the Huachucan, the other mountain people, are dying out, and without help they'll disappear in the next ten to fifteen years."

"You make it sound like you're trying to mate a couple of whooping cranes, to save the species. These are human beings, with wills of their own.

"I know that. And that's why people like me have to try to convince Don Miguel, Don Esteban, the other leaders, of the kind of danger they face. They need to learn how to save themselves."

"And what about us? Who's going to save us? Dammit, Grace, I never thought I'd hear myself say this, but I think we have something special. You feel it too."

"I feel a great deal. Yesterday may very well have been the best day of my life, Paul. But it was one day. You're a romantic man and I love you for it. But how will you feel tomorrow, not to mention next week, or next year? I just don't think I could take it if I committed myself to you and you changed your mind, or your feelings changed."

He grinned and spread his hands. "When you're Number Two you have to try harder . . ."

Her expression underwent a subtle change, a shift toward regret. "The more serious I get, the more you joke."

"It's no crime to laugh."

"No, it's not. But you can see there are still some pretty basic problems for us."

"Such as? Beside my admirable ability to save you from a tendency to deadly seriousness."

She smiled, he was relieved to see. "Paul, I'm afraid you'll laugh at me, or get angry if I tell you something that—"

"Tell me, ask me—anything, for God's sake."

She took a deep breath. "All right. I can't understand your not believing in any kind of God. A man as sensitive and intelligent as you are, how do you explain away all the evidence? How can you—"

He rolled his eyes and made the sign of the cross.

She flushed. "I knew you wouldn't understand."

"You're a religious nut! A fanatic. What kind of a question is that to ask at *this* moment? I don't have any quick answer. I don't even know if your question is right. I'd have to think about it, take some time."

"Yes," she said. "That's what I mean. I think we both need some time, to think, to look at our feelings. At least I need to, and I *can't* do it when I'm with you. Paul, I'm asking you to help me leave you . . ."

He didn't answer. He couldn't. There was nothing to do but turn and start to walk away, hands deep in his pockets, eyes searching the ground ahead as if he had lost something.

Bristol flung open the door of his suite, the bulldog face mottled and grooved, eyes puffed. "Where the hell have you been?"

Foreman went past him without answering.

On the couch, Gary McClintock and next to him Jim Sawyer. Both of them wore solemn expressions, watched Foreman's advance into the room warily.

Empty cups and a bottle of Scotch stood on the coffee table. Foreman helped himself to a drink.

"You were due here thirty minutes ago." His eyes closed and opened and he slammed his big fist into his other hand with a curious lack of force.

"Knock it off," Foreman said, and poured himself another drink.

"No consideration, that's your problem."

Foreman emptied his glass and headed for the door.

Bristol took a step after him. "Where you going? You work for me, remember. I'll say if you can go, and when."

It was McClintock who stopped Foreman. "It's Shelly. She died fifteen minutes ago."

Foreman came around. "Say again . . ."

"Some kids found her on the beach this morning. Somebody really worked her over."

Foreman took a step or two back into the room, stiff and uncertain. He looked at Bristol.

"Don't look like that at me," Bristol said. "Is it my fault she had an itch? Everybody knew it. We were having dinner with some people. She took off."

Foreman sat down.

"She drank too much," Bristol said. "You know that. Listen, I tried to stop her . . ."

"From the look of it, she'd been swimming," McClintock said. "She must have taken off her skirt, but the cops haven't been able to find it yet. She was only wearing her top and panties. Some bastard must've come across her that way. She probably tried to fight him off and he beat the hell out of her. She never regained consciousness. The cops are rounding up people."

"She said she was going to die," Foreman said.

"It's her own fault," Bristol said with a bluster he didn't feel. "Running out on me that way— You don't know what it is to live with that kind of a dame. The trouble she was. I did as much as any man could do."

Foreman went to the window. A beautiful beach day, shining, cloudless. He could almost hear the sounds of the bathers in the surf below.

"Well, I guess life has to go on," Sawyer said.

"Right!" Bristol said, gratefully. "Shelly'd be the first to say so. She'd say 'Finish the picture.' " The pouched eyes shifted quickly from face to face.

McClintock brought his hands against each other, as if in prayer. "The remaining scenes, Shelly'd be in every one of them. The mad scene, the dive, without her they . . ." He shrugged.

"Yes," Jim Sawyer put in. "And when she finds me with the Mexican girl . . . I'd hate to lose that scene."

Bristol seemed momentarily to have lost his concentration. Then he caught himself, shook his head vigorously and took over once again. "Everything can be worked out. I got a replacement in mind. Same coloring as Shelly, same build. Louise Peters is her name. We'll use her on the long shots, profiles. We'll get some radio actress later to imitate Shelly's voice, loop it into the track." Bristol felt a little dizzy, but went on. "Samantha," he muttered, repeating the name loudly. "We'll work in extra close-ups of her. Give her some lines. Foreman, you write down something for her to say. I'm going to give her star billing. Just like Gavin is using her for his cosmetics— SAMANTHA! All big letters and an exclamation point. The name goes in all the ads, all the publicity. That kidnapping . . . best break we could have . . . be an idiot not to take advantage of it . . ."

No one answered, all eyes fastened on him. "Oh, yes," he went on, more slowly now. "I talked to Theo Gavin. He's going to put up a big chunk of dough for a national tie-up between his company and *Love, Love,* if we star Samantha . . ."

Foreman stopped listening. His brain was finally clearing. Grace. He was the one who had forced things. He'd sulked and chosen to believe that she'd rejected him, when actually she'd only asked for time enough to let it happen between them. Grace hadn't wanted to commit herself to a romantic fantasy, and fantasy was his stock in trade—personal and professional.

"Okay," Bristol was saying, sounding vigorous again. "I've issued a two o'clock call to the company. Right after lunch. That gives us the morning to settle down. Then back to work. Okay, let's figure out what has to be done. Paul, I want you—"

Foreman moved across the room.

"What do you think you're doing!" Bristol yelled after him. "I've made a blueprint, a new shooting schedule. I want to go over it with you. Let's get to work."

Foreman turned to him. "No," he said. "I don't know what's really with you, Harry. I do know that you'd film Shelly's corpse and put it up on the screen if you thought you could get away with it. I faked myself out Harry. No more."

"Okay," Bristol said, "you don't like me. I don't like you either. You don't have to like a man to work with him—"

Foreman was opening the door. He glanced back. "That Shelly," saying aloud the image he'd had of her before; "a butterfly. She was a butterfly . . ."

A disturbing silence after he left. Then Bristol, erupting: "He's *right!* The bastard's right about Shelly. Get me that kind of a shot, Mac. One of those fantastic colored butterflies they have around here. Like it's hunting for some place to set down. When it does, a kid squashes the life out of it. That's the kind of crap those New York intellectuals lap up. Symbolism. We'll show the butterfly

in quick jump cuts, very surrealistic, under the opening
credits. At the end, at normal speed, then a long shot of
a woman's body—battered and bloody—on the beach, a
fast zoom in. Fantastic! Greatest idea I ever had. We'll
enter the picture at the New York Film Festival, at
Cannes, everywhere. There's no end, no end at all. . . ."
And he began to cry.

19

Foreman climbed into the Volkswagen and drove along the Costera to the Diana, turning onto the road to Mexico City. Fifty yards beyond the Pemex, he stopped for a hitchhiker.

"Mexico City nonstop," he called, as the hitchhiker came striding loosely up to the car.

"My lucky day," the tall youth said, squeezing into the seat alongside Foreman.

The VW lurched ahead, Foreman concentrating on the traffic. Up here, this was a part of Acapulco that never intruded on the world of lush hotels and spotless beaches in the lower regions of the resort. Here was where the poor lived in shacks made of wood, with roofs of corrugated paper.

Soon they were past that, curling down the eastern slope past vendors selling green coconuts. Acapulco was behind them. The hitchhiker shifted around in his seat. "You don't remember me," he said.

Foreman glanced at him. A slender youth with a smooth triangular face, vaguely familiar.

"Charles Gavin," the youth said. He grinned. "The hair, that's what's different."

"What made you cut it?"

"I didn't, *they* did. The fuzz, in Oaxaca. In some weird way I'm glad it happened, like it freed me up. Well, sort of," he amended, looking more closely at Foreman. "Hey, your face is swollen, like you've been worked over...."

Foreman nodded. "The last four days, I've been boozing, making trouble for myself. Somewhere along the line, a guy put a fist in my face. The fist won."

"I've decided I've been kind of a dumb ass."

"Welcome to the club. What brought you to the edge of wisdom?"

"A strange cat I met, more into himself than anybody I ever knew."

"And he gave you some answers?"

"Well, no. He put me in touch with myself. I at least started to think for myself, to try to figure out some things. I used to think that the world would change because I wanted it to. That my father should change because I wanted him to. Pretty ballsy, right? When it didn't happen, I dropped out. Well, it seems that nothing is about to change for me unless I make it happen. Work for it to happen. That's about where I am so far."

"That's a pretty heavy answer."

"Yeah, I guess it is."

"What do you do now? Join us old folks in the Establishment?"

"No way. But I'm going to try to find out how to make it work a little better."

"How?"

"Well, for starters, I'm going back to school." He added, a little sheepishly, "I even decided to let the old man finance me. He likes the idea. He wants to believe I've gone straight, come over to his side. I think I'll always be on the other side . . . but maybe I'll find out who I am, what, if anything, I've got inside me."

"I'm going back myself," Foreman said. "A few million years ago when I was trying to write plays . . . But first I've got something much more important to do. I'm going to find a girl. A very important girl. The fact I've got enough sense to go after her at least proves the instinct for self-preservation in Paul Foreman is not yet dead." He laughed. "No more defeats snatched from the jaws of victory—I hope."

"That sounds okay," Charles said.

They went on without speaking, the red beetle rolling along at a comfortable pace.

MEXICO CITY, *D.F.*—The tourist office this morning declared that new roads are going to be created in order to make travel easier for motorists going to and from the United States. This will increase the number of tourists who come to Mexico each year, an official predicted.

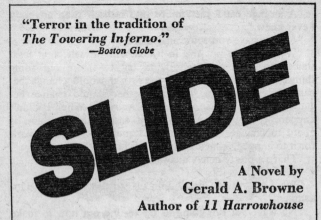

Dell Bestsellers

- [ ] MAGIC by William Goldman $1.95 (15141-4)
- [ ] THE USERS by Joyce Haber $2.25 (19264-1)
- [ ] THE HITE REPORT by Shere Hite $2.75 (13690-3)
- [ ] THE BOYS FROM BRAZIL by Ira Levin $2.25 (10760-1)
- [ ] THE OTHER SIDE OF MIDNIGHT
  by Sidney Sheldon $1.95 (16067-7)
- [ ] LOVE'S WILDEST FIRES by Christina Savage . $1.95 (12895-1)
- [ ] THE GEMINI CONTENDERS by Robert Ludlum $2.25 (12859-5)
- [ ] THE RHINEMANN EXCHANGE
  by Robert Ludlum $1.95 (15079-5)
- [ ] SUFFER THE CHILDREN by John Saul $1.95 (18293-X)
- [ ] MARATHON MAN by William Goldman ... $1.95 (15502-9)
- [ ] RICH FRIENDS by Jacqueline Briskin $1.95 (17380-9)
- [ ] SLIDE by Gerald A. Browne $1.95 (17701-4)
- [ ] SEVENTH AVENUE by Norman Bogner $1.95 (17810-X)
- [ ] THRILL by Barbara Petty $1.95 (15295-X)
- [ ] THE LONG DARK NIGHT by Joseph Hayes . $1.95 (14824-3)
- [ ] THE NINTH MAN by John Lee $1.95 (16425-7)
- [ ] THE DOGS by Robert Calder $1.95 (12102-7)
- [ ] NAKOA'S WOMAN by Gayle Rogers $1.95 (17568-2)
- [ ] FOR US THE LIVING by Antonia Van Loon $1.95 (12673-8)
- [ ] THE CHOIRBOYS by Joseph Wambaugh .. $2.25 (11188-9)
- [ ] SHOGUN by James Clavell $2.75 (17800-2)

At your local bookstore or use this handy coupon for ordering:

Dell **DELL BOOKS**
P.O. BOX 1000, PINEBROOK, N.J. 07058

Please send me the books I have checked above. I am enclosing $_____
(please add 35¢ per copy to cover postage and handling). Send check or money
order—no cash or C.O.D.'s. Please allow up to 8 weeks for shipment.

Mr/Mrs/Miss_____

Address_____

City_____State/Zip_____